from Geoffrey
1990

SYLVIA TOWNSEND WARNER

(1893–1978) was born in Harrow, the daughter of George Townsend Warner, housemaster and Head of the Modern Side of Harrow. As a student of music she became interested in research in the music of the fifteenth and sixteenth centuries, and spent ten years of her life as one of the four editors of the ten-volume compilation *Tudor Church Music*. In 1925 she published her first book of verse, *The Espalier*. With the publication of the novels *Lolly Willowes* in 1926, *Mr Fortune's Maggot* and *The True Heart* in the two following years, she achieved immediate recognition. The short stories she contributed to the *New Yorker* for over forty years established her reputation on both sides of the Atlantic.

In 1929 Sylvia Townsend Warner visited New York as guest critic for the *Herald Tribune*. In the 1930s she was a member of the Executive Committee of the Association of Writers for Intellectual Liberty and was a representative for the Congress of Madrid in 1937, thus witnessing the Spanish Civil War at first hand.

In all, Sylvia Townsend Warner published seven novels, four volumes of poetry, a volume of essays, and eight volumes of short stories. Her biography of T.H. White, published in 1967, was acclaimed in the *Guardian* as one of the two most outstanding biographies to have appeared since the war.

A writer of formidable imaginative power, each of Sylvia Townsend Warner's novels is a new departure, ranging from the revolutionary Paris of 1848 in *Summer Will Show* (1936), a 14th-century Abbey in *The Corner That Held Them* (1948), to the South Seas island of *Mr Fortune's Maggot*, and 18th-century southern Spain in *After the Death of Don Juan*.

Sylvia Townsend Warner lived most of her adult life with her close companion Valentine Ackland, in Dorset, then in Norfolk and later in Dorset once again, where she died on 1 May 1978, at the age of eighty-four.

Virago also publishes *The True Heart*, *Summer Will Show*, *The Corner That Held Them*, *After the Death of Don Juan* and her *Selected Stories* (1989).

D1513193

SELECTED STORIES
OF
Sylvia Townsend Warner

Published by VIRAGO PRESS Limited 1990
20–23 Mandela Street, Camden Town, London NW1 0HQ

First published in Great Britain by Chatto & Windus 1989
Copyright © Susanna Pinney, William Maxwell

All rights reserved

A CIP catalogue record for this book is available from
the British Library

Printed in Great Britain
by Cox & Wyman Ltd, Reading, Berks

CONTENTS

EDITORS' NOTE

This is a personal selection by Sylvia Townsend Warner's literary executors of what they consider to be her finest short stories. They have been selected from over forty years of work, from 1932 to 1977, the year before her death. The collection in which it first appeared, and its date, is given at the end of each story: two of these collections—*Scenes of Childhood* and *One Thing Leading to Another*—were published posthumously. The stories have been arranged by theme rather than chronologically. *A Stranger with a Bag* was published in the United States under the title *Swans on an Autumn River*.

Susanna Pinney
William Maxwell

A LOVE MATCH

IT was Mr Pilkington who brought the Tizards to Hallowby. He met them, a quiet couple, at Carnac, where he had gone for a schoolmasterly Easter holiday to look at the monoliths. After two or three meetings at a café, they invited him to their rented chalet. It was a cold, wet afternoon and a fire of pine cones crackled on the hearth. 'We collect them on our walks,' said Miss Tizard. 'It's an economy. And it gives us an object.' The words, and the formal composure of her manner, made her seem like a Frenchwoman. Afterwards, he learned that the Tizards were a Channel Island family and had spent their childhood in Jersey. The ancestry that surfaced in Miss Tizard's brisk gait and erect carriage, brown skin and compact sentences, did not show in her brother. His fair hair, his red face, his indecisive remarks, his diffident movements—as though with the rest of his body he were apologising for his stiff leg—were entirely English. He ought not, thought Mr Pilkington, to be hanging about in France. He'd done more than enough for France already. For this was in 1923 and Mr Pilkington, with every intention of preserving a historian's impartiality, was nevertheless infected by the current mood of disliking the French.

The weather continued cold and wet; there was a sameness about the granite avenues. Mr Pilkington's mind became increasingly engaged with the possibility, the desirability, the positive duty of saving that nice fellow Tizard from wasting his days in exile. He plied him with hints, with suggestions, with tactful inquiries. Beyond discovering that money was not the obstacle to return, he got no further. Tizard, poor fellow, must be under his sister's thumb. Yet it was from the sister that he got his first plain answer. 'Justin would mope if he had nothing to do.' Mr Pilkington stopped himself from commenting on the collection of pine cones as an adequate lifework. As though she had read his thought, she went on, 'There is a difference between idling in a foreign country and being an idler in your own.' At that moment Tizard limped into the room with crayfish bristling from his shopping basket. 'It's begun,' he said ruefully. '*La Jeune France* has arrived. I've just seen two young men in pink trousers with daisy chains round their necks, riding through the town on donkeys.' Mr Pilkington asked if this was a circus. Miss Tizard explained that it was the new generation, and would make Carnac a bedlam till the summer's end. 'Of course, there's a certain amount of that sort of thing in England, too,' observed Mr Pilkington. 'But only in the South. It doesn't trouble us at Hallowby.' As he spoke, he was conscious of playing a good card; then the immensity of the trump he held broke upon him. He was too excited to speak. Inviting them to dine at his hotel on the following night, he went away.

By next evening, more of *La Jeune France* had arrived, and was mustered outside the hotel extemporising a bullfight ballet in honour of St Cornély, patron saint of cattle and of the parish church. Watching Tizard's look of stoically endured embarrassment Mr Pilkington announced that he had had a blow; the man who had almost promised to become curator of the Beelby Military Museum had written to say he couldn't take up the post. 'He didn't say why. But I know why. Hallowby is too quiet for him.'

'But I thought Hallowby had blast furnaces and strikes and all that sort of thing,' said Tizard.

'That is Hallowby juxta Mare,' replied Mr Pilkington. 'We are Old Hallowby. Very quiet; quite old, too. The school was founded in 1623. We shall be having our modest tercentenary this summer. That is why I am so put out by Dalsover's not taking up the curatorship. I hoped to have the museum all in order. It would have been something to visit, if it rains during the Celebrations.' He allowed a pause.

Tizard, staring at the toothpicks, inquired, 'Is it a wet climate?'

But Mr Pilkington was the headmaster of a minor public school, a position of command. As if the pause had not taken place, raising his voice above the bullfight he told how fifty years earlier Davenport Beelby, a rich man's sickly son, during a lesson on the Battle of Minden awoke to military glory and began to collect regimental buttons. Buttons, badges, pikes, muskets and bayonets, shakos and helmets, despatches, newspaper cuttings, stones from European battlefields, sand from desert campaigns—his foolish collection grew into the lifework of a devoted eccentric and, as such collections sometimes do, became valuable and authoritative, though never properly catalogued. Two years ago he had died, bequeathing the collection to his old school, with a fund sufficient for upkeep and the salary of a curator.

'I wish you'd consider coming as our curator,' said Mr Pilkington. 'I'm sure you would find it congenial. Beelby wanted an Army man. Three mornings a week would be quite enough.'

Tizard shifted his gaze from the toothpicks to the mustard jar. 'I am not an Army man,' he said. 'I just fought. Not the same thing, you know.'

Miss Tizard exclaimed, 'No! Not at all,' and changed the subject.

But later that evening she said to her brother, 'Once we were there, we shouldn't see much of him. It's a possibility.'

'Do you want to go home, Celia?'

'I think it's time we did. We were both of us born for a sober, conventional, taxpaying life, and if—'

'*Voici Noël!*' sang the passing voices. '*Voici Noël! Voici Noël, petits enfants!*'

She composed her twitching hands and folded them on her lap. 'We were young rowdies once,' he said placatingly.

A fortnight later, they were Mr Pilkington's guests at Hallowby. A list of empty houses had been compiled by Miss Robson, the secretary. All were variously suitable; each in turn was inspected by Miss Tizard and rejected. Mr Pilkington felt piqued that his offer of a post should dance attendance on the aspect of a larder or the presence of decorative tiles. Miss Tizard was a disappointment to him; he had relied on her support. Now it was the half-hearted Tizard who seemed inclined to root, while she flitted from one eligible residence to another, appearing, as he remarked to the secretary, to expect impossibilities. Yet when she settled as categorically as a queen bee the house she chose had really nothing to be said for it. A square, squat mid-Victorian box, Newton Lodge was one of the ugliest houses in Hallowby; though a high surrounding wall with a green door in it hid the totality of its ugliness from passers-by, its hulking chimneys proclaimed what was below. It was not even well situated. It stood in a deteriorating part of the town, and was at some distance from the school buildings and the former gymnasium—

Victorian also—which had been assigned to the Beelby Collection. But the house having been chosen, the curatorship was bestowed and the move made. Justin Tizard, rescued from wasting his days in exile —though too late for the tercentenary celebrations—began his duties as curator by destroying a quantity of cobwebs and sending for a window-cleaner.

All through the summer holidays he worked on, sorting things into heaps, subdividing the heaps into lesser heaps. Beelby's executors must have given carte-blanche to the packers, who had acted on the principle of filling up with anything that came handy, and the unpackers had done little more than tumble things out and scatter them with notices saying 'DO NOT DISTURB'. The largest heap consisted of objects he could not account for, but unaccountably it lessened, till the day came when he could look round on tidiness. Ambition seized him. Tidiness is not enough; no one looks twice at tidiness. There must also be parade and ostentation. He bought stands, display cases, dummies for the best uniforms. Noticing a decayed wooden horse in the saddler's shop, he bought that, too; trapped, with its worser side to the wall and with a cavalry dummy astride, it made a splendid appearance. He combed plumes, shook out bearskins, polished holsters and gunstocks, oiled the demi-culverin, sieved the desert sand. At this stage, his sister came and polished with him, mended, refurbished, sewed on loose buttons. Of the two, she had more feeling for the exhibits themselves, for the discolouring glory and bloodshed they represented. It was the housewife's side that appealed to him. Sometimes, hearing him break into the whistle of a contented mind, she would look up from her work and stare at him with the unbelief of thankfulness.

Early in the autumn term, Mr Pilkington made time to visit the museum. He did not expect much and came prepared with speeches of congratulation and encouragement. They died on his lips when he saw the transformation. Instead, he asked how much the display cases had cost, and the dummies, and the horse, and how much of the upkeep fund remained after all this expenditure. He could not find fault; there was no reason to do so. He was pleased to see Tizard so well established as master in his own house. Perhaps he was also pleased that there was no reason to find fault. Though outwardly unchanged, the Tizard of Carnac appeared to have been charged with new contents—with something obstinately reckless beneath the easy-going manner, with watchfulness beneath the diffidence. But this, reflected Mr Pilkington, might well be accounted for by the startling innovations in the museum. He stayed longer than he meant, and only after leaving remembered that he had omitted to say how glad he was that Tizard had accepted the curatorship. This must be put right; he did not want to discourage the young man who had worked so hard and so efficiently, and also he must get into the way of remembering that Tizard was in fact a young man—under thirty. Somehow, one did not think of him as a young man.

Justin Tizard, newly a captain in an infantry regiment, came on leave after the battle of the Somme. His sister met the train at Victoria. There were some pigeons strutting on the platform and he was watching them when a strange woman in black came up to him, touched his shoulder, and said, 'Justin!' It was as though Celia were claiming a piece of lost luggage, he thought. She had a taxi waiting, and they drove to her flat. She asked about his health, about his journey; then she congratulated him on his captaincy. 'Practical reasons,' he said. 'My habit of not getting killed. They were bound to notice it sooner or later.' After this, they fell silent. He looked out of the window at the streets so clean and the people so busy with their own affairs. 'That's a new Bovril poster, isn't it?' he inquired. Her answer was so slow in coming that he didn't really take in whether it was yes or no.

Her flat was new, anyway. She had only been in it since their mother's remarriage. It was up a great many flights of stairs, and she spoke of moving to somewhere with a lift, now that Tim's legacy had made a rich woman of her. The room smelled of polish and flowers. There was a light-coloured rug on the floor and above this was the blackness of Celia's skirts. She was wearing black for her fiancé. The news of his death had come to her in this same room, while she was still sorting books and hanging pictures. Looking round the room, still not looking at Celia, he saw Tim's photograph on her desk. She saw his glance, and hers followed it. 'Poor Tim!' they said, both speaking at once, the timbre of their voices relating them. 'They say he was killed instantaneously,' she went on. 'I hope it's true—though I suppose they always say that.'

'I'm sure it is,' he replied. He knew that Tim had been blown to pieces. Compassion made it possible to look at her. Dressed in black, possessing these new surroundings, she seemed mature and dignified beyond her actual three years' seniority. For the first time in his life he saw her not as a sister but as an individual. But he could not see her steadily for long. There was a blur on his sight, a broth of mud and flame and frantic unknown faces and writhing entrails. When she showed him to his bedroom she stepped over mud that heaved with the bodies of men submerged in it. She had drawn the curtains. There was a bed with sheets turned back, and a bedside lamp shed a serene, unblinking light on the pillows. 'Bed!' he exclaimed, and heard the spontaneity die in his voice. 'Wonderful to see a bed!'

'And this is the bathroom. I've got everything planned. First of all, you must have a bath, lie and soak in it. And then put on these pyjamas and the dressing gown, and we will have supper.'

Left to himself, he was violently sick. Shaking with fatigue, he sat in a hot scented bath and cleaned his knees with scrupulous care, like a child. Outside was the noise of London.

The pyjamas were silk, the dressing gown was quilted and wrapped him round like a caress. In the sitting room was Celia, still a stranger, though now a stranger without a hat. There was a table sparkling with silver and crystal, smoked salmon, a bottle of champagne. It was all as she had planned it for Tim—Oh, poor Celia!

They discussed their mother's remarriage. It had been decided on with great suddenness, and appeared inexplicable. Though they re-frained from saying much, their comments implied that her only reason for marrying a meat king from the Argentine was to get away from England and the war. 'There he was, at eleven in the morning, with a carnation—a foot shorter than she,' said Celia, describing the return from the registry office.

'In that case, he must be four foot three.'

'He is exactly four foot three. I stole up and measured him.'

Spoken in her imperturbable voice, this declaration struck him as immensely funny, as funny as a nursery joke. They laughed hilariously, and after this their evening went almost naturally.

Turning back after his unadorned, brotherly 'Good night, Celia,' he exclaimed, 'But where are you sleeping?'

'In here.' Before he could demur she went on, 'The sofa fits me. It would be far too short for you.'

He told her how balmily he had slept, one night behind the lines, with his head on a bag of nails.

'Exactly! That is why tonight you are going to sleep properly. In a bed.'

She heard him get into bed, heard the lamp switched off. Almost immediately she heard his breathing lengthen into slumber. Then, a few minutes later, he began to talk in his sleep.

Perhaps a scruple—the dishonourableness of being an eavesdropper, a Peeping Tom—perhaps mere craven terror, made her try not to listen. She began to read, and when she found that impossible she repeated poems she had learned at school, and when that failed she polished the silver cigarette box. But Justin's voice was raised, and the partition wall was thin, and the ghastly confidences went on and on. She could not escape them. She was dragged, a raw recruit, into battle.

In the morning she thought she would not be able to look him in the face. But he was cheerful, and so was she. She had got off from the canteen, she explained, while he was on leave; they had nothing to do but enjoy themselves. They decided to have some new experiences, so they went up the Monument. If he wants to throw himself off, she thought, I won't stop him. They looked down on London; on the curve of the Thames, the shipping, the busy lighters. They essayed how many City churches they could identify by their spires. They talked about Pepys. She would be surprised, Justin said, how many chaps carried a copy of the *Diary*, and she asked if bullets also glanced off Pepys carried in a breast pocket. So they made conversation quite successfully. And afterwards, when they had decided to go for a walk down Whitechapel High Street and lunch off winkles at a stall, many people glanced at them with kindness and sentimentality, and an old woman patted Celia's back, saying, 'God bless you, dearie! Isn't it lovely to have him home?'

Whitechapel was a good idea. The throng of people carried some of the weight of self-consciousness for them; the wind blowing up-river and the hooting of ships' sirens made them feel they were in some foreign port of call, taking a stroll till it was time to re-embark. He was less aware that she had grown strange to him, and she was momentarily able to forget the appalling stranger who had raved in her bed all night.

They dined at a restaurant, and went on to a music hall. That night he took longer to fall asleep. She had allowed herself a thread of hope, when he began to talk again. Three Justins competed, thrusting each other aside: a cold, attentive observer, a debased child, a devil bragging in hell. At intervals they were banished by a recognisable Justin interminably muttering to himself, 'Here's a sword for Toad, here's a sword for Rat, here's a sword for Mole, here's a sword for Badger.' The reiteration from that bible of their childhood would stick on the word, 'Rat'. 'Got you!' And he was off again.

The next day they went to the Zoo. The Zoo was not so efficacious as Whitechapel. It was feeling the pinch, the animals looked shabby and dejected, many cages were empty. Two sleepless nights had made Celia's feet swell. It was pain to walk, pain to stand. She wondered how much longer she could keep it up, this 'God bless you, dearie' pretence of a lovely leave. The day accumulated its hours like a windlass. The load grew heavier; the windlass baulked under it, but wound on. He went to bed with the usual 'Good night, Celia'. As usual, she undressed and put on that derision of a nightdress, and wrapped herself in an eiderdown and lay down to wait under the smiling gaze of Tim's photograph. She felt herself growing icy cold, couldn't remember if she had wound her watch, couldn't remember what diversion she had planned for the morrow, was walking over Richmond Bridge in a snowstorm, when she noticed he had begun again. *She noticed*. It had come to that. Two nights of a vicarious endurance of what was being endured, had been endured, would continue to be endured by a cancelled generation, had so exhausted her that now she felt neither horror nor despair, merely a bitter acquiescence. Justin went on with his Hail Devil Rosary, and in France the guns went on and on, and the mud dried into dust and slumped back into mud again. People went down to Kent to listen to the noise of the guns: the people in Kent said that they had grown used to it, didn't hear it any longer. The icy cold sensation bored into her midriff, nailed her down in sleep.

Some outcry, some exclamation (she could not afterwards remember what it was), woke her. Before she knew what she was doing she was in the next room, trying to waken the man who lay so rigidly in her bed, who, if she could awaken him, would be Justin, her brother Justin. 'Oh, poor Justin, my poor Justin!' Throwing herself on the bed, she clasped him in her arms, lifted his head to lie against her breast, kissed his chattering lips. 'There, there!' She felt him relax, waken, drag her towards him. They rushed into the escape of love like winter-starved cattle rushing into a spring pasture.

When light came into the room, they drew a little apart and looked at each other.

'Now we've done it,' he said; and hearing the new note in his voice she replied, 'A good thing, don't you think?'

Their release left them no option. After a few hours they were not even astonished. They were mated for life, that was all—for a matter of days, so they made the most of it. At the end of his leave they parted in exaltation, he convinced that he was going off to be killed, she that she would bear his child, to which she would devote the remainder of her existence.

A little later she knew she was not pregnant.

Early in the new year Justin, still panoplied in this legendary and by now rather ludicrous charmed life, was made a major. In April, he was wounded in the leg. 'Nothing to worry about,' he wrote; 'just a few splinters. I am in bed, as peaceful as a pincushion.' Later, she heard that he had been moved to a hospital on the outskirts of London. One of the splinters had escaped notice, and gas gangrene had developed in the wound.

I shall be a peg leg, he thought. It's not decent for a peg leg to make love; even to his sister. He was ravaged with fret and behaving with perfect decorum when Celia was shown in—dressed all in leaf green, walking like an empress, smelling delicious. For a moment the leaf-green Celia was almost as much of a stranger as the Celia all in black had been. When she kissed him, he discovered that she was shaking from head to foot. 'There, there,' he said, patting her. Still holding his hand, she addressed herself to charming Nurse Painter. Nurse Painter was in favour of sisters. They weren't so much trouble, didn't upset a patient, as sweethearts or wives did—and you didn't have to be hanging round all the time, ready to shoo them off. When Celia came next day, Nurse Painter congratulated her on having done the Major no end of good. There had been a lot of pus; she liked to see a lot of pus.

They continued to give satisfaction; when Justin left hospital with a knee that would always be stiff and from time to time cause him pain, Nurse Painter's approval went with them. A sister was just what he wanted—there would be no silly excitement; and as Miss Tizard was a trifle older than the Major, there would be a restraining hand if called for. If Nurse Painter had known what lay beneath this satisfactory arrangement, it is probable that her approval would not have been seriously withdrawn. The war looked like going on for ever; the best you could hope for was a stalemate. Potatoes were unobtainable, honesty was no more, it was hate and muddle wherever you looked. If a gentleman and lady could pluck up heart enough to love and be happy—well, good luck to them!

Justin and Celia went to Oxfordshire, where they compared the dragonflies on the Windrush with the dragonflies on the Evenlode. Later, they went to France.

Beauty cannot be suborned. Never again did Justin see Celia quivering with beauty as she had done on the day she came to him in hospital. But he went on thinking she had a charming face and the most entertaining eyebrows in the world. Loving each other criminally and sincerely, they took pains to live together happily and to safeguard their happiness from injuries of their own infliction or from outside. It would have been difficult for them to be anything but inconspicuous, or to be taken for anything but a brother and sister—the kind of brother and sister of whom one says, 'It will be rather hard for her when he marries'. Their relationship, so conveniently obvious to the public eye, was equally convenient in private life, for it made them unusually intuitive about each other's feelings. Brought up to the same standard of behaviour, using the same vocabulary, they felt no need to impress each other and were not likely to be taken aback by each other's likes and dislikes. Even the fact of remembering the same foxed copy of *The Swiss Family Robinson* with the tear across the picture of the boa constrictor was a reassuring bond. During the first years in France they felt they would like to have a child—or for the sake of the other's happiness ought to have a child—and discussed the possibilities of a child put out to nurse, learning French as its native speech, and then being adopted as a postwar orphan, since it was now too late for it to be a war orphan. But however the child was dated, it would be almost certain to declare its inheritance of Grandfather Tizard's nose, and as a fruitful incest is thought even worse of than a barren one, they sensibly gave up the idea; though regretting it.

Oddly enough, after settling in Hallowby they regretted it no longer. They had a home in England, a standing and things to do. Justin had the Beelby Museum; Celia had a household. In Hallowby it was not possible to stroll out to a restaurant or to bring home puddings from the pastry cook, fillets of veal netted into bolsters by the butcher. Celia had to cook seriously, and soon found that if she was to cook meals worth eating she must go shopping too. This was just what was needed for their peace and quiet, since to be seen daily shopping saved a great deal of repetitious explanation that she and Justin could not afford to keep a servant in the house but must be content with Mrs Mugthwaite coming in three afternoons a week, and a jobbing gardener on Fridays. True, it exposed her to a certain amount of condolence and amazement from the school wives, but as they, like Mrs Mugthwaite, came only in the afternoons, she could bear with it. Soon they came more sparingly; for, as Justin pointed out, poverty is the sturdiest of all shelters, since people feel it to be rather sad and soon don't think about it, whereas her first intention of explaining that ever since her Aunt Dinah had wakened in the middle of the night to see an angered cook standing over her with a meat hatchet she had been nervous of servants sleeping under the same roof would only provoke gossip, surmise and insistent recommendations of cooks without passions. Justin was more long-sighted than Celia. She always knew what to do or say at the moment. He could look ahead, foresee dangers, and take steps to dodge them.

They did not see as much of Mr Pilkington as they had apprehended, and members of the staff were in no hurry to take up with another of Pilkington's Pets. Celia grew alarmed; if you make no friends, you become odd. She decided that they must occasionally go to church, though not too often or too enthusiastically, as it would then become odd that they did not take the Sacrament. No doubt a great many vicious church attenders took the Sacrament, and the rubric only forbids it to 'open and notorious evil-livers', which they had every intention of not being; but she could see a scruple of honour at work in Justin, so she did not labour this argument. There was a nice, stuffy pitch-pine St Cuthbert's near by, and at judicious intervals they went there for evensong—thereby renewing another bond of childhood: the pleasure of hurrying home on a cold evening to eat baked potatoes hot from the oven. How old Mr Gillespie divined from Justin's church demeanour that he was a whist player was a mystery never solved. But he divined it. He had barely saved Celia's umbrella from being blown inside out, remarking, 'You're newcomers, aren't you? You don't know the east wind at this corner,' before he was saying to Justin, 'You don't play whist, by any chance?' But probably he would have asked this of anyone not demonstrably a raving maniac, for since Colin Colbeck's death he, Miss Colbeck and Canon Pendarves were desperate for a fourth player. Canon Pendarves gave dinner parties, with a little music afterwards. Celia, driven into performance and remembering how Becky Sharp had wooed Lady Steyne by singing the religious songs of Mozart, sat down at the piano and played 'The Carmen's Whistle', one of the few things she reliably knew by heart. This audacious antiquarianism delighted the Canon, who kept her at his side for the rest of the evening, relating how he had once tried to get up a performance of Tallis's forty-part motet.

The Tizards were no longer odd. Their new friends were all considerably older than they; the middle-aged had more conscience about the war and were readier to make friends with a disabled major and his devoted maiden sister. In time, members of the staff overlooked their prejudice against Pilkington Pets and found the Tizard couple agreeable, if slightly boring.

Returning from their sober junketings Justin and Celia, safe within their brick wall, cast off their weeds of middle age, laughed, chattered and kissed with an intensified delight in their scandalous immunity from blame. They were a model couple, the most respectable couple in Hallowby, treading hand in hand the thornless path to fogydom. They began to give small dinner parties themselves. They set up a pug and a white cat. During their fifth summer in Hallowby they gave an evening party in the Beelby Museum. This dashing event almost carried them too far. It was such a success that they were begged to make an annual thing of it; and Celia was so gay, and her dress so fashionable, that she was within an inch of being thought a dangerous woman. Another party being expected of them, another had to be given. But this was a very different set-out: a children-and-parents party with a puppet show, held in St Cuthbert's Church Room, with Canon Pendarves speaking on behalf of the Save the Children Fund and a collection taken at the door. The collection was a master stroke. It put the Tizards back in their place as junior fogies—where Justin, for his part, was thankful to be. He had got there a trifle prematurely, perhaps, being in his mid-thirties, but it was where he intended to end his days.

He was fond of gardening, and had taken to gardening seriously, having an analysis made of the Newton Lodge soil—too acid, as he suspected—buying phosphates and potash and lime and kainite, treating different plots with different mixtures and noting the results in a book. He could not dig, but he limpingly mowed and rolled the lawn, trained climbing roses and staked delphiniums. Within the shelter of the wall, delphiniums did magnificently. Every year he added new varieties and when the original border could be lengthened no further a parallel bed was dug, with a grass walk in between. Every summer evening he walked there, watching the various blues file off, some to darkness, some to pallor, as the growing dusk took possession of them, while the white cat flitted about his steps like a moth. Because one must not be wholly selfish, from time to time he would invite a pair of chosen children to tea, cut each of them a long delphinium lance (cutting only those which were going over, however) and set them to play jousting matches on the lawn. Most of them did no more than thwack, but the two little Semples, the children of the school chaplain, fought with system, husbanding their strokes and aiming at each other's faces. Even when they had outgrown jousting they still came to Newton Lodge, hunting snails, borrowing books, helping him weigh out basic slag, addressing him as 'Justin'.

'Mary is just the age our child would have been,' remarked Celia after one of these visits. Seeing him start at the words, she went on, 'When you went back to be killed, and I was quite sure I would have a baby.'

'I wouldn't stand being called Justin—if she were.'

'You might have to. They're Bright Young Things from the cradle on, nowadays.'

By now the vogue for being a Bright Young Thing had reached even to Hallowby, its ankles growing rather muddied and muscular on the way. It was not like Celia to prefer an inferior article, and Justin wondered to see her tolerance of this anglicisation of the *Jeune France* when the original movement had so exasperated her. He hoped she wasn't mellowing; mellowness is not the food of love. A quite contrary process, however, was at work in Celia. At Carnac, even when accepting Pilkington as a way out of it, the exaltation of living in defiance of social prohibitions and the absorbing manoeuvres of seeming to live in compliance with them had been stimulus enough; she had had no mercy for less serious rebels. But during the last few years the sense of sinking month by month into the acquiescence of Hallowby, eating its wholesome lotus like cabbage, conforming with the inattentiveness of habit —and aware that if she overlooked a conformity the omission would be redressed by the general conviction that Justin Tizard, though in no way exciting, was always so nice and had a sister who devoted her life to him, so nice for them both, etc. etc.—had begun to pall, and the sight of any rebellion, however puerile, however clumsy, roused up her partisanship. Since she could not shock Hallowby to its foundations, she liked to see these young creatures trying to, and wished them luck. From time to time she even made approaches to them, solicited their trust, indicated that she was ranged on their side. They accepted, confided, condescended—and dropped her.

When one is thus put back in one's place, one finds one has grown out of it, and is a misfit. Celia became conscious how greatly she disliked Hallowby society. The school people nauseated her with their cautious culture and breezy heartiness. The indigenous inhabitants were more bearable, because they were less pretentious; but they bored her. The Church, from visiting bishops down to Salvation Army cornet players, she loathed for its hypocrisy. Only in Hallowby's shabbiest quarter—in Edna Road, Gladstone Terrace and Gas Lane—could she find anyone to love. Mr Newby the fishmonger in his malodorous den; old Mrs Foe among her sallowing cabbages and bruised apples; Mr Raby, the grocer, who couldn't afford to buy new stock because he hadn't the heart to call in the money his poorer customers owed him, and so had none but the poorest customers—these people were good. Probably it was only by their goodness that they survived and had not cut their throats in despair long ago. Celia began to shop in Gas Lane. It was not a success. Much as she might love Mr Newby she loved Justin better, and when a dried haddock gave him food poisoning she had to remove her custom—since the cat wouldn't touch Newby's fish anyhow. These disheartening experiences made her dislike respectable Hallowby even more. She wanted to cast it off, as someone tossing in fever wants to cast off a blanket.

The depression began. The increase of Mr Raby's customers drove him out of business: he went bankrupt and closed the shop. Groups of unemployed men from Hallowby juxta Mare appeared in Gas Lane and Edna Road and sang at street corners—for misfortune always resorts to poor neighbourhoods for succour. People began to worry about their investments and to cut down subscriptions to such examples of conspicuous waste as the Chamber Music Society. Experts on nutrition wrote to the daily papers, pointing out the wastefulness of frying, and explaining how, by buying cheaper cuts of meat and cooking them much longer, the mothers of families on the dole would be able to provide wholesome adequate meals. Celia's uneasy goodwill and smouldering resentment found their outlet. As impetuously as she had flung herself into Justin's bed, she flung herself into relief work at Hallowby juxta Mare. Being totally inexperienced in relief work she exploded there like a nova. Her schemes were so outrageous that people in authority didn't think them worth contesting even; she was left to learn by experience, and made the most of this valuable permission. One of her early outrages was to put on a revue composed and performed by local talent. Local talent ran to the impromptu, and when it became known what scarification of local reputations could be expected, everyone wanted to hear what might be said of everyone else and Celia was able to raise the price of admission, which had been sixpence, to as much as half a guinea for the best seats. Her doings became a joke; you never knew what that woman wouldn't be up to next. Hadn't she persuaded Wilson & Beck to take on men they had turned off, because now, when half the factory stood idle, was the moment to give it a spring cleaning? Celia worked herself to the bone, and probably did a considerable amount of good, but her great service to Hallowby juxta Mare was that she made the unemployed interested in their plight instead of dulled by it, so that helpers came to her from the unemployed themselves. If she was not so deeply impressed by their goodness as she had been by the idealised goodness of Mr Newby and Mrs Foe, she was impressed by their arguments; she became political, and by 1936 she was marching in Communist demonstrations, singing:

> Twenty-five years of hunger and war
> And they call it a glorious Jubilee.

Inland Hallowby was also looking forward to the Jubilee. The school was rehearsing a curtailed version of Purcell's *King Arthur*, with Mary

Semple, now home from her finishing school, coming on in a chariot to sing 'Fairest Isle'. There was to be folk dancing by Scouts and Guides, a tea for the old people, a fancy-dress procession; and to mark the occasion Mr Harvey, J.P., one of the school governors, had presented the Beelby Museum with a pair of buckskin breeches worn by the Duke of Wellington on the field of Talavera. 'I shall be expected to make a speech about them,' groaned Justin. 'I think I shall hire a deputy and go away for the day.'

Celia jumped at this. 'We'll both go away. Not just for the day but for a fortnight. We'll go to Jersey, because you must attend the Jubilee celebrations on your native island—a family obligation. Representative of one of the oldest families. And if we find the same sort of fuss going on there, we can nip over to France in the Escudiers' boat and be quit of the whole thing. It's foolproof, it's perfect. The only thing needed to make it perfectly perfect is to make it a month. Justin, it's the answer.' She felt indeed that it was the answer. For some time now, Justin had seemed distrait and out of humour. Afraid he was unwell, she told herself he was stale and knew that he had been neglected. An escapade would put all right. Talavera had not been fought in vain. But she couldn't get him to consent. She was still persuading when the first letter arrived. It was typed and had been posted in Hallowby. It was unsigned, and began, 'Hag.'

Reading what followed, Celia tried to hold on to her first impression that the writer was some person in Hallowby juxta Mare. 'You think you're sitting pretty, don't you? You think no one has found you out.' She had made many enemies there; this must come from one of them. Several times she had been accused of misappropriating funds. Yes, that was it: '. . . and keep such a tight hold on him.' But why *him*? It was as though two letters lay on the flimsy page—the letter she was bent on reading and the letter that lay beneath and glared through it. It was a letter about her relations with Justin that she tore into bits and dropped in the wastepaper basket as he came down to breakfast.

She could hardly contain her impatience to get the bits out again, stick them on a backing sheet, make sure. Nothing is ever quite what it first was; the letter was viler, but it was also feebler. It struck her as amateurish.

The letter that came two days later was equally vile but better composed; the writer must be getting his or her hand in. A third was positively elegant. Vexatiously, there was no hint of a demand for hush money. Had there been, Celia could have called in the police, who would have set those ritual springes into which blackmailers—at any rate, blackmailers one reads of in newspapers—walk so artlessly. But the letters did not blackmail, did not even threaten. They stated that what the writer knew was common knowledge. After two letters, one on the heels of the other, which taunted Celia with being ugly, ageing and sexually ridiculous—letters that ripped through her self-control and made her cry with mortification—the writer returned to the theme of common knowledge and concluded with an 'It may interest you to hear that the following know all about your loathsome performances' and a list of half a dozen Hallowby names. Further letters laconically listed more names. From the outset, Celia had decided to keep all this to herself, and still held to the decision; but she hoped she wouldn't begin to talk in her sleep. There was less chance of this, as by now she was sleeping scarcely at all.

It was a Sunday morning and she and Justin were spraying roses for greenfly when Justin said, 'Puss, what are you concealing?' She syringed Mme Alfred Carrière so violently that the jet bowed the rose, went beyond it, and deluged a robin. Justin took the syringe out of her hand and repeated the question.

Looking at him, she saw his face was drawn with woe. 'No, no, it's nothing like that,' she exclaimed. 'I'm perfectly well. It's just that some poisen-pen imbecile . . .'

When he had read through the letters, he said thoughtfully, 'I'd like to wring that little bitch's neck.'

'Yes, it is some woman or other, isn't it? I felt sure of that.'

'Some woman or other? It's Mary Semple.'

'That pretty little Mary Semple?'

'That pretty little Mary Semple. Give me the letters. I'll soon settle her.' He looked at his watch. 'No, I can't settle her yet. She'll still be in church.'

'But I don't understand why.'

'You do, really.'

'Justin! Have you been carrying on with Mary Semple?'

'No, I wouldn't say that. She's got white eyelashes. But ever since she came home Mary Semple has been doing all she could to carry on with me. There I was in the Beelby, you see, like a bull at the stake. No one comes near the place now; I was at her mercy. And in she tripped, and talked about the old days, telling me her little troubles, showing me poems, pitying me for my hard lot. I tried to cool her down, I tried to taper it off. But she was bent on rape, and one morning I lost all patience, told her she bored me and that if she came again I'd empty the fire bucket over her. She wept and wailed, and I paid no attention, and when there was silence I looked cautiously round and she was gone. And a day or so after'—he looked at the mended letter—'yes, a couple of days after, she sat her down to take it out of you.'

'But, Justin—how did she know about us?'

'No fire without smoke, I suppose. I dare say she overheard her parents cheering each other along the way with Christian surmises. Anyhow, children nowadays are brought up on that sort of useful knowledge.'

'No fire without smoke,' she repeated. 'And what about those lists?'

'Put in to make your flesh creep, most likely. Even if they do know, they weren't informed at a public meeting. Respectable individuals are too wary about libel and slander to raise their respectable voices individually. It's like that motet Pendarves used to talk about, when he could never manage to get them all there at once. Extraordinary ambitions people have! Fancy wanting to hear forty singers simul-taneously yelling different tunes.'

'It can be done. There was a performance at Newcastle—he was dead by then. But, Justin—'

'That will do, Celia. I am now going off to settle Mary Semple.'

'How will you manage to see her alone?'

'I shall enter her father's dwelling. Mary will manage the rest.'

The savagery of these last words frightened her. She had not heard that note in his voice since he cried out in his sleep. She watched him limp from the room as though she were watching an incalculable stranger. A moment later he reappeared, took her hand, and kissed it. 'Don't worry, Puss. If need be, we'll fly the country.'

Whatever danger might lie ahead, it was the thought of the danger escaped that made her tremble. If she had gone on concealing those letters—and she had considered it her right and duty to do so—a wedge would have been driven between her and Justin, bruising the tissue of their love, invisibly fissuring them, as a wedge of ice does in the living tree. And thus a scandal about their incest would have found them without any spontaneity of reaction and distracted by the discovery of how long she had been arrogating to herself a thing that concerned them both. 'Here and now,' she exclaimed, 'I give up being an elder sister who knows best.' Justin, on his way to the Semples', was muttering to himself, 'Damn and blast it, why couldn't she have told me sooner? If she had it would all be over by now.' It did not occur to him to blame himself for a lack of openness. This did not occur to Celia, either. It was Justin's constancy that mattered, not his fidelity—which was his own business.

When he reappeared, washed and brushed and ready for lunch, and told her there would be no more billets-doux from Mary, it was with merely tactical curiosity that she asked, 'Did you have to bribe her?' And as he did not answer at once, she went on to ask, 'Would you like potted shrimps or mulligatawny? There's both.'

They did not have to fly the country. Mary Semple disposed of the rest of her feelings by quarrelling with everyone in the cast of *King Arthur* and singing 'Fairest Isle' with such venom that her hearers felt their blood run cold, and afterwards remarked that stage fright had made her sing out of tune. The people listed by Mary as cognisant showed no more interest in the Tizards than before. The tradesmen continued to deliver. Not a cold shoulder was turned. But on that Sunday morning the balance between Justin and Celia had shifted, and never returned to its former adjustment. Both of them were aware of this, so neither of them referred to it, though at first Celia's abdication made her rather insistent that Justin should know best, make decisions, assert his authority. Justin asserted his authority by knowing what decisions could be postponed till the moment when there was no need to make them at all. Though he did not dislike responsibility, he was not going to be a slave to it. Celia's abdication also released elements in her character which till then had been penned back by her habit of common sense and efficiency. She became slightly frivolous, forgetful and timid. She read novels before lunch, abandoned all social conscience about bores, mislaid bills, took second helpings of *risotto* and mashed potatoes and began to put on weight. She lost her aplomb as a driver and had one or two small accidents. She discovered the delights of needing to be taken away for pick-me-up holidays. Mrs Mugthwaite, observing all this, knew it was the Change, and felt sorry for poor Mr Tizard; the Change wasn't a thing that a brother should be expected to deal with. From time to time, Justin and Celia discussed leaving Hallowby and going to live somewhere away from the east-coast climate and the east wind at the corner by St Cuthbert's, but they put off moving, because the two animals had grown old, were set in their ways, and would be happier dying in their own home. The pug died just before the Munich crisis, the cat lived on into the war.

So did Mr Pilkington, who died from overwork two months before the first air raid on Hallowby juxta Mare justified his insistence on constructing an air-raid shelter under the school playing fields. This first raid was concentrated on the ironworks, and did considerable damage. All next day, inland Hallowby heard the growl of demolition explosives. In the second raid, the defences were better organised. The enemy bombers were driven off their target before they could finish their mission. Two were brought down out to sea. A third, twisting inland, jettisoned its remaining bombs on and around Hallowby. One dropped in Gas Lane, another just across the road from Newton Lodge. The blast brought down the roof and dislodged a chimney stack. The rescue workers, turning the light of their torches here and there, noting the usual disparities between the havocked and the unharmed, the fireplace blown out, the portrait smiling above it, followed the trail of bricks and rubble upstairs and into a bedroom whose door slanted from its hinges. A cold air met them; looking up, they saw the sky. The floor was deep in rubble; bits of broken masonry, clots of brickwork, stood up from it like rocks on a beach. A dark bulk crouched on the hearth, and was part of the chimney stack, and a torrent of slates had fallen on the bed, crushing the two bodies that lay there.

The wavering torchlights wandered over the spectacle. There was a silence. Then young Foe spoke out. 'He must have come in to comfort her. That's my opinion.' The others concurred. Silently, they disentangled Justin and Celia, and wrapped them in separate tarpaulin sheets. No word of what they had found got out. Foe's hypothesis was accepted by the coroner and became truth.

(*A Stranger With a Bag*, 1961)

WINTER IN THE AIR

THE furniture, assembled once more under the high ceiling of a London room, seemed to be wearing a look of quiet satisfaction, as though, slightly shrugging their polished shoulders, the desk had remarked to the bookcase, the Regency armchair to the Chippendale mirror, 'Well, here we are again.' And then, after a creak or two, silence had fallen on the dustless room.

It was morbidly dustless, morbidly unlittered. Rolling up her apron, Mrs Darbyshire, the charwoman, said, 'I think that is all I can do for you today,' in tones of professional self-righteousness. Indeed, Barbara thought, there was nothing more to ask; everything, from the slight dampness on the floor of the kitchenette to the embonpoint of the cushions on the sofa, was as it should be. She had not seen such neatness for years.

The thought of someone like Mrs Darbyshire had confirmed her decision to live in London again. A London charwoman does her work, takes her money and goes away, sterile as the wind of the desert. She does not spongily, greedily, absorb your concerns, study your nose to see if you have been crying again, count the greying hairs of your head, proffer sympathetic sighs and vacuum pauses and then hurry off to wring herself out, spongily, all over the village, with news of what's going on between those two at Pond House. Not to mention the fact that a London charwoman is immeasurably better at charing.

Except that Mrs Darbyshire went away in trousers, her exit in 1950 was just as the exits of Mrs Shelley had been in the mid-thirties—the same healing order left behind, the same tonic appearance of everything wound up for a fresh start, with a filled kettle sitting on the hot-plate ready to be heated. And the flat of now, Barbara thought, in which she was again a single lady, was not very different from the flat of then; it was smaller, and the window glass, replacing glass that had been blown out in an air-raid, was of inferior quality, and the rent was a great deal higher, but the sitting-room and bedroom of the new flat were of the same sober, Victorian proportions, and, considering the housing short-age, she was lucky to get it, above all at such short notice—only two months. Two months and eight days, to be precise, for it was on the seventeenth of August that Willie broke the news, coming slowly across the sunburned lawn to where she stood repainting the front door of Pond House, little thinking how soon she would go out by it and Annelies come in.

'But why?' she had asked. 'Why must she come and *live* with you? I thought it was all over, months ago.'

'So did I.'

'But Annelies doesn't. Is that it?'

'She is so wretched,' he had said. 'So desperately, incompetently wretched. I can't let her go on suffering like this.'

While they spoke, she continued spreading the blue paint, brushing it into the knots and cajoling it round the door-knocker. Dreamily, under the shock of these tidings, there had persisted a small, steady dissatisfac-tion because the paint was not the right shade of blue.

The flat of now seemed lighter than the flat of then. This was partly because her pieces of rosewood furniture were now so much paler in tone; twelve years in a country house, with windows open and sun shining in and not enough furniture polish, had bleached the rosewood to a tint of *feuille-morte*. Outside there was a difference, too—more air, more light, welling like fountains from the bombed sites. The room was full of light, as full of light as it was full of silence. In the centre stood the rosewood table, and as she bent over it, it reflected her with the whole length of its uncluttered surface, darkened here and there with old ink-stains like sea-leopard skin.

'I shall leave you the rosewood table,' she had said to Willie. 'It's the only one that is the right height for you, and large enough to hold all your traps.'

'No, don't,' he had said. 'I shall take over the big kitchen table. It's the same height. I've measured it.'

'Very well. But you'll keep the wardrobe?'

'I'd rather not.'

'Nonsense! You must have something to keep your clothes in. Or to keep the moths in, for I suppose you'll never remember to shut the doors.'

'That's all right. Annelies has one of these compactum things. It belonged to her husband.'

'I see. How convenient.'

'My God, how I hate these practical conversations! Why must we have them? They always end like this.'

Planning ahead, Barbara had resolved that the furniture should not be arranged in the flat of now as in the flat of then. But London rooms impose a formula. Now, as then, the desk stood in the recess on the left side of the fireplace, and the bookcase in the recess on the right; the sofa had its back to the window; and, on the wall opposite the fireplace, the Chippendale mirror hung above the bureau. Later on, she thought, readjusting the sofa cushions (for Mrs Darbyshire, like Mrs Shelley, had a passion for putting square objects cornerwise)—later on, people too will regroup themselves in this room. Mary Mackenzie's hand will dangle from the arm of the Regency chair as though its rings were too many and too heavy for it, and Julian will project his long legs obliquely from the stool, and Clive Thompson will stand with his back to the room, puffing at the bookcase. They will not have kept their outlines as unyieldingly as the furniture has, but their voices will be the same, and after the first constraint we shall find a great deal to talk about. It will be best, her thoughts went on, planning, foreseeing and planning as they had done during the breathless, interminable weeks before her departure from Pond House—it will be best to get them all here together one evening, when any awkwardness can be tided over by making them a trifle drunk. But that could be later on. It was still only her third day in the flat of now, and one must have a small decency-bit of time in which to lick one's wounds and wring the sea-water of shipwreck out of one's hair. *Such privilege belongs to women* . . . One of the advantages of a solitary life is that it allows one time to verify quotations instead of trailing them about all day, hanging them on gooseberry bushes, leaving them, like rings, above the sink. *Such privilege* . . . Hermione, in *The Winter's Tale*, said it.

Shakespeare was in the bedroom, to countervail against her dislike of it. It was a dislikable room, mutilated by the remodelling, which had shorn it for a bathroom. The tree beyond the bedroom window, she thought, coming back into the sitting-room with the book in her hand—even the tree, in itself a pleasant thing, must be contemplated as a sparrow-rack, where, from the first light onward, sparrows would congregate and clatter, making sleep impossible.

She found *The Winter's Tale*, and turned to the trial scene. Here it was:

> . . . with immodest hatred,
> The child-bed privilege denied, which 'longs
> To women of all fashion. Lastly, hurried
> Here, to this place, i' the open air, before
> I have got strength of limit.

Verifying quotations would indeed be an interesting pursuit if they all turned out to be as wide of the mark as this one. If Willie had shown a spark of even modest hate, she might have known a spark of hope.

She laid Shakespeare on the sofa and presently sat down beside him. To do so was a deliberate act, for she still retained, as a vestige of the last few weeks, an inability to sit down. One says 'a glutton for work', and during her last month at Pond House she had exemplified that odious phrase, rushing gluttonously from one useful deed to another, cleaning, dispatching, repairing, turning out and destroying.

'All this revengeful housecleaning!' Willie had lamented.

'It's only fair to Annelies to get my smell out of the house,' she had replied.

In the first onset of grief, when grief was still pure enough to be magnanimous, the explanation might have been almost true, but not by the time she gave it. By then, she had no more magnanimity than a criminal on the run. There must be nothing left behind by which she could be tracked. A visual recollection of something overlooked and unscotched would strike her, as she lay sleepless—strike her violently, as though the object itself had been catapulted against her face. With her heart hammering and the blood pounding in her ears, she would begin to interrogate herself as to where, in their magpie's nest of a house, she had last set eyes on the red flannel heart embroidered with forget-me-nots, or the mug with 'William' on it that she had bought at Aberdovey.

And all the while the most damning piece of evidence had slipped her memory, and only came to light by chance.

Invalided after Dunkirk, Willie had retained from his equipment one of those metal slides that isolate the military button for polishing. Thinking that this would serve the same purpose for the brass knobs on the spice cupboard, she began to search for it in the collector's cabinet, where Willie's father had kept his birds' eggs, where Willie hoarded his oddments. In the third drawer down, she came on the letters, her sight stumbling from Annelies's crisp blue sheets to her own letters, written from the flat of then to the Willie of then. She had looked at them no longer than to think how surprisingly and for the worse her handwriting had altered during the twelve years of happy married illiteracy, when she heard Willie saying, 'I know nothing about it. Do please go away,' to the children at the back door who had come to fetch the things for the jumble sale. Slamming the drawer to, she ran downstairs to recall the children. When she went back to the cabinet, the drawer was locked. Embarrassment tied her tongue.

Three days later, looking like a good dog, Willie laid her letters on the dressing-table.

'I don't approve of what I am doing,' he said. 'But then I don't approve of anything I am doing.' After a pause, he added, 'I think I wish I were dead.'

'Not really,' she answered. 'Not really, my dear.'

They looked at each other in the mirror, then. In the mirror she watched him lay his head on her shoulder—deposit it there, as though it were a sick animal.

But it was from that hour—as though by the restitution of her letters a ghost had been laid or a cork drawn—that Willie began to recover, to ascend from being a mournful cipher in her preparations to becoming their animating spirit. The last joint days at Pond House were spent in a kind of battered exhilaration, with Willie circumventing inquiring droppers-in, beating carpets and sewing on buttons. It was not just speeding the parting guest. He had, somehow or other, to dispose of the mounting excitement with which he awaited Annelies, and to be the life and soul of Barbara's departure was at once a safety valve and a tribute to conjugality.

'Write to me, won't you?' he had said, tying on the last luggage label.

'We said we wouldn't write, except on business,' she had replied. 'It would hurt Annelies. You know how sensitive she is, how the least thing makes her suffer agonies.' (She could not deny herself this shaft, and anyhow it did not penetrate.)

'You owe me a letter, Barbara. I gave you back the others. I didn't want to, but I did. I have never been so unhappy as I was that morning.' It was true, as true as that he was now much less unhappy. 'At least write and tell me that you are settled in, that you are all right, that the roof doesn't leak, that there aren't black beetles. It might be called a letter of business, really—though it isn't.'

'I will write,' she had said.

Now she took up Shakespeare, in whose orisons all our sins are comprehended, and patted him. 'Dear Swan!' she said aloud, her voice, in the unexplored depths of the lofty London room, sounding like the voice of a stranger. She could feel her body furtively relaxing while she sat on the sofa, and beginning to enjoy itself. It sighed, and stretched its legs, and burrowed deeper into the cushions, and her nostrils quickened to the smell of furniture polish, as though there were promise in it. She had been happy in her former solitude; presently she would be solitarily happy again. Like the furniture, she would settle down in the old arrangement, and the silence of the room would not intimidate her long; it was no more than a pin-point of silence in the wide noise of London. The kettle was on the hot-plate, filled and ready to be heated. The room sat around her, attentive, ready for her to begin. But first she must write to Willie.

Crossing the room, she seemed to herself to wade through silence, as though she were wading out to sea against a mounting tide. Silence embraced her thighs and almost overthrew her. She sat down at the desk and took a sheet of paper from a pigeon-hole. The light from the window fell on the desk over her left shoulder, just as it had done in the flat of then. And, just as she had done in the flat of then, she wrote the date—the date of now—and the words 'My Dear.'

'I am keeping my promise,' she wrote. 'The flat is very comfortable. There are no black beetles, and the person overhead plays Bach by hand, which seems very old-fashioned and soothing. I have found a nice charwoman. She is called Mrs Darbyshire. She wears trousers. I hope—' The pen stopped. What did she hope?

After birthdays and Christmases there came the hour when one was set down to write the letters of thanks. 'Thank you so much for the gorgeous chocolates,' one wrote, or, 'It was very kind of you to give me that nice bottle of scent.' The chocolates had been eaten, the scent had been spilled—but still they had to be thanked for. One's handwriting sagged down the page as if from weariness, the words 'nice' or 'jolly' dogged one from sentence to sentence, and with every recommencement of gratitude the presents and the festivities became more irrevocably over and done with. One stared at the unfinished sentence and wondered what false thing to say next. Yet what she wanted to say to Willie was clear enough in her mind, clear as the printed words on India paper which had levelled themselves at her heart from that speech in *The Winter's Tale*:

> To me can life be no commodity;
> The crown and comfort of my life, your favour
> I do give lost, for I do feel it gone,
> Yet know not how it went . . .

But in real life one cannot write so plainly the plain truth; it would look theatrical. She must think of something she could legitimately hope. A hope about Mrs Darbyshire would do nicely. She wrote, 'I hope she will like me enough to look on me as a permanency.'

Oh, poor Willie! That sentence would not do at all. She tore up the unfinished letter and threw it into the grate, which Mrs Darbyshire had left neatly laid with crumpled paper and sticks and a few well-chosen lumps of coal, in case the lady should wish to light a fire in the evening; for a newly-moved-into place always strikes chilly at first, and though the autumn weather was keeping up wonderfully, almost as mild as spring, one could feel winter in the air.

(*Winter in the Air*, 1955)

IDENBOROUGH

THE car was a Rover, a 1939 model. In the December of that year Amabel's husband, Thomas Serpell, had bought it to put by, saying that at the end of a war there is no decent metal or decent leather left. It was still on blocks when, three years later, he died.

When wealthy men die, there is always a sensation of poverty, and under the stress of death-duties the executors had spoken of selling the car; but Thomas, Amabel's stepson, had cabled from Canada, where he was training pilots, that it must be kept, so it remained in the garage, draped in dust sheets and looking like a funeral trophy. Amabel also remained, living on with her mother-in-law for company, a dull, kind, preservative life, so preservative that when Thomas finally came home he exclaimed, 'Good God, Amabel, is this really you? You look like my niece!' Her smooth skin and her flowering full lips were the more remarkable for being encountered among Serpell aunts and cousins, fine large specimens of a North Country stock, brief in bloom and durable as pigskin. Amabel, an alien, had reversed this. She looked young and she felt elderly.

Her answer was defensive: 'Rather fat for a niece, Thomas.'

'Well, that will soon come off,' he said. 'You should do exercises, and swim, and play tennis.' Sojourning for so long in a new world, Thomas had brought back an embarrassing insistence on youthfulness, and smartness and spryness.

'Now we must get out the Rover,' said his grandmother, speaking as though it were a ceremonial teapot.

Thomas replied that it was scarcely worth the trouble, since in Cambridge he would use a bicycle. Thomas had also brought back a craving for culture and scholasticism and was going to Cambridge to read history.

When Thomas came north for Christmas, he brought his friend, Winter Gregory. Winter Gregory was a don, a kind of being Amabel had never set eyes on. She wished she had the sangfroid of her mother-in-law, who had never seen a don either but supposed he would eat and drink like any other mortal. After a couple of days, it was evident that he could fall in love like any other mortal, too. Amabel ceased to feel elderly, and refused his first proposal of marriage with such headlong vigour that the most cloistered and artless don might have taken hope from it. Winter was not notably cloistered. He had viewed with horror the bald solitaire diamond with which the deceased Mr Serpell had expressed his intentions of matrimony. The ring that he took with him on his second visit spelled out *Regard* with a ruby, an emerald, a garnet, an amethyst, another ruby and a quite moderate diamond. It looked very pretty on Amabel's old-fashioned small hand. There seemed no reason why the hand should not immediately become his, but she evaded marriage for over a year, and was finally routed into it by her mother-in-law's scorn for a woman of forty who hadn't the spunk to take a second husband. Her rough tongue succeeded where Thomas's encouragement had failed. Amabel had been abashed by the encouragements. It seemed to her like robbing a blind beggar to accept so much kind approval from her stepson when for the second time in her life she was violently in love, and on this occasion, too, not with his father.

The Rover preceded her to Cambridge. Thomas had given it to Winter as a wedding-present. This was so much what Thomas's father would have done that Amabel had a polyandrous impression that Thomas's father had almost done so.

Now, in the second year of their happy marriage, the car was swivelling along lanes and byroads whose banks were brooched with primroses and veined with the heavy blue of wild hyacinths still in bud. Winter had wanted to visit Amabel's birthplace in Somerset. She had not seen it since her fifth year, when her father went to a London parish, and there was very little she recognised except an archway under which he had driven her hoop. She felt a complete stranger and sightseer. It was the Cockney Winter who knew Priddy in the Mendips and the sudden violent view of the Bristol Channel from the road above

Clapton-in-Gordano, and who, saying calmly, 'We shall find it down here,' turned the car down a one-in-five rabbit-run. But it was Wiltshire, he said, as they crossed the county boundary—especially the unattended-to, undramatic country north of Salisbury Plain—that he was more at home in.

'Stonehenge,' said Amabel, catching at something she could be sure of. 'I should like to see Stonehenge.'

Without comment on her geography, he began to drive southeastward toward the smooth rampart of the chalk. On the timelessness of Salisbury Plain, Amabel suddenly became aware that the Rover looked somewhat out of date.

'You know, Winter, it's only just struck me that this car does look rather odd—spinsterish, and as if we ought to be wearing toques trimmed with autumn leaves.'

'If I had to choose between a spinster and a chromium-plated strumpet—' He broke off, and pointed ahead. 'Look!'

'Oh!' Her exclamation sounded like a cry of pity. 'Oh, Winter, is that Stonehenge?'

'Are you disappointed?'

'No! But somehow I feel so sorry for it. It is so small, so very small, and so neat.'

'Amabel, you don't know how I love you for things like that. You are the only perfectly sincere person I have ever known.'

He halted the car. Presently, he turned it and they drove away. She felt vaguely surprised. Winter's spendthrift treatment of historical monuments was something she could not get accustomed to. Thomas her husband never quitted a castle or a waterfall (he had been equally prone to both) without having, as he said 'thoroughly taken it in'. Thomas her stepson, though immune to nature and the Middle Ages, could take quite as long to absorb a portico, and talked much more. At times, she felt a certain nostalgia for the Serpell method of sightseeing. Though tiring to the legs, it was restful to the mind; there was none of this hit-or-miss, sharpshooting responsibility for saying the right thing. Having been so lucky with Stonehenge, she was the more anxiously aware of her inadequacies during the rest of the day's journey, for when they turned aside for a manor house, she could think of nothing but living in it, and when Winter stopped the car with a shout of laughter before a Baptist chapel, she asked him what he was laughing at. Above all, she was estranged by the duplicity of the landscape, so intricate and so indeterminate. After the large, hymn-tune solemnity of the North of England, it was perplexing as a fugue.

She's tired, Winter thought, and in his concern for her he lost his sense of direction, and took a wrong turning. He began to hurry, and so overshot a signpost, and had to back. It stood where the road branched left and right, and the left-hand pointer read, 'Great Wimble 9, Oxford 31.'

Sighing with relief, he said, 'There! Oxford. We shan't be long now. After Wimble, we shall strike a main road.' Even as he spoke, he noticed the right-hand pointer 'Idenborough! I had no idea we were so near it.'

'Ten miles,' Amabel said. 'And a dreadful road.'

'Yes, but Idenborough at the end of it. It's almost the loveliest small town in England, and there's quite a good inn. Why don't we spend the night there, instead of in Oxford?'

Amabel had read the name before he spoke it, and had been nerving herself to hear it spoken. It was at Idenborough, twenty years before, that she and Harry had spent a day, and two long autumn nights lying in a lumpy bed—so short a time, and yet outweighing all the rest of her life. She had gone there by train, abandoning her Thomases on the pretext of an old school friend just leaving for India. Blinded by excitement and sick headache, she had got out at a station on a branch line, where Harry was waiting on the platform, his face so stern with love that for a moment she had not recognised him, while he, glaring at the other end of the train, was so sunk in his conviction that she had changed her mind that she was compelled to take him by the sleeve and shake him before he noticed her. All rapture, all romance, and all leave-taking were sealed up under that word, *Idenborough*, and now it was a name on a signpost, and a place where she and Winter might spend the night.

'Oxford's only thirty miles on, and you wanted to show me Oxford.' Her voice shook as if she had been running.

Glancing round, he saw that she looked pale. Oxford be damned, with its bells and its buses, and its admirers settling with veneration on all the fakes! 'Oxford can wait,' he said, and turned off for Idenborough.

If only I could sometimes tell the truth, if only I could learn to speak out, she thought—and remembered how, earlier in the day, Winter had praised her for her sincerity. But now it was too late. Deceit must accumulate on deceit, and with her second husband she would visit Idenborough, where she had cuckolded her first one. Winter was assuring her how much she would like Idenborough, and comparing its grape-coloured roof-tiles with roofs in Burgundy, while, faithless once again, she sat staring ahead, licking her lips with excitement as she waited for the first recognition. The lane ran into a main road. Ahead was a wide, placid street, and the silhouette of a church tower, old and owlish. She did not particularly recognise anything, but no doubt that was because they were entering from another direction. The tower had been there, of course, for she remembered the bells chiming the hours and the quarters, and Harry saying that he had an uncle whose conversation was precisely similar. And, in fact, what did she remember of Idenborough? So little—only everything. But when Winter stopped in front of a porch surmounted by a mild bear painted plum colour, she nearly said, 'This isn't the right hotel.'

While he was garaging the car, she followed the servant to the room allotted to them, her legs moving under her like the legs of some other person, legs imperfectly attached and rather too short for her. Strewing her coat and gloves and bag on twin beds of blameless springs, she went to the window. Roofs of weathered tiles, fig trees and lilacs emerging from walled gardens, the leaden haunches of a church, and beyond, a row of tall poplars . . . She knew those trees. They signalled everything into place. The hotel where she had stayed with Harry must be at the farther end of the town. There was the true Idenborough. The poplars grew close to that hotel, aligned along a bridle-path that led to a cemetery and the gasworks. There they had walked up and down, in a gentle drizzling rain, saying that it was really too wet to stay out any longer and yet continuing to walk up and down. And there she had known the inexhaustible melancholy of youth, extending below her like an ocean and endlessly surrounding her while she floated onward, immortally buoyant and serene.

When Winter came in, she turned from the window, saying, 'I am so glad we came here instead of Oxford. Shall we go out for a little walk?'

'Not till you've had a drink. I only hope I haven't gone and overtired you, jaunting about all day. Besides, it's nearly dinner-time.'

'Well, after dinner, then?'

The drink mounted lightly to her head. All through dinner, she felt a detached, competent animation, as though she were behaving to music. Exactly on the beat, she said, 'What horrible coffee! Don't let's waste time on it. I'd rather walk round Idenborough.'

The direction of the poplar trees was so perfectly established in her mind that she felt no impatience when Winter set off in the opposite direction, talking of a town hall. A lion and a unicorn decorated the town hall, plump and suave as though they were in sugar on a biscuit. They were just what Harry would have liked, and she almost wished that they had come this way instead of going by bus to that rather tiresome village with a wishing-well. Winter liked the lion and the unicorn, too, and agreed about the biscuit. They walked down several streets, pausing to admire doorways and converse with evening cats, and finding a chemist's shop still open and lit up like an Elizabethan jewel with its coloured flasks and rosy patent tonics, they went in for the pleasure of buying something in Idenborough. The purchase of a small hot-water bottle led to a long conversation between Winter and the chemist that wound its way to leeches and local survivals of traditional remedies, such as stolen potatoes and fried mice.

When they left the shop, the twilight had changed to a blue dusk, and Amabel could hear doors being shut and bolted. But still she was not impatient, though it was apparent that Winter had something more up his sleeve, some special beauty that he was saving for the last. While she was waiting in the chemist's shop, it occurred to her that if this evening were frittered away, there would still be tomorrow morning. It would be easy to make an excuse of wanting to shop by herself in order to buy him a surprise present, and then all she need do would be to find the railway station and from there retrace her way to the hotel and the poplar trees, and on the way back she could buy a mug. Idenborough was full of shops where mugs could be bought, and when you have taken the first step of deceiving a husband, nothing is easier than to go on.

Reposing on this, she accompanied Winter down a street so narrow that there was no inducement to stop and admire anything. At the foot of the hill, the street turned sharply. She received a sudden impression of light and space, and felt the air freshened, and heard the slap of water against stone. They were on a quay, and before them extended a narrow bridge of many arches. Half-way across it, he stopped.

'Look, Amabel. That's why I wanted to bring you here.'

Behind them the town, catching the revenant light of the eastern sky, was a muddle of brown and mulberry-coloured velvets. The tower and the high nave of the church rose above it, and the sky showed through the clerestory windows. But she only looked at it long enough to steady herself, and then returned her gaze to the wide, pale river, whose waters swirled with a kind of sleepwalking impetus from between the piers of the bridge. So wide a river . . . How could they not have known there was this river? She looked along its course and saw on the far bank a row of poplar trees, rising lugubriously tall from an unlit, unbroken flatness of water-meadows.

Laying her hand on the parapet and finding it quite real, she asked, 'What river is this?'

'The Thames.'

Another strong swirl of water emerged from under the bridge and spread itself onward, as though in calm assent and confirmation.

'What did you say this place was called?'

'Idenborough.'

A small black dazzle flashed in front of her and disappeared under the bridge.

'A bat,' she said, fastening on a certainty.

Not hearing her, he went on, 'Idenborough Regis, to give it its full name. There's another Idenborough, in Bedfordshire. A dull place —though now I suppose it glitters with cinemas and garages, for there's an aerodrome near by.'

After a while, still looking down on the river, Amabel said, 'Is there anywhere you haven't been?'

There was such rancour in her voice that he was nearly stampeded into asking her if she felt tired. Taking his cue from an oncoming yawn, he replied, 'Bed, perhaps. Judging from my present sensations, I have never been to bed.'

The yawn achieved itself, and on its close he took her by the arm and began walking back to the hotel.

'I expect it's driving that old-fashioned car that tires you,' she said.

His car, his dearest possession (since one does not number a wife among possessions), which throughout their holiday of byroads and hysterical contours had behaved like a duchess—not satisfied with attacking him, Amabel must needs turn against the Rover, too. This time, he asserted himself. 'With a good car, it's mileage that counts, Amabel, not years. The same with wives.'

'Yes, but it *is* an old car, Winter. One's only got to look at it to see that. And though it's very chivalrous of you to feel affection for your old dowdy . . .'

All the way back to the hotel she talked in this strain, flagellating herself under the guise of depreciating the car, condoling with him on his faithfulness to an old car and an ageing wife. It rent his heart to hear her. It appalled his heart to admit an identity between his gentle, modest, complying Amabel and this provincial harridan at his side.

She saw his grief and his dismay, but she dared not weaken to them. If she were to change her harsh tune, if for one moment between now and when she heard him grunt and fall from her into the solitude of sleep she were to let him be kind to her, she would be done for; she would give way and tell him about Harry and the other Idenborough, and how, merely by her own despicable shilly-shallying and playing for safety, there had been no more to tell. To Winter, unjudging, unblaming, possibly even approving, it would seem next to nothing, and by length of time diminished to nothing at all. Indeed, there was not much of it: two nights and a day, a rapture so inattentively, unbelievingly entertained that she did not even know what county Idenborough was in. Unbelievingly entertained, weakly lost, negligently remembered (for months at a time she did not give it a thought), yet it was all she had. Thinking this, she reversed the thought. She was all it had. It existed by her secrecy; to speak of it would be to dismiss it, like the small crystal world of a bubble, into common air. Any infidelity but that.

(*Winter in the Air*, 1955)

THE FOREGONE CONCLUSION

SHE planted a high Spanish comb in her pubic hair and resumed her horn-rimmed spectacles.

'There! That's as much as I shall dress.'

'You look very improper.'

'I *am* improper.' Her young voice was quelling.

Love warmed her. It did not warm him. He moved nearer the gas fire and repelled the thought of his overcoat. He would soon be in it and on his way home. But politeness requires that after making love one must make a little conversation.

'I heard a record of that new Icelandic bass, last night.'

They met for the first time six months before at a concert, simultaneously turning to each other and saying 'Well!' as if they had simultaneously been dropped from a cloud to find themselves in Row K, Seats 18 and 19. After the first hush the applause exploded. The conductor waved the orchestra to rise. The applause redoubled. Speech was out of the question, and so they continued to look at each other.

Ignoring his Icelandic bass, she said, 'You look perfectly proper—all you need is your umbrella. I can't think how you do it in time.'

'The practice of years, Lucy. You'll dress as quickly when you are my age.'

It was that glint in her voice which had birdlimed him, though when he suggested she should come on to Pagliacci's Sandwich Bar—for Mahler left one famishing—it was merely a fostering concern to supply anything so young, so vital, so exceedingly thin, with the means to keep it alive. But by the third sandwich the glint in her soft voice, her precise diction—even with her mouth full—her pell-mell opinions had entangled his curiosity, and he invited her to the Berlioz 'Te Deum' under the same conductor. She came dressed in leather and spangles—height of her fashion, he supposed—and spoke hardly at all. Afterward he saw her home, and stayed.

'When I am your age . . .' she broke off.

The conversation was not going very well. The lovemaking had not gone very well, either. On an impulse of atonement he got up and wrapped her in his overcoat.

'"And custom lie upon thee—" How long have you had this splendid coat?'

'A good ten years.'

'And how many Lucys, how many lucky Lucys—No, I didn't say that; I'd rather be magnanimous. Suppose I fall asleep in it? You'd never have the heart to turn me out into the snow; you'd have to stay the night.'

He stooped to kiss her. She evaded him, walked stiffly to the piano, sat down, and began to play a Scarlatti sonata.

The coat swamped her; she looked like some grotesque bear. Her hands, her narrow naked feet were as touchingly out of scale as she was out of scale with the gaunt Victorian proportions of her bed-sitting room, where the smell of gas contended with the smell of pineapple and muscadet. Before the pineapple there had been sole cooked with grapes, avgolemono. He had often begged her to entertain him less extravagantly, said he would be as pleased with bacon and egg. She wouldn't listen. In their beginning, he tried to feed her by going to restaurants. Halfway through a meal their impatience hurried them away.

But even the young can't subsist on love and an occasional banquet; her ghost's earnings couldn't amount to much. 'What's your job?' he'd asked at Pagliacci's. 'I'm a ghost', she replied. For the flash of a moment he believed it. Ghosts, she explained, write other people's books for them, haunting the reading room of the British Museum for facts.

The Scarlatti sonata—she was playing more accurately than usual and not so well—twirled its tail and ended.

'Have you done anything about getting the man from the gas company to see to that leak?'

She shook her head and began another sonata.

The man from the gas company; the warm dressing gown she never put on; the vitamin pills; the visit to the oculist—of course, she was bored by his solicitudes, the more so since she didn't attend and he had to renew them over and over again. In their beginning, love made these insistences lighthearted—a wooing dance where he strutted, she flustered; now they had become so habitual that twice he had forgotten that a particular request had been complied with. No wonder such inquiries fell on her like something to be shrugged off. *And custom lie upon thee with a weight heavy as . . .* as what? As earth? As lead? As a methodical civil servant with a wife, two dull daughters, an OBE, and old enough to ber her father.

She had left off playing and sat staring at the Louis Philippe wall clock he had given her, and which she had been pleased with and seldom remembered to wind up.

'Four-fifteen', she reported.

It was because of the resemblance between the gentle, precise chime of the clock and her voice that he had chosen it; and because it had pleased her, his solicitude extended to it and he reset and wound it each time before leaving.

'I must be going, my sweet.'

Habit and daily conformity sequester what may be the loveliest thing in the person we love. When they dropped from a cloud into Row K, Seats 18 and 19, Lucy's face was turned toward him. So it remained: to think of Lucy was to think of her face so turned; it had become the familiarised representative of her voice. As she began to rid herself of his coat, and her small head on its tulip-straight stem emerged, he realised with intensity that it was the nape of her neck he loved beyond all else. He clasped her and the coat together and felt her tremor through the coat. Dislodged by his embrace, the comb fell on the floor. 'Poor object', she said and laughed to herself.

'Damn your comb! Lucy, Lucy, you do know I still love you? You do know?'

' "Still" is not a word to use to a lady.'

He was within an inch of shaking her.

She picked up the comb and carried it off, leaving him with the overcoat. Opening a drawer, she took out the warm dressing gown, put it on, and tied the cord. He could see why she didn't wear it: its crimson leeched the colour from her mouth, its woollen amplitude vulgarised her. It was another of her sensible mistakes. She had put it on out of good manners, and, once he was away, she would tear it off and trample on it.

'What will you do after I've gone?'

'I shall wash up. Then I shall write a sad poem. Then I shall go to bed and cry myself to sleep.'

He asked because he could not bear to go away without her voice in his ears.

'Good luck to the poem. Kiss me.'

She kissed inattentively, more occupied in putting something in his pocket.

'It's to read in the Underground.'

'Is it a poem? Shall I read it now?'

'Read it in the Underground.'

He knew it was dastardly, going away with Lucy's poem in his pocket when he should have insisted on reading it there and then. The reading would not have taken long. Lucy's poems were brief—six lines at most—obscure, and residually trite. He never knew what to say about them. The best he could have done would be to say they reminded him of nursery rhymes. And they did not; they reminded him of those small, solidified, semi-transparent blobs of resin which ooze from old plum trees and taste of rain. He could not have praised it; she could infallibly see through him, though she could not always see through herself. Better that it should be in his pocket, doing no harm. He would fit it into his morning-after letter, tomorrow.

The train was standing at the platform; he jumped in, just as the doors were about to close. The light, the warmth of the car, the drone of speed overcame him. He yawned and yawned. His eyes watered so that he could hardly read her poem.

She had headed it with the date.

17th January.

We can't keep it up—this poor pretence. You know it as well as I do. You have grown tired of our love. Not of me, perhaps. But there is no instantaneity left between us. You will not even know that tonight is the last night.

Thank you and goodbye. Lucy.

I don't want to stay friends.

He drew a deep breath. Presently he got out at the right station.

(*The New Yorker*, 1973)

AN ACT OF REPARATION

Lapsang sooshang—must smell like tar.
Liver salts in *blue* bottle.
Strumpshaw's bill—why 6*d*.?
Crumpets.
Waistcoat buttons.
Something for weekend—not a chicken.

So much of the list had been scratched off that this remainder would have made cheerful reading if it had not been for the last item.

Valerie Hardcastle knew where she was with a chicken. You thawed it, put a lump of marg inside, and roasted it. While it was in the oven you could give your mind to mashed potatoes (Fenton couldn't endure packet crisps), bread sauce and the vegetable of the season—which latterly had been sprouts. A chicken was calm and straightforward: you ate it hot, then you ate it cold; and it was a further advantage that one chicken is pretty much like another. Chicken is reliable—there is no apple-pie-bed side to its character. With so much in married life proving apple-pie-beddish, the weekend chicken had been as soothing as going to church might be if you were that sort of person. But now Fenton had turned—like any worm, she thought, though conscious that the comparison was inadequate—declaring that he was surfeited with roast chicken, that never again was she to put one of those wretched commercialised birds before him.

'Think of their hideous lives, child! Penned up, regimented, stultified. They never see a blade of grass, they never feel the fresh air, all they know is chicken, chicken, chicken—just like us at weekends.

Where is that appalling draught coming from? You must have left a window open somewhere.'

'What do you think I ought to get instead? I could do liver-and-bacon. But that doesn't go on to the next day.'

'Can't you get a joint?'

A joint. What joint? She had never cooked a joint. At home, Mum made stews. At the Secretarial College there was mince and shepherd's pie. No doubt a joint loomed in the background of these—but distantly, like mountains in Wales. When she and Olive Petty broke away from the college to share a bed-sitting room and work as dancing partners at the town's new skating rink their meals mainly consisted of chips and salami, varied by the largesse of admirers who took them to restaurants. Fenton, as an admirer, had expressed himself in *scampi* and *crêpes Suzette* —pronounced 'crapes', not 'creeps'—with never a mention of joints. Grey-haired, though with lots of it, he was the educated type, and theirs was an ideal relationship till Mrs Fenton, whom he had not mentioned either—not to speak of—burst out like a tiger, demanding divorce. The case was undefended. Six months later to the day, Fenton made an honest woman of her. Brought her down to earth, so to speak.

Marriage, said the registrar, was a matter of give-and-take. Marriage, thought Valerie, was one thing after another. Now it was joints. Sunk in marriage, she sat at a small polished table in the bank, waiting for Fenton's queries about his statement sheets to be thoroughly gone into, meanwhile enjoying the orderliness and impersonality of an establishment so unlike a kitchen or a bedroom.

And at an adjoining table sat the previous Mrs Hardcastle who for her part had come to withdraw a silver teapot from the bank's strong room, examining with a curiosity she tried to keep purely abstract the young person who had supplanted her in Fenton's affections. Try as she might, abstraction was not possible. Conscience intervened, compunction and stirrings of guilt. It was all very well for Isaac; he had not drawn Abraham's attention to the ram in the thicket. It was all very well for Iphigenia, who had not suggested to the goddess that a hind could replace her at the sacrificial altar. Isaac and Iphigenia could walk off with minds untroubled by any shade of responsibility for the substituted victim. But she, Lois Hardcastle, writhing in the boredom of being married to Fenton, had snatched at Miss Valerie Fry, who had done her no harm whatever, and got away at her expense. And this, this careworn, deflated little chit staring blankly at a shopping list, was what Fenton had made of her in less than six months' matrimony.

'Oh, dear!' said Lois, and sighed feelingly.

Hearing the exclamation and the sigh, Valerie glanced up to discover who was taking on so. She could see nothing to account for it. The woman was definitely middle-aged, long past having anything to sound tragic about. Indeed, she looked uncommonly healthy and prosperous, was expensively made up, wore a wedding ring, had no shopping bags—so why should she jar the polish and repose of a bank by sighing and exclaiming 'Oh dear?' Leg of lamb, leg of pork, leg of . . . did nothing else have legs? A bank clerk came up with a sealed parcel, saying 'Here it is, Mrs Hardcastle. If you'll just sign for it.'

'Here, you've made a mistake! Those aren't Mr Hardcastle's—' As Valerie spoke, she saw the parcel set down in front of the other woman. Fenton's other one. For it was she, though so smartened up as to be almost unrecognisable. What an awkward situation! And what a pity she had drawn attention to herself by saying that about the parcel. Fortunately, Fenton's other one did not appear to have noticed anything. She read the form carefully through, took her time over signing it, exchanged a few words with the clerk about the time of year before he carried it away. Of course, at her age she was probably a bit deaf, so she would not have heard those give-away words. The give-away words sounded on in Valerie's head. She was still blushing vehemently when the other Mrs Hardcastle looked her full in the face and said, cool as a cucumber, 'Mrs Lois Hardcastle, now. What an odd place we've chosen to meet in.'

Pulling herself together, Valerie replied, 'Quite a coincidence.'

'Such a small world. I've come to collect a teapot. And you, I gather, are waiting for Fenton's statement sheets, just as I used to do. And it's taking a long time, just as it always did.'

'There were some things Mr Hardcastle wanted looked into.'

Not to be put down, Mr Hardcastle's earlier wife continued, 'Now that the bank has brought us together, I hope you'll come and have coffee with me. I'm going back to London tonight, so it's my only chance to hear how you both are.'

'I don't know that I can spare the time, thank you all the same, I'm behindhand as it is, and I've got to buy a joint for the weekend.'

'Harvey's or Ensten's?'

'Well, I don't really know. I'd rather thought of the Co-op.'

'Excellent for pork.'

'To tell the truth, I've not bought a joint before. We've always had a chicken. But now he's got tired of chicken.'

Five months of love and chicken . . .

'I'm afraid you've been spoiling him,' said Lois. 'Keep him on cold veal for a few weeks and he'll be thankful for chicken.'

'I hadn't thought of veal. Would veal be a good idea?'

'Here come your statement sheets. Now we can go and have some coffee and think about the veal.'

'Well, I must say, I'd be glad of it. Shopping gets me down.'

Tottering on stiletto heels and still a head shorter than Lois, the replacement preceded her from the bank, jostling the swinging doors with her two bulging, ill-assembled shopping bags. Lois took one from her. It was the bag whose handle Fenton, in a rush of husbandry, had mended with string. The string ground into her fingers—as fatal, as familiar, as ever.

The grey downs grew into lumps of sin to Guenevere in William Morris's poem, and as Fenton's wives sat drinking coffee the shopping bags humped on the third chair grew into lumps of sin to Lois. They were her bags, her burden; and she had cast them onto the shoulders of this hapless child and gone flourishing off, a free woman. It might be said, too, though she made less of it, that she had cast the child on Fenton's ageing shoulders and hung twenty-one consecutive frozen chickens round his neck . . . a clammy garland. Apparently it was impossible to commit the simplest act of selfishness, of self-defence even, without paining and inconveniencing others. Lost in these reflections, Lois forgot to keep the conversation going. It was Valerie who revived it. 'Where would one be without one's cup of coffee?'

For, considering how handicapped she was with middle age and morality, Fenton's other one had been putting up a creditable show of sophisticated broadmindedness, and deserved a helping hand—the more so since that sigh in the bank was now so clearly explainable as a sigh of regret for the days when she had a husband to cook for. Lois agreed that one would be quite lost without one's cup of coffee. 'And I always think it's such a mistake to put milk in it,' continued Valerie, who with presence of mind had refused milk, black coffee being more sophisticated. Two sophisticated women, keeping their poise on the rather skiddy surface of a serial husband, was how she saw the situation. For a while, she managed to keep conversation on a black-coffee level: foreign travel, television, the guitar. But you could see the poor thing's heart wasn't really in it; grieving for what could never again be hers, she just tagged along. Yes, she had been to Spain, but it was a long time ago. No, unfortunately, she had missed that programme. 'I never seem to have enough time. Do have another cake.' She seemed to have time enough now. The cake lay on her plate, the coffee cooled in her cup; still she sat brooding, and frowned as though she were calculating some odds, hatching some resolution. Could it be that she was going to turn nasty? All of a sudden, she looked up and exclaimed, 'I know. Oxtail.'

'I beg your pardon?'

'Oxtail. Instead of a joint. Come on.'

Well, if it made her happy . . .

It certainly did. A wife Fenton hadn't given her an idea of, a wife as animated and compelling as a scenic railway, swept Valerie to the butcher's, summoned old Mr Ensten himself, made him produce a series of outlandish objects totally unlike Valerie's conception of what could be called a joint, chose out the most intimidating of the lot, stiff as a poker and a great deal longer, watched with a critical eye as he smote it into coilability, swept on to a greengrocer to buy carrots, garlic, celery and button mushrooms, then to a grocer's shop, bafflingly small, dusky and undisplaying, where she bought peppercorns, bay leaves and a jar of anchovies, finally to a wine merchant where she bought half a bottle of claret. Whirled on in this career, consulted and assenting over God knew what next, abandoning all thought of the rest of her shopping list, Valerie fell from gasps to giggles. Why peppercorns, when pepper could be got ready ground? Why anchovies, when there was no thought of fish? And garlic? Now it was claret.

'And a taxi, please.'

As though it were perfectly normal for wine merchants to supply taxis, the taxi was fetched. Valerie was put into it; the parcels and shopping bags were put in after her.

'Seventeen Windermere Gardens,' said Lois.

Once, escaping from the Secretarial College, Valerie and Olive Petty bought half-crown tickets for a Mystery Drive. The bus, thundering through a maze of small streets, had taken them past the Corporation Gas Works into the unknown. It had dived into woods, skirted past villages with spires and villages with towers, shown them an obelisk on a hill-top, a reservoir, a bandstand, an Isolation Hospital, a glimpse of the sea, a waterfall, a ruined castle. Then, with a twirl through some unidentifiable suburbs, it set them down by the War Memorial, a stone's throw from the Secretarial College. Now it was to be the same thing. The Mystery Shopping Excursion would end at 17 Windermere Gardens. All that remained was to say something calm and suitable.

'Such an unexpected pleasure to meet you. You've quite changed the day for me.'

'But I'm coming, too. I'm coming to cook the oxtail. I hope you don't mind.'

'Mind? My God, I'd be thankful! And more.'

The ring of sincerity transformed the poor girl's voice. To say 'transfigured' would, however, be going too far. Transformed it. Unmuzzled it.

No act of reparation, thought Lois, sitting in the taxi, can be an exact fit. Circumstances are like seaweed: a moment's exposure to the air, an hour's relegation to the past tense, stiffens, warps, shrivels the one and the other. The impulse to ease even a fraction of the burden she had imposed on that very different Miss Valerie Fry of the divorce proceedings—an impulse first felt in the bank as an amused acknowledgement of a faint sense of guilt, which at the word 'joint' had fleshed itself in the possibility of a deed, and a compassion against which she had soon ceased to struggle—for only someone in a state of utter dejection could have eaten three of those appalling little cakes—would fit neither the offence nor the moment. Probably even the medium was ill chosen. She happened to like oxtail herself, but very likely the girl would have preferred rolled ribs. Only one static element would resist the flux of time: Fenton's planet-like, unconjectural course. The Borough Offices where he worked as an architect closed at midday on Saturday. The planet-like course then took him to lunch at the Red Lion, and then to a healthful swim in the public baths, and then to his club; and he would be home at six.

'I'm afraid, as I wasn't expecting you, there won't be more than bread and cheese,' said the voice, now back in its muzzle.

'Nothing I should like better. It will give us more time to cook in. When does Fenton usually get home?'

'Four, or thereabouts.'

Even Fenton wasn't the same. She glanced with admiration at the young person whose society was two hours more alluring than hers had been; then at her wristwatch.

'Well, if I don't dawdle over my bread and cheese, that should be long enough. At any rate, it should be well on its way by then.'

'By then? All that time to cook a tail? You *must* be fond of cooking!'

The tone of spontaneous contempt, thought Lois, was just what anyone trying to apply an act of reparation might expect, and therefore what she deserved.

The taxi turned down Windermere Terrace. Seeing the iteration of small houses, each carefully designed to be slightly at variance with the others, each with a small identical garage and small front gardens for demonstrations of individuality, Lois observed that in some of the gardens the ornamental shrubs had grown larger, in others had died. They entered the house.

'I should think it must feel a bit queer to you, coming back like this,' Valerie said.

'No. Rather homelike. What a pretty new wallpaper—new wallpapers, that is.' A pink wall with squiggles, a blue wall with stripes, a yellow wall with poodles, kiosks and the Eiffel Tower, a black wall with marbling. And did Fenton come home two hours earlier to gaze on these?

'I put them all on myself. And one with fishes in the bathroom. I expect you know your way to the bathroom?'

'I must not, will not, be censorious,' said Lois to herself. And Valerie, arranging ready-sliced bread and processed cheese for two, muttered to her four walls, when she was left alone with them, 'If she goes on being a condescending old ray of sunlight, I'll murder her.'

There was no time to expect that Lois knew her way to the kitchen. She was in it in a flash.

'I haven't really got around to decorating this yet. To tell the truth, I'm not all that struck on cooking.'

'Where do you keep the large stewpan?'

The large stewpan was traced to the cupboard under the stairs, where it held jam pots and spiders. But at some time it must have been used, for Lois had left it clean. The cooking knives were rusty, the wooden spoons had been used to stir paint. Moths and skewers were in every drawer she opened. Without a flutter of pity, of compunction, of remorse, of any of the feelings that should accompany an act of reparation as parsley and lemon accompany fried plaice or red-currant jelly jugged hare, Lois searched, and cleaned, and sharpened, and by quarter to three the oxtail was in the large stewpan, together with the garlic, carrots, bay leaves, peppercorns and celery.

'What about the mushrooms?' Valerie inquired. She had rubbed the mushrooms and did not intend to see them slighted.

'They go in later on.'

'Well, as you seem to be managing all right, perhaps I'll . . .'

'Yes, do.'

One of the things Fenton particularly liked about Valerie was her habit of awaiting him. A man likes to be awaited. At the end of a dull day's architecture, to find a wife quietly sitting, undistracted by any form of employment, not even reading a book, but just sitting and waiting and ready to look pleased is very agreeable. Today he happened to be forty minutes later than usual, a conversation with a man called Renshaw having delayed him. His expectations were forty minutes livelier, and as he closed the garage and walked towards his door he said to himself that there was really quite a dash of the Oriental in him. The discovery of this dash—he had not been aware of it till Valerie—had even reconciled him to the prospect of baked beans or scrambled eggs on cold toast, if such was the price of being awaited. Besides, he always had a good substantial lunch at the Red Lion. But today Valerie was awaiting him amid a most exhilarating smell of cooking. It would be gross to comment on it immediately: to mulct her of the caresses of reunion, to fob off her proper desire to hear what he had been doing all day. And though she did not comment on his unpunctuality, he was at pains to tell her of his unforeseen encounter with Renshaw—not the Renshaw who skated and had been instrumental in bringing them together but his cousin E. B. Renshaw; to recount what E. B. Renshaw had said and to give a brief account of his character, career and accomplishments as a slow bowler. Only then did he say, 'No need to ask what you've been doing. What a wonderful smell! What is it?'

'Oxtail.'

'Of course! Oxtail. I thought I knew it.'

'Do you like oxtail?'

'Immensely—when it's not out of the tin. I can smell that this isn't.'

'Oh, no!'

He snuffed again. Lois had added the mushrooms and the anchovies and was now administering claret.

'Delicious! What's in it?'

'All sorts of things. Button mushrooms.'

Her smile struck him as secretive—no wonder, with this talent up her sleeve. And all performed so casually, too, so unobtrusively; for there she sat, reposeful, not a hair out of place, none of the usual cook's airs of flurry and inattention, not a single 'Just wait one moment' while he was relating his day and the meeting with E. B. Renshaw.

'When will it be ready?' he said with ardour.

'Not just yet. Do you like my nail varnish? It's new. I bought it today.'

'Very pretty. Do you think you ought to go and stir it?'

'Oh, no! She'll do all that.'

'She?' Had Valerie gone and got a cook? A cook from whom such odours proceeded would demand enormous wages, yet might almost be worth it. 'She? What she?'

'Your other wife. She's in there. She's been doing it all the afternoon.'

'Do you mean Lois?'

'Of course I mean Lois. You haven't any other wives, have you?'

This pertness when referring to his previous marriage was customary, and did not altogether displease. Now he didn't even notice it. He had a situation to grapple with, and the better to do so removed part of it off his knee.

'How did this happen?'

'We met at the bank—she'd gone there for some teapot or other. We couldn't sit there glaring at each other, so we began to talk.'

About him, of course. What confidences had been exchanged? What invidious—

'She told me you liked cold veal.'

A total misrepresentation. Lois had always been malicious, seizing on some casually expressed liking to throw in his teeth. 'What else did she say?'

'Nothing much. I had to do most of the talking. And before I knew where I was, she was wanting to come and cook you an oxtail. I couldn't very well stop her, could I? Of course I paid for it. The worst of it is, she was in such a rush to get here that I hadn't a chance to ask Strumpshaw about that sixpence, or to get the waistcoat buttons or the right liver salts or your China tea. She isn't what I'd call considerate.'

'I shall have to go and see her.'

He would have to open the kitchen door, take the full assault of that witching smell, see Lois cooking as of old—an unassimilable answer to prayer. For of course she mustn't come again, she mustn't go on doing this sort of thing; nor was he a man to be won back by fleshpots. Yet he knew himself moved. Poor Lois, making her way back almost like an animal, forgetting her jealousy, her prejudice, all the awful things she had said at the time of the divorce, trampling on convention and *amour-propre*, just to cook him a favourite dish. What had impelled her to do this? Remorse, loneliness, an instinctive longing to foster and nourish? For many years her feeling for him had been almost wholly maternal—which made her insistence on the divorce even more uncalled-for. What had set it off? Seeing the teapot, perhaps. They had both been fond of the teapot. It was Georgian.

Or was it all a deliberate scheme to lure him back?

He sprang to his feet, straightened his waistcoat, left the sitting room, entered the kitchen. It was empty. She had gone. Tied to the handle of the stewpan was a visiting card, on the back of which she had written: 'This will be ready by seven. It should simmer till then. *Don't let it boil.*'

(*A Stranger with a Bag*, 1961)

LAY A GARLAND ON MY HEARSE

I T was difficult, short of giving one's whole mind to the subject, to keep an accurate census of the Meridens at Foxholes. Just as one had become accustomed to Teresa and Egbert, Teresa and Egbert would return to Canada and Roy, Geraldine, Rosemary, Peter, and the twins, arriving from the Scilly Isles, took their place. Almost literally took their place. For Foxholes was a smallish house, and when the larger consignments of Meridens were in residence it was nothing for three Meridens to sleep in one bed. In summer, of course, it was easier. All the Meridens were hardy—'Quite gipsies, really,' as they said, indicating a row of camp-beds extending down the central path of the kitchen-garden.

So, on the whole, it was safest not to dogmatise about the number of the Meridens. One just said that they were a large devoted family, that though fate and economics had scattered them over the British Empire, family affection brought them back to pay long visits to old Mrs Meriden. Then one might add how lucky it was that old Mrs Meriden still had her wonderful old Sarah, what a mercy it was that old Sarah still kept about so well, what a loss it would be when old Sarah no longer kept about—though of course Rosalind helped a good deal.

The very involutions of the Meriden's family devotion made it harder to number them. For instance, should Egbert, Jasper, and Bunny be counted as Meridens, or merely as the Messrs Twillicoat, Hobson, and Webb whom Teresa, Faith, and Dorothy Meriden had married? I always reckoned them as one and a half Meridens; and the four daughters-in-law, Geraldine, Mary, Mary mi., and Molly, summed up, in my estimation, to three and a quarter Meridens. But then I have always been fond, in a piddling way, of arithmetic. Old Mrs Meriden spun no such filigrees. They were all her dear children, she made no distinction between the bond and the free. The grandchildren were even more her dear children. The instant they were born she swallowed them whole.

Besides the Meridens, there were the Meriden animals. Each of them had a terrier or two, whether Teresa was in Canada or in Kent her bloodhound was at Foxholes: there were cats, Blue Beveren rabbits, a poultry-yard and the 'household pony'—a faithful surly creature who pumped water and went on errands. All these animals had names. Most of the Meriden's inanimate belongings had names also—fantastic names: the umbrella-stand was called La Tosca and the lawn-roller Dr Johnson. So ready were they with their christening wit that if I were having tea at Foxholes I never took a piece of bread-and-butter without preparing myself to hear a sprightly chorus exclaim:

'Oh look! She's taken Esmeralda!'

But however confused one might be as to the number of the Meridens, one could always be sure of Rosalind Meriden.

Rosalind was the youngest daughter, and unmarried, and always at home.

Always busy, too. Rosalind helped in the house and helped in the garden, and took the dogs for walks, and managed the Blue Beverens entirely, and was marvellous with all the children, and wonderful with old Mrs Meriden, and the life and soul of the Women's Institute. She also drove the car, and every winter she played her fiddle in the Chorsley Operatic Society's production of a Gilbert and Sullivan. Always at home, and always busy, Rosalind's days, as she said herself, went by in a flash.

Rosalind's flashing days had carried her to the age of thirty, when Mr Wilcox came to live at the newish bungalow in the Foxholes lane. He was a widower, a red-faced, grey-haired, globular man with a toothbrush moustache and round, goggling, codfish eyes. He sweated a good deal, but if by accident you touched him he invariably felt cold. He had a daughter who was at school, he had a weak heart, he had retired from a Bank in the Midlands to live quietly on his moderate means and breed bulldogs.

It was certain that Mr Wilcox and the Meridens should establish contact, the conjunction of bulldogs and terriers made this inevitable. What no one had foreseen was that, even in the moment of kneeling in the road opposite Mr Wilcox, each of them grasping the hinder end of a fighting dog, Rosalind should fall in love with Mr Wilcox at first sight.

Love, as the poet Hogg sang, is like a dizziness. It will not let a poor body go about his business. Walking up the Foxholes lane, holding her bleeding terrier and humming inattentively, Rosalind forgot that she had gone out in order to buy stamps for the weekly letters to the far-flung Colonial Meridens. When old Mrs Meriden observed on this omission Rosalind, forgetting that it was tea-time, set out instantly for the post-office and remained away for nearly an hour. In the spiritless winter dusk she leaned on Mr Wilcox's gate, staring at his bungalow, at his lighted windows, at his newly planted rose-bushes, emblems that Mr Wilcox had come for good, that he was not merely a dream; she heard his bulldogs barking, and smelled his dinner cooking. When she turned away it was with a heavy sigh. An hour ago she had fallen in love, and already it was a hopeless love, and Rosalind had begun to pine.

I fear we all took it for granted that Rosalind should love unrequited. All the Meriden women are cut from the same cloth. Plain as children, even plainer in maturity, in their late teens they develop a certain carnal freshness and lusciousness: the quality which the French call *beauté du Diable* and the English, more poetically, bloom. Their eyes are bright, their lips look moist, and a smell of new milk exhales from them. After a year or so, their bloom goes off, and the eyes that had been bright become beady, and the moisture dries on their lips which remain slack and over-large, and the smell of new milk decomposes into the ordinary smell of poor mortal flesh—flesh kept clean, but still subject to the various discommodities of humanity—varied by stronger fleeting gusts of old dog, garden mould, or Californian Poppy.

So Rosalind, whose bloom had long ago faded, pined. But being of a very honest disposition, and completely unselfconscious, she doubled her pining with a perfectly open pursuit of Mr Wilcox. Wherever he might be met, there was she. If he spoke to her, she flushed with pleasure, and if he did not speak to her, she spoke to him. As Mr Wilcox's heart forbade him to play tennis, Rosalind played tennis no more, giving it as her excuse that she was too old to run about: and then she would go and sit by Mr Wilcox. As Mr Wilcox fancied religion, Rosalind became a devout church-goer, and having failed to persuade Mr Wilcox into the Operatic Society she resigned from it herself. After a few years she began to call him Prospero. His name, actually, was Esmé.

The bulldogs were an invaluable pretext, and during the holidays she also cultivated Mr Wilcox's daughter Olivia. Olivia was a stony, shallow little baggage, she was abominably rude to Rosalind, and told everyone that Rosalind Meriden's one idea in life was to marry Mr Wilcox. This information was, of course, quite superfluous.

As for the Meridens, they did what they decently could to detach Rosalind's steadfast attentions from Mr Wilcox. For one thing, they unanimously and quite properly thought him not fit to black her boots; for another, they wished those attentions to return to themselves. The dizzying nature of love made Rosalind much less satisfactory as a daughter, sister, sister-in-law, and aunt. Almost every night they heard Rosalind crying in her bedroom. They pitied her a good deal, especially for the first few years. As time went on Rosalind's unrequited love, like any other infirmity of long standing, became a matter of course. Even so, the assembled Meridens made a protest when, on Christmas Eve, Rosalind remarked that instead of staying at home to fill the children's stockings she was going down to The Rosery to rub Prospero's legs before he went to bed.

'Nonsense!' said old Mrs Meriden. The rest of the family froze into a disapproving silence, glancing at Roy Meriden, the head of the family, for a lead. Roy slowly removed his pipe from his mouth and said: 'I say, Rosebags. Isn't that going a bit too far?'

'It's only five minutes' walk,' she answered. 'That's nothing.' And leaving them to scramble over the misunderstanding, she stumped out.

When Rosalind had been pining for nine and a half years Olivia Wilcox got married. It was a showy wedding, and she insisted on Rosalind being a bridesmaid. I don't think I have ever seen a more painful sight than Rosalind as a bridesmaid, wearing an arch period dress of shell-pink taffetas and a little mob-cap on the side of her large head. She had made up her face for the ceremony, her first experiment in face-painting. It was so derisively bungled that I could have sworn that Olivia had done it for her. There she stood, listening to Olivia and Olivia's gigolo bandying their vows, with tears streaming down her face, crying as frankly, as despairingly, as she cried in her bedroom at night. Afterwards she got appallingly drunk on champagne, and pursued

Prospero about the room with a hired gold chair, begging him to sit down and rest his heart.

A month later she shot like a champagne cork into rapture. Mr Wilcox asked her to marry him, asked her if she could ever come to love a lonely middle-aged man. He would have asked her before, he added, but it had not seemed fair to her youth to do so.

With groans of wrath and relief the Meridens gave their consent; and before the week was out the omnivorous placid Mrs Meriden was prepared to look on Esmé as another of her dear children, only needing the wedding day to be as full-blooded a Meriden as any of the rest. There was to be a short engagement, already there was a diamond engagement ring.

Meanwhile Rosalind went round telling everybody how happy she was and licking up congratulations like a bear licking up honey. It was really embarrassing to see one's half-hearted assentings vanish into that candid maw, I could only hope that when it came to the point she would swallow Mr Wilcox with the same uncritical egoistic satisfaction.

The wedding was going to be embarrassing too.

For Rosalind was determined upon a very grand wedding, a wedding with every traditional floridity. She was to wear white satin, with a six-yards train and a wreath of orange blossom. Four bridesmaids, two pages, culled from the third generation of the Meridens, were to follow her. There was to be a three-tiered wedding-cake, a marquee on the lawn, heaven only knows how many camp-beds in the kitchen-garden.

A bevy from the Women's Institute was to strew rose-leaves before her, a bishop, raked out of old Mrs Meriden's past, was to conduct the service, and the dogs were to wear white satin favours.

All this, needless to say, was Rosalind's own devising. But in the mood she was in no one could have stopped her, even Prospero was swept along by her enthusiasm. Indeed, now that she was sure of him, Rosalind became in a way rather inattentive to her Prospero. He was in every way perfection, and he was hers. With that she dismissed him; all her energies, all her excitement, surging about the wedding, and the trousseau, and the honeymoon, and the refurnishing of the best bed-room at The Rosery.

One evening, when the invitations had been sent out and replied to, and the champagne ordered, and the wedding-dress tacked together;

when Foxholes was filling up with relations arriving and wedding presents being unpacked: one summer evening Rosalind and Prospero went for a lovers' stroll, and strolled down Foxholes lane.

'This is the very place,' she said, 'where first we met.'

'So it is,' said Prospero.

'Poor Henry J. Ford!'

There was a questioning silence, and she added:

"Henry J. Ford was the dog that fought your dog. He died four years ago. Poor old Henry!'

'I remember it quite distinctly. I thought then, This is a brave little girl. You were wearing a blue muslin dress.'

'No, I wasn't. It was in November.'

'Blue serge. That's it, blue serge.'

Mr Wilcox laid his arm round her waist.

'Ten years ago, eh?'

'Ten years ago, Prospero.'

Mr Wilcox's face came nearer.

'And have you loved me a long time?' he enquired tenderly, 'a long, long time?'

Taking a surer hold, discarding a puff of cigar smoke, Prospero bent down for a kiss. The cigar smoke must have obscured his vision, he did not notice that Rosalind's doting expression had changed, even in that moment, to a look of bewildered incredulity.

'Leave me alone, Prospero! Let go!'

He let go with alacrity, looking to see what threatened him—a wasp, maybe, or some pin.

'I can't marry you. I won't.'

'Rosalind!' Prospero's voice expressed pain.

'No! It's impossible. All these years you've kept me waiting, all these years I've been miserable, everyone knew I was in love with you, you knew it as well as they did. But you never troubled to ask me till Olivia was married, till you wanted to make sure of a woman to look after you. You selfish beast, you selfish cold-blooded beast! But I see it now, thank God I've seen it in time! For I would rather die than marry you.'

'You can't!' gasped Mr Wilcox.

'*I can!*

'I can, I can,' she exclaimed. 'I hate you, I'm revolted by you, I'm done with you. This very evening, the moment I get home, I shall write an announcement saying that the wedding won't take place' . . . she put out her tongue, licked up a tear . . . 'and send it to the *Morning Post*!'

(*A Garland of Straw*, 1943)

THEIR QUIET LIVES

THE window was shut. Outside was an April sky, tufted with small white clouds, and a semi-rustic landscape dotted with red-roofed new bungalows whose television masts controverted the anarchy of some old apple trees, a sufficient number of which had been preserved to justify the title of The Orchard Estate.

Once again, Mrs Drew consulted her watch. The watch was attached to her bosom by a matching enamel brooch; to turn its face upwards and bend her own over it involved a certain degree of effort, and made her grunt. But though there was a clock on the mantelshelf, she preferred to consult her watch. For one thing, it had sentimental value; her husband had given it to her as a honeymoon present, fifty years earlier. For another, she could trust it. Audrey had more than once forgotten to wind the clock.

Three minutes to eleven. No doubt her Bovril would be late. Dr Rice Thompson had said repeatedly that with a digestion like hers regularity was everything. But one does not expect too much. One has learned not to. Two minutes to eleven. At eleven precisely, the door burst open. Audrey came in with her stumping tread.

'Mother! Mother! Did you hear? The cuckoo?'

'What, dear?'

'The cuckoo. The first cuckoo.'

'What, dear? Has something gone wrong?'

There was nothing wrong with the tray, that she could see. The toast was nicely browned, the pepper caster had been remembered. So why did not Audrey put it down?

'The first cuckoo, Mother. Spring has come.'

'Who has come? I wish you'd tell me. I can stand up to bad news better than suspense. And do put that tray down. If you aren't careful, you'll slop it.'

Audrey put down the tray and slopped it as she did so.

'The cuckoo, Mother.'

'Oh. The cuckoo. . . . I can't hear it.'

'No. It's left off.'

So much confusion and nonsense about a bird that came year after year and more or less at the same date. But the Bovril was delicious. It swept down her, a reviving tide, and renewed her interest in life.

'Has the paper come?'

'Not yet.'

'Tchah! It's always late now. Why is it always late?'

'Because it comes with the milk.'

'But it has always come with the milk.'

'Yes. But now there are all these new houses, you see, all having milk, so the milkman takes longer to get to us.'

'I don't see at all.'

For the last eighteen months this conversation about the newspaper and the milk had taken place daily.

But everything, thought Audrey, is more or less daily. Daily, her brother Donald caught the 8.5 in order to reach his office at 9 with a few minutes in hand to feed the city pigeons. Daily at 10.50 she squared the crust off two slices of bread and put them in the electric toaster to accompany the eleven-o'clock Bovril. Daily at 2.30 she arranged her mother on the sofa for an afternoon sleep and had an hour or so to herself. Daily at 5.55 the bell of St Botolph's sounded its twenty strokes and she slipped off to Evensong. Nightly at 10.30, having settled Mother in bed and emptied the sink basket, she noted down the day's expenses, wrote in her diary and read the Psalms for the day. The milkman, the postman, the baker, the BBC announcers—all rolled round in a diurnal course along with Wordsworth's Lucy; though Lucy rolled unconsciously, being dead.

Luncheon, too, was daily; and today it involved both mincing and sieving, so she would have to set about it immediately. As she was leaving the room, her mother said, 'By the way, you'll have to order extra milk if . . .' There she stopped.

'If what, Mother?'

'If you make a milk pudding.'

Poor Mother! It was sad to see her trying to assert her former hold on life.

'Yes, Mother. I'll remember.'

Hearing the door close, Mrs Drew chuckled. Good Lord, that had been a near thing! It was no part of her plan to mention Betty Sullivan until she was sure of her. Fortunately, she had kept her head, and turned it off with a pudding.

The milkman came in his diurnal course, and Audrey carried in *The Daily Telegraph*. Mother turned with avidity to the Deaths. When other helpers fail and comforts flee, when the senses decay and the mind moves in a narrower and narrower circle, when the grasshopper is a burden and the postman brings no letters, and even the Royal Family is no longer quite what it was, an obituary column stands fast. On days when it failed to record the death of someone Mother knew, it would almost certainly provide a name familiar to her, and this would be dwelt on with speculation and gathering confidence.

Today the name was Polson.

'Polson. Gertrude Polson. Pepper, please; you never put in enough pepper nowadays. I met her at Malvern. We were staying in one hotel and she was staying in another, and we met at the lending library. Such a charming woman, and I'm almost sure her name was Gertrude. She looked frail even then, though. Gertrude Polson, in her eighty-seventh year. I don't suppose you remember her.'

'I don't think I do.'

'No, you wouldn't. We were at Malvern in 1917, when you were three. There was a Mr Polson, too—he etched or something. But the announcement doesn't mention him, it just says that she died peacefully in a nursing home at Castle Bromwich. I expect there was a divorce.'

In some ways, Mother's presumptive deaths were even better than her valid ones. They afforded her more scope. But though Mrs Polson brightened lunch, tea was clouded by the usual disappointment. 'Where are the letters? Hasn't the post come?'

'Yes, it's come. But there were no letters for you this afternoon.'

'No letters? Are you sure? Did you look carefully?'

'Yes, Mother. Two for Donald, and a circular for me. Nothing else.

'Are you sure there wasn't a letter for me? With a Devon postmark?'

'Were you expecting a letter from Devonshire?'

Mrs Drew looked at her daughter as though seeing her steadily and whole, and said, 'Fool!'

At 5.55 the bell of St Botolph's rang for Evensong. Audrey went to church through an exquisite evening, the evening of the day when she had heard the first cuckoo; and prayed to be made perfect in patience. Mrs Drew continued to extort patience till her bedtime.

'What's wrong with Mother?' Donald inquired when Audrey came downstairs to empty the sink basket. 'Has anything upset her?'

'She didn't get some letter she was expecting—from Devonshire. I do wish she could get more letters, poor old thing!'

'Perhaps she'll have one tomorrow.'

The expected letter, addressed in a curly, dashing hand and postmarked Exeter, was in the morning post. Mrs Drew tore it open, read it with obvious satisfaction, replaced it in the envelope and said she would have a poached egg for her breakfast. It was after she had drunk her eleven-o'clock Bovril that she remarked, 'There's not much on a duck, so I think you had better order a couple. Why are you looking at me like that? Didn't you hear me? I said, order a couple of ducks.'

'But ducks are still very expensive, Mother. It's only April, you know. And one duck is more than enough for three.'

'Four.'

'Four ducks?'

'No! Two ducks. Four people. Betty Sullivan's coming. I suppose you can remember *her*, at least.'

'Oh yes. She was your great friend when you were a girl, wasn't she? And married a lawyer. What day is she coming?'

'The day after tomorrow.'

'How nice! You will enjoy seeing her again. For lunch?'

'To stay.'

'Over the weekend? I'll get the spare room ready.'

'For a couple of months.'

'Months, Mother?'

'Months, Audrey. Or longer, if she likes. And I wish you'd go and have your ears syringed. I'm not strong enough to have to say everything twice over. And don't bother about the spare room. She'll be bringing a lot of luggage with her—she's giving up the lodgings she moved into after Gerald Sullivan died and that odious daughter-in-law of hers insisted that they'd inherited the house and moved into it with a pack of children. It can't possibly all get into the spare room, so she will have to have your room and you can have the spare room. Has the paper come?'

'Not yet. It comes with the milk, you know.'

'That's no reason for it to be late.'

'It isn't late, Mother. It comes later, that's all. But, Mother, about Mrs Sullivan . . .'

'Well?' Mrs Drew's neck crimsoned.

'I didn't know she was a widow,' said Audrey hastily. For though Mother's blood pressure would sooner or later carry her off—whereby everything would be greatly simplified—Audrey did not wish to bring on a stroke in order to avert Mrs Sullivan. That must be Donald's part. A son has more authority. And it was only fair that Donald should undertake Mother occasionally, instead of talking about Quietism and leaving everything to her. After a few words about Mrs Sullivan's widowhood (which, bursting on Mrs Drew through the column of Deaths, had called forth a letter of condolence, and a renewal of former intimacy), Audrey said no more and spent the afternoon tidying the spare room.

Nuns, she recalled, are contented with their narrow cells. Considering the spare room in this light she felt that with a transference of pillows and a removal of all the pictures and ornaments she might be quite happy in it. For one thing, it would make a change; for another, it was at the other end of the passage from Mother; for yet another, it was definitely more cellular, and so might be thought of as a sort of ante-cell to the little whitewashed room under a beehive roof that awaited her in South Africa. 'We will take you at any moment,' Sister Monica had said. 'Just send a cable and a get a plane.'

Chief among the things which Mrs Drew's blood pressure would ultimately simplify was the matter of her children's religious vocations. Audrey's was the more compact. She was an oblate of an Anglican sisterhood, and at a retreat she had met Sister Monica, on leave from the daughter house in Africa. By the end of the retreat Audrey felt sure of her vocation and Sister Monica had provisionally accepted her. It was only a question, as the nun remarked, of keeping her passport up to date and waiting on the Lord. While Audrey waited on the Lord, Donald was going through more complicated spiritual adjustments. There were times when he even thought of becoming a Buddhist. Just now he felt almost certain that he would become a Roman Catholic and enter a contemplative order. But all this had to be kept from Mother, who prided herself on despising all forms of religion impartially—though if she were to discover Donald's present way of thinking she would be ready to shed the last drop of his blood for the Protestant faith.

Instead of coming straight back from Evensong Audrey intercepted Donald at the station and told him about Betty Sullivan. He pooh-poohed it, with every sign of alarm. 'I shan't say a word about it,' he declared, 'unless Mother does.' And while Audrey was getting dinner he retired to the tool shed and oiled the lawnmower.

The lawnmower had been put away dirty—he would not say by whom—so he had to clean it, too. He could not but think it unfair that he, working all day in the office, should find himself expected to deal with poor Mother's vagaries the moment he got back. That was a daughter's part. And it was all very well for Audrey to secrete a vocation to be a nun in Africa, but here and now her vocation was to be a daughter in Middlesex.

At 7.30, Mother sat down at the head of the table, made sure that the pepper caster was within reach, and said, 'Audrey, have you remembered to order those ducks?'

Audrey glanced meaningly at Donald, who said, 'Duck? Are we going to have roast duck? How delightful!'

'No, Mother. We can't afford them. I asked, and they are twenty-five shillings each. Isn't it wicked?'

Disregarding the moral issue Mother said, 'And may I ask who pays for the food in this house? You haven't got that power of attorney yet, you know.'

Donald raising his voice remarked, 'Audrey, this is very nice soup.'

Audrey's silence and Mother's ominous sotto-voce 'Not yet, not yet, not yet!' drove him to speak again.

'By the way, Mother, returning to the duck, do you particularly want a duck? I might be able to find a cheaper one in London.'

'I never said I wanted a duck. I want two ducks. I wish you and Audrey would listen to me occasionally, and not wink at each other. You're as bad as Betty Sullivan.'

'Who is Betty Sullivan?' 'Does Mrs Sullivan wink?' Donald and Audrey spoke simultaneously.

'Of course she winks. She's always winked. But in her case, it's nervous. It only comes on when she's angry. And it's quite uncontrollable; she can't be blamed for it. Not like you two, winking at each other all through meals, like semaphores.'

Donald started. Audrey had kicked him sharply on the ankle. 'We seem to have lost sight of the duck,' he began. 'As I said, if you want a duck, I might be able to—'

'I said nothing of the sort. I said I wanted two ducks. And I mean to have them. I don't call five shillings a great deal for a duck.'

'Twenty-five shillings!' shouted Donald, roused at last.

'Twenty-five shillings, if you like,' said his mother airily. 'Are we going to have anything besides soup, Audrey?'

Donald could be relied upon to put up a pretty good fight when money was concerned so Audrey took her time over dishing up the braised lamb. Their voices grew increasingly louder, increasingly alike. Donald was certainly engaged; she would leave him to it for a little longer. In the event, she left him too long. When she took in the lamb, he was saying, 'Well, I wash my hands of it.' The lamb was eaten in silence. During the pudding there was a little conversation about the cuckoo.

Apparently Donald had also washed his hands of the washing up, which he ordinarily helped in. When Audrey returned to the sitting room he had turned on the wireless and was listening to a talk about the thraldom of writers behind the Iron Curtain. Mother's neck was no longer crimson. Her hooked nose, which in moments of wrath asserted itself as it would when she lay dead, had sunk back into the mass of her face and she looked as composed as a sea anemone digestively sealed on its prey. Excerpts from *The Merry Widow* followed the thraldom of Soviet writers. Donald continued to listen. When she had settled Mother in bed, he was having a bath. She waited for him to come out, and pounced.

'Well, Donald. So you've decided to give in.'

'No. Not exactly. But I think we should give way. Not to the ducks, of course. That's palpably absurd, and you must get round it. But give way about this Sullivan person. After all, she is our mother.'

'You mean, Mother is.'

Donald for a moment looked exactly as Mother had done before ejaculating 'Fool!'

'As you say, Audrey, she is our mother. Her life is monotonous, she lives in the past, she has never realised that her money is only worth half what it was twenty years ago. She has set her heart on seeing Mrs Sullivan. Anyhow, it won't be for long. They are bound to quarrel. Mother quarrels with everyone after a week. Are we to grudge her this little pleasure?'

Stalking down the passage in his bare feet and his plaid dressing gown, he looked positively apostolic. Even in the nursery she had made it her business to shelter her little brother. The little brother was now going bald. The sheltering process had gone on too long.

Two days later, and with a great quantity of small pieces of luggage, Betty Sullivan arrived.

'Betty!'

'Poppy!'

'After all these years!'

'But I'd know you anywhere!'

They continued to exclaim. Audrey continued to carry the small pieces of luggage upstairs. One of them was so unexpectedly heavy that she exclaimed, too. Mrs Sullivan turned round. 'And is this your Audrey?'

'How do you do.'

'Why, you might be your great-aunt! Poppy, isn't she exactly like your Aunt Ada? Don't bother with that parcel, dear. It can stay. Poppy! You'll never guess what I've brought. All my old snapshot albums.'

Though Mrs Sullivan's face was more ravaged than Mother's she had kept some modicum of her waist and seemed the younger of the two. In fact, as Audrey realised when called on to look at a snapshot of two pigtailed girls in skirts down to their ankles, Poppy and Betty were exact contemporaries. Now they sat on the sofa with the albums, elatedly identifying people with names like Bertie and Nina.

Ducks require basting, so Audrey had to forgo Evensong. The oven door was open and the basting in process when Donald looked in.

'What's she like? She seems to talk a—You don't mean to say you bought those ducks?'

'I gave way, Donald. After all, she is our mother.'

'Well, I suppose it's too late now. But I wish you hadn't.'

Having left the kitchen, Donald speedily returned. 'Audrey! What's this frightful smell all over the house?'

'I expect it's Mrs Sullivan's scent.'

'Good God! But it's everywhere.'

'She's been everywhere. Mother's been showing her round. She put some on Mother, too. It's called *Méfie-toi*.'

While Poppy and Betty continued to evoke the past—to recall hockey matches, blue voile, fox terriers, confirmation classes, the Bishop's boots; while Mother, animated by these feasts of memory, grew increasingly demanding and autocratic and Audrey increasingly jaded and fatalistic, Donald was being driven frantic by *Méfie-toi*. He bought aerosols, he sprayed the bathroom with disinfectant, he soaked his handkerchief in citronella and pressed it convulsively to his nose whenever Mrs Sullivan came near him. He pressed it so convulsively that after a few days his nose became inflamed. Mrs Sullivan, calling him her poor boy, insisted on applying a cooling lotion—one of the *Méfie-toi* series. Trying to remove the stink from his nostrils with carbolic soap and a nailbrush, Donald rubbed himself raw. This wasn't so obvious in the train, for there he could hold up his newspaper. But one cannot walk through the streets of London with a newspaper before one's face, and it seemed to him that people were either looking at his nose or avoiding looking at it. Then Holiday, with whom he lunched on Tuesdays, said to him, 'You ought to take care of that nose, Drew.' The same evening, when he turned to Audrey for sympathy, she blinked at him as though he were a very long way off and remarked that she had a pain in her stomach. Donald replied that he was sorry to hear it—Audrey had expressed no sorrow about his nose—and added that it was probably colic, arising from the richness of the food since Mrs Sullivan had been with them. As Audrey did the cooking, the remedy was in her own hands.

Two evenings later Audrey fell off her chair during dinner and lay writhing on the floor. When they tried to pull her up she screamed. Dr Rice Thompson was sent for, and she was taken to hospital in an ambulance and operated on for acute appendicitis.

When Audrey came round from the anaesthetic and saw only strange faces bending over her she gave a sigh of relief and burrowed back into unconsciousness. Some time later—how much later she did not know or care—she opened her eyes and there was Donald. A voice from somewhere said, 'Not more than five minutes, Mr Drew.' Donald sat down and gazed at a kidney basin.

'How are you all getting on?' she asked.

'Splendidly!'

'Oh.' She felt a vague relief and also a vague surprise. 'I'm so glad.'

'You needn't worry about us. Betty got Hannah.'

Hanna. Hanna in the wilderness. Probably some kind of patent food. Well, if it satisfied them. . . . Then her conscience woke up and told her that poor Donald was putting a brave face on it. 'What is—'

At the same moment Donald continued, 'Hannah is her old servant. Betty telegraphed and Hannah came by the next train, and does everything. I must say, Betty has been very helpful. I've never eaten better pastry. And Betty's arranged with her to stay on for a week after you're back to ease you in.'

'Oh. Where does she sleep, this Hannah?'

'She's sleeping out. She fixed it up with the greengrocer. He's a Wesleyan, too. They're thick as thieves, and he lets her have asparagus for next to nothing. I could never be a Wesleyan myself—but there's something rather beautiful in such a simple outlook.'

No one is wholly pleased at learning that he has been replaced by someone who does as well or better. Only by exerting her lower nature, by reflecting on such domestic offices as cleaning round the bathroom taps and washing the milk bottles, was Audrey able to repose on the thought that Betty Sullivan's Hannah, lodging at Powell's and coming in to get Donald's breakfast, would be there when she got home.

Betty Sullivan arrived in a hired car to fetch Audrey away and throughout the drive was everything that was kind and everything that was hospitable. 'I want you to feel as free as if you were staying in a hotel,' she insisted. 'A nice restful little hotel, where you've only got to ring a bell. I've put one of your mother's bells in your room. It's absurd for her to have five hand bells, even if they do have associations. So you've got the one that Madge Massingham-Maple gave her as a wedding present. She never really cared for poor old Madge.'

'How is Mother?'

'In wonderful form. Top-hole. Fit as a flea.'

Audrey had scarcely greeted her mother before she was being put to bed. Tea, with homemade cake, was brought in by Hannah. It was a Saturday, and presently she heard Donald mowing the lawn. The millennium could not last. The bills would be appalling. Mother looked dangerously red. Betty had somehow got at the best tea service and Hannah would undoubtedly break it. Sooner or later, there would be the devil to pay, and *Méfie-toi* would hang about the house for months. Meanwhile she would make the most of this unexpected sojourn in a nice restful little home where she had only to ring Madge Massingham-Maple's bell.

But nothing whatever went wrong. Hannah was an excellent manager as well as an admirable cook and seemed prepared to stay on indefinitely. So, of course, did Betty Sullivan, but this was not altogether a matter for regret. Not only was Betty an adjunct to Hannah; not only was she contributing, and pretty handsomely, to the household expenses; but since her arrival Mother had become a changed being, a being with an interest in life. They talked untiringly about their girlhood—about the winters when they went skating, the summers when they went boating, the period when they were so very pious, the period when they were pious no longer and sent a valentine to the curate: the curate blushed, a crack ran out like a pistol shot and Hector Gillespie went through the ice, the fox terriers fought under old Mrs Bulliver's chair, the laundry ruined the blue voile, the dentist cut his throat in Centry Wood, Claude Hopkins came back from Cambridge with a motor-car and drove it at thirty miles an hour with flames shooting out behind, Addie Carew was married with a wasp under her veil. From time to time, they pursued themselves into their later years—into marriage, maternity, butter coupons, the influenza epidemic, the disappearance of washstands, poor Lucy Latrobe who took to drink, Mr Drew going out for an evening paper and being brought back dead, Addie's pretty granddaughter rushing from one divorce to the next. But over these years the conversation did not flow so serenely. There were awkward passages where Betty boasted, where Poppy criticized. So presently they travelled back to the days of their youth, and told the same stories over again and laughed with inexhaustible delight at the same misfortunes. The windows stood open, summer curtains frisked in the breeze and Mother felt so well that she and Betty made several excursions to London, to choose new chair covers, to lunch at little places in Soho.

Audrey and Donald wallowed in unprincipled peacefulness—to Audrey, at any rate, it seemed unprincipled, for she was ill-acquainted with pleasures not snatched from the jaws of duty.

'Do you know what I've been thinking?' said Donald. They were in the garden, collecting slugs by twilight. From the kitchen came the sound of Hannah washing up, from the sitting room the story of Hector Gillespie going through the ice.

'No, what?' she said apprehensively.

'That now's your time.'

'Now's my time?'

'Now's your time. To get away. If you went to Africa now, Mother would scarcely notice it. Listen to her! She's completely happy, living in the past. And if you go, Betty will certainly stay on. It would be just the excuse she needs for staying here, in reach of London.'

'But if now's my time, isn't it your time, too?'

'It's not so urgent for me. And not such plain sailing.'

'You're thinking Mother couldn't live without you—without your salary?'

'I'm thinking nothing of the sort,' he said with acerbity. 'Betty's very well off. You've only to look at her—you've only to smell her to know that. Besides, I happen to know.'

'But how? Did she tell you?'

He scooped up another slug with his teaspoon and dropped it into the jar of salt water.

'As a matter of fact, I sent Lorna—my secretary—to the Probate Office to have a look at Gerald's will.'

A voice from indoors exclaimed, 'Betty, you've got that wrong again! You always get it wrong. Bertie Gillespie was dancing with me—not with Mabel.'

'Very well, very well. Have it your own way, dear.'

Their tones made it apparent that Betty Sullivan was winking, that Mother's neck was crimsoning. From time to time, they had these girlish tiffs.

'But, Donald—I shall have to tell her.'

'You can tell her that Sister Monica has invited you to go there for a month, to convalesce.'

Such resourcefulness, such solicitude for her vocation, such readiness to stand aside and let her get away. . . . Poor Donald! How she had misjudged him! For years she had thought him selfish. Yet now he stood beside her, a strong brotherly presence, prepared to suffer in her stead—not only Mother, either; for he suffered as much as ever from *Méfie-toi*, which was why he was sharing the slug hunting, and why he often did not come home till the last train, making a supper of sandwiches on the Embankment or in some quiet city churchyard in order to avoid it. For years, Audrey had been misjudging Donald; and within half an hour she was misjudging him again. The more she thought of it, the more penetrating became her impression that Donald had something up his sleeve and was trying to get rid of her.

Feeling in some vague way menaced, she took refuge in a precautionary inertia. The way of escape stood open—at least, Donald assured her it did. Mother needed her no longer, infinitely preferring Betty's company and Hannah's cooking. Nothing tied her to a home where, since she slept in its spare room, she was already in part a stranger. She had not even to buy an outfit, for when she arrived at the convent she would put on her novice's habit. Inoculations, topee, sunglasses—everything would be provided. She had only to make up her mind. But instead of letting itself be made up, her mind drifted away to suppositions and excuses. Was she well enough? Had Sister Monica really meant it? Oughtn't she to wait till Mother died? Was she sure of her vocation? What was Donald really up to? And when Donald inquired if she had written to the convent, if she had found out about flights, she put him off with adhesions, old letters that must be sorted and disposed of, a bank manager that must be visited.

'I warn you, Audrey. Time is getting short.'

'What do you mean? Why is it any shorter than it was last week?'

'It is a week shorter. Didn't you hear Mother yesterday evening?'

'Yesterday evening? Yes, they did have rather a tiff, but they often have tiffs. And then they make it up again.'

'Before very long, they'll have a tiff and not make it up again. Mark my words, Audrey. Time is getting short. Don't say I didn't warn you.'

These words provoked the inevitable reaction. Audrey laughed in an elder-sisterly way and said that if Donald had seen as much of Mother as she had done, he wouldn't think much of yesterday evening. Donald, his nose standing out like Mother's at its most embattled, said he would say no more, and added that he would be away for the weekend.

The sight of Donald going away with a little bag, to mind his own business instead of hers, restored Audrey's confidence in her purpose. She checked her passport and sent a cable to Sister Monica; on Monday she would go up to London and book her flight. All this took no time at all, and she spent the afternoon tearing up old diaries and parcelling clothes to be sent to the Church Army. Walking to Evensong through a downpour of thundery rain, she seemed to be moving under an invisible umbrella that sheltered her from alternatives and second thoughts far more efficiently than the visible umbrella, which had holes in it, sheltered her from the downpour. In the same heavenly frame of mind she walked home and entered the house.

The sound of violent altercation came from the sitting room.

'I tell you, you've got it wrong. You've been singing it wrong ever since I first knew you.'

'Well, that's a lie, anyhow. You first knew me when we were at the kindergarten—and they hadn't been published then. We're not so young as you try to make out, Betty.'

'I didn't know you at the kindergarten—not to call it knowing. I merely disliked you, because you sat on your hair and never left off saying so.'

'I can sit on it to this day.'

'Well, suppose you can? Is that the be-all and end-all of existence? But we're not talking about your hair, Poppy. We're talking about the Indian Love Lyrics. And I tell you again, you get it wrong. It goes like this: "Less, pom-pom-pom, than the dust, pom-pom-pom, be-Neath, pom-pom, thy chariot Whee-heel." The way you sing it, it sounds like a hymn.'

'The way you sing it, it sounds like a railway accident.'

Terrified of what she might overhear next, Audrey crept away. Her umbrella was still in her hand. She opened the kitchen door. 'Hannah. May I leave my umbrella to drip in the sink?'

Hannah sat at the table, shelling peas. 'Leave it where you like, Miss Drew. I don't know what Mr Powell thinks he's doing, calling these fresh garden peas. Maggots in every pod! I've got more than a mind to throw the whole lot back in his face.'

Audrey crept away from the kitchen. She went up to the spare room, fell on her knees among the tidy confident parcels for the Church Army, and prayed with her hands over her ears. During dinner she tried so slavishly to speak peace to Mother and Betty that they unitedly bit her head off. Well, if it united them. . . .

For the time being, it did. Sunday might almost have been called a day of rest, if it had not been for Hannah, who slammed in and out looking harried and injured, and when offered praises of a gooseberry tart replied ominously that no one could say that she hadn't always tried to give satisfaction. The next day, as is usual after Sunday, was Monday. Audrey had dedicated Monday to seeing her bank manager and booking her passage. But she did neither, for in the course of discussing whether their next outing should be to Windsor or Box Hill Mother became so curt and Betty so bridling that she was afraid to leave them alone together. All day she longed, as she had never thought it possible to long, for Donald's return; and when she saw him at the gate, she rushed out and drew him into the tool shed.

'Donald! It's too awful! You were quite right, I feel it will break up at any moment, and Betty and Hannah will go off in a huff—for Hannah's furious, too, and has turned against Powell. And now we shall never get away.'

'You're leaving on Wednesday—the day after tomorrow.'

'The day after tomorrow?'

'I knew you'd put off doing anything, so I fixed it all up this morning. I couldn't get a direct flight, so you'll have to change at Amsterdam, and spend a night in Athens, and go on from there by a plane that carries freight and one or two passengers. But you'll find it all perfectly easy and straightforward.'

'The day after tomorrow!'

'You can make some excuse—the dentist or something—and travel up with me on the 8.5. And I'll see you off. So all you've got to do now is to pay me for your tickets and behave as if nothing were up.'

'And tell Mother.'

'I will tell Mother.'

'*You* will tell Mother? Donald, do you mean it?'

'Certainly. I shall tell her that evening, when I get back. I've been thinking it out. It will be far better to tell her then, when it's all past praying for. The shock will draw them together.'

She stared at him. In the dusk of the tool shed his face was smug and moon-like—as the face of some all-sufficing, all-managing, miraculously intervening angel would naturally be.

'I'm hungry,' he said. 'Let's go in and hurry up Hannah. And we'll have a bottle of Graves. I feel like celebrating.'

On Wednesday, after a day during which her efforts to exercise a calming influence brought down on her a lecture from Betty about showing more consideration for Poppy's blood pressure and a considered critique from Mother wherein her stupidity, her virginity, her grovellings at St Botolph's, her lifelong failure to exhibit a spark of initiative and her parsimony over buying new toothbrushes were severally laid forth and enlarged on; after a night of being alternately devoured by conscience and by a conviction that one or other of those planes would crash, Audrey caught the 8.5 with Donald. He accompanied her to the airport, assuring her from time to time that once she was on the plane everything would be easy and from time to time glancing covertly at his watch. At the airport they had twenty minutes to wait. Donald ordered coffee. His conversation was repetitive, and he seemed to have something on his mind. Remembering what lay before him, Audrey thought this was only reasonable. They sat at a little table and round them other people sat at other little tables, and it was as though this were some unnaturally hospitable out-patients' department. Another group of doomed travellers, these doomed to perish on a flight to Brussels, was summoned and rose up. The doors opened on a roar of propellers, and closed behind them. Swallowing with terror, Audrey said, 'Donald, I shall pray for you this evening. When will you do it? Before dinner or after?'

'Do it? Oh, tell Mother, you mean. As soon as I get back. After all, I shall have to explain why you're not with me.'

'About quarter to seven.'

'Or thereabouts. They should be back from their outing by then.'

'I'm afraid she will be very angry.'

'Yes. That's what I'm counting on.'

The surmise that Donald had something up his sleeve darted back and transfixed her. 'Counting on?'

'Yes. You see, I shall be killing two birds with one stone. First I shall tell her about you going off to Africa. Then about my marriage.'

'Donald! Are you going to marry?'

'I am married. I married Lorna—my secretary—ten days ago. And I've been waiting to get you safe off to Africa so that I can begin with that, and draw the worst of her fire. As a matter of fact, I mean to say that you promised to break the news to her at the weekend while I was away —and that you forgot to. It can't hurt you, you'll be safe out of it. And it may make a great difference to me.'

'Then if there's a crash and I'm killed, it will serve me right!' The words burst from her. It was as if her fear, raw and bleeding, had been torn out and lay on the table between the coffee cups. 'Donald, I must go back! I can't think why I gave in to you. How could I do such a thing? Leave Mother without a word? Why, it might kill her. Oh, poor Mother! And you wouldn't have the slightest idea what to do for her. You've never even seen her in one of her attacks.'

'Hannah will be there.'

'I must have been mad to think of it. And just to make things easier for you—for that's all it amounts to. Really, Donald, for cold-blooded selfishness . . . Why are you looking at me like that?' He continued to look at her. 'No, I must go back. I must be there when you tell her about your being married. Besides, if I'm there, you won't have to tell her. You'll be able to leave everything to me. As usual!'

Donald appeared to be considering this. Then he shook his head. 'No, Audrey. I know what I'm about, and it will be far better if you are out of the way. For years, you've been getting on Mother's nerves—'

'Oh!'

'—and she's been getting on yours. Look at the state you're in now, working yourself up, as if planes crashed every time someone who's left a mother is on board. Besides, everyone with a vocation goes through something of this sort. Think of St Chantal, walking over her son's body. Concentrate on your vocation, Audrey. They're expecting you. The tickets are bought. You can post a letter to Mother from Amsterdam, if you want to—in fact, I think you should. It's all perfectly straightforward, and by this evening . . .'

'Attention, please,' said the impartially summoning voice.

'Oh, poor Mother, poor Mother!'

'Audrey! Pull yourself together. People are beginning to look at us.'

That did the trick. Appearing only moderately distraught, Audrey let herself be put on the plane, sank into an embracing seat, fastened her belt and began to read the advertisements. As the plane taxied interminably along the runway, everything became a certainty. A few minutes of remorse; then an explosion in which her cry for forgiveness would be lost. The plane rose. She looked down on reeling buildings, roofs fleeing like frightened sheep, a surprising quantity of trees. A moment later, she forgot everything in the realisation that she was going to be sick.

In Athens a cable was handed to her: 'MOTHER DIED CLIMBING BOX HILL.'

(*A Stranger with a Bag*, 1961)

A SPIRIT RISES

'B UT why,' said the ageing man to the ageing woman, 'why did your father keep a rocking horse in his study?'

'Was that odder than the carpenter's bench?'

'Yes, decidedly. In fact, I think all schoolmasters should do carpentry for a hobby. It would be a relief to drive something in with a hammer from time to time. But a rocking horse—a large rocking horse. Why?'

'Everything was larger in those days—rooms, rocking horses—'

'The British Empire—'

'Table napkins.'

(She saw once again the long room, running the whole width of the house. At one end was the fireplace, with St Jerome above it, his bald, studious head eternally bent, his small lion for ever waiting for a word of recognition. At the other end of the room was the carpenter's bench, with its array of tools, and near by it the rocking horse. The rocking horse was a dapple-grey, with tail and flowing mane of silvery horsehair. The saddle and harness, scuffed with usage, were of crimson leather, and it was mounted on rockers, painted green. And as a child, looking up into its flaring blood-red nostrils, she had always felt an uneasy sense of pity. Surely anything so red must be a representation of pain?)

'I suppose it was rather large.'

'Ten hands from floor level,' he replied.

They had not met for over forty years, and now they met by chance in a crowded room, introduced to each other as strangers. They talked with a kind of stiff intimacy, like children at a party.

(The room was a half basement, he remembered: dusky, shabby, smelling of books, wood shavings, tobacco, and sometimes glue. Its windows looked out on a steeply rising bank where ferns and irises grew and autumn scattered fallen leaves from a Virginia creeper. The bookshelves lining the walls gave it an additional sombreness, and as there were heaps of books on the floor as well as that demoniacal cat one needed to pick one's steps.)

'Ten hands. An easy leap for Daniel. Do you remember Daniel, curled up on the saddle?'

'Daniel!' he exclaimed. 'I was just trying to remember its name. What an alarming beast!'

'You should have known Jael. Daniel was mutton compared with Jael.'

'Why did he choose such savage cats?'

'Jael chose him. She met him in the street and followed him home. And nothing could dislodge her.'

'I don't wonder. I felt much the same.'

(The man, dead for so many years, now entered the room carrying a large stoneware jar of ink. The cat fastened herself round his leg, intending to climb up him. The jar slipped from his hand. As it hit the floor, the cork flew out, and a fountain of ink spurted up, drenching everything except the cat. This incident she knew only by hearsay, but on the ceiling a corona of spattered ink, like a satanic halo, remained to bear witness.)

'Why are you so circumstantial about the rocking horse's height?'

'I measured it, one day when I was waiting for him. I believe it was the only time he kept me waiting. Some ass had waylaid him.'

'He didn't suffer asses very gladly.'

'My God, no! No need to tell one of his pupils that.'

(Laying a hand over a title, for instance, he would inquire what the essay was about, adding that though it didn't matter which end of a worm you took hold of, a given theme should be approached with more respect—if only as a formality of thanks to the bestower. Then, sitting beside him, you watched him read on, slowly, carefully, giving his whole mind to it, while you felt increasingly sick as you remembered passages lying ahead—the eloquent, the learned, the judicious passages you had been so pleased with at the time of writing; and finally you went off, walking on air because now and henceforward you would know how to set about it.)

'There has never been anyone like him,' he said.

Their hostess came up.

'Philip, I'm very sorry to drag you away. But Anna says that unless you mean to miss the first act—'

'She's quite right. We must go. Oh dear, now I shall never know about the rocking horse. But it's been extraordinarily nice meeting you like this.'

'It was his nursery rocking horse,' she said, suddenly relenting. 'He kept it to ride on.'

'He rode on it?'

'And read at the same time.'

'Like Shelley. Thank you.'

Till that moment, she had been fobbing him off, teasing a curiosity she had no intention of satisfying, caressing a private malice, honouring an ancient grudge. It had touched her to meet this grey-haired man who still remembered his teacher with such living piety. But for all that, he had been one of them, one of those special pupils who came thronging between her and her birthright, whose voices rose and fell behind the study door, who learned, who profited, who demanded, who endeared themselves by their demands, who were arrayed for the ball while she, her father's Cinderella, went barefoot like the cobbler's child in the adage. So why should she admit him to her patrimony, to a memory which she and she alone possessed? Then, because in that sad, submissive, 'Now I shall never know,' he had seemed to be saying farewell to her father and not to her at all, she relented, sending him away with a picture in his mind.

But the picture was incomplete. A figure was lacking from it.

At the date of the picture, she had no consciousness of those pupils arriving to supplant her. Perhaps they had not even begun to arrive, for at that time her father was a young man, a junior master at the foot of the ladder. Certainly at that time he had more leisure. The sounds of carpentering ascended through the house; he fitted new limbs to her wooden dolls and showed her how to bore holes with a gimlet. He strolled into the garden, snuffing the sweetbriar or hunting for slugs among the auriculas; he was chief mourner at many tadpole funerals. When her mother was out for the afternoon, he would fetch her down to have tea with him—in summer under the hawthorn where you could hear people walking and talking in the road behind the tall wooden paling, in winter below St Jerome, where the fire and the reading lamp changed the rest of the room into a cave. After tea, she would stay on till her bedtime, pulling out from the lower shelves books she couldn't read and methodically replacing them while he wrote at his desk, a cat dripping from his knee, or sat on the dapple-grey horse, reading and gently rocking. Because of the blood-red nostrils, which had a different reality from the rest of the animal, she was afraid of the horse. He must have known this, for he never urged her to ride on it. But one rainy summer afternoon he called her to him and pulled her up to sit on the saddle-bow before him. Holding her round the middle with his right hand, holding a book in his left, he began to read aloud.

> 'Little Ellie sits alone
>   'Mid the beeches of a meadow,
> By a stream-side on the grass,
>   And the trees are snowing down
>   Doubles of their leaves in shadow
>   On her shining hair and face.'

Nursery rhymes she knew, and hymns, for the cook sang them; and a godmother had tried to teach her to say various little poems by rote. This, too, rhymed and ran. But it was different. A calm steady rain was falling, and through the open windows came coolness and the smell of wet grass. The raindrops splashed on the flagged walk at the foot of the bank, the rockers kept up a gentle thunder on the wooden floor.

> And the steed it shall be shod
> All in silver, housed in azure,
> And the mane shall swim the wind;
> And the hoofs along the sod
> Shall flash onward and keep measure,
> Till the shepherds look behind.

The rocking horse was keeping measure, the silver rain was falling in order to be silver, everything ran together and was one thing. She relaxed, abandoning her weight to the hard body behind her, leaving her legs to dangle, rubbing her head against her father's shoulder. The grasp tightened round her, the voice went on. Just as the rocking horse kept measure, just as the rain fell in order to be silver, the voice went on in order to be poetry. It was familiar, and made itself unknown. Lulled and held and enchanted, happier than she had ever been before, she knew for certain that presently she was going to weep; but to weep as she had never wept before, to weep in acquiescence and delight and participation in a whole, as the rain fell in acquiescence to the grey skies, as the ferns on the bank spread out their fronds under the rain. She knew, too, that the rocking horse was bearing them towards a sad ending: that Ellie would die, or the knight be killed before he could be shown the swan's nest. But that was not why she would weep.

Down at the convent they had begun to ring their bell. It was a single bell, high-pitched and over-sweet. 'Ting, ting, ting,' it said in a precise, mincing voice. But presently the iterated single strokes began to trail an echo after them, an echo that swelled and vibrated till the syllables of the bell were almost unheard in it and became a rod of sound that pierced one through like a crystalline gimlet. To this tranquil agonizing cry Ellie found the nest gnawed by rats and the wild swan flown. Her tears fell and fell. He made no attempt to check them. After a while, but now not reading from the book, he began again: 'O what can ail thee, Knight-at-arms . . .'

(*A Spirit Rises*, 1962)

THE LEVEL-CROSSING

SINCE 1927 Alfred Thorn had kept the level-crossing where the road from Wellbury to Kingsfield crosses the railway. Before then he had worked in the goods-yard at Paddington. A rupture ended that employment, and the company, since he was a steady man and no drinker, transferred him to the Kingsfield L.C.

For over forty years a Londoner, and living always in the narrow, noisy, shabbily cosy district of North Paddington, he found it strange to live in the country, that was so bare and calm; and going out at night to set the gates for the passage of the 12.41 up goods train he had almost feared the heavy summer whisper of the trees, the moorhens squawking under the bridge. With a kind of homesickness he would recall the night turn in the goods-yard, the figures under the raw arc lights, his mates shouting, the soft whine of the wind along the metals and how once, seeing a train come in with a white crust still lying on the tarpaulins, he had said to himself: It's snowing in the country. And a picture was in his mind, a picture based on a Christmas card: a white landscape, a church spire, a sunset glowing between bars of cloud like the coals in a grate.

With his first winter came snow: so sudden and so heavy a fall that before he could swing back the large gates closing off the road he had to shovel the snow to one side. Some winters it snowed, some not. There was more variation in the winters than in the summers. But the years became pleasant to him, for he had taken to gardening, and the driver of the 11.5 would lean out of the cab to wave a gesture of approval towards Alfred Thorn's well-trenched celery or dark autumnal dahlias.

He was unmarried; but as a level-crossing keeper must have a companion, someone to take his place should he be suddenly disabled, he had brought with him his niece, Alice Hawkins. As a child she had been pretty, and when she went out to her first employment as a kitchen-maid it was taken for granted that in a year or two she would be married, and peeling potatoes for a household of her own. But one morning, pouring kerosene on an unwilling kitchen fire, she set fire to herself. They thought she would die of her injuries, but she lived on, her face so frightfully scarred that no one now could think of a husband for Alice, and never another word came from her wried mouth. From shock and terror she had lost the power of speech.

At first Alfred had found it painful to be companioned by this pitiable creature, from whom the flames seemed to have burned off youth and sex and personality, leaving but the morose industry of a machine. Though her hearing was only a little impaired, words appeared to have no more meaning for her. Only very rarely would she feel the impulse to communicate, and then she would scrawl a sentence on a piece of paper, usually no more than a household request for hearth-brick or a new scrubbing brush. But insensibly a kind of harmony grew up between them, his pleasure in her good cooking and cleanliness complementing her instinct to serve; and his old bachelor habits—the easy-chair always drawn forward at the same angle, the pipe lit at the same hour, the coat hanging from one nail and the lantern from another—giving her a sense of security, of being insured against another disaster. She lived by the trains almost as much as he, and though she would not go to the shop or to church, she would go out, almost with gladness, to work the level-crossing gates.

There was an element of monasticism about their lives. As the monk charts his days by lauds and matins, vespers and compline, Alfred Thorn lived by the four expresses, the ten locals, the six clanking goods, his being always attentive to the note of the signal that linked him to the organisation of the Great Western Railway as the chime of the bell links the monk to the organisation of Christendom.

The declaration of war in 1939 imposed many changes on the railways. Duplicated notices came to Alfred Thorn advising him of altered runnings and trains that would run no longer. His life was dislocated. In the last war, too, his life had been dislocated—soldiering had sent him hither and thither, the chiming of high explosive had been the mad timepiece he lived by. But these new days seemed reproachfully empty, empty as the autumn landscape, the bare stubble-fields, the trees growing shabby and furtively casting their leaves. And in the lengthened intervals between the clicks of the signal the noise of the river seemed as loud and intimidating as it had seemed on his first coming.

There were fewer trains; but the traffic across the metals increased. Army lorries, army cars, tanks, and riders on motor-bicycles roared past the level-crossing gates. More and more soldiers were coming into the district—'to be given a lick,' said the postman, 'before they go over.' One day early in October a billeting officer came to the house, asking Alfred if he could put up soldiers, and how many.

'If I sleep on the couch downstairs, there's my bedroom. It's a fair-sized room. But it has only a single bed.'

'This will take five,' said the officer. 'Never mind about the bed. Put it away. They'll sleep on the floor.'

On Sunday evening the men came. It was a wet, windy evening, and their arrival seemed to darken the house. The rain dripped off them, their feet scraped heavily on the floor, they stacked their equipment in every corner. Sourly humorous, they complained of the delays on their train journey. They had been travelling for eleven hours, and of those hours, nearly five, they said, had been spent in waiting on platforms or in sidings.

'We could have marched it in the time.'

'And kept a fair sight warmer.'

'Yeah! *He* could have marched it, anyway. Twenty miles an hour's nothing to him—look at the size of his feet.'

'It wouldn't have been twenty miles an hour. What's twenty elevens? Two hundred and something. You telling me it's two hundred miles from there to here?'

'Well, how far is it, smarty?'

Out of their fatigue a dispirited wrangle flickered up. Alfred and Alice served them with sausages and potatoes and a great deal of cocoa. One of the soldiers—he was a sharp-faced fellow, they called him Syd —remarked:

'You'll be out of pocket by this, you know. They don't allow you'll feed us.'

'We don't often have company,' said Alfred.

They were all very young. He felt embarrassed among them. His life during the last years had gone on so quietly, so regularly, that he had not thought of himself as growing older. Suddenly he saw himself an elderly man.

When the meal was over for politeness' sake they hung about a little, lighting cigarettes, staring at the pictures on the walls, the fancy calendars, the enlarged photographs of Alfred's parents, the framed certificate of his Friendly Society, the crayons of dogs and roses that Alice had done at school. Now Alice got up. It was time to set the gates for the 9.37. Thinking of the rain, Alfred said:

'I'm going.'

But the words were hardly out of his mouth before he remembered her shyness, her deformity. Now she would be left alone with them. The train was late. By the time it had passed and he had reset the gates nearly quarter of an hour had gone by. When he got back to the house the curly-haired boy they called Ikey had sunk to the floor and was asleep with his head propped against Syd's knees. The others were in the back-kitchen helping Alice wash up. Later on, after they had stumbled upstairs, Alfred Thorn remembered the feeling that had weighed on him as he stood waiting for the 9.37. It had been a feeling of shame as for some failure of hospitality. Now he identified it, remembering their complaints of the journey, the many delays, the cold. He found himself speaking aloud. 'It's a bad thing.'

Alice looked up. She nodded her head in agreement, nodded violently. Her expression was harsh and mournful. They were at cross-purposes, but he did not explain his thought. War, too, was a bad thing, at any rate most women thought so.

Agreeing with the billeting officer he had acted on impulse, worrying afterwards as to whether Alice would suffer, her long privacy laid open to the glances of five strange young men; and he had bargained with his uneasiness, planning to do this and that so that she need not come in contact with them. She had made no comment on the news of their arrival, only writing down a list of extra groceries. When they arrived she began to cook for them as a matter of course.

'My niece is dumb,' he had said, that there might be no awkwardness over speeches of thanks.

Ask for their washing, she wrote next morning. And that afternoon she wrote again, sending him to the village shop for sultanas for a cake, darning-wool, oranges, cigarettes, seven pounds of sugar for making apple jelly. At the shop he was told that there were no sultanas and that a pound of sugar was all that he could be spared. When Alice heard this she stood a little while, her face working. Then she put on her hat, the hat she had left London in twelve years before, and went out. What happened at the shop he would never know, but she brought back all she wanted.

She feels like a mother, he thought.

A week later he was thinking: She feels happy. Yet how did he know it? She manifested no outward happiness. Sombre and reserved, she moved from oven to table, took up plates to refill them, clawed at a tunic that needed mending. They praised and thanked her, and gave her presents: boxes of chocolates, gloves, a potted chrysanthemum brought from the town by the carrier; and she accepted her presents so flatly, so ungraciously, that it seemed to Alfred that such acceptances could only be felt as rebuffs. And yet he knew well that between Alice and the soldiers there was an intimacy that would never exist between the soldiers and himself, though it was with him that they talked and joked, played games and swopped tobacco.

'It's like that in every family,' he told himself. 'It's always the mother means most to the boys.'

They were good boys. Syd and Ikey he thought of as the eldest and the youngest, the Reuben and the Benjamin; for it was difficult to remember that there was less than a year's difference in age between them, for Syd was already lined and sharp-spoken, while Ikey, his long lashes gleaming as he screwed up his eyes in fits of laughter, seemed no more than a child. In between came Joe, Ivor, and Wallie. Nicer young fellows you couldn't ask for. Well-mannered too, and more refined than boys had been in his day. Oh, it was a pity you couldn't look at them without seeing the khaki, without remembering the advertisement that said: *Four Out of Every Five*, and the five pictured faces with the black squares laid across four of them. Then, out of the blue, it happened.

Supper was over and cleared away, and the boys were in the back-kitchen, washing up, and he had gone out for the 9.37. Tonight it was almost on time. The trains running so unpunctually had irked him, and watching the clouds of rosy steam fade on the sky he felt a warmth of pleasure, thinking: Tonight, they can't laugh at me. I've got the laugh on them. For they had found out his foible, teasing him night after night when the last local kept him dawdling with his hand on the gate-lever.

Out of the dark box which was his home came the noise of the soldiers scrimmaging at the wash-bowl—a splash, feigned cries of horror and anguish, Ikey's wild warbling giggles.

And so unheard he entered the front room.

Ivor sat in the easy-chair and Alice, folding a table-cloth, stood near him. He pulled her down on his knees—a gentle, dreamy movement, the movement almost of a sleeper. With one arm about her waist he held her there; and then, his eyes averted, he began to stroke her face, her ruined cheek and chin. She sat stiff and unmoving, staring in front of her, her red hands quietly folded on the table-cloth. Even when tears began to roll down her cheeks and through his caressing fingers, she did not move her hands.

The first thought went no further than: This is cruelly awkward for me. He wanted desperately to go away. But his duty was clear: he must put a stop to it. There could be no doubt as to how to speak; for a young man pulling a girl down on his knees, a girl ten years older than he and as frightful as a figure at a fair, was one thing only: a thief, an abuser of hospitality.

He walked forward, his footsteps tramping. Still holding Alice, still stroking her face, Ivor looked up.

'I mean to marry her.'

As for the words, they might have been the words of any boy caught out, a boy who says: *I mean to give it back, I mean to mend it*. But the voice spoke something quite different, and made the words sound formal and irrevocable, like a vow, or a sentence given in court.

'You don't know what you're talking about. You'll be off to France at any moment now—and she's ten years older than you.'

He spoke gloomily, hating the words as he uttered them. Here was a young man who in a month might be dead, and a woman who since her girlhood had been doomed to a life not much better than death; and because he himself was old, and would soon be death's due, he must needs scold them out of their moment's happiness. From the next room came another burst of laughter. It was more than he could bear. He groaned, and sat down, and buried his face in his hands.

When he looked up they were sitting just as before, only Alice had left off crying. Now she got up, slowly, smoothly, as though all her life she had been getting up off a young man's knee, and came over to him. As presently she, dumb Alice, moved her lips; and a faint hiss came from her as though she were shaping the word, *Please*.

'It's one thing or another, my lad. Either you clear out, or you act square by the girl and marry her.'

'I mean to marry her.'

Then you'd better act openly about it, and tell the others.

The words were on his lips but he did not speak them, for at that moment the others came in. Joe proposed a game of Rummy, the evening went by like any other evening; and when Alice and Alfred were left alone she straightened the room, made up his bed on the couch, kissed him and went off to bed, just as usual.

The more he thought of it, the worse it seemed. Such a match could only bring misery to both of them—if it came to a match. And if it did not? Going out for the 12.41, the calmness, the serenity, of the moonlit night seemed to throw scorn on his perplexity. The goods train rumbled past, and with all his being he yearned to throw himself into one of those trucks, to be carried to Paddington, back to the goods-yard, back to his lodging in the cosy, shabby street, back to his former strength and the cocksureness of youth. But here he stood, old and puzzled, and of no use to anyone.

Most of the night he lay awake worrying. He worried about Alice, then his thoughts would wander off to the problem of who would take her place if she married and left him. But she might marry, and yet remain with him, and bear a child. A level-crossing is no place for a child, and if the war went on long enough, or Alice were widowed by it, the child would be of an age to stagger on to the track or out into the road, and be run over. How long would the war go on? How much higher would prices go? When would the air raids begin? There was a movement overhead, and in an instant he was on his feet, shaking with rage. No! There should be no such doings under his roof. The next minute he heard a window closed, and the footsteps recrossing the floor, and a sigh, and a creak of the boards as the closer of the window settled again to his sleep. Overcome with shame and misery Alfred lay down also. What would he think next? What had come over him that he should nurse such suspicions, such jealousy? And what was to be done about Alice?

In the morning he looked at her narrowly, anxiously. There was no change of expression in her marred face, no lightening of her tread, no outward indication of love or the astonishment of love. Yet somehow from her dull unchanged face and unchanged mechanical serenity there streamed a conviction of being loved and being triumphant. As for Ivor, he was no more and no less than the others: a boy in a hurry who would be punished if he were late for school.

Sorrow is not so self-sufficient as joy. Alfred Thorn had meant to deal with his trouble unaided, to say no word of the matter. But when the soldiers came back at the end of the day he buttonholed Syd, and took him into the dusky garden.

'Something's happened that shouldn't have. Ivor says he wants to marry my Alice.'

'Does he?'

There was so little surprise in the words that Alfred Thorn exclaimed in instant furious suspicion:

'Did you know about it, then? Has he been talking about it?'

'Not a word. But I'm not altogether surprised. He's been looking at her a lot.'

'Looking at her? What sort of looking?'

'Just looking.'

'Oh, well, I don't like it. What makes a boy like him run after a girl like her?'

'She's a very nice girl. She's very kind.'

'But she's dumb! And her face. Her face, you know. Those scars.'

'Perhaps he likes the scars.'

'Likes them? *Likes* them?'

Shaking with anger he glared into the young man's face. But it gave him back no look of irony or insolence—unless it be insolent for a young man to look so calmly on an old man in a fury.

'People do, you know. Some people. It's psychological. For him it might be just the attraction.'

'I don't know what you call it. I call it plain disgusting. Morbid, I call it.'

'You can't blame the boy for being morbid if he's made that way.'

'Oh, can't I? You'll see if I can't blame him.'

'Well, Mr Thorn, you'd be wrong. What you're feeling is something very old-fashioned. Nowadays—'

But Alfred Thorn had turned his back, and was stumping off. Reaching the garden gate he paused, and shouted:

'Tell her I shan't be in till the 9.37.'

He went off down the railway track, lurching from sleeper to sleeper.

'Maybe a drink will comfort him,' thought Syd. He considered the old man to be stupid, and certainly in the wrong; but he had a responsible nature and felt a soldierly impulse to tidy him. It had been such a happy household till now.

Alfred Thorn, however, was not walking to the public-house. A mile farther down the track the Wellbury branch line came in, and here was a signal-box. A signal-box can be a very comfortable place, standing above the cares of the common world, warm in winter, in summer airy, with a mug of tea on the window-sill. Now he was going to the signal-box for shelter, to take sanctuary in his profession. It was as good as he'd hoped. The tea was strong, and they talked of railway matters, and Vincent Jones sang his song of 'Crawshay Bailey had an engine,' and laughed, and said that war would never change Wales, and perhaps not change England much either. But the clock hung on the wall, and the reminders of time rang and chirped through the conversation, and too soon it was time to go back for the 9.37.

It was a cloudy night, and cold, with a gusty November wind. The moon had not risen yet. The wind droned in the telegraph wires; though he walked with bent head he could know when he was approaching another telegraph pole by the heavy throbbing that spread into the air. He felt fretted and discouraged. It was hard to leave Vincent Jones, a man of his own age and profession, and return to a pack of soldiers—five young men all banded together against an old man, laughing at him up their sleeves, teasing him about the trains being unpunctual. And so he would wait outside the house till the 9.37 had gone through.

Walking to and fro he had an impression that someone was near by. There were no footsteps on the road, no sounds but the wind crying through the wires and along the metals, and the rustle of trees, and the shed-door rattling. But he cried out:

'Is anyone there?'

No answer. One of those boys, he thought, following me out to tease me, on the chance of the train being late. Late it was, too. The third quarter had struck and still it was not signalled. A bicyclist came down the road, his light a low wobbling star, and dismounted.

'You can cross. She isn't signalled yet.'

The bicycle was edged through the wicket-gate and wheeled across the track. The rider was young Harry Foley, and as he rode off he cried:

'Good-night, Mr Thorn. Hope you don't wait much longer. Don't catch cold. There's a lot of the 'flu about.'

That's how the young think, thought Alfred. Hoping is easy work for them. But as the minutes went by his grievance faded from his mind, shouldered aside by anxiety at the train's delay. Ten o'clock had struck. Something must have happened. An accident? An air raid?

From cold, from anxiety, he began to walk up the line. A creature of his profession, part of the organisation of the Great Western Railway, he set out on the up line, and turning came back on the other. His foot struck against something lying in his way. It was heavy, yielding, human. Dead? No, alive! For it rose up, and tried to run. But in the darkness he caught it, and found himself holding on to a man, dressed in tight-fitting clothes of coarse woollen cloth.

'Now what's this? Who are you?'

'I—I must have been asleep.'

'Ivor!'

'Yes, it's me, Mr Thorn.'

The boy was shaking with cold and his teeth chattered.

'Now what are you up to? What were you doing here?'

'I must have fallen asleep. I was waiting.'

His voice was senseless, he spoke as though still heavy with a dream.

'Waiting? What for?'

'The 9.37. *Where is it?*' he cried out suddenly. 'Oh, damn your trains, they're always late!'

'You'd best tell me what all this is about,' said Alfred Thorn.

'I can't stick it,' lamented the boy. 'It's no use. I can't go through with it.'

'Now, now,' said the old man. 'You've got worked up, that's what it is. You're young, and it's hard for you. But you mustn't act so silly, boy. War's a thing one gets used to like everything else. Lots of people come through it, and none the worse. I was in the last war myself, I know what I'm talking about.'

'It's not the war.'

'Not the war? What is it, then?'

'Marrying Alice. I can't go through with it.'

The signal rang. Alfred took the boy by the arm and began towing him along the track-side.

'It's her face. I thought it would help, but it doesn't. From the moment I set eyes on her—'

He paused, shuddering.

'That's right,' said Alfred. 'You tell it from the beginning.'

'In Camberwell—I come from Camberwell—there was an exhibition got up by some Peace people or other. And I went in for a look. I'd never thought about war till then. They had a lot of photos. Photos of people wounded in the last war, and still alive to this day.'

His voice rose into a scream. When he began again it was in a whisper.

'The worst of them was a man with half his face shot away. Ever since I've been trying to forget it. But I couldn't. Then this happened, and I was called.'

'I said all along it was too young,' said Alfred.

'When I saw Alice—she isn't so bad, though, nothing like so bad—I couldn't bear to look at her. Then I thought: Suppose I do look at her? Maybe I'll get used to it. Then I couldn't but look at her. It fascinated me. Then I thought: If I could only touch her face, stroke it, then somehow I could get used to it, forgive it. *For that's what will happen to me!* I know it, I've known it all along.'

Now they had reached the level-crossing, and stood by the gate.. Touching the smooth cold surface Alfred felt that they had overcome the worst, reached some kind of assurance.

'And she sat so still, letting me stroke her. I couldn't help it, it was like something that would go on for ever. And then you came in, and I thought: It's got to be like this.'

From far off, through the curtaining wind, came the faint regular pulsing of the engine, a feeling on the ear-drums rather than a sound.

'But it's no use, no use! I can't go through with it. When I begin to realise it I know I can't.'

A delicate rosy light bloomed on the darkness. The train was audible now.

'So I came out here to end it all. But the train didn't come. I lay down on the line, I must have dropped off to sleep. We've been hard at it all the day.'

The train came thundering on, its full steam-voice armoured in clankings and clatterings. It was not possible to speak and be heard. At last, Alfred could say:

'Well, you can't marry her, that's certain.'

As he spoke his hand pressed the lever and the gates swung back, leaving the road clear. A couple of cars went through.

'But who's going to tell her?'

'I can't, Mr Thorn.'

'I don't fancy it either.'

In the silence that followed they knew themselves drawn together, sharing for the first time a common emotion, a common uneasiness. Ivor pulled out a packet of cigarettes.

'Maybe Syd could. He's best at explaining.'

But Alice did not hear it from Syd. The next day they came in with the news that they were to be sent off for a course of machine-gunning. There was a flurry of departure, and on the morrow, early, they were gone. 'I'll write,' Ivor had said.

Two days later the letter came. He saw her reading it, a slow task, for she was little used to letter-reading. She folded it up, and put it back in the envelope, and laid the envelope on the mantelpiece under the tea-canister. He watched in an agony of pity and embarrassment. He dared not speak, and she could not. Her face became deeply flushed, and the more hideous for being so.

After a while his honour broke down, and being alone in the room he looked under the canister. The letter was gone.

Early in December new soldiers arrived, and the policeman brought another billeting notice. Awkward with compassion, and speaking almost harshly, Alfred said:

'You've only to say if you don't want them, Alice.'

She found her pencil, and wrote:

Let them come.

Did she hope in some obscure romance of her heart that the new batch of soldiers would bring her another lover, and a kinder one? Was she bent on proving to herself that the wound of Ivor was only a surface wound, and healing? It was impossible to say. She looked after these as efficiently, as commandingly, as she had looked after those others, and moved among them firmly, and seemingly content. Alfred thought: She'd rather have them than be alone with me. And perhaps she put their unconsciousness of her tragedy between herself and his knowledge. As Christmas neared she began to make preparations, baking and icing a Christmas cake, buying coloured paper garlands and looping them across the ceiling. Gipsies came through the village selling mistletoe. One of the soldiers bought a bunch and brought it in. She nodded approvingly, and hung it in the centre of the room.

Late that afternoon she went into the garden to fetch the washing. She stood there for some time, staring about her. In her attitude there was something of release and sudden boldness, as though she had come out of prison. Perhaps the wind, blowing her hair and fluttering her skirts, had blown this look on to her. On her return she took up her pencil and wrote on a slip of paper, and handed it to Alfred. She had written the word *Snow*.

For a minute he thought it was something for Christmas.

'Snow, Alice?'

She pointed out of the window at the calm cold sky and the bare landscape, and nodded her head decisively.

When, a few days later, the snow came, and all the railway traffic was disorganised, she went about with a queer look of triumph, and began to treat him more affectionately, as though her prophecy coming true had reconciled them and put them back on the old footing.

(*A Garland of Straw*, 1943)

A SPEAKER FROM LONDON

Mrs Benton had always believed in showing consideration. Consideration for others cost so little and meant so much. Consistently practised, consideration for others became a habit and cost nothing at all. Now with the ease of habit she turned to the less well-furred woman beside her and said:

'Dear Mrs Mabberley, may I throw myself on your kindness? May my poor Miss Tomlinson—my secretary, you know—come in and warm herself at your hearth while we are at the meeting? I really don't like to leave her in the car. The poor thing has had influenza and I'm afraid she got chilled to the bone dealing with that puncture.'

Mrs Mabberley, less accomplished in showing consideration than Mrs Benton, replied that if Miss Tomlinson did not mind being left alone and sitting in the kitchen? . . . 'We haven't sufficient coal for two hearths,' she concluded rather acidly.

'But of course! Who wouldn't love to sit in the kitchen? I always say, this war has taught us to appreciate out kitchens. An Aga?'

'An Esse.'

'Quite, quite perfect!' Mrs Benton glanced at her watch. 'If you wouldn't mind showing us the way? Miss Tomlinson! Mrs Mabberley says . . .'

Mrs Mabberley said: 'But wouldn't she really prefer to come to the Village Hall and hear you speak?'

'No, no! She has far too many opportunities to hear me speak. Besides, she's got a really terrible cough.'

Mrs Benton's tone of voice implied that not only had Miss Tomlinson many opportunities, but that she slighted them. With a last effort to safeguard her groceries Mrs Mabberley said:

'If you hear anyone moving about the house, Miss Tomlinson, don't be worried. It'll only be the Rector.'

As the two ladies walked briskly towards the Village Hall Mrs Benton observed:

'I always feel that it's a little inconsiderate to ask my poor Miss Tomlinson to listen to my talks. After all, my message is really for Youth.'

Mrs Mabberley obliged with a titter. She also reflected that she was fifty—but a Rector's wife must be eternally young.

Mrs Benton continued: 'A poor thing, but mine own. And really, it's so difficult to get anything like a secretary nowadays, that I'm thankful for her. I've had her Reserved.'

Meanwhile Miss Tomlinson had taken off her hat and her gloves, wiped her glasses, which the change from an outdoor to an indoor climate had misted, sat down at the kitchen table and pulled a pen and a wad of thin letter-paper from her bag. Turning over the pages already written, she went on with her letter.

. . . this everlasting war. Sometimes I wonder if you will even recognise me when we meet again. I expect I shall be sick. Something silly, anyhow, or it wouldn't be me. Perhaps we had better agree to carry a flower so as to know it's us. The price of flowers is awful. Two-and-six for a dozen snowdrops. But I have to buy them sometimes, all the same. I can't do without flowers, they make such a difference.

She paused, and read, and added a mark of exclamation after the word *sick*. Her pen trailed on the page. Suddenly she began to write again.

What a Godsend! I have a whole hour to write in. Mrs B. is doing her lecture, and thank God this time she has let me off. I coughed all the way here and it must have worked; anyway, she has gone off, having graciously arranged that I should sit in the Organiser's kitchen. It's just the sort of kitchen you'd expect, with one of those posh cookers like a family vault, and everything so neat and hungry-looking it's enough to give one the creeps. When we have a kitchen we'll have a proper fire you can poke up, and blue and white china and a geranium on the window-sill, and a smell of bacon, and a cat. I wish there was a cat here, I could do with some company. But there's nothing but a rector, and he hasn't shown up yet. She mentioned, though, that he would be round and about. Just a gentle reminder that if I stole a currant I'd be heard doing it. What beasts these people are. The war means nothing to them.

The spurt ended. She looked back over the written pages and numbered them. She had a typist's handwriting, hasty, irregular, and unformed. She herself resembled her handwriting; for her wearied middle-age was yet callow and gawky, and the lines in her face had no maturity, they were as though some abrupt ageing process had seized and fixed the grimace of a schoolgirl.

She shivered, and coughed, and began to walk about the room to warm herself. Presently she discovered a battered *Good Housekeeping*, tucked away beneath cookery books; and for a while she read it, and a look of melancholy greed appeared on her face. But it did not hold her long. She gave a conscious laugh, replaced it, and went back to her letter. Slowly she wrote:

Sometimes I feel so blue, darling, I don't know what to do with myself. And then I hear Mrs B. doing her bloody piece about how after all one has only to remember our brave men and our own small troubles seem such small things, don't they? And then she gives one of her wistful grins, and bears up even if her tea is late. The war means simply nothing to these people, simply a wonderful opportunity to be paid six hundred a year by the Government for going round telling kids what splendid fun they'll have being killed. Only now it's going down mines and scrubbing floors. I look at her and think of you . . .

The sound that had been the Rector on his prowls hardened into a light resolute tapping. There was a man looking at her through the window, and smiling. As she rose he moved away and she heard his footsteps pause on a doorstep. She found her way to the back-door and opened it.

'Good afternoon, Miss. Excuse me interrupting you but . . .'

He eyed her consideringly and went on:

'. . . but I saw you writing. I suppose you wouldn't care to buy a couple of pencils?'

He opened a case, pulled out pencils and blocks.

'I've got thin paper, too, air-mail stuff.' Sliding it into her hand, he said: 'You can take my word for it, a letter from home makes all the difference. You can't write too often, I know.'

She looked at him.

'Seems queer to be doing this,' he said, 'after fighting in Africa.'

'What?'

'It's just another hard-luck story,' he said, dismissingly; and allowed enough silence, and then went on: 'You wouldn't think it, would you, to look at me? And you wouldn't think it either, after all the speeches they make and the bits in the papers about heroes and all. But I was a Desert Rat all right, believe it or not. That's why I know what letters mean. You go on writing, my dear. And I hope he comes back luckier than I did.'

'But . . .'

'Yes, I know. Where's my disability money and all that? Why am I on the road selling rotten pencils and job-lot paper?'

He looked at her.

'Bit of red tape got tied in the wrong sort of knot. That's why.'

'Wait a minute,' she said. 'I'll be back in a minute.'

Out of their kitchen store-cupboard she took tins of salmon, of meat, of treacle, of peaches, cartons of tea, slabs of chocolate, and packed them in a carrying-bag and remembered to add a tin-opener. As she worked she could hear him on the door-step, shifting from foot to foot, and she hurried to fill the bag and carry it to the door.

'I can't get at their whisky,' she said. 'It's locked up. But some of these things you could swop. Now go!'

He began to thank her, saying that he would never forget her, that the world was a queer place and maybe they'd meet again, that the chap who had her was a lucky one, that girls like her were what a man fights for.

'Go, go away!' she cried. 'Go away before I begin to believe in you.'

He went, and dived with gratitude into the church, where he repacked the stuff in his case. He might be able to get away with it, but she wouldn't. There would be hell let loose when it was discovered. At the bottom of the carrier there was a pound note, so she'd pinched the housekeeping money into the bargain. She must be one of those delinquents, he decided. A lot of them were leased out as servants, especially in places like rectories. Yes, that was it. A delinquent.

For some reason this conclusion eased his mind, and he quitted the church more comfortably than he had entered it.

(*The Museum of Cheats*, 1947)

THE FIFTH OF NOVEMBER

FEELING the need for a little repose and luxury, Ellie, on her way
back from the carpet factory where she worked, turned aside into
the church of St Mary Ragmarket. She had done so before at various
times, and could enter without feeling constrained to put on any
particular behaviour, to bow the knee and adapt the heart to the
presence of a ciborium that, wrapped in a striped veil, presented a rather
Turkish appearance, to avoid the melancholy stare of the figure on the
cross, to admire the architecture, or to apprehend interruption. The
church stood in the old part of the town, whose venerable slums were in
process of being cleared away and replaced by industrial buildings. The
fairground from which it took its name was now occupied by a bus depot,
and the remaining streets and alleyways did not house a church-going
population. Though St Mary Ragmarket had been the parish church of
one of the Pilgrim Fathers, whose ancestors knelt among the embla-
zoned figures in its armorial east window, and as such was visited by a
certain number of pilgrim Americans, the proportion of American
visitors in a town like Thorpe is small at any time, smaller still in
November; and at 6 p.m. on a November evening any American visitor
would be pursuing livelier interests. Ellie could feel pretty sure of having
the church to herself.

The door closed behind her, and the noises of traffic, though still
audible, passed into a different dimension of sound. Her sense of
hearing relaxed. Her eyes recovered from the joggle of dark streets and
devouring headlights. She saw instead the composed clear-obscure of
the dimly lit interior, where, as if she were a fish in a pool, the dark pews,
the glimmering effigies, the blackness of the glass in the traceried
windows surrounded her like rocks and fronded waterweeds. But when

she sighed with relief, no bubble rose to the surface. Nothing corroborated her sigh.

As she expected, the church was pleasantly warm. Warmth is one of the outward signs of the variety of English churchmanship known as High—an atmosphere in which ciboriums, images of the Blessed Virgin, sanctuary lamps, stands for holding votive candles, and shallow wadded mats referred to as 'kneelers' are in their natural clime. In churches known as Low one finds, instead of kneelers, hassocks, which themselves are high. It varies inversely. Ellie knew all this, not because she was religiously inclined but because, in the days before calamity forced her down in the world, she had been on the fringe of the class called educated, with a mind sufficiently at leisure to enjoy noticing things, and speculating over them, and reading books from the public library in order to learn more exactly about them. But this was a long time ago, and the scraps of knowledge she had then accumulated lay like a heap of dead leaves, broomed away into an unfrequented corner of her mind and only stirring now and then, and only the lightest and least significant of them stirring, at that. The Reformation of the English Church had come about, men had burned at the stake and a faith as fiery had blown the flames, Jesuit missionaries had been disembowelled at Tyburn, Laud's hands had fluttered in blessing through the prison grate, Quakers had been whipped through the streets, Newman had torn himself weeping from the mother he abjured, and as a result of all this anguish and altercation Ellie knew that St Mary Ragmarket could be relied on to provide warmth, repose, and a sense of luxury.

They were being provided as usual, and with them the amplitude of the nave, the remoteness of the roof, a serene faint smell of wax polish and candle wax, an uncluttered spaciousness; but tonight, for some reason, the quiet and the solitude had taken on a different quality, and were silence and emptiness. No building had ever been so totally silent, so totally uninhabited. It was as if the fabric had grown up, and endured through the centuries, without anyone ever knowing about it or ever coming here. It was as though it were unvisitable, like a place in a dream, a dream into which she had got by mistake and out of which she would never pass. Perhaps the difference lay in herself. For tonight, though her body was relaxing like a cat on a familiar hearth, her mind would not relax. It was as though she were waiting, helplessly, ignorantly, rigidly waiting—as during the air-raid winters one had waited—for some dreadful thing that was about to declare itself, some inevitable, shattering recognition that would presently explode from within her. She ransacked her memory for a possible cause—a tap left running, a bill unpaid. She ran through the familiar rota of familiar dreads—Mother dying, herself taken ill and carted off to hospital, the rent raised, her job lost, another war, a purely hypothetical illegitimate son of Father's, specious and bullying, turning up to prey on them. There was no quiver of response. It must be nerves. For everything was just as usual. Her day had been no more tiring or uncongenial than usual. She was going home, as usual, where as usual she would get supper and serve it to Mother in her wheelchair, talk for a while, put her to bed, wash up, set things to rights, and go to bed herself, with the door ajar, so that she would wake up at any call from the adjoining room. Other women led lives quite as restricted, and much sadder, having no one to love. She had her mother, who, together with the habit of love, had survived thirty years of poverty and had been, till only a short while ago, a supporting and even a reviving person to go home to. For it was only in these last few years—four years, six years?—when deafness had closed her in, and given her the stunned, inattentive expression it was so painful to see, that acquaintances had begun to say she was wonderful for her age, and quite a character, and that Ellie would feel quite lost when she passed on.

This was the sort of acquaintance they were now reduced to—people who thirty years ago would only have been deserving old dears for Mother to give port wine and blankets to, people to whom it would be inconceivable that thirty years ago Mother walked on three-inch heels with the gait of a queen, subjugated everyone she met, and could kiss the wall behind her. Then, too, she was wonderful for her age—but no one would have dared say so. This was the being whom Father deserted, going off with a smug slut whose petticoats dangled below her skirts. 'I can do without him,' Mother had declared. 'Alimony is as good as matrimony at my age.' It was a brave boast, and while the alimony lasted, it held. Then, during the slump, he died, penniless. She mourned him briefly and tempestuously, and afterward began to pick holes in him.

Poor Mother!

It was time to think of getting back to her. Pauses for repose and luxury in St Mary Ragmarket seldom exceeded ten minutes, and tonight, since St Mary Ragmarket was not living up to Ellie's expectations, there was the less reason to linger there. Yet she wanted to linger; or rather, she was reluctant to quit it for streets where she would certainly encounter more of those horrible Guys. It was the Fifth of November, and at every turn she had met groups of children bearing their dummy towards the bonfire, on a chair or in a handcart, and assailing her with, 'Penny for the Guy.' It was curiously shocking to be confronted with these effigies, stuffed with straw, bedizened in human rags, sagging forward over the string that fastened them by the waist to their conveyance. It was mortifying not to be able to spare the penny. As she walked on, the chant pursued her like a hail of pebbles:

'Guy, Guy, hit him in the eye!
Hang him on a lamp-post and never let him die.'

Nevertheless, she rose and went to the door. As she opened it, she heard a spurt of sound, the sizzling uprush of a rocket, an outburst of young yells. Then a voice said, 'Now for the squibs!' Remembering the squib that had burned a hole in her stocking, she drew back into the church; and to kill time and combat the sense of silence and emptiness, she began a tour of examination. Presently she came to the stand for votive candles. It was an iron frame supporting three tiers of branching sockets. All were empty. Only a few had remnants of candle grease in them, and in these, as she discovered by poking, the grease was hardened and quite cold. Below was a platform, and on it were candles in a container, a box of matches, a few match ends, and a slotted box fastened to the stand by a chain and lettered 'CANDLES FOURPENCE EACH.' Fourpence apiece for such puny specimens! No wonder the sockets were empty.

Even while this reflection was passing through her mind, she had dropped four pennies into the box and taken a candle.

Though what does one burn a candle for, and to whom, and why? What deity or demiurge did she think to invoke? Certainly not that presiding white plaster Virgin near by, to which she had taken an instant dislike because its expression of pigheaded meekness recalled the woman Father had gone off with. Not God, that Maker and Manager of all things visible and invisible, of whom it is declared by the Prophets that He is above the heavens, and who is therefore, presumably, above bribes. And on whose behalf—her luckless own, her irremediable

mother's? And why? Out of all the things that can be done for fourpence
—still, in spite of the rise in the cost of living, quite a considerable
number—why pick on this?

Meanwhile, she was painstakingly fixing the candle to stand firm and
upright. When it was settled to her satisfaction, she struck a match and
held the flame to the wick, which after a momentary halfheartedness
took fire and began to burn independently. Oh, no need to ask why! The
answer was in the act. The dated confident little flame, the minute dated
warmth, the wax gently yielding—by bringing this about she had
brought a new light and a new warmth into the cavernous world. She had
created an impersonal good, a good that would benefit no one and harm
no one, impose no obligation and fulfil no duty. Looking at her candle,
now burning so diligently and composedly, she felt a kind of delighting
trust in it. How far it spread its beams! How pleased it looked! How
bravely it burned, the phoenix of its kind, among those yawning empty
sockets! She had another four pennies; and although eightpence is
two-thirds of a shilling, which is the economic unit of a slot meter, yet, if
only out of gratitude—gratitude for having experienced a purity of
gratitude such as she had not felt since childhood—she must light a
second candle, a votive candle to the first. She tried it in one socket and
another, to see where it looked best. When this was decided on, and the
candle firmly established, she struck a match. As if she had provoked an
echo, there came from outside an answering spurt, a rushing sizzle as
the rocket tore upwards, a thud.

The match burned unheeded in her hand. Only when it scorched her
finger did she throw it down.

With a spurt and a sizzle and a thud, a realization had exploded in her
mind. Those dummies, those frightful pitiable dummies! They were
exhibitions to her of what her mother was becoming, had almost
become. The horror they aroused in her only corroborated and proclaimed an abhorrence she had not dared to admit. It was with abhorrence that she now looked at her mother. Abhorrence must have been
there for months, disguised as a flinching pity. And now, knowing the
truth, she must go home and experience it.

She lit the second candle, stared at its magicless flame, and went to
the back of the church, where it was darkest and sternest, to sit for a
while longer. She would be late. Mother, clutching at her last pleasure, a

nice hot supper with something tasty, would be angry at having been kept waiting. She would scold, in her flat voice, and afterwards she would weep. She was eighty-four; hunger, suspicion, and self-pity was all that was left to spice her dreary days. Ellie, telling herself that she must somehow scratch up a handful of courage—or if not courage, compassion, and if not compassion, common sense—sat waiting for the candles to burn out. The first died easily. The second flared and struggled. After this, there was no excuse to remain. She remained, sitting bolt upright, her head gradually drooping forward.

She became conscious of a stir of cold air, and heard footsteps approaching. She did not move. The footsteps slowed, drew level with her, and halted, creaking slightly. She did not look up, but out of the corner of her eye she saw a straight black garment reaching to the floor—a cassock, and within the cassock, no doubt, a rector. He coughed, drew breath to speak, thought better of it, coughed again, again drew a breath.

'Good evening! Jolly of you to come in like this.'

She made no reply. After a moment or two, he moved on. She stumbled to her feet and hurried out of the building, knowing that never again would she set foot in it.

When the door had closed behind her, he gave a movement of the shoulders that could have been a shrug if habit had not made it an acknowledgment of a burden. Once again he had done the wrong thing. He had spoken when he should have kept silence. Surely, there had never been a visitor more patently in need of a kind word than this poor old girl, so gaunt and derelict, her bony, coarsened hands clamped on her shabby handbag. But it had been the wrong thing. He had offended her, and she had fluttered away like some ungainly bird. Perhaps a notice in the porch saying, as much to him as to others, 'Persons entering this Church will not be spoken to' . . . Better phrased, of course. If by some extraordinary chance—a forgotten glove (but had those hands ever been gloved?), a change of heart—she were to return . . . But she did not return.

His purpose resumed him. He went to the altar rail, knelt down, and began to pray for the soul of Guy Fawkes.

(A Spirit Rises, 1962)

APPRENTICE

THE front door, where the officers came in, was level with the street; but the house being built on a slope, from the narrow garden at the back one looked over a wall, and there, six feet below, were the heads of the passers-by. Not often, though. Not many people, and no officers, went down the narrow muddy lane, on the farther side of which was another wall, and another slope, and the upper boughs of an old pear tree.

Perched on the wall was a small stone summer-house, no bigger than a sentry-box. It had eight corners, a little spire, and a window like a church window, only the glass had been broken during the fighting. From the window one could look down into the lane, or across, over the roof-tops of the lower town, over the river and the forest, to the mountains. The mountains were stony and jagged. They were so close that one could imagine they echoed back the noises of the town—the jangling churchbells, the clear bugle notes from the garrison barracks, the cry of the goat that was tethered in the garden of the pear tree; though after a few weeks the goat cried no more, so someone must have eaten her.

'My house,' said Lili. As the autumn was fine and warm they gladly allowed her to spend most of her time there. Lili was a sweet child, and Major von Kraebeck made quite a pet of her. Still, it was better to have her out of the way, for what is sometimes amusing is not always amusing.

Whoever Lili's father had been—and Irma honestly did not know —there could be no doubt that he had been all right. No Jewish blubber-lips had befouled a healthy German maiden on that occasion. Lili's eyes, set as closely in her face as the imbedded jewels in an old-fashioned ring, were flax blossoms to corroborate her flaxen hair.

Her limbs were solid and straight, her flesh, as Anna remarked, was like the most expensive face-cream. Though she was only ten years old she was already rounded and womanly. She was a quiet child, quiet in a healthy un-morbid way, as though, without any break, she would develop from a model baby to a model woman.

So Lili kept house in the gazebo, sometimes eating a biscuit, sometimes thrumming on her guitar, sometimes inscribing picture postcards to send to her friends. For though Poland was a detestable country, it was rather grand to be in Poland.

As usual, all thanks were due to Major von Kraebeck. His interest in Irma extended to the whole establishment, to the three other doves and the dove-mother, and to Lili, who was his littlest dove. He managed everything; even the formalities of Lili ceasing to be educated he managed; and when they arrived he had a lovely house for them, victuals, bedding, clothes, cosmetics, everything of the best. He had even remembered to collect toys for Lili.

The people who used the lane were all Poles. They were poor and shabby, there was nothing interesting about them, except sometimes the extraordinary things they carried. They carried mirrors, saddles, gramophones, mattresses, statues, cooking-pots. Once an old man went by carrying a large gold clock that chimed in his arms. They went down the hill with their strange burdens; and after a while they would come back again, and sometimes they would have exchanged what they had taken for beetroots or cabbages, but sometimes they would bring back what they had carried down. They walked slower on the way back, because it was all uphill. Some of them looked at the mountains, but no one ever looked up at Lili.

A Polish woman came to the house to clean. She came at nine in the morning, and somebody had to get up to let her in. Quite often Lili did. Like a dead leaf the woman would whisk down the stairs, and then one would hear sounds of scrubbing, chopping wood, washing dishes. She was no fun at all, she was silent and looked cross, and she had a skin disease. Helge said that it was not wholesome that she should wash their dishes, but Madam Ulricke said it was nothing infectious, it was only because her blood was so poor.

One day there was a crash, and the noise of chopping ceased.

'Oh God, she's gone mad! She's begun to break things,' cried Helge.

And Lili's mother said:

'Why on earth did we ever let her get hold of the axe?'

They clustered together at the head of the cellar steps, listening.

No sound came. They talked in whispers about barring the door, or sending for a Gestapo man. After a while came the sound of a heavy sigh.

'That's just a fit,' said Madam Ulricke, and went down to the cellar. The others followed her, and Lili went too.

There on the cellar floor sat the woman, swaying and looking round her as though she wondered where she was, and the axe lay beside her. She had not broken anything. Her face worked, and suddenly she was sick, holding her shawl to her mouth. When she took the shawl away there was nothing much on it, just some green slime.

Madam Ulricke went to the larder, and unlocked it, and brought out milk, and gave it to the woman. At the first sup the woman looked astonished, and frowned. She put up her hand as though to take hold of the cup, then she put it down again, folding it in the shawl. Madam Ulricke cut a slice of bread, and put butter on it. It was the good butter, but even so the woman did not seem to notice it. She ate slowly, like an old machine that needed oiling, and as she swallowed, she choked. Suddenly the saliva began to stream from the corners of her mouth, and Helge said what a pig she was, no better than an animal, hay was what she needed, not butter.

'Just about what she's been getting,' said Madam Ulricke. 'That was grass that she sicked up.'

'Pooh! Why should she eat grass? We pay her, don't we?'

'Suppose she had children, though?' Irma's eyes filled with tears. 'She would starve to feed them. Any mother would. If my Lili . . .'

'Starving? Fancy! Is she really starving?'

Anna stared at the woman with interest. Madam Ulricke nodded.

'I know starvation when I see it. You girls have never seen it, but I have. After the last war, we starved.'

'Ah, the brutes!' exclaimed Helge. 'They starved us. Now *they* shall starve, Poles, French, Russians, English, all of them! And we shall eat and guzzle. Give me something to eat now, something good.'

Madam Ulricke went to the larder again. They heard her moving dishes, breathing thoughtfully. The woman sat on the ground, panting and dribbling. Madam Ulricke came out with a bowlful of food; there was lard, cheese, coffee, eggs, the carcase of a fowl, and two goose drumsticks stuck out. Helge said she didn't want any of that.

'You won't get it, my girl.'

'What? Is that for her? All that?'

'Yes. I went hungry once. Now I feed well, thanks to our Leader. I don't want to turn my luck.'

Helge laughed, but the other girls became tender and excited. They ran about collecting more food—chocolate, herrings, dumplings—which they rammed into the bowl. At intervals they turned to the woman, smiled, and made gestures of bestowal. Madam Ulricke hauled her to her feet, put the bowl in her arms, pulled the shawl over it, and pointed to the back door. The woman looked round like a cat and ran off. Her behaviour, so ungrateful and insensitive, was disappointing. She had not finished her work, either.

Yet to Lili it seemed very nice to feed the starving. It was exciting, it made one feel good. Before they came to Poland she had had a little dog, and she always enjoyed feeding it, throwing biscuit and seeing him dash after it, holding the bone above his head while he begged and rolled his eyes. It occurred to her that she could feed the starving from her summer-house. She would feed children; no one could much object to that, for they would be Polish children only, all the Jews had been put away.

She began to save and purloin. When she had a basketful of scraps she carried it to her summer-house and sat there, waiting for children.

Before long four children appeared, children whom she already knew by sight. As usual, they were dragging a sledge with bits of wood on it. Some of the wood was already charred. It came from the suburb where the bombs had fallen, everyone went there to steal wood.

'Here!'

She leaned forward and emptied the basket. What a pity, she had meant to throw the bits one by one. The biscuits, the dried plums, the shrimp-heads, and the orange scattered on the muddy road, and the orange began to roll downhill. The children let go of the sledge; it, too, began to run down the hill. Just like the little dog, they dashed to and fro, snatching up bits of food. They even barked, or something very like it.

When they had picked up everything they went after the sledge.

'Here! Here I am!'

She called at the top of her voice. They began looking for more food; at last they looked up and saw her. She held out her hand, as though more were coming. They stared. She had no more, but at least they had seen her.

For hours after she nursed a violent impression of the contrast between them and herself. There she had leant with her smooth plaits swinging, so plump and white-skinned and smiling so graciously; and there they had stood, turning up their wizened sallow faces, and blinking their sore eyes. They all had swelled bellies. It was funny, it made them look greedy and not starving at all. But of course they must be starving, one could see that by their hollow cheeks, their stringy necks, the toes that came out of their torn shoes, toes so thin that they looked like rats' claws.

That afternoon Major von Kraebeck brought a box of chocolates. She sat on his knee and ate them from between his lips, which made them rather sticky.

'Aren't you lucky?' said Irma. 'Luckier than the poor little Polish kids.'

Lili tweaked out another chocolate.

'They look so funny, the Polish kids! They all have big bellies and yellow faces. They are like little monkey mothers. Boys and girls, they are all like little monkey mothers.'

The Major exploded with laughter, and said he must tell that to the mess. Lili tried to think of another clever remark about the Polish children (she was not often so successfully clever), but before she could do so he had set her down and told her to run away.

Though everyone was so good-humoured, something warned her to keep her summer-house game a secret. The fat Captain was always telling Helge stories about typhus, and Helge saying they should be like the brave men in the English story, who shut themselves up during a plague and would have nothing to do with anyone outside their village. As time went on it became rather a bore collecting the scraps. There was always plenty of cigar-ends, of course, and bits of orange-peel, but real food was harder to come by. It was a good hour when the idea came to her of wrapping pebbles in the fancy papers that had wrapped sweets. They looked charming, and most life-like. The sledge children still paused under the summer-house, though now they were not so excited that they let the sledge run away, and once the boy, finding a pebble in his mouth instead of a sweet, spat it out and threw it at her. Then they came no longer. Perhaps they were dead. There were other children, though, all ugly and with swollen bellies, and ready to eat anything, who paused and looked up enquiringly.

It occurred to her that instead of just throwing food down it would be much better sport to lower it on a string. For then she could dangle it, lowering it and drawing it up again; and quite a little food would last out as long as a basketful. This was delightful: so delightful that she became a much better thief, stealing sprats and little cakes, and taking the bones and crusts that Madam Ulricke put by for the charwoman. And naturally the poor children enjoyed their bits much more when they had jumped for them a little, and fought among themselves. Back in Germany Lili had learned in school how what you fight for and take from others is sweetest of all.

But there was one boy who would not jump, who would not beg. There was nothing to make him so proud, he was just a Pole, and as thin as the others, his eyes were inflamed, his belly was swollen, his hands were covered with open chilblains. Only his hair looked rather strong. It was black, and grew straight up off his forehead, like a forest. Twice when the other children had been jumping for crusts he stopped on his way up the hill, and spoke angrily to them. The first time they listened, and walked away. The second time he scolded them they paid him no heed, but jumped on. After that he always walked by with his nose in the air.

He was stuck-up, and a spoil-sport. Cruel, too, for he tried to prevent the poor hungry children from getting their crusts. Lili hated him. She hated him, and she thought of him. She wondered how tall he was—it was difficult to tell from above. She wondered if he was an orphan and if he had ever worn a hat. She wondered if he had gipsy blood. She wondered if he had lice in his hair, and one day, seeing him scratch his neck savagely, she knew that he had, and was delighted. She hated everything about him: his upstanding black hair, the recollection of his sharp voice, the old satchel he carried under his arm. No doubt he thought himself a scholar, a professor. Sometimes she even wondered if he were not a Jew; he might have been hidden when the others were carted off. The only thing about him which she did not hate was his regularity: every afternoon he came up the hill, late, when the river mists were rising. And sometimes she even hated his regularity, he was like some hateful medicine which she had to swallow day after day.

Her regularity began to match his. Every afternoon she waited for him, and kept the best, the most tempting bit to dangle in front of him. If some grown-up person went along the lane at the same time that he did, so that she could not carry out her fishing game, she was furious. Sometimes, hearing him approach, she thought how much she would like to tumble down a stone, a heavy stone, on top of that black head. One day, perhaps, she might. But not until she had hooked him. That must come first. He must eat from her hand, as the others had done, and look up, and be grateful.

Time went on. It grew cold, a damp wind blew away all the leaves from the pear tree and even the topmost pear that no one could reach. Looking at the forest you could almost hear the wolves howl. You could hear the Poles howl quite plainly. The women had rioted, breaking the windows of the fashionable baker's shop to get at the cakes and golden crescents within. Irma and Helge and Anna and Lisl, even Madam Ulricke, had been terrified, and had run about the house hiding away food and wine and their best clothes in case the Polish women should break in. Anna had pulled her shoes and stockings off, and put a shawl over her head, saying that she would pretend to be a peasant; and the others had laughed hysterically, pointing to her white feet and crimson-varnished toe-nails. On the next day the charwoman was dismissed, for the officers said it was not safe to have her about the house, she might let in the others, and as for the housework and the washing-up, the girls could manage it for themselves; and Major von Kraebeck sent in a soldier to chop wood and see to the great stove. The girls were angry, they did not like housework, they had not come to Poland to be drudges. The soldier grew very fond of Madam Ulricke, they would stay a long time in the cellar together, making the stove burn up, Madam Ulricke said. When they came out the soldier would lay his head on her bosom and weep, and say how greatly he longed for home. And Madam Ulricke would make him hot milk.

All these things were observed by Lili, for now that the charwoman came no more she was being more useful. But still in the afternoons she went to her summer-house to wait for the boy; for in the afternoons nobody wanted her. And now she had finer and more tempting baits, for being so much in the kitchen she picked up many good things.

The boy still came by at the same time. She often heard his footsteps long before she could see him, for the mists from the river swelled higher and higher, all the lower town was blotted out in fog. He came up out of the mist and was gone, and never once did he look at the bait she dangled before him. And day after day she fretted more, foreseeing that quite soon it would be dark before he came by.

For three days and nights the wind howled and the rain lashed against the windows. On the fourth morning the wind fell, the air was like ice-water, and snow lay on the mountains. The people who went along the lane shaded their eyes against the brilliant sunlight, and pulled their clothes closer round them against the motionless cold, and an old man carrying a cello to the pawnshop slipped on the ice and fell groaning. The cello groaned too as it fell, it skidded down the hill and crashed against a post and was broken, and the old man went after it on all fours, howling like a beast.

The sun, the tingling air, the snow on the mountains, the excitement of wearing for the first time a little fur coat and a pair of fur gloves, all gave Lili a sense of confidence. Today, surely, her luck was in!

'Bake cinnamon buns,' she said to Madam Ulricke. 'Bake cinnamon buns, and I will wash all the glasses and polish the saucepans too.'

'Why do you want cinnamon buns?'

'To eat in my house,' she replied boldly.

'Heavens, child! It is far too cold to play there now.'

'No, it is lovely! I will sit there and eat my buns with my gloves on, and look at the sunset, and pretend I am grown-up, and engaged to be married to a General, or a Minister.'

But to fix the bun on the string she had to pull off her gloves. And the air seemed to bite away her flesh, so warm and plump, as though it would give her rat's-paw hands, like any Polish child. Then she sat down to wait.

Other children came by, and looked up at her, and held out their rat's-paw hands. But she paid no heed to them, she could not be bothered with them now. She waited. And the colours of the roof-tops changed, the river grew pale as lead, the forest seemed to come nearer. The church bells jangled, the sky became almost green. The bun was quite cold now. She ground her teeth with impatience. But still she felt sure of him.

At last he came with his black head and his satchel. And today, for the first time, he looked for her as he was approaching. She could not discern much, for already dusk was falling, only that his face was white, and that he was looking at her. Then, just as though to tantalise her, he turned away and leaned on the wall, staring at the river and the forest and the mountains—as though he had not seen them every day of his life. She could see by the movement of his narrow shoulders that he was out of breath.

She tried to whistle softly and prettily, as one whistles to a bird. But her lips were stiff with cold; instead of a whistle she could only manage a squawk.

At last he turned away from the mountains and came on up the hill, walking slowly; and slowly she lowered the bun.

She lowered it so cleverly that it bobbed against his face. Then she whisked it up again.

He leaped after it. He almost caught it. It was frightful that anyone could leap like that.

The satchel dropped from under his arm. His head jerked backward, he fell, and lay in the road, quite still. Quite still, she watched him.

Presently she began to count. Fifty, fifty-one. If I reach a hundred, she thought, and he does not move, I shall think he's dead. Seventy-seven, seventy-eight, seventy-nine. . . . She reached the hundred, and went on counting, frozen in an ecstasy of amassing. She had counted up to eight hundred and ninety when a man came along the lane. It was annoying, she did not want anyone to come by, and the rhythm of his footsteps threw her out in her count. Seeing the boy he stopped, and then knelt down beside him. To her it was obvious that the boy was dead, and at last the man was convinced of it too. He got up, and dusted the frost off his knees. Then, as though an idea had struck him, he stooped again, and pulled the boy straight, crossing his hands on his breast and smoothing the strong hair. Then he took a handkerchief from round his neck, and began to spread it over the boy's face, but changed his mind, and put on the handkerchief again, and knotted it carefully. Then he went away.

So it was true, really true. The boy was dead. He had died of cold and hunger before her eyes, just as they said. Dozens of them were dying so; but hearsay is one thing, seeing with one's own eyes another.

Poor boy! He should not have been so proud, so unpleasant. If he had taken her gifts earlier he might still be alive. It was not her fault that he had died so horribly of starvation. It must be really terrible to die like that, really terrible to be dead.

There was the poor bun, still dangling.

Hastily she pulled it up, and ate it.

(A Garland of Straw, 1943)

A RED CARNATION

No other word had been used; the order had run: Prepare to depart for manœuvres on June 20th. And accordingly manœuvres was the word which darted about the barracks, echoed from the walls, was mixed with the clatter of knives and spoons and tin dishes, sounded an overtone on the band-music. Even in one's thoughts one continued obediently to use the word.

But every one knew it meant Spain.

Others had gone, many others. By now there was nothing remarkable or dramatic about going to Spain. It was the soldier's duty to fight the Red menace. Whether one was sent east or west it was the same duty, wherever the compass needle swung there the German soldier must march at the word of command. Wherever those red flames sprang up there the German soldier must go, to trample them out under his strong boots.

Kurt Winkler looked at his boots with new appreciation. Such fine boots, good leather, thick soles! . . . At first it had hurt his feet, wearing such boots; now he was used to them, could not imagine himself without them. It was a pity that one could not take one's boots with one when one's army days were over.

The Spanish Reds actually fought in rope-soled sandals.

The word to be said was manœuvres, but the word in his heart was Spain. And for the fiftieth time he found himself flooded with excitement, with pleasure, with a childish and unsoldierly yielding to romance. Spain! He would see Seville, the orange trees, the bullfights, those girls who made cigarettes. He would walk about holding a red carnation between his teeth.

The blood began to dance in his limbs. He clattered up the stairs, caught hold of Heinrich's arm, plump as a girl's.

'Heinrich! Tomorrow we start for manœuvres, eh?'

'Shut up!'

'Why, good Lord!'

'Well, you pinched me.'

Heinrich's voice was sullen, his blue eyes looked flat and dark in his round face, they were like two pools of water reflecting the colour of a thunder-cloud.

'Anyhow—it's serious.'

That was true, that was certainly true. Kurt was ashamed of himself. Again, for the fiftieth time, he had let himself be run away with by this childish and unsoldierly excitement. Spain? What was Spain? A battle-field merely, a preliminary battlefield. East or west, wherever the red menace shows itself, there must the German soldier go, strong, disciplined, practical. Heinrich understood this, he had a serious nature, he thought a great deal. Kurt felt ashamed of his levity.

By the next morning all his excitement was obliterated. The moment of departure, the early-morning, ordinary-seeming lorry ride to the station, all the well-managed masquerade that he had foreseen and whose drama he had tasted beforehand—he hardly realised these things were taking place. His thoughts were absorbed by Heinrich Fiedler, who, in the small hours of the morning had gone to the lavatory and cut his throat.

The non-commissioned officers were furious. At this last moment, when everything was so well prepared, every detail polished and exact, to make a gap in the ranks!—such an act was mutiny, was treachery. Why the hell couldn't he have slit his throat a few days earlier?

Naturally, no mention of this bad beginning was allowed. 'Heinrich Fiedler!' The name was called. Then a condemning silence. 'Ludwig Mueller.' 'Present.' After that, no more of Heinrich Fiedler.

And this, of course, was right. Heinrich Fiedler was not only dead, but disgraced. His memory must be thrown away while the life of the stalwartly-living went on. For all that, Kurt could not remove his thoughts from this astonishing disaster. He travelled through the dislustred day feeling hollow and dumbfounded, feeling as though he were going to be sick. Every now and then he recalled with surprise that he was going to Spain.

On the boat he was sick. Not because of the waves, for the sea was as flat as a mill-pond, but because of the heavy smell of engine oil, because of the overcrowding and lack of the exercise to which, in his soldier's life, he had grown accustomed, and because of the disgusting sensation of having water underneath one, shifting, unstable, unknown, instead of good solid earth. But he was only sick for one day, and recovering from physical misery he seemed to have recovered from Heinrich Fiedler too. He began to think about Spain once more, he fished out his phrase-book and dictionary. He had bought them the day after the news came. On board ship there was an unusual amount of leisure, he began to study.

It was a foolish civilian phrase-book, old-fashioned as they always are. With a sensation of losing his dignity he read the sentences in which the traveller asked the way to the cathedral or paid a laundry bill. The dictionary was more useful, he learned a lot from the dictionary. And at night, listening to the noise of the boat, rocked on the indifferent bosom of the sea, he rehearsed the things he would say in Spain. *Good afternoon. We have come to bring you victory.* That was how one would greet the peasants. To the women one would say, *Have no fear. I am here to protect you from the marxists* . . . or something a little tenderer. Children one would greet with *Grow up into a good fascist and patriot.* Whom else would one meet in Spain? Priests, of course. He could not frame a greeting for priests. Advanced nations know that religion is all bunkum. Presently he was able to hold most satisfactory imaginary conversations in Spanish.

It was disconcerting when the sergeant tossed his phrase-book overboard, saying that the less he talked to the inhabitants the better, that good German would be all the language he would need. Some of the phrases stayed in his mind, though. He could almost feel them in his mouth, forbidden sweets. But the dictionary he put obediently away, hiding it behind his cork jacket.

They docked at night. No one had known that this was about to happen; after supper they had gone to bed, to be awakened with the order to stand-to and prepare for disembarkation. No one knew, either, which port it was, and they were not told. Soldiers do not ask questions. Waiting on the lower deck they whispered among themselves. The port was Cadiz. The port was Seville. One man asserted that it was Valencia.

Then a peevish voice remarked that the Reds were in Valencia, and another voice replied, with a laugh: 'All the better. We land, and finish them off.'

At last the order came and they began to clatter down the gangways. The ship rode high; for a moment Kurt had a view of the city rising beyond the docks. It was twinkling with lights, a pinkish haze embowered it, like vapours from a stage cauldron, and it seemed to him that he heard music.

The quays were ill-lit. They seemed unpopulated except for the soldiers, standing in their ranks like a clipped garden. One could hear the shuffling of feet, occasionally there was a hollow clanking noise, followed by a sigh of steam and a jet of water. The reflection of the gangway lamp spread in oily circles. Sure enough, floating down there was any amount of orange-peel.

In Spain, he was now in Spain. It must be Spain, for they had passed through the Straits of Gibraltar. It was a pity that they had not been allowed to arrive by day. Still, the city was awake. In Spain gay life persists all night long, and presently he would be riding past cafés and flood-lit fountains, and girls would throw flowers from balconies, and he would catch a red carnation and hold it between his teeth.

The order to march was given. They turned into a street winding between tall warehouses. It was cobbled, and had tram-lines. The tram-lines made an endless hallucinating path. After a while the warehouses thinned out, and gave place to factories and yards, and after that they passed through a district of mean houses, where their passage aroused the barking of dogs and thin cock-crowings. It became obvious that they were leaving the city behind. Even into the countryside the tram-lines persisted. An astonishingly cold wind blew across the fields and brought clouds of dust with it. The men began to sneeze.

Dawn was breaking when they halted at a small railway station. The only other building in sight was about a mile away: a large barrack-like place with a high wall around it. Their train was in; and the old-fashioned engine, large and lumpy like a peasant woman, had steam up. There was a coach for the officers, and a hunchback was climbing in and out of it, shaking a feather whisk. Her head was bundled up in a white shawl, her feet were bare. The rest of the train was cattle-trucks.

It was rather wounding to be treated like this; but any shelter was grateful against the cold wind, and when they had settled down in their trucks hot weak coffee was served round. The trucks were clean. Cleaned for us, he thought; for the Spaniards are notoriously a dirty lot. The doors were closed, now the next stage of their journey was beginning. Kurt settled himself where he would be able to observe the country through a crack. But though the engine continued to let off steam it did not start. Rays of sunlight began to pour through the chinks, presently a herd of goats came by, bleating and pattering. They were driven across the rails, and a voice was answered briskly by another voice. They were speaking Spanish, of course. Fancy waiting for a herd of goats! The goats' cries died away, still the train remained in the station. When at last it got under way the jolt barely roused him from sleep.

When he woke the train was once more at a standstill, and the truck had grown stiflingly hot. He woke remembering that he had forgotten to take his dictionary from its hiding-place. Knowing quite well that this was so, nevertheless, he began to pat his pockets and rout in his knapsack. As he moved the sweat sprang out all over him.

'Winkler! Don't fidget.'

He looked through the crack. All he could see was a bush that had small leaves. It was smothered with dust.

Then the door was unbarred, and they were told to get out and relieve nature. The violence of the sun was like a blow. The landscape extended pale and lifeless, as though the light had stunned it. A line of stony mountains lay along the horizon, they were wrinkled, like a crumple of wrapping paper, and it was impossible to say if they were near or far. Looking again at the dusty bush he saw that it was dotted with small white flowers. A shout of laughter came from his companions. One of them had noticed that the ground was swarming with ants, and a competition to drown the ants was taking place. Farther down the track the cooks were preparing breakfast.

They travelled all day. At intervals the train halted, always in places as bare and pale as the first. Everyone agreed that this was a worthless country, and Fridolin Kuh grumbled that such a country might as well be left to the Reds, no one else could want it. The engine-driver sat on the step of the cab with his legs dangling, and poured wine into his mouth, holding the bottle away from his lips. At each halt they egged one another on to go forward and talk to him, but each time that a group began sneaking off a non-commissioned officer would order them back.

After a halt where the railway track ran beside a dry riverbed they travelled for a long time, and dusk gave way to darkness, and the noise of the wheels seemed to alter. Then again they halted, but the doors remained barred. They heard an old-fashioned mechanical piano playing quite close by, and presently a thick tenor voice took up the tune. After the song there was stamping and clapping and cries of approval. Listening drowsily, Kurt found that he could understand what was being said. Spanish was an easy language then, he had learned it better than he supposed, and the loss of the dictionary was not so serious after all.

'Do you hear that, boys? That's some of ours. Sounds good, eh?' He realised that the singer and the shouters were German.

Everyone was delighted to think that there were comrades so close, and answering shouts and snatches of song came from the trucks, but at the same moment the train got going again, just as though the driver had done it out of malice.

At last they detrained at a station no larger than the one they started from, and just as solitary. The new road also had tramlines, and inverted the morning's march from country into mean suburbs, from suburbs to yards and factories. They might have been back where they started from, only there was no sea.

Left wheel! The tramlines went on, the men turned into a road which began to mount steeply uphill, past a cemetery, past large villas, each standing behind a high pale wall. Looking at the cypresses and the fantastic silhouettes of the balconied and turreted villas Kurt felt that at last he was in Spain. Ten minutes later, as Fridolin Kuh remarked with pleasure, they were back in Germany.

The barrack was a large building in modern style. The Republicans had built it, they were told, to house lunatics and cretins. Now it was put to a better use, swarming with healthy young men, ringing with healthy boot-treads, smelling of healthy meat and dumpling. A garden even had been laid out for the lunatics, and planted with young trees. This was now a parade-ground, and the few saplings that remained were broken and dying. Everything was splendidly managed, day by day swinging by as though to a march-tune. Even the sun, rising above the white wall, burning the dew off the dying saplings, bleaching the sky to a midday pallor, declining into a coppery mist, seemed to be on parade. In such a life—short of active service the most congenial a young man can ask for—Kurt should have been happy. But on the whole he was not happy. Analysing his discontent, he told himself that he was bored and frustrated, that nothing short of the noblest could satisfy him, and that having come to Spain to root out marxism he could not be happy till he was doing it. Meanwhile, there were other small rubs and annoyances. The relation between his detachment and the earlier arrivals was not good. The first lot were sour and clannish, and behaved as though they owned the place. There was a good deal of petty thieving, an unwillingness to share or lend—as though a sense of being besieged had developed from the state of being in a foreign country. No one felt very well. You'll soon get it, the old lot told the new. Sure enough, before long the new arrivals began to suffer from headaches, shivering fits, and diarrhœa. In a fit of confidence Karl Heidler, one of the first lot, told Kurt that this was because of a bunch of flowers which Corporal Schutz had brought in one evening, flowers bestowed on him by a young lady. They were bright magenta-coloured flowers, Heidler said, and carried fever, though they had no scent. There had been a row, and the nosegay had been thrown into the furnace; but the fever persisted.

Only the non-commissioned officers, it appeared, were allowed to go into the town. For himself, said Heidler, he wouldn't trouble to go. It was unhealthy, the prices were exorbitant, and there were beggars at every turn.

'All the same, it would be nice to see Spain.'

'You'll see it fast enough,' Heidler replied. 'There's an inspection on Wednesday.'

The inspection was carried out by a Spanish general. He was a short man with a worried expression, and at brief intervals he scratched himself. His staff, who accompanied him, all seemed to belong to one and the same family. They were singularly tall and thin, they had blankly supercilious faces and sagging lower lips. It was not romantic.

Yet romance there must be. All the stories, all the songs, all the movies, stressed the romance of Spain, and they could not all be mistaken. Besides, had not a political lecturer described to them how in marxist Spain the singing and dancing and traditional piety and gaiety had been overwhelmed by squalor and starvation?—whereas this was nationalist Spain. So Kurt cultivated Corporal Heidler, listened to his ailments and gave him aspirins and unwaveringly admired the photographs of Corporal Heidler's birthplace and relations; for Heidler was, as Kurt told himself, the gateway to romance. And at the same time he did all in his power to be made a corporal himself.

At last the gateway—none too willingly—allowed him passage. One of the officers had been given a dog, and the dog was coming by train, and a car must go to the station to meet it. Heidler had been told to drive the car, and Schutz, who spoke Spanish, was to go with him to collect the dog from the station officials.

Ill-naturedly they spoke to him of this, remarking how unfortunate it was that they, who didn't want to go, should be going, while he, who would give his ears to go, must stay behind.

'Destiny is often like that,' said Schutz.

'The fortunes of war,' added Heidler.

'Only gold,' said Schutz, 'can overcome destiny. By the way, would you like us to do any shopping for you?'

'No. I don't think I need anything.'

Schutz raised his light eyebrows. Heidler laughed.

'No brandies for you today, honoured corporal. He does not wish us to drink his health.'

'But—But of course, I should be delighted. I should be proud.'

'Actually,' said Schutz, 'I do not feel much inclined to get drunk just now. I have a splitting headache. *I* don't want to jolt down to that filthy station and jolt back with a filthy dog. If Winkler really yearns to go instead of me, why shouldn't he?'

'And leave me to deal with all those station clerks? I can't speak a word of their beastly talk.'

'I know a little Spanish,' said Kurt.

'H'm. Do you? First I've heard of it. What's dog in Spanish?'

'Perro.'

Heidler looked at Schutz. Schutz nodded.

'First-rate! And what's brandy?'

Conversation in a restaurant. Bring me more bread, more butter, one of your best cigars. This coffee is too weak, too strong. This fish is not fresh. The phrase-book had vanished through the porthole, a loose page, snatched by the wind, fluttering lightly upward, like a bird. Heidler laughed.

'I'll teach him on the way down,' said Schutz.

The car was large and low, a very grand car. He sat in the back seat, crouching in order to see as much as possible. By daylight the villas were even more romantic, their turrets roofed with blue or emerald-green or orange tiles, their balconies smothered with brilliant creepers. And that, its magenta blossom colliding with a burst of scarlet geraniums, must be the fever flower.

'There's the bull-ring.'

He saw a vast expanse of brick wall covered with posters. Farther on a door in a dark porch opened, a woman in black came out, behind her was a brief revelation of candlelight and gilding. The woman unfortunately was ugly and quite old.

As they neared the station the town became pretty much like any other town, though in front of the station was a row of palm-trees. They could not be very good specimens, though: they were short, and the leaves were scanty, and quite a dull colour. Round about the entrance to the station were quantities of beggars. Some were cripples, some nursed babies, some displayed sores. A monk and some nuns were standing near by, dispensing alms, he supposed. Religion had kept Spain a backward country, yet there was something quite touching in this old-world piety, this old-world charity. As the three soldiers approached the beggars began to shout and scream, the cripples hitched themselves forward; but the religious persons swept imperiously to the front rank and held out boxes. They were beggars too.

'Now we will hear you talk Spanish.'

Kurt flushed. He began to doubt the efficacy of the phrase he had rehearsed on his way down. *Un perro. Ferroviaria.* But there should be a verb and he could not remember many verbs. All around were people talking Spanish, and he could not understand a word they said. At least he could begin with saying Good-afternoon. Politeness often makes a good impression. *Buenas me*—that was as far as he got. Schutz elbowed him aside and began to question the porter in a loud voice. Schutz's Spanish he could understand quite well.

The porter was explaining something. He kept on using the same word, suddenly it became clear to Kurt that the porter was telling them to hope. Why hope? What had they to hope for? And where was the dog?

'God, what a filthy country,' exclaimed Schutz.

'Why, what's wrong? Surely the Reds are not advancing on us?'

'The train's late. We've got to wait for two hours, he says. Idiot!'

'Just nice time for a drink,' said Heidler. 'Come on, Winkler. Now you can pay for your ride.'

They entered the station café, ordered brandies, and began to smoke. The café was large and nearly empty. It had a bar crammed with every sort of drink. On the walls were patriotic posters, showing the militiamen as monkeys, showing a hairy red hand throttling a young lady with well-developed naked breasts between which a black cross dangled primly. Above the bar was a large clock. Kurt paid for the second round of brandies also.

After a while he suggested that they might move on to another café.

'Why?' said Heidler. 'They've got eats here too, if you're hungry.'

'Well, we might see more.'

'That's a good idea,' said Schutz to Heidler. 'Let's order something salted, and have beer with it.'

Heidler beckoned to the waiter. Schutz gave the order, Kurt paid. He half rose, smiled appealingly at Schutz, made himself look boyish. Schutz smiled back.

'Well, as long as you're back on time. . . . If you find anything worth our attention, come and tell us.'

Leaving the station he was again assailed by beggars, by nuns with collecting boxes, and by a little girl in a long skirt of tattered yellow cotton. She pursued him, screeching and giggling. At last he threw down a coin. Afterwards, looking cautiously back, he saw that she had returned to her pitch, and was turning a somersault in front of a nun.

This had been very unpleasant. One could not love such children, children so unchildish. He began to walk slowly, keeping close to the shop-windows, staring at their displays. There was nothing beautiful, nothing out of the way. He would have preferred to walk on the other side of the street, where there was a row of flower-stalls. The flowers were marvellous, not just those red carnations, but really expensive flowers; but the flower-stalls were too near the station, the little girl might come after him again. It was very hot, much hotter than up on the hill. Presently he looked at his watch. Only ten minutes had gone by since he left the others.

One shop led to another shop. His ears became accustomed to the sound of Spanish. Large grand cars tore past, honking continuously. Then he heard a strange noise . . . a fine tinkle of falling water. He looked about, and saw, opening out of the street, a passage, and beyond the passage a little square. He waited till someone else turned down the passage, and then followed.

The square had arcades all round. It was like a cloister, but it also looked Moorish, as of course, it should do. In the middle was a small fountain. The jet of water was feeble and intermittent, it seemed as though something might be blocking the feed. But still, it was a fountain. There were some more palm-trees—no better than those by the station, presumably this was not a part of Spain where palm-trees were at their best—bushes of a dark-leafed shrub, and two stone benches. As there was no one about he sat down. The houses round the square were tall, so tall that all the lower half of the square was in shadow. Only on the upper walls was there sunlight. It shone on a line of washing hanging from one shuttered window to another. Somewhere a canary was singing.

He began to be very happy. This was a moment he would remember all his life . . . a corner of old Spain. And he had found it entirely by himself. It was undoubtedly picturesque, yet no one else had found it. There were no directing notices, no artists, no one paused with a camera, and though there were a few shops under the arcades not one of them showed the slightest preparedness for lovers of the picturesque. Sparrows hopped around, the canary continued to sing, a woman called to a child, two priests walked by, the fountain tinkled. If only someone would begin to play the guitar, everything would be perfect.

He looked at his watch. Over half an hour had passed. Heavens, what a long time he had wasted loitering here, when there was so much more to see! How would it sound if he were questioned, and could only reply: 'I sat in a little square watching a fountain'? He would be teased to death.

He sprang up and went to the mouth of the passage, assuring himself that from thence the station was in sight. Then, sure of his retreat, he set out to explore.

At the farther end of the square was another passage. It took him into a narrow street that was cobbled, and shady, and highly picturesque.

Almost the first thing he saw was a great hooded archway with carving on it. One would have expected such an entrance to lead into a church, but actually it led into a garage. How on earth could such large cars turn in such a narrow street? After a little thought he became pleased with this mixture of medieval and modern, surely most typically Spanish? A church-porch leading to a garage, that was something one might well talk about, for it was both funny and characteristic. Darkening the next turning was a building, so square, so massive, that it must be a prison. An old prison, a prison of the Inquisition. Even now the few slit windows high up in the blank walls of greasy ancient stone kept their iron bars. People were strolling in and out of the prison, women mostly, then came a party of young girls, walking stiffly, shepherded by nuns. Looking again he saw that the prison was surmounted by a Gothic spire, was a church. Remembering the beggars at the station—there would certainly be beggars at a church too—he turned off into a yet narrower street.

This street was very dull, and he kept on thinking that he would turn back. But he did not do so. A soldier of the Third Reich never turns back. Here there were more people about; women carried red and green peppers or very inferior cauliflowers in string bags, children played cards in the road, an old, old man sitting on a rush chair on a pavement nursed a goggle-eyed baby that must surely be an idiot. The cobbles were covered with dirt and refuse, and for a while he tried to pick his way. Then he saw a group of men watching him, and though none smiled he felt they were laughing at him, so after that he walked straight ahead, keeping in the middle of the road. Presently he realised what a loud noise his boots made. Treading on cobbles between tall house-fronts of stone he was in a stone sounding-box. His seemed to be the only footsteps in the street; the other passers-by were wearing rope-soles, some even went barefoot.

He turned off again. This street was narrow too, stonily echoing. Obviously it was very old, yet it was not picturesque; there was no colour, no incident, no gaiety. Even the children spoke little, darting past him like a shoal of minnows. He had certainly got into a poor bad part of the town.

Then he became aware of a smell.

During his ramble he had, of course, noticed many smells. By the station there had been a smell of boiling shell-fish and hot black clothing. In the little square there had been a smell of cooking in oil. By the church there had been a violent smell from a urinal hollowed in the wall. After that he had traversed smells of garbage, garlic, piss, sour wine, and from the old man nursing the idiot had come a strong smell of cockroaches.

But this smell was different.

Naturally, he had not grown up in a palace. He knew as many bad smells as the next fellow. There was the smell of antiquity: dry-rot, cobwebs, mildewed walls; there was the smell of poverty: greasiness of bad fat, the close woollen fustiness of old clothes; there was the smell of sickness, of bad teeth and bad stomachs, the charnel smell of decay, the smell one commonly calls drains. Nasty as they were, and socially deplorable, yet they had also a certain geniality, they had a flattering fulsome welcome like ageing prostitutes, they reassured one's sense of being a man, and comfortably at home in the world. Even the stink of decay could give one a queer thrill.

But this smell had not a breath of welcome. It was evil, not base. It expressed a stony antiquity, a poverty beyond food or clothing, an immaterial sickness, a cold-blooded excrement, the excrement of fishes, perhaps, a decay, not of a corpse but of a ghost. It was everywhere, unanswerable as the smell of the sea. It was full of despair and lassitude, and yet it was quite inhuman, and yet it was like a curse.

He felt himself daunted, yes, really quite inexplicably frightened. The flower that carried fever had no smell at all, they said. But a smell like this might even drive one mad, shrivel one into idiocy, into cretinism, like some newly invented poison-gas. If he could see any sort of tavern he would buy a glass of spirits. He still had enough left for one drink. And then he would turn back at once. After all, he had seen a church-porch leading to a garage, that was something to tell the others. Very likely they would not even ask him what he had seen.

And still he walked on, thinking that there must be a tavern quite close.

At the street corner a group of women and children were waiting outside a closed door. On the door was a nationalist poster, above it was a crucifix of stone. As he went by they turned, and looked at him. How terribly thin they were, how sickly-looking, how mirthless! Even the children were haggard. This was what marxism had done to the joyful, carefree people of Spain. Out of his fear and confusion a correct kindly thought sprang to attention. He was here to defend these miserable beings, to lead them to a glorious efficient future. He raised his hand, and cried:

'*Arriba España!*'

One of the children laughed. Its mother instantly cuffed it. Otherwise there was no sign of response. They looked at him with blank faces. He had the strange feeling that each one of them was looking at him out of a pale stone house with shuttered windows. Then another of the children made a grimace at him, and spat. Presently they turned their backs on him. He was ignored, left alone with the smell, knowing himself hated.

And I am dying on their behalf, he thought dolefully. Till now it had never occurred to him that in coming to Spain to fight he might also have come to Spain to die. But from then till the hour of his death the conviction never left him.

(*A Garland of Straw*, 1943)

OVER THE HILL

LIKE a stone into water death drops a weight into the ground, and the ripples spread. A movement is set up, things are changed —sometimes a life, sometimes the position of an ornament on a chimney-piece. When one old gentleman died at Nice, where his young wife had taken him for his health because she did not like the English winter, another old gentleman in Dorset was moved from the east side of a hill to the west. It seemed to him that he had been moved much as a chimney ornament might be—plucked up and set down elsewhere without a word of warning; but that was because he was deaf, and did not hear his granddaughter telling her husband that now, with the estate being sold piecemeal, the time had come to buy the flint cottage, for live next door to Mrs Loppet she would no longer.

The flint cottage stood a good half-mile out of the village, and was grand. It had a gentry-like staircase, ascending from the passage to the landing instead of leading from the front kitchen into a bedroom; it had a wall round it instead of a fence, the door opened with a little key instead of a large one, and the pump was said to embody several modern ingenuities. Besides being grand, it was damp; but damp in a grand manner, not just damp here and there where a wall needed repointing, but imperceptibly damp all over, an unalienable freehold damp.

From the moment of arrival old Jacob knew what he was reminded of. Once, many years ago, he had gone on a journey to Salisbury, and at Yeovil Pen Mill he had been put for some time in a waiting-room. The flint cottage was like the waiting-room. The fire smoked, and the new pictures all represented the kind of place to which one is invited to travel by train.

'Come and sit here, grandfather, and warm yourself while I settle things.' But he sat down by the window instead and looked out. The waggon which had brought him with the last load was going back to the village. It vanished, and he was looking at the hill.

Every indentation of its dull, serene slope was familiar to him, and every mutation of stars that the year hung above it, for while he still worked he had been a shepherd, and the flint cottage was on the way to the sheepwalk. When this aspect of the hill met his eye he knew that sight of the village lay beyond it, and quickened his steps. Now he sat still, and it hid the village from him.

So the hill, however familiar, was changed in his eyes. It had been a landmark; it was now a barrier. It had been a rise of ground over which he walked; now it was a bulk. And staring at it day after day he began to think of it in terms of weight, and those uncounted tons of chalk and loam seemed to lie heavy on him.

He had time to think, time to have queer fancies. For many years Jacob had not walked without a stick, and his stick had been mislaid in the move. With an old man's obstinacy he would not use any stick but his own, and though his granddaughter offered him her umbrella, and her husband cut an ash-plant, for it irked them to see him sit moping always in the same place, he was not to be shaken.

It was almost three weeks before the stick was found.

'I knew you'd be rare and pleased,' she said, when she brought it to him. He did not show much pleasure, eyeing it heavily as though it were another train to catch. But late that afternoon, when no one was observing him, he went out and walked over the hill. It was a brilliant autumn day; the smoke rose straight into the air. He knew every chimney, he told the mumbling outlines of the thatched cottages like a flock, and there, late with her washing as usual, hung on the line Mrs Loppet's purple bloomers, and all the little Loppets' pinafores. Beyond the washing were his own apple-trees. The leaves had hung on late this year; the trees still looked bushy. Some believe in pruning, some do not.

And then he remembered that now he lived in the flint cottage, that the trees were his no longer.

But he would not turn back, though for the next fifty yards with every step he seemed to leave his bowels behind him. Once fairly into the village, things were easier. Neighbours were there, shouts of greeting reached his ear, he was asked after his health, and the common demeanour conveyed that by moving beyond the hill he had become something rather rare and lofty. So he was able to pass his cottage with a cold, safe heart, and going to the inn he became merry, and boasted about the new abode that could provoke so many free drinks. On the way back he was not even aware that his feet had stayed before the old entry; for Mrs Faux, whom neither age nor liquor could abate, had him by the arm and was seeing him home.

'I'll see 'ee home-along, daddy, to thee's country estate. 'Tis town 'ouse and country 'ouse with 'ee now, I reckon.'

Mrs Faux's kingdom was not of this world. She could cure warts, bring back a lover, and overlook cattle, and so she could afford to praise the flint cottage on this evening visit, tweaking open all the cupboard doors, endangering the patent pump by frolicking with it, and giving to all she pried into its meed of admiration and belches, careless that her own cottage was wattle and daub and that her well ran dry. But even so she could not be immune from a twinge of envy, and on the morrow it was natural for her to say, 'Old Jacob do be turned a sloppy drinker.'

It was quite true. Jacob, who had once had a head like iron, now became maudlin and peevish on half a pint of cider. But the young people put no obstacle in his way when he went over the hill to the inn. The old fellow had few pleasures, he was failing, and they gave him the liberty given to an old dog, too old to chase the fowls or do anything but dodder from one interesting gate-post to another. They knew he would not come to any harm; he would not even get wet. For he retained his weather sense, and by looking at a March cloud could tell if he would have time to walk back before the hail came clattering, or no. People used him as a weather-glass; a woman seeing him turn back to the cart-shed for shelter would run to fetch in the dish-clouts from the line. But long and enforced exposure to the weather had been the price of his cunning, and rheumatism was in his bones. The flint cottage did not agree with him, his fingers grew too stiff to clasp the stick he leaned on—one day, just on the brow of the hill, he stumbled, fell, and could not get on his feet again. As he twisted himself about, complaining, he discovered that he had gained a new view of the village, for, having fallen on his back, he now saw it the wrong way up. At this discovery he ceased to struggle and lay in a tipsy content, pondering this novel aspect of creation, until a passer-by came and righted him, and led him home.

This seemed likely to be his last view of the village. Lying heated in the wind he had caught a chill, and when he was allowed out of bed again he had forgotten how to walk, and it was not worth while to teach the art to so old a baby. So he sat by the window and looked at the hill.

Although he had lived for a year at the flint cottage, walking home to it as duly as the sheep in the Green Park walk at nightfall to the summit of their hill, the fancy that it was a waiting-room had never quite left him. Now, with nothing to do but wait, this fancy became strong. Turning over in his mind the contradictory facts that this was a place to wait in only, and that his family were living, scrubbing, cooking, and eating in it as though it were a dwelling like any other, he reconciled these in the conclusion that they must all be living in the flint cottage until the time came when they would return to the old home. A waggon had brought them. A waggon, surely, would come to fetch them back. It was a long time in coming; but then he had waited a long time at Yeovil Pen Mill.

His deafness had so closed in on him that he had little to say to the outside world, and awaited the waggon for the most part in silence. But at last, hearing him for the ninth or tenth time complain of its delaying, his granddaughter listened more attentively, and understood what was in the old man's mind.

'What am I to say?' she asked her husband. 'He's so childish, I shan't ever make him understand we are here for good. Yet I don't like not to say anything, the poor soul does fret so.'

'Tell him it's coming next week,' he replied. 'Weeks—years—he won't notice no odds. 'Tis this year, next year, some time, never, with he nowadays.'

The advice was good. Elsie was a quick-witted woman and could always find some excuse why the waggon should not come till next week.

'It's haysel, grandfather, and the farmers are working to carry it before the moon changes.'

After the hay harvest came the oats, the corn, the barley. Then the hurdles must be carried into the fields where the ewes were to be penned, or Mr Lovel had loaned his waggons to the new clergyman, who had such a deal of furniture, or the horses were ploughing.

This policy kept the old man pretty quiet, but in other ways he was increasingly a trouble. He was now so stiff that he had to be shoved and supported up and down stairs, and little Daphne had to sit by him at meals to guide the spoon to his mouth. It would have been simpler to keep him in bed, but he insisted, with weeping and rage, that he must be where he could look out of the side window whence he would see the hill, and watch for the first sight of the waggon coming to fetch him from the waiting-room.

'Will it come next week, Elsie?'

'It's coming today, grandfather. You watch out for it, for it's coming at last.'

He watched, but no waggon came. Nothing came over the hill but a car, a thing of no interest to him. But hearing the horn Elsie jumped up and cried, 'Here 'tis—here 'tis!'

The car stopped at the door.

'Silly cow thee be if thee don't know waggon from one of they motoring cars.'

'Yes, but this be come instead of the waggon. Now let me straighten you, so's you can start tidy.'

She was very quick, and flurry had reddened her face as if with shame. Before he knew what had been done to him Jacob was in his hat and coat, and standing before the car. There was a passenger inside already, a woman, wearing a cloak and veil. She was a strong woman. While Jacob was doddering on the step of the car she leaned forward and gave him such a haul as he in old days had given to a sheep stuck in a ditch.

The wind blew Elsie's bobbed hair across her eyes and he noticed that she was hatless. Through the open door he saw the furnished house.

'Where be furniture to bide then? 'Baint 'ee going to bring furniture?'

' 'Tis all right,' she shouted, leaning flushed into the car. 'You be going first, we will come after you.'

The door slammed between them, the car jolted back and forth; having turned, it went over the hill. There was the village, that he had last seen inverted. Now it was the right way up once more. But that was about all he had time to notice, for the car went swiftly, carrying him to the county town infirmary.

(*The Salutation*, 1932)

A WIDOW'S QUILT

'EMMA loves museums,' said Helena, 'and I think it's good for her to look at things being still, for a change, instead of that incessant jiggety-jog of television. Not like us when we were young, Charlotte —though you were never so tied to the box as I was.'

'I hated watching people breathe.'

The sisters were visiting the American Museum at Claverton, in Somerset. It was Charlotte's first visit.

'Do you come here often?'

'Yes. It's an easy run from Bristol, and I enjoy buying fancy jams from their shop. Expensive. But traditional things are always expensive. And Henry likes them. You should take something back to Everard.'

'Remind me to.'

Emma was staring into a quiescent period parlour. 'That clock doesn't strike,' she said. 'Why doesn't it strike, Mummy? Hasn't it got an inside? Is it too old to be wound up?' Other visitors smiled, murmured, seemed inclined to enter into conversation. 'Now I want to see the blue dogs.'

They moved on into the quilt room. It was hung with pieced and appliqué quilts, brilliant as an assembly of macaws. Emma ran from one to another, identifying the blue dogs in an appliqué miscellany of rosebuds, hatchets, stars, kites, apples, horsemen, and shawled ladies encircling Abraham Lincoln in a stovepipe hat, quitting them for a geometrical pieced design of lilac and drab.

'Queen Charlotte's Crown—that's for you, Aunt Charlotte. And here's Fox and Geese.'

'Darling! Don't touch.'

One would always have to be being patient, thought Charlotte. On the whole she was glad she did not have a child. Her attention was caught by a quilt that stood out from the others, dominating their rich vivacity with a statement of dulled black on white. She moved towards it.

'That's a widow's quilt,' said Helena. 'Narrow, you see, for a single bed. I suppose you made one for yourself, when your husband died. Or your friends made it for you. Rather grisly.'

'I think it's a hideous quilt,' Emma said.

They descended to the shop, where Charlotte was reminded of the something she must take back to Everard, and chose horehound candies. Then Helena drove her to the station, and she made her platform thanks and farewells. 'I particularly enjoyed the quilts,' she said. 'One doesn't see enough blue dogs.'

But between Bath and London Charlotte sat in a dreamlike frenzy, planning the construction of her own black-and-white quilt. Built up from hexagons, and narrow, it would not be more than a winter's work, once she had assembled its materials: half a dozen exact geometrical hexagons; heavy paper, over which she would tack her patches; fine needles for the small stitches; a couple of sheets. The black would not be so easily found—that lustreless soot-black, dead-rook black. Perhaps she might find some second-hand weeds in the Chelsea fantasy boutiques. Or should she qualify the white unanimity of the sheets by using a variety of blacks already available? There were remains of the official blacking-out curtains drawn over the windows at home during the war, kept to come in useful, her mother had said, and still kept in the inherited piece box from which she had pulled fragments of chintz for the patchwork cushion cover started for Great-Aunt Emma but never completed. There was the black shawl bought at Avignon; some black taffeta; some sateen; quantities of black velvet. As she recalled these varieties of black, the design of her widow's quilt shaped itself to her mind's eye. In the centre, a doubled, even a trebled ring of black velvet hexagons massively enclosing the primal hexagon of white wedding-dress brocade. Extending to the four corners of the quilt, long black diagonals, the spaces between interspersed with star-spangled black hexagons not too close together, and for a border a funeral wreath of black hexagons conjoined.

Dizzied, she got out of the terminus because everyone else was doing so, and took a wasteful taxi to the usual address without realising she was going home.

Next morning, as soon as Everard had tapped the barometer, put on the indicated topcoat, and left for his office (he was a partner in a firm that sold rare postage stamps), she chose the pair of sheets and went out to buy the fine needles, going on to F. Wilkens, Electrician and Household Repairs—for during the night it had occurred to her that the basic hexagons would be much more satisfactory if they were exact to measure and cut out of tin. F. Wilkens, oddly calling them templates, knew exactly what she meant, and would have them ready in half an hour. She spent the interval in the Health Food Shop, buying Everard's muesli, then collected the templates and went back to the flat in Perivale Mansions. By the time he returned she had assembled most of the double garland of black velvet round the wedding-dress brocade, folded it away in a pillowcase, and prepared supper.

That night her pleasure in the progress of the black velvet garland was soured by seeing it as so much done already. At this rate, the quilt would be snatched from her hands, no more to the purpose than a daisy chain. Patch after patch would lessen her private entertainment; the last patch in the border of black hexagons would topple her over the edge to drown in the familiar tedium. She did not want to make another quilt, or any other kind of quilt. This was her only, her nonpareil, her one assertion of a life of her own. When Everard left for his office, she hardly dared take out the pillowcase. While stitching in the first white hexagons, she realised the extent of even a single-bed quilt. She need not despair for some time yet.

By midday it was raining steadily. The barometer's counsel of an umbrella was, as usual, justified. The sound of rain was agreeable to work to. It rained. She worked. Between two and three in the afternoon, finding herself extremely hungry, she ravaged the larder for an impromptu meal—unwontedly delicious, since she fed on the tinned delicacies.

The weekend jolted her out of her contentment. Two days of Everard at home she was inured to, but to waste two days without setting a stitch in the quilt was torment. She festered in idleness; she had never hated his company more. And it increased her exasperation that he should be unaware of it.

Yet as time went on, and the quilt enlarged, and weekends fell into the pattern of her existence as though they were recurring hexagons of an unassimilable material which she would presently unpick, her disposition changed; she was complacent, she was even benign. Strange, to think that Everard, whose demands and inroads had compelled her to such an abiding rancour that seeing the widow's quilt had given her a purpose in life, should have supplied this soothing influence. Meanwhile she went on with the quilt, never losing sight of its intimations and in the main preserving her original scheme—though the diagonal had to be revised: the single black line lacked emphasis, and had to be changed to a couple of lines hedging a band of white. This, in turn, involved a reconsideration of the corners. The solution had been found (there was exactly the right amount of the black shawl to supply its hexagons) when Christmas stared her in the face—and Everard. She could not securely hope that his seasonal influenza would keep him coughing in bed and out of her way; but she was on fire to get at the revised corners, and told herself that a little publicity would be the surest safeguard of the secrecy which was an essential ingredient in her pleasure. On Christmas Eve Everard came home to find her with the quilt on her knee. He glanced at it warily, as though it were something that might disagree with him. When it was there next day and the day after, he mentioned its presence.

'What's that, Charlotte—all those bits you're sewing together?'

She displayed it.

'How nicely you've done it. What's it for?'

'In time it will be a quilt.'

'Oh. So it's not finished yet.'

'No. Not yet.'

She stitched in another hexagon.

'Do you make it up as you go along?'

'I saw one like it in the American Museum.'

'In a museum. How interesting. Was that black and white too?'

'Yes. It's a traditional pattern. It's called a magpie quilt.'

'Magpie? Magpie? Oh, because it's black and white, I suppose. Quite imaginative.'

She stitched, Everard pondered.

'I wonder the United States Post Office doesn't use these old designs—now that they go in for so many commemorative stamps.'

She thought of the blue dogs, but refrained.

By the New Year Everard's cough was so insistent that he had to give up taking his temperature. She foresaw herself stitching her widow's quilt at his bedside. Instead, his partner brought a Puerto Rican violet for his opinion. Finding it spurious, Everard felt equal to going back to his office.

With the enlarging days the quilt gathered momentum. It outgrew the pillowcase and had to be folded away in a bedspread. Each morning it seemed to have grown in the night; each day it was more responsive, more compliant. The hexagons fitted into place as if drawn by a magnet. It had a rationality now, a character; the differing blacks superimposed a pattern of their own, as well-kept fields do with the various tints of their crops. She was so much at ease with it that she could let her thoughts stray as she worked—not so far as to make a mistake, though. She hated mistakes, even those she could unpick. But looking forward to the time when she would rightfully sleep under it, her mind made excursions to places where she might go as a quiet travelling widow. To Lincolnshire, perhaps, with its 'fields of barley and of rye' bordering the river—a sinuous, slow-flowing river with no conversation, effortlessly engulfing the chatter of Tennysonian brooks. Then, on the one hand, a quiet cross-country bus would show her Boston Stump outlined against the pale eastern sky, or, catching a train at Dukeries Junction Station, she would survey the Vale of Beauvoir.

Not since her marriage had she gone beyond the Home Counties, and these had only been visited at licensed holiday seasons: a dab of green at Easter, in August a smear of summer with Everard's cousins in Surrey. Meanwhile, she had travelled a great deal in theory, studying guide-books and ordnance maps and railway guides, even a list of bus routes in East Anglia which had chanced her way. The row of Methuen's Little Guides in the bookcase on her side of the bed had assured her in detail of the existence of what imagination left visionary: churches (E. E., Perp., restored in 1870), the number of different species of bat in Essex, an almshouse or a gasworks, a disused bridge, a local industry, an extensive prospect of rolling country, a forgotten battlefield, a clay soil, a sandy loam, floodmarks, plantations of conifer, a canal. On the whole, it was the dullish Midlands she preferred; romantic extremities, like Cornwall, could come later.

She was stitching away at Everard's demise—every hexagon brought it a step nearer—when Helena, who was in London to visit her dressmaker, came on to Perivale Mansions. After a momentary gasp, Helena admired the quilt, now three-quarters done.

'And what are you going to stuff it with?'

'Stuff it?'

'It would have to be interlined and stitched through to the backing, you know. Otherwise it wouldn't be a quilt. The one you admired in the museum has harps outlined in stitching—I suppose she felt strongly about Ireland.' She talked on about New England quilting bees, and left before Everard was due to return.

There was nothing for it but to swallow the shock, be glad that the quilt could continue into summer, and decide on the stitched design which should complete it. Not harps, anyhow. A speedy crisscross would be about as much as she could manage. For with the added weight of the backing and the interlined padding, the quilt would be too heavy to handle comfortably, could become a drudgery—another marital obligation, almost another Everard.

She began to make mistakes, straying from the order of her design, choosing the black sateen when it should have been the fustier black of the curtain material. Twice she sewed in a hexagon back side uppermost. The thread tangled, slid out of the needle's eye. When she came to re-thread a needle, she had to make shot after shot at it, holding the needle with a grip of iron, poking the thread at it with a shaking hand. Her heart thumped. Her fingers swelled.

If I were sensible, she thought, I would take to my bed. But the voice of reason reminded her of Everard's disconsolate fidgeting, his dependence on her (Where do I find the toaster? Oh dear, the milk has boiled over again! What am I to mop it up with?) when she had rheumatic fever. She was not in a fit state to be an invalid. The widow's quilt, even if at the moment it was thwarting her intentions, was the more enlivening companion.

She was in the last corner now. It was mid-March, and the east wind was howling down the street like the harlot's curse, when the last of her misfortunes, the silliest and most derisive, tripped her: she had no more thread. She shook some of the ache out of her back, put on her thickest coat, eased her swollen hands into gloves, grimaced at the barometer, and went downstairs and out. It was as though the wind had whirled her out of herself. She was loose again, the solitary traveller, and back in Lincolnshire. She took the narrow road across the saltmarsh flats between her and the sea. They stretched on either hand, featureless, limitless. Nothing would gainsay their level till the enormous breakers reared up, one driven forward on another, and fell with a crash and a flump on the beach. The wind streamed through her; she fought it with every step, and was one with it. At the corner of Perivale Street and Sebastopol Terrace a burly holidaymaker off an advertisement was blown overhead, exclaiming 'Skegness Is So Bracing!'

She had to struggle for breath before she could ask for thread and civilly agree with the shopwoman that the wind was quite savage, wasn't it. And, indeed, as she walked back she could hardly walk straight. The wind was still roaring in her ears when she stood in the hallway of Perivale Mansions, with the stairs in front of her—three flights, each of seventeen steps. She paused on the first landing. The roaring in her ears had changed and was now loud beats on a gong. Twice seventeen was twice seventeen. She mounted the second flight. The gong beat on, but irregularly—thunder to the flashes of lightning across her eyes. At the foot of the third flight she stumbled and fell. She saw her gloved hands clutch the air. A little paper bag fell from one of them. Two reels of thread escaped from it, rolled along the landing, and went tap-tapping down the stairs. Another of her misfortunes. Her lips tried to grin but had turned to lead. The wind had blown out all the lights, and down in the hallway the sea rose higher and higher. A seventh wave, a master wave, would surge up the stairs she had climbed so painfully, thrust its strength beneath her, carry her away like a wisp of seaweed. She was still vaguely alive when Everard almost tripped over her. He called 'Help! Help!' and blew the police whistle he always carried on his key ring.

'There was something wrong with her heart,' he said to Helena, who came next morning. 'It might have happened at any moment. You can imagine what a shock it was to me. I think I must move.' He had not much to say, but he talked incessantly. 'At first I thought she had been killed. You can imagine what I felt. There is so much violence about nowadays—no post office is safe. I never felt easy leaving her. But it was something wrong with her heart. She was everything to me, everything, my poor Charlotte. Where do you think I should go?'

Helena had picked up the quilt and began folding it.

'And there's that quilt. What should we do about it? It's not finished, you see. Poor Charlotte, so unfortunate! It's a magpie quilt.'

'Magpie?'

'Yes, because it's all black and white—like the birds, she said.'

'I see.'

'I can't very well take it with me. Yet it would be a pity to throw it away. Could you take charge of it, Helena? It would be a weight off my mind if you would. You'd know how to finish it, and I don't suppose it would take you very long. Not that there's any hurry now. And then you could keep it, to remember her by. I'm sure she'd like you to have it. It meant a great deal to her.'

(*One Thing Leading to Another*, 1984)

BUT AT THE STROKE OF MIDNIGHT

S HE was last seen by Mrs Barker, the charwoman. At ten minutes to eleven (Mrs Ridpath was always punctual, you could set your watch by her) she came into the kitchen, put on the electric kettle, got out the coffee-pot, the milk, the sugar, the two pink cups and saucers, the spoons, the coffee canister. She took the raisin cake out of the cake tin, cut two good slices, laid them on the pink plates that went with the two cups, though not a match. The kettle boiled, the coffee was made. At the hour precisely the two women sat down to their elevenses. It was all just as usual. If there had been anything not just as usual with Mrs Ridpath, Mrs Barker would certainly have noticed it. Such a thing would be quite out of the common; it would force itself on your notice. Mrs Ridpath was never much of a talker, though an easy lady to talk to. She asked after Mrs Barker's Diane and David. She remarked that people in the country would soon be hearing the first cuckoo. Mrs Barker said she understood that the Council were poisoning the poor pigeons again, and together they agreed that London was no longer what it was. Mrs Barker could remember when Pimlico was a pleasure to live in—and look at it now, nothing but barracks and supermarkets where they treated you with no more consideration than if you were a packet of lentils yourself. And at eleven-fifteen she said she must be getting on with her work. Later, while she was polishing the bath, she saw Mrs Ridpath come out of the bedroom and go to the front door. She was wearing her grey and had a scarf over her head. Mrs Barker advised her to put on a mac, for it looked like rain. Mrs Ridpath did so, picked up her handbag, and went out. Mrs Barker heard the lift come up and go down, and that was the last she knew. It was Saturday, the day when she was paid her week's money, and she hung about a bit. But Mrs Ridpath didn't come back, and at a quarter past one she left. Her credit was good, thank God! She could manage her weekend shopping all right, and Mrs Ridpath would pay her on Monday.

On Monday she let herself in. The flat was empty. The Aga Cooker was stone-cold, the kitchen was all anyhow; the milk bottles hadn't been rinsed, let alone put out. The telephone rang, and it was Mr Ridpath, saying that Mrs Ridpath was away for the weekend.

By then, Aston Ridpath was so determined that this must be so that when Mrs Barker answered him he waited for a moment, allowing time for her to say that Mrs Ridpath had just come in.

For naturally, when he got home from his office on Saturday (the alternate Saturday when he worked during the afternoon), he expected to find Lucy in the flat, probably in the kitchen. There was no Lucy. There was no smell of cooking. In the refrigerator there was a ham loaf, some potato salad, and the remains of the apple mousse they had had on Friday. It was unlike Lucy not to be there. He turned on the wireless for the six o'clock news and sat down to wait. By degrees an uneasiness and then a slight sense of guilt stole into his mind. Had Lucy told him she would not be back till after six? He had had a busy day; it might well have slipped his memory. It was even possible that she had told him and that he had not attended. It was easy not to attend to Lucy. She had a soft voice, and a habit of speaking as if she did not expect to be attended to. Probably she had told him she was going out to tea, or something of that sort. She sometimes went to picture galleries. But surely, if she had told him she would not be back in time to get dinner, he would have noticed it? By eight o'clock it became obvious that she must have told him she would not be back in time for dinner. No doubt she had told him about the ham loaf, too. She was thoughtful about such matters—which was one reason why her conversation was so seldom arresting. It would not do to seem inattentive, so he would eat and if there was time before she got back, he would also wash up.

He ate. He washed up. He hung the dishcloth on the rail. In some ways he was a born bachelor.

The telephone rang. As he expected, it was Golding, who had said he might come round that evening with the stamp album he had inherited from an uncle who had gone in for philately. He didn't know if there was anything in it worth having; Ridpath would know. Golding was one of those calm, tractable bores who appear to have been left over from ampler days. Every Sunday he walked from Earls Court to St Paul's to attend matins. Now he arrived carrying a large brown paper parcel and a bunch of violets. 'Lucy's out,' said Aston, seeing Golding look round for somewhere to dispose of the flowers. 'She's gone out to dinner. Have a whisky?'

'Well, yes. That would be very pleasant.'

The album turned out to be unexpectedly interesting. It was after eleven when Golding began to wrap it up. His eye fell on the violets.

'I don't suppose I shall see Mrs Ridpath. I think you said she was dining out.'

'She's dining with some friends.'

'Rather a long dinner,' said Golding.

'You know what women are like when they get together,' said Aston. 'Talk, talk, talk.'

Golding said sympathetically, 'Well, I like talking too.'

Golding was gone. As Aston picked up his violets, which would have to be put into some sort of vase, he realised with painful actuality that if Lucy wasn't back by midnight he would have to do something about it—ring up hospitals, ring up the police. It would be necessary to describe her. When one has been happily married to a woman for nearly twenty-five years it is too much to be expected to describe her. Tall. Thin. Knock-kneed. Walks with a stoop. Brown eyes, brown hair —probably safer to say grizzled. Wearing—How the hell was he to know what Lucy would be wearing if she had gone out to dinner? If he were to say what occurred to him, it would be tweeds.

Suppose she had not gone out to dinner? Suppose—for fiction is after all based on real life—suppose she had gone off, leaving that traditional note on her pincushion? If she had a pincushion. He walked into their bedroom. There was a pincushion, a very old and wilted one, but there was no note on it. He could see no note anywhere. There were some letters on her desk. He read them. They were from shops, or from friends, recounting what the friends had been doing.

If only he had listened! If only she had not got into this unfortunate trick of mumbling! For she would certainly have told him whom she was going out to. 'Aston, I'm having dinner with . . .' It seemed as if he could almost recapture the words. 'Aston, I'm going . . .' Could she have continued, 'away for the weekend'? For that would explain everything. It was perfectly possible. There were all those friends who wrote to her about flying in Hovercrafts to the Isle of Wight, visiting Leningrad, coming back from cruises to the West Indies. Why shouldn't she be spending the weekend with one or other of these Sibyls or Sophies? It was April, a season when it is natural to spend weekends in the country—if you like that sort of thing. Only a few weeks ago he had remarked that she was looking tired and would be the better for country air. An invitation had come; mindful of his encouragement she had accepted it. He could now almost swear he had heard the words 'Aston, I am going away for the weekend.' No doubt she had also told him where. He had failed to remember it, but one cannot remember everything.

He ate some biscuits, went to bed with a clear conscience, and was asleep in five minutes.

In the morning his first conscious thought was that Lucy was away for the weekend. The conviction was so strong that presently he was able to imagine her being brought breakfast in bed—brown-bread toast, honey, piping-hot coffee; he could positively see the tray. There she would lie, listening to the birds. If it had not been for that unlucky moment of inattention, he would have been able to construct some approximation of the surrounding landscape. London is surrounded by the Home Counties. Somewhere in the Home Counties—for if she had told him she was going to Yorkshire or Cape Wrath he would surely have registered the fact—Lucy was having breakfast in bed. He was glad of it. It would do her good. Thinking affectionately of Lucy, he lay in bed for some while longer, then got up and made his breakfast. The bacon took a long time to cook. He had omitted to riddle the stove overnight; the fire had choked and was almost out. He looked about conscientiously to see if Lucy had left any food he ought to heat up. He did not want to be found with any kind provisions uneaten. When Lucy went to visit her cousin Aurelia in Suffolk, she always left, he remembered, quantities of soup. This time she had left nothing. No doubt she had said, at that moment when he wasn't attending, that he had better eat out.

Accordingly, Aston ate out. His mind was at rest. Wherever Lucy might be, she could not be with Aurelia and would return from wherever it might have been his own normal Lucy. During those Suffolk absences all he could be sure of was that Aurelia was leading Lucy, whether up a windmill or to Paris, by the nose, and that what he received back would be Aurelia's Lucy: talking in Aurelia's voice, asserting Aurelia's opinions, aping Aurelia's flightiness, flushed, overexcited, and giggling like a schoolgirl. Thoroughly unsettled, in short, and needing several days to become herself again. Family affection is all very well, but it was absurd that visits to a country cousin—a withered virgin and impecunious at that—should be so intoxicating that Lucy returned from them as from an assignation, and acknowledged them as such by leaving him with such quantities of soup. Even when she went to Aurelia's funeral she provided it; and came home saying in Aurelia's voice that cremations would be all right if they weren't so respectful. But now there was no soup and his mind continued to be at rest till he was in the bathroom brushing his teeth before going to bed and noticed Lucy's sponge. It was a new sponge; he had given it to her for Christmas. There was no excuse for leaving it behind. Apparently she had not taken anything—not her hand lotion, not her dusting powder. Examining Lucy's dressing table, he saw that she had taken nothing from that either. In a moment of blind panic he fell on his knees and looked for her body under the bed.

This was probably due to Wordsworth's tiresome trick of staying about in one's memory. If Lucy had been christened Angelina, he would not have been under the same compulsion to suppose she was dead. Lucy (his Lucy) kept Wordsworth beside her bed. He looked up the poem and found that on this occasion Wordsworth was mistaken, though in the following lyrics he had lost her and it made a great difference to him. Then he remembered that Samuel Butler had wickedly put it about that Wordsworth, aided by Southey and Coleridge, had murdered Lucy. This meant returning to the sitting room for Butler. Half an hour with Butler recalled him to reason. Lucy must have forgotten to pack her sponge and had bought a new hairbrush.

But the sponge and the hairbrush had shaken him. He did not sleep so well that night, and when he got up to a cold, companionless Monday morning the reality of Lucy's absence was stronger than the ideality of her breakfast tray floating somewhere in the Home Counties, and he hoped very much she would soon be back—by which time Mrs Barker would have put things straight, so that there would be nothing to impede him from saying, 'And now tell me all about it.' For that was the form of words he had decided on.

When he came back that evening everything had been put straight. But still there was no Lucy.

Anxiety hardens the heart. Addressing the absent Lucy, Aston said, 'I shall ring up Vere.' Vere was his sister—a successful widow. He did not like her very much and Lucy did not like her at all. She lived in Hampstead. He rang up Vere, who cut short his explanations by saying she would come at once and grapple.

She came with a suitcase and again cut short his explanations.

'I suppose you have told the police.'

'Told the police, Vere? Why the hell should I tell the police? It's no business of theirs. Nothing would induce me to tell the police.'

'If Lucy doesn't reappear and you haven't told the police, you'll probably be suspected of murder.'

As Aurelia walked toward the Tate Gallery she noticed that she was wearing a wedding ring. Her first impulse—for she was a flighty creature—was to drop it into a pillar-box. Then some streak of latent prudence persuaded her that it would be more practical to sell it. She pulled it off—it was too large for her and revolved easily on her finger—and dropped it into her bag. She remembered that there had been a second-hand jewellery shop a little farther along. She had sometimes looked in through its wire-meshed windows at coral earrings and mosaic brooches of the Colosseum, St Peter's, and other large celebrities. Once, long ago, she had bought herself an unset moss agate there. It was only a simulacrum of moss, but the best that then presented itself. The shop was still in its old place. She went in and presented the ring. The jeweller looked with compassion at the sad middle-aged woman in a mackintosh with a wisp of greying hair plastered to her forehead by the rain. To judge by the ring, she must have known better days. It was both broad and heavy, and he could give her a good sum for it. 'I'm afraid I must ask for the name,' he said. 'It's a formality.'

'Aurelia Lefanu, Shilling Street, Lavenham.' She smiled as she gave the address.

Well, at any rate, the poor thing loved her home.

The same unaccountable streak of prudence now told Aurelia she must do some shopping. Stockings, for instance. It was raining harder, and her feet felt wet already. One need suggested another, and impressed by her own efficiency she bought some underclothes. Finally, as it was now raining extremely hard and she had collected several paper parcels, she bought a tartan grip. The Tate would be full of people who had gone in to shelter from the rain; but they wouldn't be looking at the Turners. Joseph Mallord William Turner, staring from under his sooty chimney-pot hat, sucking in colour as if from a fruit, making and remaking his world like some unendingly ambitious Jehovah and, like a Jehovah, peopling it with rather unsuccessful specimens of the human race, was hers and hers alone for the next hour. When she left the gallery, Joseph Mallord William Turner had got there before her. The rain had stopped. A glittering light thrust from beneath the arch of cloud and painted the river with slashing strokes of primrose and violet. The tide was at the full, and a procession of Thames shipping rode on it in blackness and majesty.

'Oh!'

In her excitement she seized the elbow of the man beside her; for he too was looking, he too, no doubt, was transfixed. Touched by her extreme emotion and her extreme wetness, he said, 'I'm hoping to catch a taxi. Can I give you a lift? It's going to pelt again in a moment, you know.'

'I've forgotten to take out my bag. Could you wait an instant?'

Seeing its cheapness—indeed, he could read the price, for the tag was still hanging from it—he supposed she was some perpetual student who would be much the better for a good square tea. She had a pretty voice.

The light grew dazzling. In another minute a heavier rain would descend; if he could not secure the taxi that had just drawn up to discharge its passenger, there would be no hope of another. He hauled her down the steps, signalling with her tartan bag, and pushed her in.

'Where can I take you?'

'Where? . . . I really don't know. Where would be suitable?' And gazing out of the window at the last defiance of the light, she murmured, '"Whither will I not go with gentle Ithamore?"'

He gave his own address to the driver. The taxi drove off.

Turning to him, she said, 'Marlowe, not me, I'm afraid it may have sounded rather forward.'

'I've never been called Ithamore in all my life. It's a pretty name. What's yours?'

'Mine's a pretty name, too. Aurelia.'

So it was in London that she breakfasted in bed, that Sunday morning, wearing white silk pyjamas with black froggings—for however cleverly one goes shopping one cannot remember everything, and she had forgotten to buy a nightdress. In all his life he had never been called Ithamore. In all his life he had never met anything like Aurelia. She was middle-aged, plain, badly kept, untravelled—and she had the aplomb of a *poule de luxe*. Till quite recently she must have worn a wedding ring, for the dent was on her finger; but she bore no other mark of matrimony. She knew how to look at pictures, and from her ease in nakedness he might have supposed her a model—but her movements never set into a pose. He could only account for her by supposing she had escaped from a lunatic asylum.

She must be saved from any more of that. He must get her out of England as soon as possible. This would involve getting him out of England, too, which would be inconvenient for Jerome and Marmor, Art Publishers, but the firm could survive his absence for a few weeks. It would not be longer than that. Once settled at Saint-Rémy de Provence, with Laure and Dominique to keep an eye on her, and with a polite subsidy, she would do very well for herself—set up an easel, maybe; study astronomy. She would feel no need for him. It was he who would feel need, be consumed with an expert's curiosity.

She had spoken of how Cézanne painted trees in slats, so he drove her through the beechwoods round Stokenchurch and along a canal to a hotel that concealed its very good cooking behind a rustic Edwardian face. Here she said she was tired of eating cooked food, she would prefer fruit. She was as frank as a nymph about it, or a kinkajou. This frankness was part of her savour. It touched him because it was so totally devoid of calculation or self-consciousness. It would have been remarkable even in a very young girl; in a middle-aged woman showing such marks of wear and tear it was resplendent. It was touching, too, though rather difficult to take, that she should be so unappreciative of his tact. He had led her to a prospect of Provence; he had intimated that he sometimes went there himself; that he might have to go there quite soon; that he hoped it might be almost immediately, in order to catch the nightingales and the wisteria. . . .

'Will you take me, too?' she inquired. To keep his feet on the ground, he asked if she had a passport.

On Monday morning he rang up Jerome and Marmor to say he had a cold and would not be coming in for a few days; and would Miss Simpson bring him a passport-application form, please. The form was brought. He left Aurelia to fill it in while he went to his bank. As this was a first application, someone would have to vouch for her, and he would ask Dawkins to do it. Dawkins was closeted with a customer. He had to wait. When he got at him, Dawkins was so concerned to show that the slight illegality of vouching for someone he had never set eyes on meant nothing to him that he launched into conversation and told funny stories about Treasury officials for the next fifteen minutes.

'Aurelia! I'm sorry to have left you for so long. . . . Aurelia?'

Standing in the emptied room he continued to say, 'Aurelia'. The application form lay on the table. With a feeling of indecency, he read it. 'AURELIA LEFANU. Born: Burford, Oxon. 11th May 1923 Height: 5 ft. 10. Eyes: Brown. Hair: Grey.' The neat printing persisted without a waver. But at the Signature of Applicant something must have happened. She had begun to write—it seemed to be a name beginning with 'L'—and had violently, scrawlingly erased it.

She had packed her miserable few belongings and was gone. For several weeks he haunted the Tate Gallery and waited to read an unimportant paragraph saying that the body of a woman, aged about forty-five, had been recovered from the Thames.

'If you haven't told the police—' The thought of being suspected of murdering Lucy left Aston speechless. The aspersion was outrageous; the notion was ridiculous. Twenty years and more had passed since they were on murdering terms. But the police were capable of believing anything, and Vere's anxiety to establish his innocence was already a rope round his neck. Vere was at the telephone, saying that Mr Ridpath wished to see an officer immediately. There appeared to be some demurring at the other end, but she overcame it. While they waited, she filled in the time by cross-examining him. When did Lucy tell him she was going away for the weekend? How did she look when telling him? If he wasn't quite sure that she had done so, what made him think she had? Had she been going away for other weekends? Had he noticed any change in her? Was she restless at night? Flushed? Hysterical? Had her speech thickened? If not, why did he say she mumbled? Had he looked in all her drawers? Her wardrobe? The wastepaper baskets? Why not? Had she drawn out money from her post-office savings? Had she been growing morbid? Had she been buying cosmetics, new clothes, neglecting the house, reading poetry, losing her temper? Why hadn't he noticed any of this? Were they growing apart? Did she talk in her sleep? Why did she never come to Hampstead? And why had he waited till Monday evening before saying a word of all this?

When the police officer came, she transferred the cross-examination to him. He was a large, calm man in need of sleep, and resolutely addressed himself to Aston. Aston began to feel better.

'And you were the last person to see Mrs Ridpath?'

Interrupting Vere's florid confirmation, Aston had the pleasure of saying 'No', and the further pleasure of saving her face. 'My sister has forgotten about our charwoman. Mrs Barker must have seen her after I did. She came up in the lift just as I was leaving for work.'

The police officer made a note of Mrs Barker and went away, saying that every endeavour would be made. 'But if the lady should be suffering from a loss of memory, it may not be so easy to find her.'

'Why?' said Vere. 'I should have thought—'

'When persons lose their memory, in a manner of speaking they lose themselves. They aren't themselves. It would surprise you how unrecognisable they become.'

When he had gone, Vere exclaimed, 'Stuff and nonsense! I'm sure I could recognise Lucy a mile off. And she hasn't much to be recognised by, except her stoop.'

Bereft of male companionship, Aston sat down with his head in his hands. Vere began to unpack.

She was in the kitchen, routing through the store-cupboard, when Mrs Barker arrived on Tuesday morning. She said, 'Well, I suppose you know about Mrs Ridpath?'

Mrs Barker put down her bag, took off her hat and coat, opened the bag, drew out an apron and tied it on. Then, folding her hands on her stomach, she replied, 'No, Madam. Not that I know of.' Her heart sank; but a strong dislike is a strong support.

'Well, she's gone. And Mr Ridpath has put it in the hands of the police.'

'Indeed, Madam.'

'Not that that will be much use. You know what the police are like.'

'No, Madam. I have had no dealings with them.'

'They bungle everything. Now, why three packets of prunes? It does seem extraordinary. She was the last person in the world one would expect to do anything unexpected. Did she ever talk to you about going away? By herself, I mean?'

'No, Madam. Never.'

Mrs Barker had no doubt as to where Lucy had gone. She had gone to the South of France—to a pale landscape full of cemetery trees, as in the picture postcard, not sent by anyone, which she kept stuck in her dressing glass and said was the South of France. Remarking that she must get on with her work, Mrs Barker went smoothly to the bedroom, removed the postcard, and tucked it into her bosom.

Loath as she was to admit that her sister-in-law could have a lover, Vere was sure that she had eloped. (Men are so helpless, their feelings so easily played on.) She was sure that Lucy's detestable charwoman knew her whereabouts and had been heavily bribed. A joint elevenses was when she'd catch the woman and trip her into the truth.

This was forestalled by Mrs Barker bringing her a tray for one at ten-fifty, remarking that Madam might be glad of it, seeing how busy she was with her writing: and quitting the room with an aggressively hushed tread. Vere believed in leaving no stone unturned. Though she was sure that Lucy had eloped, this didn't seem to have occurred to Aston yet. A series of confidential letters to Lucy's friends might produce evidence that would calm his mind. Not one of the tiresome women had signed with more than a given name, so the envelopes would have to be directed to 'Sibyl', 'Sophie', 'Peg', and 'Lalla'; but a 'Dear Madam' would redress that. The rest would be easy: a preliminary announcement that she was Aston's sister and was writing to say that Lucy had left home for no apparent reason since she and Aston had always seemed such a happy couple; and that if Lalla, Peg, Sophie, or Sibyl could throw any light on this, of course in strictest confidence, it would be an inexpressible relief.

More she would not say; she did not want to prejudice anyone against Lucy.

All this took time. The friends might know each other and get together; it would not do if her letters to them were identical. It would suggest a circular. Her four letters done—for she did not propose to write to people like the linendraper in Northern Ireland who regretted he could no longer supply huckaback roller towels—she would get to work on Mrs Barker; differently, this time, and appealing to her feelings.

It was in vain. However, she managed to get the woman's address from her, so she rang up the police station and stated her conviction that Mrs Barker knew what she wouldn't say and should be questioned and, if need be, watched. As Vere was one of those people who are obeyed—on the fallacious hypothesis that it tends to keep them quiet —an inspector called that afternoon on Mrs Barker. He could not have been pleasanter, but the harm had been done; everybody in the street would know she had been visited by the police. Both the children knew it when they got in—David from school, Diane from her job at the fruiterer's. 'Mum! Whatever's happened?' 'Mum! Is anything wrong?'

The sight of them turned the sword in her heart. But she did not waver. Go back to those Ridpaths she would not; nor demean herself by asking for the money she was owed, though it might mean that the payments on David's bicycle and the triple mirror in Diane's bedroom could not be kept up. Pinch, pawn, go on the streets or the Public Assistance—but grovel for her lawful money to that two-faced crocodile who set the police on her she would not. She drew on her savings; and comforted herself with the thought of the two-faced crocodile down on her knees and doing her own scrubbing. The picture was visionary. Vere was on a committee—among other committees—of a Training Home for Endangered Girls, and whistled up an endangered mental deficient in no time.

'Now, now.' Aurelia adjured herself, gathering her belongings together. 'Now, now. Quickly does it. Don't lose your head.' Going down in the lift she was accompanied by the man in Dante—the decapitated man who held his head in front of him like a lantern and said through its lips, 'Woe's me.' But fortunately he got stuck in the swing door. She was alone in the street and knew that she must find a bus. A taxi would not do, it must be a bus; for a bus asks you nothing, it substitutes its speed and direction for yours, it takes you away from your private life. You sit in it, released, unknown, an anonymous destiny, and look out of the window or read the advertisements. A bus that had gone by at speed slowed as a van came out of a side street. She ran, caught up with it just as it moved again, clambered in, and sat down next to a stout man who said to her, 'You had to run for it, my girl.' She smiled, too breathless to speak. Her smile betrayed her. He saw she was not so young as he took her for. She spent the day travelling about London in buses, with a bun now and then to keep her strength up. In the evening she attended a free lecture on town and country planning, given under the auspices of the London County Council. This was in Clerkenwell. During the lecture she noticed that her hands had left off shaking and that for a second time she had yawned quite naturally. Whatever it had been she had so desperately escaped from, she had escaped it. Like the lecture, she was free. It had been rather an expensive day. She atoned for this by walking to King's Cross and spending the night in the ladies' waiting room. It was warm, lofty, impartial—preferable, really, to any bedroom. The dutiful trains arrived and departed—demonstrations of a world in which all was controlled and orderly and would get on very nicely without her. Tomorrow she would go to some quiet place—Highgate Cemetery would do admirably—and decide where to go next.

It was in Highgate Cemetery, studying a headstone which said 'I will dwell in the house of the Lord for ever', that Aurelia remembered hostels. The lecturer in Clerkenwell had enlarged on youth hostels. But there were middle-aged hostels, too—quiet establishments, scenes of unlicensed sobriety; and as youth hostels are scattered in wild landscapes for the active who enjoyed rock-climbing and rambling (he had dwelt on rambling and the provision of ramblers' routes), middle-aged hostels are clustered round devotional landmarks for the sedentary who enjoyed going to compline. She had enough money to dwell in a middle-aged hostel for a week. A week was quite far enough to plan for. Probably the best person to consult would be a clergyman. There was bound to be a funeral before long. She would hang on its outskirts and buttonhole the man afterward. 'Excuse me,' she would begin. 'I am a stranger. . . .'

'Excuse me,' she began, laying hold of him by the surplice. He had a sad, unappreciated face. 'I am a stranger.'

Thinking about her afterward—and she was to haunt his mind for the rest of his life—Lancelot Fogg acknowledged a saving mercy. His Maker, whom he had come to despair of, an ear that never heard, a name that he was incessantly obliged to take in vain, had done a marvel and shown him a spiritual woman. His life was full of women: good women, pious women, energetic, forceful women, blighted women, women abounding in good works, women learned in liturgies, women with tragedies, scruples, fallen arches—not to mention women he was compelled to classify as bad women: bullies, slanderers, backbiters, schemers, organisers, women abounding in wrath; there were even a few kind women. But never a spiritual woman till now. So tall and so thin, so innocently frank, it was as if she had come down from the west front of Chartres into a world where she was a stranger.

There was nothing remarkable in what she had to say. She wanted to find a hostel somewhere away from London—but not far, because of paying for the ticket—where she could be quiet and go to compline and do some washing. He understood about washing, for being poor he sometimes tried to do his own. But her spirituality shone through her words; it was as if a lily were speaking of cleanliness. Spirituality shone even more clearly through her silences. While he was searching his mind for addresses, she looked at him with tranquil interest, unconcerned trust, as though she had never in her life known care or frustration —whereas from the lines in her face it was obvious she had known both. She was so exceedingly tranquil and trustful, in fact, that she gave an impression of impermanence—as if at any moment some bidding might twitch her away. Non-attachment, he remembered, was the word. The spiritual become non-attached.

'Would Bedfordshire be too far?'

'I don't think so. I should only be there a week.'

He had remembered one of the women in his life who had been kind and who now kept a guest-house near a Benedictine monastery. He gave her the address. She thanked him and was gone. So was the funeral party. The grave was being filled in with increasing briskness. That afternoon, he must preside at the quarterly meeting of St Agatha's Guild.

The mistake, thought Aurelia, had been to dwell on compline. Doing so she had given a false impression of herself. The recommended Miss Larke of St Hilda's Guest-house had no sooner let her in than she was exclaiming, 'Just in time, just in time! Reverend Fogg rang up to say you were coming—the silly man forgot to mention your name, but you are the lady he met, aren't you?—and that you would be going to compline. I'm afraid we've finished supper. But I'll keep some soup hot for you for when you get back. And here is Mrs Bouverie who will show you the way. She's waited on purpose.'

'How do you do? How kind of you. My name is Lefanu. Is the abbey far away?'

'If we start now we'll make it,' said Mrs Bouverie.

They started. Mrs Bouverie was short and stout and she had a short stout manner of speech. Presently she inquired, 'R.C. or A.C.?'

Aurelia was at a loss. The question suggested electricity or taps.

'Roman or Anglo?'

Aurelia replied, 'Anglo.' It seemed safer, though it was difficult to be sure in the dark.

'Mrs or Miss?'

Aurelia replied, 'Miss.'

She had felt so sure that she would be fed on arrival that this day, too, she had relied on buns, resisting those jellied eels which looked so interesting in the narrow street that twisted down to the river—for instead of going straight to the guesthouse she had spent an hour or so exploring the town to see if she'd like it. She did like it. But she had never eaten jellied eels.

She had never been to compline, either. This made it impossible to guess how long it would go on, or exactly what was going on, except that people were invisibly singing or reciting in leisured tones. If she had not been so hungry, Aurelia decided, she could have understood why compline should exercise this charm on people. There was a total lack of obligation about it which was very agreeable. And when it had mysteriously become over, and they were walking back, and Mrs Bouverie remarked how beautifully it ended a day, didn't it, Aurelia agreed —while looking forward to the soup. The soup was lentil. It was hot and thick, and she felt her being fasten on it. The room was full of chairs, the chairs were full of people, the television was on. She sat clasping the mug where the soup had been. But it wilted in her grasp. She knew that at all costs she must not faint. 'Smelling salts!' she exclaimed. A flask of vinegar was pressed to her nose, her head was bowed between her knees. When she had been taken off to be put to bed with a hot-water bottle, Mrs Bouverie announced, 'She's Anglo.'

'Naturally. They are always so absurdly emotional,' said a lady who was Roman.

Miss Larke returned, reporting that the poor thing was touchingly grateful and had forgotten to bring a nightdress.

In the morning Aurelia woke hungry but without a vestige of gratitude. The sun shone, a thrush was singing in the garden, it was a perfect drying day.

Aurelia, the replacement of Lucy, was a nova—a new appearance in the firmament, the explosion of an ageing star. A nova is seen where no star was and is seen as a portent, a promise of what is variously desired: a victory, a pestilence, the birth of a hero, a rise in the price of corn. To the man never before called Ithamore she was at last an object of art he could not account for. To Lancelot Fogg she was at last a spiritual woman. To the denizens of St Hilda's guest-house she was something new to talk about—arresting but harmless. At least, she was harmless till the evening she brought in that wretched tomcat and insisted on keeping it as a pet. If Lancelot Fogg had not recommended her so fervently, Aurelia with that misnamed pet of hers would have been directed to lodgings elsewhere. It was bad enough to adopt a most unhealthy-looking tomcat, but to call the animal Lucy made it so much worse; it seemed a deliberate flout, a device to call attention to the creature's already too obvious sex.

'But why Lucy, Miss Lefanu? Surely it's inappropriate?'

'It's a family name,' she replied.

Lucy developed on Aurelia's fourth evening at the guest-house. She was again accompanying Mrs Bouverie to compline when a distant braying caught her ear. Looking in the direction of the braying, she saw a livid glow and exclaimed, 'A circus!'

'It's that dreadful fair,' Mrs Bouverie replied. 'As I was telling you, my brother-in-law who had that delightful place in Hampshire, not far from Basingstoke, such rhododendrons! I've never seen such a blaze of colour as when they were out. . . .'

When she had seen Mrs Bouverie safely down on her knees, Aurelia stole away and went off to find the fair. Fairs, of course, are not what they used to be, but they are still what they are, and Aurelia enjoyed herself a great deal till two haunted young men in frock coats and ringlets attached themselves to her, saying at intervals, 'Spare us a reefer, beautiful. Have a heart.' For they, too, had seen her as a nova. At last she managed to give them the slip and hurried away through the loud entrails of a Lunar Flight. This brought her to the outskirts of the fair, and it was there she saw the cat lying on the muddied grass under the bonnet of a lorry. Its eyes were shut, its ears laid back. It had gone under the lorry bonnet for warmth, and was paying the price.

When she came back with a hot dog, it had rearranged itself. In its new attitude she could see how thin it was and how despairingly shabby. She knelt down and addressed it from a distance. It heard her, for it turned its head away. The smell of the hot dog was more persuasive. It began to thresh its tail. 'You'll eat when I'm gone,' she said, with fellow-feeling, and scattered bits of hot dog under the bonnet and began to walk away—knowing that its precarious balance between mistrust and self-preservation could be overset by a glance. She had left the fairground and was turning into a street full of warehouses when she saw that the cat, limping and cringing, was following her. She stopped, and it came on till it was beside her. Then it sat down and raised its face toward her. Its expression was completely mute—and familiar. The cat was exactly like her cousin Lucy.

When she picked it up it relaxed in her arms, rubbed its head against her shoulder, and purred. The cat took it absolutely for granted that it should be carried off by a deity. Still throned in her arms, it blinked serenely at the mortals in the guest-house, sure that they soon would be disposed of.

There were a great many things to be done for Lucy. His suppurating paw had to be dressed, his ears had to be cleaned and his coat brushed, food had to be bought for him, and four times a day he had to be exercised in the garden. In the intervals of this, his fleas had to be dealt with. Using a fine tooth comb she searched them out, pounced on them, dropped them in a bowl of soapy water, resumed the search. It was a dreamlike occupation: it put her in touch with the infinite. Twenty. Thirty. Forty-seven. Fifty-two. From time to time she looked sharply at the bowl of soapy water and pushed back any wretches that had struggled to the rim.

The total of fleas went up in bounds. The money in her purse decreased. Even using the utmost economy, stealing whenever she conveniently could, having sardines put down to Miss Larke, she would not be left with enough to pay for a second week at the guest-house. Lucy's paw healed slowly; it would be some while yet before he could provide for himself. She noticed that Lucy's paw was increasingly asked about; that suggestions for his welfare multiplied.

'I wonder why you don't put an advertisement in the local paper, saying "Found." All this time his real owners may be hunting for him, longing to get him back.'

Aurelia looked deeply at the speaker. It might be worth trying. There is no harm in blackmail, since no one is obliged to give in to it. On the other hand, it is no good unless they do.

She composed two letters: 'Unless you send me fifty pounds in notes, I shan't be able to come back.' 'Unless you send me fifty pounds in notes, I shall be forced to return.'

Combing out fleas to a new rhythm of 'he loves me, he loves me not,' she weighed these alternatives. The second would probably have the stronger appeal to Aston's heart. Poor Aston, she had defrauded him too long ⌐f the calm expansion of widowerhood. But the stomach is a practical organ; the first alternative might be the more compelling. She did not, of course, mean to return, in either case. Since her adoption of Lucy, she had become so unshakably Aurelia that she could contemplate being Lucy, too, so far as being Lucy would further Aurelia's designs. But Lucy, the former Lucy, must be Aurelia's property. There must be no little escapades into identity, no endorsing of cheques, no more slidings into Lucy Ridpath. That was why the money must come in notes. Even so, who was it to be addressed to?

It was time for Lucy to scratch in the garden. For the first time, he tried to scratch with both hind legs. Everything became easy. Whichever the chosen form of the letter demanding money with menaces, Aurelia, signing with a capital L., would ask for the money to be directed to Miss Lefanu, *poste restante*. Lucy had been Lefanu when Aston married her. He could not have forgotten this; it might even touch his heart and dispose him to add another five pounds. All that remained was to decide which letter to send, and to post it from Bedford, which was nearby and non-committal. The envelope had been posted before she realised that both letters were enclosed.

'Lucy's handwriting,' said Aston. 'She's alive. What an infinite relief!'

'I never supposed she wasn't,' said Vere. 'Still, if it's a relief to you to see her handwriting—it doesn't seem such a niggle as usual, but that's her 'L'—I'm sure I'm glad.'

'But Vere, on Monday evening, on *Monday evening*, you said I must ring up the police or I should be suspected of murdering her.'

'So you would have been. They always jump to conclusions. Well, what does Lucy say?'

The letters had been folded up together. The first alternative was uppermost.

'She seems to have got into some sort of trouble. She says she can't come home unless I send her fifty pounds.'

'Fifty pounds? Where is she, then. California?'

'The postmark is Bedford. She's gone back to her maiden name.'

'Fifty pounds to get back from Bedford. Fifty pounds! She must have got herself mixed up in something pretty fishy. Yes. I heard only the other day that Bedford is an absolute hotbed of the drug traffic. That's what she wants the money for. Poor silly Lucy, she'd be wax in their hands. Aston! You'll have to think very carefully, apart from this absurd demand for money, about having her back. If she were here alone all day with no one to keep an eye on her—What does she say on the second sheet?'

'Is there a second sheet? I hadn't noticed. She says—Vere, I can't make this out. She says, "Unless you send me fifty pounds in notes I shall be forced to return."'

'Nonsense, Aston! You're misreading it. She just made a fair copy and then put them both in.'

'But Vere, she says unless I send her the money she will be forced to return.'

'She must be raving. Why on earth should she expect you to pay her to keep away? Let me see.'

After a pause, she said, 'My poor Aston.'

Her voice was heavy with commiseration. It fell on Aston like a wet sponge. His brief guilty dazzle of relief (for as long as Lucy wasn't dead he really didn't want to live with her again; what he wanted was manly solitude, and he had already taken the first steps toward getting shot of Vere) sizzled out.

'Poor Lucy! I must send her something, I suppose.'

'Yes, you ought to. But not too much. Ten pounds would be ample. What's Bedford? No way at all.'

When Aurelia called at the post office, the clerk handed her two letters. She opened Aston's first.

Dear Lucy,

I will not try to persuade you. The heart has its reasons. But if a time ever comes when you want to come back, remember there will always be a door on the latch and a light in the window.

I will say nothing of the anxiety your leaving without a word has caused me.

—Aston

Four five-pound notes were enclosed.

The other letter was from Vere. It ran:

Aston is now recovering. I will thankfully pay you to keep away.

This letter was accompanied by ten ten-pound notes.

Aurelia bought Lucy some tinned salmon and a handsome travelling basket. But for the greater part of that afternoon's journey, Lucy sat erect on her knee looking out of the window and held like a diviner's twig by his two front legs. She relied on Lucy to know at a snuff which station to get out at, just as he had known how to succeed in blackmailing—for while she was debating which of the two letters to send he had leaped onto the table, laid his head on her hand, and rolled with such ardour and abandonment that she forgot all else, so that both letters went off in the one envelope. Relying on Lucy, she had chosen a stopping train. It joggled through a green unemphatic landscape with many willow trees and an occasional broached spire. Lucy remained unmoved. She began to wonder if his tastes ran to the romantic, if high mountains were to him a feeling—in which case she had brought him to quite the wrong part of England. In the opposite corner sat a man with leather patches on his elbows, paying them no attention. Then at a station called Peckover Junction two ladies got in, and resumed (they were travelling together) a conversation about their grandchildren. From their grandchildren they turned to the ruin of the countryside—new towns, overspill, and holiday camps.

'Look at those caravans! They've got here, now.'

'Don't speak to me of caravans,' said the other lady.

Disregarding this, the first lady asked if there were as many as ever.

'More! Such hideosities at poor Betcombe . . . and the children! Swarming everywhere. I shall never find a tenant now. Besides, all these new people have such grand ideas. They must have this, they must have that. They don't appreciate the past. For me, that's its charm. If it weren't for the caravans, I'd be at Betcombe still, glorying in my beams and my pump. Do you know, it was eighteenth century, my pump?'

'Would you like me as a tenant?' said Aurelia. 'I can't give you any references just now, but I'd pay ten shillings a week. No, darling!' This last remark was addressed to Lucy, who had driven his claws into her thigh.

'Ten shillings a week—for my lovely little cottage?'

'A pound a week.'

'Really, this is so sudden, so unusual. No references . . . and I suppose you'd be bringing that cat. I'm a bird-lover. No, I'm afraid it's out of the question. Come, Mary, we get out here.'

For the train was coming to a halt. Both ladies gathered their belongings and got out. From the window Aurelia saw them get in again, a few carriages farther up.

'You're well out of that,' observed the man with leather patches. 'I know her place. It's a hovel. No room to swing a cat in, begging your cat's pardon.'

Lucy rounded himself like a poultice above his scratch. Aurelia said she expected she had been silly. The train went on. An atmosphere of acquaintance established itself. Presently the man asked if she had any particular place in mind.

'No. No exactly. I'm a stranger.'

'Because I happen to know of something that might suit you—if you don't object to it being a bit out of the way. It's a bungalow, and it's modern. If you're agreeable, I'll take you to see it.'

It was impossible not to be agreeable, because he was so plainly a shy man and surprised at finding himself intervening. So when he got out she got out with him, and he took her to a Railway Arms where she and

Lucy would be comfortable, and said he would call for her at ten the next morning.

He was exactly punctual. When she had assured him how comfortable she and Lucy had been, there seemed to be nothing more to say. Fortunately, he was one of those drivers who give their whole mind to driving. They drove in his van. It was lettered 'George Bastable, Builder and Plumber', and among the things in the back was a bathtub wrapped in cellophane. They drove eastward, through the same uneventful landscape. He turned the van into a track that ran uphill—only slightly uphill, but in that flat landscape it seemed considerable. 'There it is.'

A spinney of mixed trees ran along the top of the ridge. Smoke was rising through the boughs. So she would have a neighbour. She had not reckoned on that.

But the smoke was rising from the chimney of a bungalow, and there was no other building there.

He must have got up very early, for the fire was well established, the room was warm and felt inhabited. The kitchen floor was newly washed and a newspaper path was spread across it.

'You'd find it comfortable,' he said.

'Oh, yes,' she said, looking at the two massive armchairs that faced each other across a hideous hearth mat.

'It hasn't been lived in for three years, though I come out from time to time to give a look to it. But no damp anywhere—that'll show how sound it is.'

'No. It feels wonderfully dry,' she said, looking at a flight of blue pottery birds on the wall.

Lucy was shaking his basket.

'May I let your cat out? He'd like a run, and I daresay he'd pick up a breakfast, bird's-nesting.'

Before she could answer, he had unfastened the lid and Lucy had bounded over the threshold. How was she to answer this man who had taken so much trouble and was so proud of his bungalow?

'Did you build it yourself?'

'I did. That's why I know it's a good one. I built it for my young lady. When I saw you in the train, you put me in mind of her, somehow. So when you said you wanted somewhere to live—' He stared at her, standing politely at a distance trying to recapture the appearance of his nova in this half-hearted lady, no longer young.

The house had stood empty for three years. She had died. Poor Mr Bastable! Aurelia's face assumed the right expression.

'She left,' he said.

'How *could* she?' exclaimed Aurelia.

This time, there was no need to put on the right expression. She was wholeheartedly shocked at the behaviour of Mr Bastable's young lady—and if the young lady had come in just then she would have boxed the ungrateful minx's ears. Instead, it was Lucy who trotted in, looking smug, with fragments of eggshell plastered to his chops, sat down in front of the fire, and began cleaning himself. Mr Bastable remarked that Lucy had found a robin's nest. He was grateful for Aurelia's indignation but shy of saying so. He suspected he had gone too far. Somewhat to his surprise he learned that Aurelia would like to move into his lovely bungalow immediately. He drove her to the village to do her shopping, came back to show her where the coal was kept, gave her the key. Watching him drive away she suddenly became aware of the landscape she would soon be taking for granted. It sparkled with crisscrossing drains and ditches; a river wound through it. A herd of caravans was peacefully grazing in the distance.

Happiness is an immunity. In a matter of days Aurelia was unaffected by the flight of blue pottery birds, sat in armchairs so massive she could not move them and felt no wish to move them, slept deliciously between pink nylon sheets. With immunity she watched Lucy sharpening his claws on the massive armchairs. She had a naturally happy disposition and preferred to live in the present. Happiness immunised her from the past—for why look back for what has slipped from one's possession? —and from the future, which may never even be possessed. Perhaps never in the past, perhaps never in the future, had she been, could she be, so happy as she was now. The cuckoo woke her; she fell asleep to Lucy's purr. In the mornings he had usually left a dent beside her and gone out for his sunrising. Whatever one may say about bungalows, they are ideal for cats. She hunted his fleas on Sundays and Thursdays. He was now so strong and splendid that for the rest of the week he could perfectly well deal with them himself. She lived with carefree economy, seldom using more than a single plate, drinking water to save rinsing the teapot, and as far as possible eating raw foods, which entailed the minimum of washing up. Every Saturday she bought seven new-laid eggs, hard-boiled them, and spaced them out during the week—a trick she had learned from Vasari's *Lives of the Artists*. It was not an adequate diet for anyone leading an active life, but her life was calculatedly inactive—as though she were convalescing from some forgotten illness.

On Saturday evenings Mr Bastable called to collect the rent and to see if anything needed doing—a nail knocked in or a tap tightened up. He always brought some sort of present: a couple of pigeons, the first tomatoes from his greenhouse, breakfast radishes. As the summer deepened, the presents enlarged into basketloads of green peas, bunches of roses, strawberries, sleek dessert gooseberries. But as the summer deepened and in spite of all the presents and economies Aurelia's wealth of one hundred and twenty pounds lessened, and she knew she must turn her mind to doing something about this. She could not dig; there was no one but Mr Bastable to beg from. The times were gone when one could take in plain sewing. Surveying the landscape she had come to take for granted, she saw the caravans in a new light—no longer peacefully grazing but fermenting with ambitions and cultural unrest.

By now they must have bought all the picture postcards at the shop. She had always wanted to paint. For all she knew, she might turn out to be quite good at it. Willows would be easy—think of all the artists who painted them. By now the caravaners must be tired of looking at real willows and would welcome a change to representational art. She took the bus to Wisbech, found an arts-and-crafts shop, bought paper, brushes, gouache paints, and a small easel. That same evening she did two pictures of willows—one tranquil, one storm-tossed. Three days later, she set up the easel on the outskirts of the caravan site and began a caravan from life. It was harder than willows—there were no precursors to inspire her—but when she had complied with a few suggestions from the caravan's owner she made her sale and received two further commissions. By the beginning of August she was rich enough to go on to oils—which was more fun and on the whole easier. It was remarkable how easily she painted, and with what assurance. The demand was chiefly for caravans. She varied them, as Monet varied his haystacks. Caravan with buckets. Caravan with sunset. Pink caravan. One patron wanted a group of cows—though his children were cold towards them. She evaded portraits, but yielded to a request for an abstract. This was the only commission that really taxed her. Do as she might, it kept on coming out like a draper's window display. But she mastered it in the end, and signed it A. Lefanu like the rest.

By the end of September she had made enough to keep her in idleness till Christmas—when she would have thought of something else.

Winter would bring a new variety of happiness—slower, more conscious, and with more strategy in it. The gales of the equinox blowing across the flats struck at the spinny along the ridge, blew down one tree, and shook deadwood out of others. Here was an honest occupation. She set herself to build up a store of fuel against the winter. It was heavy work dragging the larger branches over the rough ground clogged with brambles and tall grass, but Lucy lightened it by flirting round her as she worked, darting after the tail of the branches, ambushing them and leaping on them as they rustled by. She was collecting fuel, Lucy was growing a thick new coat; both of them were preparing their defences against the wintry months ahead. Mr Bastable said that by all the signs it would be a hard winter, preceded by much rain and wind. He advised her to get her wood in before the rain fell and made the ground too soggy to shift it. If she manages the first winter, he thought, she will settle. Though she was an ungrateful tenant, or at any rate an inattentive receiver, he wanted her to settle; it delighted him to see her making these preparations. Later on, he would complete them by chopping the heavier pieces into nice little logs. Taking Mr Bastable's advice, Aurelia decided to get the wood in, working on till the dusk was scythed by the headlights of passing cars, till Lucy vanished into a different existence of being a thing audible—a sudden plop or a scuffling. She never had to call him when she went indoors. By the time she was on the threshold he was there, rubbing against her, raising his feet in a ritual exaggeration. He was orderly in his ways, a timekeeper. He took himself in and out, but rarely strayed. When she came back from selling those unprincipled canvases, he was always waiting about for her, curled up on the lid of the water butt, drowsing under the elder, sitting primly on the sill of the window left open for him. He was happy enough out of her sight, but he liked to have her within his.

So she told herself, later on, that foggy, motionless November

evening when he had not come in at his usual time. She had kindled a
fire, not that it was cold—indeed, it was oddly warm and fusty; but the
fog made it cheerless. It was a night to pull the curtains closer, listen to
the snap and crackle of a brief fire, go early to bed. She had left the
curtains unclosed, however. If Lucy saw that a fire had been kindled, he
would be drawn from whatever busied him. He was a very chimney-
corner cat, although he was a tom. Twice the brief fire died down, twice
she made it up again. She went to the door, peered uselessly into the
fog, called him. It was frightening to call into that silent, immediate
obscurity.

'Lucy. Lucy.'

She waited. No Lucy. She must resign herself to it. Tonight Lucy was
engaged in being a tom. As she stood there, resigning herself to it and
straining her ears, she felt the damp of the foggy air pricked with a fine
drizzling rain. A minute later, the rain was falling steadily; not hard but
steadily. She had not the courage to go on calling. The pitch of her voice
had frightened her; it sounded so anxious. She went indoors and sat
down to wait. On a different night she would have left the window open
and gone to bed. And in the morning Lucy would have been there, too,
and in her sleep her arm would have gone out and round him.

With the rain, it had become colder. She added coal to the fire. It
blazed up but did not warm her. She counted the blue pottery birds and
listened. She listened for so long that finally she became incapable of
listening, and when there was a sound which was not the interminable
close patter of rain she did not hear it, only knew that she had heard
something. A dragging sound . . . the sound of something being dragged
along the path to the door. It had ceased. It began again. Ceased.

When she snatched the door open, she could see nothing but the rain,
a curtain of flashing arrows lit by her lighted room. A noise directed
her—a tremulous yowl. He struck at her feebly when she stooped to
pick him up, then dragged himself on into the light of the doorway. She
fell on her knees. This sodden shapeless thing was Lucy. He looked at
her with one eye; the other sagged on his cheek. His jaw dangled. One
side of his head had been smashed in; his front leg was broken. When
she touched him he shrank from her hand and yowled beseechingly.
Slowly, distortedly, he hitched himself over the threshold, across the
room, tried to sit up before the fire, fell over, and lay twitching and

gasping for breath. When at last she dared touch him, his racing heartbeats were like a machine fastened in him. She talked to him and stroked his uninjured paw. He did not shrink from her now, and perhaps her voice lulled him as the plumpness of his muscular soft paw lulled her, for he relaxed and curled his tail round his flank as though he were preparing to fall asleep. Long after he seemed to be dead, the implacable machine beat on. Then it faltered, stumbled, began again at a slower rate, fluttered. A leaden tint suffused his eye and his lolling tongue. His breathing stopped. He flattened. It was inconceivable that he could ever have been loved, handsome, alive.

'Lucy!'

The cry broke from her. It unloosed another.

'Aurelia!'

She could not call back the one or the other. She was Lucy Ridpath, looking at a dead cat who had never known her.

The agony of dislocation was prosaic. She endured it because it was there. It admitted no hope, so she endured it without the support of resentment.

The rain had gone on all the time and was still going on.

Lucy Ridpath's mackintosh was hanging in the closet, ready to meet it. Mrs Barker had advised her to put it on and she had done so. Tomorrow she would put it on again when she went out to dig a hole in the sodden ground for the cat's burial. It is proper to bury the dead; it is a mark of respect. Lucy would bury Lucy, and then there would be one Lucy left over.

She sat in the lighted room long after the light of day came into it. Then she put on the mackintosh and took up the body and carried it out. The air was full of a strange roar and tumult, a hollow booming that came from everywhere at once. The level landscape was gone. The hollow booming rose from a vast expanse and confusion of floodwater. Swirling, jostling, traversed with darker streaks, splintering into flashes of light where it contested with an obstacle, it drove toward the river. Small rivulets were flowing down from the ridge to join it, the track to the road was a running stream. In all that water there must be somewhere a place to drown.

With both hands holding the cat clasped to her bosom, she walked slowly down the track. When she came to the road, the water was halfway to her knees. A little farther along the road there was a footbridge over the roadside ditch. It was under water but the handrail showed. She waded across it. The water rose to her knees. With the next few steps she was in water up to her thighs. It leaned its ice-cold indifferent weight against her. When a twig was carried bobbing past her, she felt a wild impulse to clutch it. But her arms were closed about the cat's body, and she pressed it more closely to her and staggered on. All sense of direction was gone; sometimes she saw light, sometimes she saw darkness. The hollow booming hung in the air. Below it was an incessant hissing and seething. The ground rose under her feet; the level of water had fallen to her knees. Tricked and impatient, she waded faster, took longer strides. The last stride plunged her forward. She was out of her depth, face down in the channel of a stream. She rose to the surface. The current bowed her, arched itself above her, swept her onward, cracked her skull against the concrete buttress of a revetment, whirled the cat out of her grasp.

(*The Innocent and the Guilty*, 1971)

ABSALOM, MY SON

HAVING escaped the fall of high explosives, incendiaries and guided missiles, and having been preserved from requisitioning or billeting because of the age and reputation of its owner, in 1948 Matthew Bateman's house in Kent was totally destroyed by an ordinary civilian fire. It was empty at the time, and the cause of the fire was never ascertained. A farm-hand, on his way to the morning milking, noticed smoke rising from the valley, and a moment later saw a trophy of flame leap up as the thatched roof fell in.

It was a roof which in earlier years had sheltered many visitors. The headlines, 'Well-Known Writer's House Burned Down: Total Destruction of Kenton Mill-House,' revived memories of rooms darkened with books and lit with the tremulous reflection of water, of a reedy voice, and a bony hand stroking a jackdaw, and of a quantity of slightly macabre bric-à-brac—blotched shells, scowling daguerreotypes, the Emblems of the Passion in a bottle—placed with old-maidish precision on fringed mats. Several such readers wrote to condole, to offer hospitality or to search, even, for that white blackbird, an empty house. These offers were politely refused by Miss Loveday Patterson, writing on Matthew Bateman's behalf.

And so, at the age of seventy-three, Matthew Bateman found himself possessed of the clothes he stood up in and those in a small leather suitcase, two pairs of spectacles (those on his nose and those in his pocket), a watch, a fountain-pen, a pistol, a signet-ring, a note-book, the mss of two novels which, published in the early twenties, had established him as a man of letters, and the ms. of an unfinished novel, earlier in date. These mss had been lent to an exhibition in Maidstone, which he had opened afterwards, spending the night on which his house caught fire at a hotel there. He also retained Miss Loveday Patterson, who had accompanied him to Maidstone, and had been his secretary for so long that she really might be counted as part of his personal estate.

He heard the news of his loss in silence, and bore it with acid stoicism. 'It is your *books* that I grieve for!' exclaimed Mrs White, the lady who had got up the exhibition. 'It might be worse: at least, I have read them,' he answered. Condolers, reporters and friends in need came to the hotel in quantities, and after two days of this he told Loveday Patterson to go in search of a furnished house without neighbours or telephone and not to come back until she had found it. Thirty-six hours later she returned with news of a bungalow (called High Hope) already rented, coals delivered and a charwoman arranged for. 'It's on a hill,' she said.

'I hate hills,' he replied.

'And I found out in the village that the two ladies it belongs to tried to run it as a café, but couldn't make it pay because they kept such large black dogs—they bred dogs, too—that strangers were afraid to go near it. Then all the dogs died of distemper, and one of the ladies had a nervous breakdown and is in a mental home, and the other has gone to work in a hostel near Birmingham.'

'Did they bury the dogs in the garden?' he inquired.

'Yes. But I wouldn't call it a garden. It's just a patch of rough ground, with horseradish all over it.'

'Horseradish is practically ineradicable. I like the horseradish.'

She had mentioned the horseradish and the deaths of the dogs on the established principle of mentioning the disagreeables first, in order to get them over and wipe them out with the subsequent agreeables; and also because honesty is best. She had been with Matthew Bateman for twenty years, at first as secretary and housekeeper, then, as time went on and times worsened, as cook and partially laundress and sometimes nurse. Statistically and clinically, she knew him thoroughly, and if she had been less conscientious, she might have known him humanly. But devotion to duty browbeat her intuitions and imprisoned her in a state of cautious astonishment. Intuition now told her that she could not hope to improve on the dogs and the horseradish, but to herself she only said that Mr Bateman had a sense of humour, and that with a sense of humour one can overcome anything—so she could go off with a quiet mind and buy him winter underclothes.

On the day they moved in, seeing him get out of the hired car and walk resolvedly unnoticing towards what would now be his front door, she was thankful that she had bought them thick. The wind of the autumn equinox plied the macrocarpus hedge that sheltered High Hope from its total absence of neighbours, and the lean sinewy branches bowed as if in a grotesque homage to the new owner. A plane flew over. The cloud hid it, but the gusty wind carried its noise like an intermittent shouting. As they entered the house, they heard the first spikes of rain hit the windows.

'It won't take me a minute to get tea,' she said. He did not answer. He had walked towards a bookshelf, and stood staring at it. When she came back with the tea-tray, he was standing in the same place, a book in his hand.

In her first visit of inspection she barely glanced at the books, only noticing that they were battered, miscellaneous and not Mr Bateman's kind of book. Mr Bateman's kind of book would have to come from the London Library, wrapped in the darkest and toughest brown paper. How nice it would be if Mr Bateman, nourished by the London Library, should spend the winter comfortably making extracts about astrologers, complying with Mr Crocker the publisher's wish for a companion volume to the book about almanack-makers which had sold so well during the war. Mr Bateman had called it a pot-boiler; but as far as she could see, it had cost him quite as much pains and needed retyping quite as often as the books that were all out of his head. And it had sold much better. Meanwhile Mr Bateman, book in hand, had sat down to let his tea get cold; and only his surroundings, and the social category of the tea-cup, and the nature of the book divorced him from the process of letting his tea get cold at Kenton Mill-House.

Book by book, reading with unswerving, unsmiling attention, Mr Bateman traversed the High Hope bookshelves. He read *The Scarlet Pimpernel* and *The Green Hat* and *The Blue Lagoon* and *The Lilac Sunbonnet*, and *The Revised Prayerbook of 1927* and *Lassie* and *Rin-tin-tin* and *The Memoirs of Marie of Roumania* and *The Story of San Michele*. He read the works of Barrie and Milne, and old copies of *Vogue* and *Good Housekeeping*, and bound volumes of *The Girl's Own Paper*, and *Gone with the Wind*, and *The White Cliffs of Dover*. Roused to helpfulness by news of his burned house, or possibly aware of the increased sales value of

anyone publicly pitiable, editors wrote and asked him when they might
have another article, even if they had never had one, and publishers
suggested that he should write introductions to their reprints of lesser
classics. These letters, having typed envelopes, were opened by Loveday
Patterson, who was pleased to see them. Mr Bateman's finances had
suffered by the ebb-tide which catches all writers who have become well
known without ever having been popular. Keeping her voice suitably
impartial, she read them aloud. But barely raising his eyes from *The
Intimate Life of the Tzarina* or *Opening a Chestnut Burr*, Mr Bateman
asked her to write to the fellow and say he'd think about it.

He's relaxing, she thought; and having found this benign explanation,
settled down to do a little reading and make herself some new clothes;
for her possessions, naturally, had been burned with his. As secretary to
a distinguished man of letters, Loveday made a point of reading
high-class books, and got them from a lending library. She could only
afford the cheap subscription, so by the time she got them they were a
year or so out of date, but they were still high-class.

He read, she read and knitted. And then, with laceration, like one
startled from a deep dream, Matthew discovered that he had read every
book in the house. Awakening with a sigh, he looked round on his new
surroundings. There, exhaling in a long perspective, was the landscape
of yet another autumn; and here, so close at hand as to be almost
perspectiveless, was Loveday Patterson, growing old in his service, but
still fresh-coloured, prompt and trim.

'Loveday, who was the fellow who wanted an introduction to *Peter
Wilkins*?'

'To *Peter Wilkins*, Mr Bateman? I think it was Butler and Bugler.'

'Tell him I'll do it.'

For Peter Wilkins, creature of an eighteenth-century romancer who
wrote but this one book, being shipwrecked on a desert island, wooed a
feathered mistress, half woman, half bird; and having mastered his first
mistrust of such a being, got children on her and put her into European
dress. Just so, thought Matthew, writers substantiate their first amours
with poetry, and make novels, and publish them. All this is a parable, and
should be written down. But as usual the first impetus was caught and
strangled in thickets of analogies and qualifications. Poor Loveday typed
and retyped, and each revision was a stage further away from his

intention. The Introduction to *Peter Wilkins* was limping towards its final stage of completion and nausea when the postman brought a registered packet. The Maidstone exhibition had closed, and Mrs White returned his three manuscripts together with a letter aptly hoping that he was at work on another of his delightful books.

'Tell her I wish she were at work in a soap factory,' he commanded, and later in the day signed unprotestingly a note of polite acknowledgment. In the interval he had begun to read the unfinished novel—his first child by his feathered love, begotten before he had put even a rush ring round her finger or tied an apron before her sex. Oh dear, thought Loveday Patterson, there he is with a manuscript—so unsettling! For while in a state of being in manuscript, Mr Bateman was always quite unlike his usual self: only an attempt at dictation had been worse. This was a manuscript out of the past, and unpacking it, and noticing that it had come back from the exhibition with its pages a trifle jostled, she had felt as calmly about it as if it were a shirt come back from the laundry with a ravelled cuff: she would set it to rights and put it away. But he had taken it, and now it had taken him. There he sat, straining his eyesight over the waning ink, his cheeks flushed, his lips moving, his hand with the veins standing out on it trembling with impatience as he turned over two flimsy pages for one. She stood with the signed letter to Mrs White in her hand, looking down on him, and it was as if she saw the rash coming out. If only he would let her type it!—for that is why a properly established writer keeps a secretary—to wash and clothe and cradle these reeking fragments of creation. There was not much of it, she could rattle it off in no time. But it wouldn't do to say so now.

He became conscious of her, and glanced up. His expression was brilliantly serene, a glance from another world; as if he were a boy going fishing. 'Is that you, Loveday,' he said. 'Off to bed? That's right, that's right.' She went to her sitting-room, took the cover off her machine, and sat down to write to her married sister in Canada. 'You will be surprised at my new address,' she wrote, half-knowing that Phoebe would omit to notice it, 'but it does not mean what you might think, for I am still with Mr Bateman.' Canada was a long way off, but the man on the yonder side of the wall was further away than Canada.

Before going to bed that night, Matthew strolled out among the horse-radish. It was the first time since the arrival at High Hope that he had felt an interest in the weather. The wind was blowing from the south-west, the air was soft, the sky overcast. It smelt of rain. He went to bed deeply satisfied, knowing that the following day would be wet and stormy, the most propitious weather for his purpose, which was to write. This time, he would really write: freely, dashingly, leaving out all the stuffing and nonsense, observing nothing but his own intentions, going where he pleased, even if it meant going where he had notoriously gone before, unharnessed to any purpose except to please himself, as he had written when he lived in the harsh Arcadia of youth. He would take up the unfinished story, and finish it, and nothing of his doubtful later self should get into it, except the technical skill of the practised hand. Not for nothing had his middle years vanished in smoke. This negligible little box he now inhabited was, in fact, the perfect container for the deed he proposed. As for Loveday, he would put her under hatches. She could be sent off on excursions of pleasure.

The following day was so extremely wet that he could not in conscience pack Loveday out to enjoy herself. He told her not to bother him, and she obeyed. The gale whirled him into the dusk before he remembered to feel hungry. During the night the storm blew itself out.

'Loveday, have you ever been to Rochester?'

'Yes, Mr Bateman. I've been there several times, to a dentist.'

'Ah! Well, have you ever been across the Thames on the Gravesend Ferry? No? Now that's a thing everyone should do. This would be an excellent day for it. You'd better start at once.'

Smoke, shipping, the pale estuary horizons: the mind's eye prospect delighted him, he would have gone himself if he had not had better fish to fry. 'Tomorrow,' he added, 'you might go to Canterbury. I know you've been there before, but one cannot go too often to Canterbury.'

The weather continued implacably fine, and after a couple of days it became necessary to send Loveday for a breath of sea air at Ramsgate. He was getting to a stage when the combination of a high barometer and Loveday fidgeting about on tiptoe might be fatal. When he was over this precarious bridge, where the inexperience of the original narrative had to be underpinned by knowledge of real life and yet preserve its air of fortuitous infallibility, things would be easier. Loveday could stay at home and the woman could come to scrub.

'I think you had better spend a night at Ramsgate, while you are about it.'

She put on her look of being a bear that can dance no longer, and said that if it were the same to him, she would much prefer not to. He had to give way. But the thought of her return that evening irked him. It shortened the day. Two separate interruptors, a gipsy selling clothes-pegs, and a man coming to read the electricity meter, shortened the day still further. When he had eaten the tray luncheon that Loveday had left for him, he realised that for the moment, only for the moment, he had written himself to a standstill. He would have coffee, and then he would go for a walk.

The coffee-pot was on the stove, it only needed heating. This time, instead of leaving it to boil, boil over, and boil away, he remained in the kitchen. One of Loveday's lending library books was on the window-sill. Without looking at the title, he opened it at random and read on till the coffee boiled.

The recollection of what he had read stayed pleasantly with him as he walked. The book had shadows in it: though what Norman Leigh (he had noticed the name as he put the book down: it was a name unknown to him) meant by calling such an unbedizened piece of work *Reverse the Sun* was another matter. Perhaps it was something astrophysical. Titles change like women's hats. He must find a title for his old story made new, for *The Bride of Smithfield* smacked of the twenties and wouldn't do. His mind went back to his own affair. He hit on a possible answer to a difficulty which had hampered him all that morning, and he turned home.

He saw a bicycling woman dismount at his gate and walk with a dreadful positiveness up the path. Instantly deciding on the worst, he foresaw his afternoon laid waste by Mrs White. She had come to 'look him up', her car had broken down, but at the garage, inflexible as a tiger on the trail, she had borrowed a bicycle.... It was the girl from the post-office with a reply-paid telegram. Loveday had met a friend at Ramsgate, and would spend the night there if he had no objection. He scribbled his permission, went jubilantly into the house that was now so much more his own, and settled down to work.

His hand was out. The expedient he had carried back did not fit. Words lay on the page like drowned flies. All his renounced obesities came back to him, qualifications and evasions muddied every sentence. It was worse than the Introduction to *Peter Wilkins*. He threw the day's work on the floor, washed his face and hands in cold water, and began again, leaving the botch to clear itself, and taking up the narrative farther on where the manuscript petered out. He fell into a conversation, and three hours later the conversation was still going on, weakly sparkling like a squib that wouldn't lie down and die. His head ached, his wrists were furrowed where he had clawed them. He walked into the kitchen to find himself something to eat, and immediately his spirits began to revive. Triviality released him into self-respect, and he sang to himself as he wandered about collecting the ingredients for a curry. Carrying his tray into the sitting-room, he turned back, daunted by the smell of smoked tobacco and labour-in-vain. The kitchen smelled gaily of onions and India, and he would eat his supper there. His hand went out for Loveday's book. This time, he would begin at the beginning, and find out what the young man was up to—he was bound to be young, nowadays they were all young men. Seeing the first page so branded with over-anxiety, and finding the curry so accomplished, he muttered to himself that malt does more than Milton can, that if he consulted his own pleasure, he would drown his books, dismiss Loveday, and devote himself entirely to the satisfactions of cookery. After the first few pages—quite properly a little stiff, for if you cannot begin like Byron it is much better not to try to—*Reverse the Sun* seriously delighted him. He began to match his reading to the book, pausing to consider, turning back to compare one stroke with another. After those annihilating gallops over the High Hope course, just to be reading so was pleasure in itself. At times he stopped quite uncritically, halted by sheer astonishment at finding something so unforeseeably well managed. Yet though the book astonished him, it was congenial too, the fruit of a congenial mind: a scrupulous, searching, disdainful mind, with a vein of black bile. It was against this Calvinistic melancholy that the details of the narrative stood out with such brilliance, as though they were reeds and dragonflies taunting the vision of a drowning man. He read it to the end, and went to bed thinking of it, and thinking of the letter he would write to Norman Leigh. Words slipped through his mind, a little greasily from having been fingered by every reviewer. Rare . . . judicious . . . distinction . . . originality . . . authenticity . . . Plagiarism! That word didn't slip! It seized on him, as ice is welded on a warm hand. The fellow was a plagiarist, an aper, a purloiner! And how near he had been to writing to congratulate his ape! He sat up in bed, shaking with fury. 'Blast his impertinence,' he said: and the exclamation doddered, because he had taken out his teeth.

He lay down again, stiffly humiliated, and tried to compose his feelings. These things happen, he told himself. Young hawks pick out old hawks' eyes, each generation begins its course with such a stirrup-cup; and at the end of a career of honest work with small thanks for it, there is even a sort of compliment in being found worth stealing from. 'Dear Mr Leigh'—the letter might be sent, after all—'Thank you for your kind attention to my writings. I am gratified to find that they have been of use to you.' But his resentment could not be sneered away. It had too much grief in it. He grieved for the brief duration of his pleasure in the book, he grieved for his dreamily decaying wits, and his grief was made weightier by a sense of bereavement. For the time was gone by when he had enjoyed his reputation of singularity, of being the only writer to write like Matthew Bateman. In *Reverse the Sun* there had been something corroborative, a look of kindred—so he had thought, till the look of kindred was reshaped into a pasteboard mask held before a thief's face. How could he have become so dull that he did not recognise his own imitation? Loveday herself could not have failed to notice it. Everyone must notice it. His anger, once more charging ahead, plunged him into another morass. Why should anyone notice it? He was known by his reputation, not by his books. At best, a few people reading Norman Leigh might remark on a slight influence of Matthew Bateman, which it was to be hoped would soon be shed.

He could bear it no longer. He had drugs beside him, and in the next room there was alcohol, but for him there was only one reliable form of dramming. He got up, dressed and went grimly to his desk. With the beard poking from his jaws, he sat till the first blade of sunrise thrust through the curtain-chink. Writing fluently, he had covered a dozen pages. He drew them together, astonished to find so much accomplished. Perhaps, after all, he might live to be grateful to Loveday's lending library author. Mettled by jealousy, roused from being the unique Matthew Bateman into being a competitor, he had not done so badly. He sorted the new pages into order, and was laying them down, when a sentence caught his eye. It wouldn't do. He was ringing it, when another sentence grimaced at him from further down the page. He read more attentively. Everything he had written that night smelled of Norman Leigh.

Too tired for any more rages, he groaned, and looked out of the window, rubbing his cheeks. Here was another day. The sky was clouding over, the macrocarpus hedge twitched before an oncoming wind. It would be a day to write in; but as things stood, it was the day when Loveday would come back. Before she came, there would be brewers, bakers and candlestick-makers coming to the door, and he must shave and spruce himself. That meant the electric kettle. He walked into the kitchen. It retained the previous night as a bed retains an act of carnality. The meal was still on the table, the unwashed saucepans stood hardening on the stove, the sink was littered with onion peelings and grains of rice. Lying in the crumpled cretonne lap of the armchair, and occupying the whole kitchen, was *Reverse the Sun*.

He heard time falling like drops of water from the clock on the wall. Time cannot be put back, the book was there, and he had read it, and it could never be unread. But it remained that the deed should never be known, and so he would put the book back on the window-sill whence he had taken it. Holding it at arm's length, he crossed the room with it, and stiffly set it down. He was turning away when a further initiation into criminality told him that he might have left a crumb in it, or a shred of tobacco. He took hold of it by the covers, and gave it a shake. The action tossed him into bodily fury, and he shook it long and savagely. It was only when the noise of the fluttered pages reminded him of a bird's wings that he was able to control himself and put it down. The paper jacket had slipped awry. He straightened it, and before he could stop himself he had begun to read the publisher's note on the inside flap.

Norman Leigh, whose death from poliomyelitis at the age of twenty-six cut short . . .

It was as if he had heard his whole being utter a shout of triumph.

Slowly, an agony of shame overwhelmed him. He did not know what to do.

At last something stirred in his cavernous discouragement, and was remorse. He turned to the first page, and began to read. There it was, that rather stiff, rather defensive opening: the scabbard, with the blade of a purpose lying in it.

The postman, and after him the woman who brought the milk, passing the kitchen window saw Miss Patterson's old gentleman standing within, reading a book. When they knocked and got no answer, they concluded that Miss Patterson's old gentleman must be deaf, and left parcels and milk on the doorstep. Later, when his legs began to tremble with fatigue, he went down on his knees to read. By then, however, there were no more daily comers, to conclude that he was praying. When cramp began to eat away his power of concentration, he hauled himself to his feet, drank some cold coffee, and settled down in the armchair.

For a long time after he had finished the book, he sat thinking. One thing still perplexed him: whether the evocations of himself (and a second reading made them unmistakably plain) were deliberate imitation or the expression of a mind like his own and working with a similar intention. He would have liked to know this; but he never would know, and, after all, it was not so very important. It was more significant that Norman Leigh, writing like Matthew Bateman, had written a better book than ever Matthew Bateman had set his name to; and would not write another. He was dead, this young man who had already matched and surpassed him. Matthew Bateman, so long and complacently a man without a match, lived on, a man without an heir. Putting the book down on the table, he laid his cheek against it, and fell asleep.

Waking much later, he retained a steadied sense of bereavement and a steady knowledge as to what must be done. First, the kitchen must be put in order. Then he must straighten his bed; finally, his desk. He went at it calmly, too much fatigued to be conscious of any additional effort. Once only he was impeded by an uncertainty of purpose, and that was when he came to the manuscript on his desk. But after a glance at the bookshelf, he let it be. Those deplorable favourites had taken their chance, and so should this. He took the pistol from the drawer, and checked that it was in order. A minimum of oil and attention will keep such things in condition, though they lie for years unused and unthought-of. The habit of carrying it with him when he travelled had conveyed it to Maidstone, and now it was here. A last thought struck him. He went from room to room opening the windows. The air flowed in, impartial and absolving. Air flows in, soul flies out. But that is for the housebound deathbed; for his part, he had no notion to die anywhere but out of doors. Blood, so unseemly on a carpet, soon assimilates itself to earth.

He went out, and into the patch of ground at the back of the house where the dogs were buried and the horseradish grew. Frost had already touched the strong-grown serpentine leaves. Their edges were fraying, their green was blotched as if with rust. Rubbing one against another in the slow wind, they made a grating noise, one might almost call it clanking—or would that be a Gongorism? One must be on one's guard against . . . He remembered that the obligation to be on one's guard was now at an end. All he had to do was to decide whether to shoot through the eye or the ear. The eye is infallible, yet most people flinch at that who flinch at nothing else, and prefer to blow their brains out through the ear. He would wait for the robin to end its little stanza, and then he would shoot himself through the eye.

The robin flew up. Loveday's voice, a little out of breath, said, 'Oh, Mr Bateman, are you after that rat? He's about here every evening. But you won't get him now, for I saw him run into the hedge as I came out.'

'Oh! Did you? Well, so here you are. Did you enjoy yourself at Margate?'

'Oh, yes, Mr Bateman. I had a very nice time. The sea looked so calm, I quite wanted to go on it.'

Ramsgate was where he had advised her to go, Ramsgate was where she had been. But Loveday knew that this was not a moment in which to be geographical. It was enough that she had come back, found all the windows open and that manuscript blown all over the floor, and Mr Bateman up to no good. Up to no good: she would not allow herself to think more explicitly. To do so would not help him or her. Talking of the blueness of the sea, the whiteness of the cliffs, the devastations of war, the unexpectedness of sitting down on a bench and finding Lucy Petter, whom she had not seen for years, sitting at the other end of it, she stood conversing among the horseradish, wearing shoes that had become too tight for her and a hat like an apple-turnover.

'You really ought to go to the seaside for a few days yourself, Mr Bateman. It's wonderful! When I woke up this morning, and heard the waves—I can't describe how I felt; but somehow, it did seem so extraordinary.'

Little by little, she got him indoors, and sitting down, and fed. He shivered; and when he spoke, though what he said was ordinary enough, his voice sounded as if it had not been used for a twelvemonth. It looked to her, she said, as if he might have a cold coming on, nothing likelier than that he should have got chilled waiting about for that rat. The pistol was still in his trouser pocket. When she had given him a hot whisky and seen him settled in his bed, she carried off his suit to give it a good brushing.

'No waves tomorrow, poor Loveday,' he called through the closing door. A weight fell off her heart: he was not planning any more excursions for her. Whatever it might be that she had been sent out of the way of, whatever the solitary drama whose last act she had interrupted, it was at an end. But, to be on the safe side, she dropped the pistol into a larder crock containing haricot beans. The larder looked as if a hurricane had raged in it. He must have been putting things tidy: but she would leave it so until tomorrow. Tomorrow. She sighed, stooping to take off her shoes. At this time yesterday evening she and Lucy Petter were sitting in the ice-cream parlour, and Lucy was saying, 'Secretary? It strikes me that you're nothing but an old man's darling. What future is there in that, my girl? The future—that's what you should keep your eye on.' 'But Mr Bateman is a very distinguished writer, Lucy.' 'Distinguished writer? He must be, if that's all he pays you, and gets away with it.' Lucy's diagnosis had frightened her. During the journey back she had reasoned fright into prudence, and she entered High Hope quite resolved to tell Mr Bateman that she needed to find another post—a post where she could keep in better practice and use her shorthand. Now all that was out of the question. She could not think of leaving anyone who looked as lonely as he had done, standing in that derelict patch you couldn't call a garden. She would write to Lucy, telling her that High Hope would continue to be her address, but giving no reason. And before going to bed she would finish that book from the library, and have it done up ready for the postman to take in the morning, so that she could get another.

(*Winter in the Air*, 1955)

BOORS CAROUSING

IT was still raining, it was half-past two in the afternoon. Mrs Gainsborough had gone home, and would not be back till she came at half-past six to see about his dinner: he had his house to himself and the long afternoon before him.

No one would come interrupting in, the rain would see to that. Though country neighbours too often look on a snow-storm or an easterly gale as prevenient to a rousing walk and a call round about tea-time, this was summer rain: it would keep them at home, disapproving—irrationally, since the rainfall of an English summer is higher than the rainfall of an English winter. But they were not governed by reason.

He walked into the hall and took his telephone receiver off its stand. It began to utter the soft, duteous growl it would keep up till Mrs Gainsborough came and replaced it. He stood listening to the only noise in the silence of his house. A heavenly and nourishing silence. No little footsteps on the stairs, no little smears of jam on the stair-rail. Magdalen and her brats had torn themselves away that morning. True, in the loving moment of riddance he had sketched an invitation for Christmas; but Christmas was a long way off, and by then, he hoped, his brother-in-law would be out of his job in Army Education and enforcing his natural dislike of intellectuals. All through his lovely empty house rang the noise of the rain, singing in the gutters, lisping against the window-panes, plashing on the flagged walk; and in his mind's ear he heard the most melodious rainfall of all, *l'eau qui tombe dans l'eau*, the rain falling into the swollen river that washed the foot of his garden and tugged at his Chinese willows. To look through the windows of a Georgian house at a Chinese view. . . . He sighed with contentment at his lot and went back to his library.

With a whole afternoon before him in which to write, it would be slavish, he thought, and sinning his mercies, to begin to write immediately. He would read for a little first. The act of reading, the effacement of mind in a kindred mind, *l'eau qui tombe dans l'eau*, puts one in the best frame for the act of writing. He would read for a little, then he would settle down to write; and seriously, working on his philosophical novel where he aimed to apply the narrow brush of Jane Austen to a Tiepoloesque design; for the charms of philosophy are usually obliterated by a style of revolting romanticism, all tufts and vapours. With Magdalen in the house he had found it almost impossible to get on with the novel; he had written short stories, a prey to human nature—which is poison and dram-drinking to the serious artist.

Half an hour later he put down his book, saying *Damn!* A knock on the front door had resounded through the house. Sitting motionless, he listened, and presently there was another knock.

'Blast these people who can't use the bell!' he muttered. Life in the country had taught him that there are two kinds of visitors: those who ring the bell and those who knock. Those who ring the bell are at least semi-educated and can be relied upon, after three or four rings, to use their wits and go away. Those who knock are the poor and humble, accustomed to being kept waiting, accustomed to being ignored. With the pertinacity of the down-trodden they are capable of knocking for an hour on end.

A third knock sounded, no louder than the first. After an interval, no longer or shorter than the previous intervals, there was a fourth knock. Exclaiming: 'And in five months' time it will be the carol-singers!' he rose and marched off to open his door.

'Oh, Mr Kinloch! I see it's you, Mr Kinloch. I am so sorry . . .'

'Do come in.'

'No, no, I wouldn't interrupt you for the world. I just came to ask you—such a silly question, really. Do you think it will go on raining?'

'Undoubtedly, I should say. Do come in.'

'I said to myself, I'll just run up and ask Mr Kinloch. I felt sure you'd have a barometer. I'm Miss Metcalf, you know.'

She was wearing a sou'wester, and the rain poured off it, and from under the brim and behind the raindrops she peered at him—like an elderly mermaid, he thought, who had taken to country life. Her name was Metcalf, and she was a maniac. So far, so good.

'Miss Metcalf,' she repeated. 'I live down by the river.'

Dort oben wunderbar. He repeated his invitation to come in.

'I don't know if you've noticed how the river is rising. All this rain, of course. I'm so worried about the rabbits. There are eight young ones.'

He said that probably their doe would look after them.

'But she can't. She's in the same boat. At least, it's a coop really, a sort of coop.'

'Dear, dear!' he said. 'But I wish you'd come in. You are getting so needlessly wet.'

She stared at him desperately.

'It only needs lifting. If it could be lifted on to the table—for I always keep a table in the garden, it's so nice in summer and one can put things on it—everything would be all right. But it *is* rather heavy, and the rabbits get so nervous and rush about like a shipwreck. . . .'

'I'll come at once,' he said, dimly and gloomily realising an appeal to his manly strength.

At his gate there was a moment of awkwardness, for he turned to the left and set off briskly towards the village. She followed him tugging at his sleeve.

'It's the other way, Mr Kinloch. I'm Miss Metcalf, you know. I daresay you thought I was Miss Hancock. *She* lives by the church.'

They turned about, and splashed down a lane and across a sopping meadow where an indeterminate track led into a grove of willows and alders which was also, apparently, a rubbish-tip for the village, since some old iron bedsteads and disused oil-heaters glowered rustily among the tree-trunks. Beyond this, suddenly and surprisingly whitewashed and neat, was Miss Metcalf's dwelling, like a bandbox abandoned on the river's brim by someone who had committed suicide. And the river, just as Miss Metcalf had said, had risen enough to be washing over its banks and round a rabbit-hutch. He clasped the hutch—it was revoltingly cold and slimy—and lifted it on to a table.

'It seems a pity,' he said, for somehow he had to overcome her pelt of thanks and apologies for having troubled him, 'to keep such a handsome mahogany table out of doors.'

'Oh yes, Mr Kinloch, I often think so myself. But what am I to do?

There is no room for it indoors and it belonged to my father. He was the rector, you know.'

So that was who she was! He had often heard her story and no doubt he had heard her name as often; but the two had become disconnected in his memory. Miss Metcalf's father had been the Reverend Thomas Metcalf, sometime Rector of this Parish and now resident under a very ornate and informative tombstone, which did not, however, mention that he had drunk himself and his fortune out of existence, which was why poor old Miss Metcalf lived where and how she did and was a trifle eccentric, you know.

But it seemed to him a charming place to live, if one did not object to being flooded from time to time and kept oneself uncompromised by rabbits. Her view was better than his own; for one thing it included his house, and at exactly the right distance to be seen at its best. Fortunate Miss Metcalf, who could gaze down the river all day at his south elevation, while screened from the world by her thicket of willows, alders, and old bedsteads! No one was likely to come knocking at her door. A time might come—a time might come too easily, if the housing shortage continued and he could no longer fend off impertinent enquiries as to how many bedrooms he had and whether he did not feel quite lonely all by himself in such a large house—when he might be very comfortable here. He did not suppose she would live for ever—and surely she and her rabbits would be much better off farther—so to speak—inland.

Meanwhile Miss Metcalf had become somewhat sprightly and was asking him in for what she called 'just a wee drappie'. It was now too late to refuse, so he followed her under a trellised porch that was like Niagara, and past what he believed to be a mangle to her parlour. Anyhow, he was pleased to, for he wanted to see the inside of her place.

There was this much to be said for it, it was totally unrestored; and with a very small expenditure and the right kind of fixings one could make the room very agreeable indeed. He noted the alcoves on either side of the hearth, their shelves now sagging beneath cloth-bound divinity and The Badminton Library, but worthy of his Montesquieu, and the latticed windows, so very jessamy, and the delicate original fire-place hidden behind that appallingly burly anthracite stove. One could make of it just such a room as de Quincey enjoyed those winter evenings in—omitting Margaret and the ruby-coloured laudanum. Of course one would have to put in drains and electricity and that sort of thing. Meanwhile he sat compressed between a portentous sideboard and a portentous table with an oil-lamp in its centre, and opposite him sat Miss Metcalf, backed by a harmonium and offering him cigarettes. No wonder she kept tables in the garden. He had never seen so much furniture, and all so frightful, in his life. The room was icily and cleanlily cold, and smelt of honest poverty. How on earth she cleaned it, how on earth she scrubbed the encumbered oil-cloth . . .

Miss Metcalf remarked that she would have a little one too, to keep him company.

Yet the room did not look damp, it was just because she kept no fires.

'How I wish I had a siphon! If I had known all this was going to happen, I would have gone to the grocer. Say When.'

He said. But would to God he had accepted it neat! For this was pre-war whisky, relict of the Reverend Thomas Metcalf's deep cellar, strong and smooth as silk. Fortunately she had obeyed his saying of When with instantaneous accuracy. One could see she was a drunkard's daughter, and well-trained.

'Personally I should never be surprised to wake up and find myself floating down the river—away and away! This is such a treacherous time of year, don't you think, and how one dislikes seeing swallows on telegraph wires! Do have another! To keep the cold out.'

Yes, one could be uncommonly cosy here, listening to the river and the trees, hearing the oil-lamp purr (for sentiment's sake one might keep an oil-lamp and use it from time to time, though de Quincey evenings would demand candles), reflecting on one's deep ensconced solitude. No one would come to stay in such a house as this. They could not. He would turn the second bedroom into a bathroom.

'I often wonder where I should get to. Out to sea, perhaps. But even in mid-Atlantic I should remember your kindness to my rabbits. Beverens, you know. I could not bear to eat them.'

He glanced across the table. She also was keeping the cold out, and it had greatly improved her. Sister to the beauty of the young leaf is the beauty of the skeleton leaf, having the last skirmish of its vegetable blood before the winter sucks it into the mould. She had pulled off her sou'wester. Her cropped hair was white as thistledown, and when she laughed, a wrinkle appeared on her long sheep's nose. But was this the last bottle of Mr Metcalf's whisky, or would it be possible, possible . . . ? No doubt she was all filial piety, the daughters of abominable fathers always are; but five guineas would be more to her advantage: with five guineas she could light a roaring fire in that deserted Moloch's altar there.

'I see you are looking at that picture, Mr Kinloch.'

The walls of the room were plastered with things in frames, and he was not consciously looking at any of them. But now he followed the direction of her glance to the picture above the mantelpiece. It was a large steel-plate engraving, luridly brilliant. *Kermesse*, perhaps, or possibly *Boors Carousing*.

'It is a very fine specimen, I believe. And very valuable. My dear father thought the world of it.' Leaning across the table, her light whiskied breath on her cheek, she exclaimed, 'Sometimes I think I will take it down! *But if I did*,' she said, '*what can I put in its place?*'

'Why need you put anything?'

'Oh, I must, I must! Because, you see, if I took it down, there would be the patch on the wallpaper. The different-coloured patch where the wallpaper hasn't faded. It would always be there to remind me.'

'True.'

True, indeed. It would always be there to remind her. Absent or present, the boors would always be carousing. Morning, noon, and night Miss Metcalf would see those drunken, grinning faces, those paunches, overturned flagons, and wrinkled boots, those frank vomits and idiot rejoicings. Morning, noon, and night it would remind her of the Reverend Thomas Metcalf who had drunk himself to death and left her stupefied and penniless. Absent or present, it would taunt her with an inherited alcoholism, a desperate maidenly desire for strong drink.

Even at this moment, overset by her confidence, she had begun to whimper, and the first tears were rolling gaily down her flushed cheeks. In compassion and horror Adam Kinloch got up and made his hasty farewells.

Midway in the meadow he stopped and wrung his hands. The poor old wretch, the hapless elderly Iphigenia! Chance and the swollen river had brought her to his door, but only as another chance, and the swollen river, might have carried her past it. *Regrettable death of one of our oldest parishioners, Miss Metcalf, daughter of the late Revd. T. Metcalf, once Rector of Little Bidding. The deceased lady presumably fell into the river whilst attending to her rabbits, to which she was devoted. All those who knew her will feel her loss.*

All those who knew her! He began to walk on again, his hands in his pockets. All those who laughed at her, and hinted about her, and never went near her. There was nothing for it, he would have to pull himself together and be neighbourly to Miss Metcalf, take her for drives, ask her to tea, give her fur gloves at Christmas. Perhaps he could find a nice cheerful water-colour of some Welsh mountains to replace the *Boors Carousing*. But really the kindest thing to do would be to walk down with a bottle from time to time, and tipple with her. He would sit in her father's chair, and as the evening wore on, and the chairs creaked louder, she would scarcely distinguish him from the Reverend Thomas; all would be as it was, she would be a girl again, sipping from father's wonderful glass, and feeling proud to sit up so late like a grown woman. What a story she would make!

'You to the life!' he said aloud. 'Do nothing for her, but put her into a story.' The admission released him. He quickened his pace, he bounded up the steps to his door, he let himself in, he threw off his wet coat, he glanced at his wrist-watch. It was four o'clock. It was still raining. With a long sigh of relief he walked sedately into his library, sat down, and pulled a writing-pad towards him.

(*The Museum of Cheats*, 1947)

ON LIVING FOR OTHERS

EXPLAINING that he wished to walk home across the fields, Hugh Whiting left his suitcase at the station, to be picked up later in the day.

'Didn't think to see you back so soon,' said the booking-office clerk, who four hours earlier had issued him a return ticket to London and watched him board a local train. 'Hope nothing's wrong, sir.'

'Nothing at all, Parker. I changed my mind. Silly to go to London on a day like this.'

The words made Parker more conscious of the warm air, the blue sky. He strolled to the doorway and watched Mr Whiting go down the road and turn off into a grassy track, walking with an easy rhythmical stride. The young porter came out to see what Parker was looking at.

'Pretty good for a man of his age,' said Parker, as if he took pride in it.

'Regular old bachelor, isn't he?'

'Bachelor in his way, may be. He was married when he came here first. But she died. He went away for a couple of years, then he came back to Badknocks, and there he's lived ever since.'

The track led to a group of farm buildings, where the footpath branched off through the fields. They were beanfields, and fields of standing hay. The beans had just come into bloom. The clusters of black-and-white flowers gave out a smell like that of lilies, but with a lighter sweetness. Oboe, Hugh thought, not clarinet. The distinction had occurred to him many years before, and every summer recurred. He was a composer—eminent rather than well known. The course of time that had made him eminent had also made him somewhat out of date. The reason he had packed the suitcase and taken the ticket for London was that on that same afternoon the Ferrabosco Society was performing a seventeenth-century masque he had orchestrated for them. A meeting of the Advisory Committee would follow, and afterward he was to dine and sleep at Adela Turpin's flat, where he would find Humphrey Dudgeon, whose opera on Hannibal was in rehearsal for the Aldeburgh Festival. If only he had not made that silly joke. . . . One should never make jokes on the telephone; the acoustics aren't right for it. To his inquiry how a sufficiency of elephants could be got on to that small stage Adela had replied, 'But it's *opera da camera*, darling!' Thoughts of this, and of the Advisory Committee, where Hilda Carpentras would repeat that the 'cello is no real substitute for the viola da gamba and everyone would snub old Jones, assailed him even before his local train reached its first stop. By the time it had got him to the main-line junction, he had turned from stoicism to opportunism, telling himself, as he walked up and down the platform, that if he had stayed at home a sense of duty would have teased him into doing something about Mrs Pilkington's Mass, a commission he had spent the last six months in wishing he had never accepted. If the London train had not been late, presumably he would have got into it. But it was late. This was the last straw, and he clutched it. He sent off telegrams of apology, ate some buffet sandwiches, and when the local train came in, which it did with exact punctuality, he returned by it. Now he was walking through the smell of bean flowers, which would not have happened if he had not set out for London. And tonight he would lie down in his fourposter bed with the quickened appreciation of knowing how nearly it had been exchanged for a skimpy divan in Hampstead.

He reached the summit of a gentle rise and looked down, like a returning Ulysses, on the landscape that had been his for so many years. He could see his ilexes but not the house itself. A tune that came to him long ago and had associated itself with this first view of the ilexes resumed its easy hold on him. It wasn't much of a tune, and he had never made anything of it, but at this point of the walk it would come up and link arms with him, as though it had waited to meet him there, and for the rest of the way would accompany him, step for step. He was grateful for its company, for he was wearing his town shoes, and by the time the path brought him into the lane they were hurting his feet. The rope-soled shoes he gardened in lay in the porch and sitting down on his doorstep he changed into them. Then he tried the door. It was locked.

Audrey, excellent creature, had finished her cleaning and gone home. He let himself in. Audrey had closed all the windows but left the inner doors open, so that the air should circulate. He saw that everything was just as he'd left it, just as it should be. All he had to do was to go round and open the windows. But first he must get rid of those shoes. He could not put them down on anything in the passage, for there was nothing to put them down on. Julia had said, 'Let us leave the passage just as it was, so that there will always be something to remind us of how we felt when we first walked in.' And the passage had remained just as it was, with the row of pegs, and the wallpaper of gaudy roses on the low ceiling, under which her coffin had been carried out. Holding his shoes he went upstairs and into the bedroom.

A man and a girl were lying asleep on the fourposter bed. The girl was Audrey. She lay on her back with her mouth half open. The man lay sprawled across her, with his head on her breast. Their lovemaking had cast them into so deep a sleep that neither of them stirred. Ugly, and dishevelled, and disquietingly life-size, they had nothing beautiful about them—only a nobility of being completely unaware.

Hugh was half-way down the stairs before he realised that the man's face was known to him. It was the face of the Rural District Council's rodent officer, a stocky young man who from time to time came to the door offering to put down rat poison, and whom he as often turned away. But as he had never before seen him half naked and asleep, the recognition had been delayed. Now his laggard fury exploded. It was the outrage committed against his bed that angered him. His bed, his honourable lonely bed, had been dishonoured, like a Shakespearean bed. And by a rodent officer! If it had been a plain ratcatcher he could have laughed it off, so much are we at the mercy of a word. But a rodent officer had usurped his bed, and he felt ready to roar like Othello.

The flare of rage, with no action to feed on, quivered out, and left him to grope between desolation and embarrassment. With the pleasure of return torn from him, and made an interloper in his own house, he stood there, still clasping the pair of shoes, and could have wept over his disappointment. But if you are an old man, and employ a young woman to scrub your floors with her strong red arms and her willing nature, and go off on a summer's morning and return unlooked for, you have no one but yourself to blame if your return is not what you expected of it.

On his desk lay the *Canzona* for contralto and two bassoons, and in the kitchen was the coffee-pot. But there was nothing for it; unfortunate righteous householder that he was, he must creep away like a criminal and leave an untroubled exit for the lovers. Since the shoes could not be left, mutely accusing, at the foot of the stairs, he stepped cautiously into the sitting-room, where they could be concealed under the sofa; and at the same moment, as though he had provoked it, there was a vague languishing sound overhead, a yawn that shaped itself into an endearment—Audrey waking to her rodent officer.

He thrust the shoes under the valance and stole out of the house and down the path, glancing guiltily from side to side. But there was no one in sight, to betray him by bursting into conversation. Still undecided where to shelter himself, he turned down the lane, past the pond and Mr Duke's barn and the milestone, past all the things he had noticed with temporary leave-taking when the taxi drove him to the station that morning. One thing had become quite certain. He would resign from the Ferrabosco Society. If it had not been for that inept organisation he would not now be wandering comfortless, and driven into the embraces of a bramble patch because an approaching car was too wide for the lane. As it passed him, it slowed down. It stopped. A voice said, 'Isn't that you, Mr Whiting?' A man and a woman got out and bore down on him, the woman saying, 'I knew it was you. I never forget a face. I'm Candida Pilkington, you remember, and this is my husband. We're touring Suffolk, and we thought we'd call in on you to ask how my Mass is getting along. How lucky to catch you like this.'

'Very lucky,' Hugh said. So it was, in a sense; very lucky for the pair slumbering in his fourposter bed. 'Particularly lucky for me,' he added. 'I'm on my way to the church, and now you will be able to give me a lift.'

He had not the slightest idea what was to be done with them, but at least he could show them the church. They were papists, but that was no reason why they should not conform with the decent customs of England, one of which is church-showing. He must also show them who was master.

So he watched them turning the car, without essaying helpfulness, and when they had finally done so he got in as though he were accustomed to bestowing these little favours.

'Are you having a music festival?' Mrs Pilkington's manner indicated a matching readiness to bestow little favours. 'I do think it's such a step forward, using your Anglican churches for festivals. Poor things!'

'Ours is a very small church. Turn to the right.'

'All over pews, too, I suppose. Those fatal pews! Now, in Portugal—'

'Take care of that dog! It's deaf. Personally, I'm in favour of pews. People must sit down somewhere.'

The dog was bearing this out. Mr Pilkington halted, sounded his horn, and then said to himself in a subdued way, 'Silly of me, of course.'

The money was his, as well as the wife, poor wretched man, thought Hugh. 'It's a very old dog,' he went on. 'And being old, it has not much to be interested in except its fleas. So I dare say we shall be here for some time. Tell me about Portugal.'

Portugal and the dog accounted for nearly ten minutes. Ten minutes would seem no time at all to Audrey and her lover. Allowing them, say, another hour for dalliance and fond farewells, and adding a quarter of an hour to that, to keep on the safe side, and subtracting Portugal and the dog, one hour and five minutes must somehow be disposed of before he could invite the Pilkingtons to his house. . . . Stay! Audrey, warm-hearted and domesticated, would certainly give the rodent officer tea. Two hours and five minutes. The hour was now three-forty-five. By six he might call Badknocks his own again. . . . But, no, not at all! There was the six-o'clock news broadcast to be reckoned with; the rodent officer would scarcely leave before he had heard the cricket results. Cricket results and fond farewells. . . . Better say six-thirty.

'Harold! Why don't you get out and move that dog? I can see Mr Whiting is worrying about the time.'

If he had said he was going to the village he could have made something of this. But he had committed himself to the church, and so must do what he could with it. The church had much to offer. They might look through the burial register for Pilkingtons. Or a notice about swine fever in the porch might lead to a visit to Paigle Farm, where Mrs Duke would give them tea.

'Here we are. I don't suppose I shall be long. Perhaps you'd rather wait outside?'

This was mere hopeful foolishness, since he felt assured that nothing would prevent Mrs Pilkington from coming into the church in order to animadvert on its deficiencies. There was nothing about swine fever, so he showed them in.

'If I were to be taken into a church blindfolded,' she said, 'I should know from the moment I was inside what form of faith—'

'Nice little church,' interposed Mr Pilkington.

'So should I,' said Hugh, with blandness.

After a slight pause, Mrs Pilkington observed, 'I can't see why you shouldn't have a festival here, Mr Whiting. It's quite large enough. Too large for the congregation, I've no doubt.'

'We might talk about that. But first of all, I've got to measure some organ pipes. Where would you like to sit?'

One should never go out without a piece of string in one's pocket. Hugh never did, and now he furtively tied some knots in it. When he had measured a rank of visible pipes and scribbled on a piece of paper, he called out encouragingly that now he was going on to the diapasons. Secluding himself in the usual organist's den behind the organ case, he spent the next half hour reading *Thirty-Two Voluntaries by Caleb Simper*, a work that he found there. He read with professional attention, coming to the conclusion that Simper missed a lot of opportunities.

Another expedient suggested itself to him.

'Well, that's over,' he said as he emerged from behind the organ case. 'I'm sorry if I kept you waiting, but one can't hurry over these things. Now, since I've got you here, I'll take you up on the tower.'

'Mr Whiting, before you do that—'

The tower door was locked. 'I expect the key's in the vestry,' he said. 'I won't keep you a moment.'

'—there are one or two little suggestions I'd like to make,' Mrs Pilkington went on.

She'd like to make suggestions, would she? Disregarding the woman, he hurried into the vestry. A bunch of keys was rather imperfectly concealed behind a fire extinguisher, and probably one or other of them would fit the tower door; but this was of less importance now, since a far fruitfuller and more congenial expedient had met his eye.

He returned, jingling the keys.

'One or two little suggestions, Mr Whiting,' Mrs Pilkington repeated.

He began trying the keys.

'About my Mass.'

Her Mass, indeed! The fourth key turned the lock. The opened door disclosed a narrow cascade of steps, with a dead rook lying on one of them.

'Harold has no head for heights,' Mrs Pilkington said.

Hugh had no stomach for dead rooks, and found he could temper justice with mercy. He locked the door, and waved the Pilkingtons into a pew, and leant against a pillar, looking down on them—which he could do handsomely, since he was both long and lean.

'I am proposing to write this Mass strictly *a capella*, Mrs Pilkington. It will be for five voices.'

'Why, we've got more than that, I can assure you. Sneckheaton is a very musical neighbourhood and there isn't much our choir won't undertake.'

'Five vocal parts. The number of voices singing a part is more or less immaterial, provided there is a proper balance of tone. I hope your tenors are under control. North Country tenors are apt to be aggressive.'

This was a mistake, for by incensing Mrs Pilkington's racial loyalty he renewed her determination to make that Mass her own. A sort of solo for Jimmy Rawson, who could have sung in opera only he wouldn't leave his mother, was one of the suggestions she had at heart; another was places where the congregation could join in; another that *Hosannas* should be sung, *pianissimo*, by a small body of trebles in the loft, to bear out the sense of *in excelsis*. 'And what was the last thing? I know it was very important. Harold, what was the last thing? Oh yes, I remember. *Et in unam ecclesiam.* Mr Whiting, I want that section to be all in unison, and thoroughly emphatic. I want it to stand out, with a real broad, compelling melody; for, as I see it, that's one of the vital spots in the creed, and we can't make too much of it.'

There was this to be said for her suggestions, Whiting thought: they helped to pass the time. By now Audrey might be thinking about tea. He was.

'Well,' he said briskly. 'If you'll come into the vestry I will give you an idea of the music I have in mind—on the harmonium.'

'On a harmonium?'

'A harmonium.'

'But why can't you play it on the organ? Can't you play the organ?'

'I prefer the harmonium for *a capella.*'

The vestry faced north. It smelled of mice, paraffin, and ink. When Hugh opened the harmonium, a cloud of dispirited dust rose slowly into the air, and when he tried the pedals, a smell of mouldy leather was exhaled. He eyed the stops. Diapason, reed, bourdon, dulciana. He pulled out dulciana, and the knob fell off in his hand. But it was a game old instrument, and came snoring and tottering back to life under the easy rhythmical tread that Mr Parker had admired earlier that afternoon.

'Are you comfortably settled? Good! Now we'll begin. *Kyrie eleison.*' For the next thirty minutes, he extemporised in the key of G, drawing freely on Caleb Simper for his material, but chastening it. At intervals, he cast them a guiding word, or drew their attention to a canon at the octave. His guiding cry at *Et expecto* was answered by a snore from Mr Pilkington, who from then on snored as methodically as a ground bass. The harmonium also threw in some touches of its own, not so easily reconciled with strict *a capella* style as Mr Pilkington's snores; but in the main it answered to the helm. As for Mrs Pilkington, she stayed mute as a mousetrap.

I wonder what she's hatching, Hugh thought. He also wondered how much longer his ankles would hold out, for the bellows demanded a discreetly adjusted supply of wind, and discretion is a much greater tax on the ankles than fervour.

Wondering about his ankles, and Mrs Pilkington, and how Audrey and the rodent officer were getting on, he allowed his attention to stray from Caleb Simper and engage itself with Hugh Whiting, whose demands presently became rather engrossing and led him into the mixolydian mode and a five-four measure. Here a passage seemed to him so interesting that he paused to memorise it.

'And is that the end?'

As she spoke, Mr Pilkington suspended his ground bass.

'That is the end.'

'Oh. You didn't say so.'

He replaced the knob on dulciana and closed the harmonium, giving it, since he couldn't treat it to a bran mash, a grateful pat.

'Well, Mr Whiting, I'm afraid I've got to be frank. I don't like it.'

'No?'

'No. I feel it lacks sincerity.'

Just so, with the same uninspired acumen, she would have said to the fishmonger, 'That herring's not fresh.' He was on the brink of esteeming her, when she continued, 'Mind you, we'll pay for it.'

'Naturally. One does, when one has commissioned a thing. Shall we go out, and look at tombstones?'

For, after all, he could not esteem her, and he did not suppose that the hypothetical fishmonger would have esteemed her, either. Fishmongers resent bad manners; they are not marble slabs. Discarding the thought that he would get Pilkington's cheque having done uncommonly little to earn it, he began to question him about the tour through Suffolk.

'One thing's disappointed me,' said Pilkington. 'I did hope to see a man-orchis.'

'A man-orchis? Well, if you take the lane that goes off behind the Wesleyan Chapel and follow along it till you come to the second signpost, and turn left, and left again just after a bridge, and on till you come to an old windmill, and get out there, and go through a white gate—'

He broke off. They were now in the churchyard, and beyond the churchyard wall was the rector, hurrying forward with welcoming looks to greet a young man. 'Here you are! I had almost given up hopes of you. Don't apologise, don't apologise! Better late than never.'

The young man he had almost given up hopes of was the rodent officer.

The warmth of the sun and the blue of the sky and the blackness of the rector and the smell of the churchyard yews and the ache in his ankles and all the outrages of that interminable afternoon, from his dishonoured bed to Mrs Pilkington's acumen, together with the residual surliness that accompanies the knowledge that one has been behaving rather disgracefully, all melted, for Hugh, into a harmonious and Amen-like realisation that he could now go home. And alone; for Mrs Pilkington was getting into the car.

'Hurry up, Harold! We really must be getting on.'

'Yes. We really must be getting on,' said Harold. He said it in an undertone, as though addressing only himself, and just as he had said 'Silly of me, of course' after sounding the horn at the deaf dog. No doubt he often addressed himself, not having much expectation that remarks addressed to others would be attended to, except possibly in the confessional. 'Goodbye, Whiting. It's been a very interesting afternoon. Very interesting. I'm afraid we've taken up a great deal of your time.'

'Harold!'

Harold lingered, as though he were waiting for something he knew wouldn't happen, then turned and walked to the gate. How extraordinary, thought Hugh, that those two may have lain together as obliviously as Audrey and the ratcatcher.

'Goodbye, Mr Whiting,' Mrs Pilkington said.

'Stop! Stop, I'm coming with you,' Hugh called.

Since Mr Pilkington was at the wheel, the car stopped. Hugh got in. He said to Mrs Pilkington, 'Your husband wants to see a man-orchis —*Aceras anthropophora*—and he won't find the place unless I go with him.'

Mr Pilkington made unerringly for the Wesleyan Chapel, followed the lane behind it, kept on past the first signpost and at the second turned left, and left again after crossing the bridge, and drew up beside the old windmill. There was no need to guide him; the directions were written on his heart. Mrs Pilkington stayed in the car, remarking that they didn't want her—her acumen again—and that she'd rather sit quietly with a book. They walked for a couple of miles over heathy pasture land, for the most part in silence. Mr Pilkington appeared to be in a species of trance, and Hugh was tired. When they neared the place where the man-orchises grew, he sat down and left Mr Pilkington to find them for himself. Mr Pilkington strayed and gazed and strayed and gazed, and watching him Hugh reflected on the pursuit—so arduous and so haphazard—of other people's pleasure, and how, in the course of that afternoon, quite without volition or design and totally against his preconceived notion of how he would spend it, he had been instrumental in the pleasure of three people, only one of whom it had ever occurred to him to wish to please, and that one with no more than a very moderate and unspecifying impulse to be pleasant, since the utmost he did by way of pleasing Audrey was to praise her for not disturbing his papers, give her presents at Christmas and Easter, and tip her when she had done something that pleased him. Yet she, and that fellow who was even now preparing an excruciating death for some harmless church mice, and Pilkington—where would their rounded pleasures be if chance had not impressed him to drudge and trudge and moil on their behalf? Chance, and weak-mindedness, since he could perfectly well have hidden in his own garden and never met the Pilkingtons at all. Not that his motives had been entirely pure. It was to spare his own feelings as well as to spare Audrey's that he had slunk from the house. It was as much to wipe Mrs Pilkington's eye as to gladden Mr Pilkington's heart that he had set out for the man-orchises. But he was not interested in the nature of his motives. A pure motive is a barren theme; no speculation branches from it; it is incapable of contrapuntal development. Indeed, his motives, even though impure, had counted for very little. Fortuity and a resolute illusion of free will had shaped his course, wrenching him away from the rational intention of a quiet afternoon under his own roof and hurling him unprepared into a career of living for others. It was a very disorderly way to live. Yet there were people who made a practice of it; and though they were usually wan and fractious, they got on somehow; they brushed their hair and caught their trains and kept out of Bedlam. No doubt it was largely a matter of technique, of keeping in practice. It must be admitted that in the matter of living for others he was out of practice. He was a selfish dog—a quiet, cleanly, abstemious, and selfish dog. And his legs ached, and midges were biting him, and he wanted to creep back into his kennel.

Pilkington was beside him, saying rather sternly, 'I hope you don't take unreliable people to see them—people who might dig them up.'

'You're the only person I've taken.'

Pilkington flushed with pleasure. I've managed that quite well, thought Hugh—though in fact he had spoken defensively and with no intention to please.

Seeing the man-orchises had conjured up a new Pilkington. All the way back, he held forth about wild flowers—those that are regional, those that are true rarities, those that are escapes, those that are dying out through the actions of man. The war, he said, had done incalculable harm, turning the British flora upside down. He knew a great deal, and was rather boring. Fairies are said to live on nectar and the scent of flowers, and Pilkington was like a fairy who had just had a good meal. His eupepsia swept him over the reunion with Mrs Pilkington; he quelled her resentment by being so much more aware of his own satisfaction, and in the end she was forced in self-defence to say that she had been enjoying her book, and had seen a weasel.

'Mr Whiting looks tired,' she remarked.

'Oh dear, I hope not.'

'What he needs is some brandy.' She produced a flask and a cup, stating that one should always take brandy with one, and that she always did. Nothing could render her less unamiable, but it was admirable brandy. Hugh began to feel more like his usual self, and when they assured him that the least they could do was to drive him home, he said that it would be even better if they would first drive to the station, where he had a suitcase waiting to be picked up.

(*A Spirit Rises*, 1962)

PLUTARCO ROO

THE world is full of stories of artists who would not prostitute their talents and so died hungry. The world is almost equally full of stories of artists who did prostitute their talents and so died regretful. This is the story of an artist who preserved his ideals and found a steady market for them. It is true that as an artist he was not of much account, but as a human phenomenon he was a rare specimen. The world is singularly bare of stories which have both a happy and a moral ending.

Plutarco Roo was a Mexican, born in the second half of the last century. Being of extremely mixed race, he doubtless carried in him the strands of many national cultures—Spanish, Aztec, Mixtec, Totonac, Zapotec, and possibly Chihuahuan—but these elements were more of a fertilising than a formative influence; they composed, as it were, an anonymous humus from which flowered an art essentially empirical and of the nineteenth century.

His mother was a hard-working woman of the town. When she died, Plutarco was taken by some good nuns who kept an orphanage. There he was considered satisfactorily pious and adequately industrious, but his creative gifts went unperceived and uncultivated. Plutarco's favourite nun was Mother Remedios, who made the cakes which are sold for All Souls' Day. These cakes are made of sugar in the shape of skulls. The name of a dear dead person is scrolled on to the skull by means of a forcing-pipe, together with some ornaments of tears, lilies, etc. They are bought for picnics in the cemetery, and at the close of the picnics the affectionate relatives eat them.

Under the teaching of Mother Remedios, Plutarco Roo became adept at tears and lilies. He could also put very expressive eyeballs into the sockets, though not every client approved of this variant, considering eyeballs too naturalistic. When the time came for Plutarco to make his living in the world, he was apprenticed to a pastry-cook.

Plutarco Roo's talent was definitely for colour and arabesque. The sculptural element in confectionery made no appeal to him; his buns were uncouth, his crescents unsymmetrical. But his decorative impulse, unfolding with the profusion of a tropical spring, heaped ornament on ornament and ran riot in cochineal and saffron. The pastry-cook accused him of stealing inordinate quantities of sugared rose petals, violet petals, angelica, and small silvered balls in order to eat them. It is true that he stole. But it was not to devour. He kept his thefts in small paper bags under his mattress, and at the hour of siesta, when the pastry-cook and his family were asleep, Plutarco would re-knead a very old and grimy piece of dough (which he also kept under his mattress) and emboss it with various experimental mosaics and floral designs.

He had been reared piously. Now his piety took on a fervent quality. His eyes opened to the delights of religous art, to the hues, surpassing any cochineal or sap green, of nineteenth-century stained glass, to the more than meringue-like suavity of saintly draperies and saintly complexions. He took to wandering from church to church during his working hours. This placed the pastry-cook in a difficult position. It is one thing to track down an idle apprentice to the wine-shop or the market place, whence he can be haled back with a kick and harsh words. It is quite another matter to hale him from the sanctuary where he is kneeling in devout contemplation before an image of St Mary Magdalene.

For some years Plutarco Roo and the pastry-cook continued in this uneasy relationship. As time went on Plutarco's feeling for religious art so outpaced his earlier passion for pure arabesque that he left off stealing rose petals. The pastry-cook indulged a hope that after all he had not been sold such a bad pennyworth by the good nuns and that there was some prospect that the young man might sober down into a useful tradesman, the more so since he was now of an age when he might reasonably be expected to abate some of his religious fervour and begin to attend to the things of this world.

It was with the design of luring Plutarco's attention to the things of this world that the pastry-cook delegated to him the icing of a cake ordered by Don Isidro Barca. This cake, it had been intimated, must be of a grand and festive appearance, an appearance, indeed, semi-nuptial, since it was intended to celebrate the fifth anniversary of Don Isidro's successful introduction to Doña Mercedes Valles-Bosch, the most admired soprano of the town opera company. 'Make it as lively as possible,' said the pastry-cook. 'Take all the doves. A lyre or two also would look well and be appropriate.'

Plutarco was working on the cake till the last possible moment; that, maybe, was why the pastry-cook did not go into all the details as closely as he might have done. It seemed very ornate, very sumptuous, in fact very much what it should be, only rather too sticky. And when, on the morrow of its delivery, Don Isidro Barca came stormily into the shop and slammed it down on the counter, stickiness was the pastry-cook's first thought. 'Such a cake,' he said excusingly, 'takes a long time, takes much thought.'

'Such a cake,' exclaimed Don Isidro, 'takes deliberate malice. But it doesn't take long, or need great perspicacity, to decipher the venomous intention of such insinuations. Look at this! Is that a Cupid? And at this! Is that meagre visionary a nymph? And what do all these harps mean, and all these doves and lilies? I asked for a cake, not for a shrine of the Immaculate Conception. Have I been a Liberal, and a freethinker, and a man of the world for fifty years to be offered a monument of reactionary Gothic? So much for your cake!' And with his cane he whacked the edifice.

Enough unbroken icing remained for it to be quite clear that Plutarco had allowed admiration for religious art to outrun the scope of his material. And as Don Isidro was a man of influence and a good customer, the pastry-cook dismissed Plutarco there and then.

Plutarco did not hesitate over what to do next. He went to a house of Carmelites and asked to enter the religious life. Love of God, he explained, was his motive. Love of art would be his dower. He promised to paint for them such pictures of paradise and of the saints as would make their establishment renowned throughout Mexico and visited by Americans of the North. The Superior seemed unconvinced. For some time Plutarco spoke of art and of vocation, but made little headway. Many young men, said the Superior, felt like this, especially when they had just lost a job. Not many young men, retorted Plutarco, lost their jobs so honourable as he, and he told of the cynical behaviour of Don Isidro Barca and of the treachery of the pastry-cook.

'Persecuted by a Liberal,' murmured the Superior thoughtfully. 'Have you witnesses for this?'

'Ask him yourself,' replied Plutarco. 'Ask the pastry-cook. Ask, above all, to see the cake. That will show you what sort of artist I am.'

Plutarco was accepted for a novitiate. A novitiate is a very active experience. Plutarco had no time for practising art, and not much time even for thinking about it. He grew despondent; but just then a small earthquake took place, which caused a great deal of dust. It became imperative to spring-clean the chapel. A local firm of ecclesiastical decorators was called in. Statues were scrubbed with soda and wire brushes, altar-pieces were renewed, the chapel became almost unrecognisably clean and spruce. At the close of these doings the Superior walked round with the firm's proprietor, and during their conversation the proprietor remarked: 'You've got some fine old masters here. Several undoubted Correggios and three Murillos at least. All they need is a little renovation.' The Superior said that renovations were costly.

'On the contrary. Such expenses repay themselves in a month. A little paragraph in the newspapers: "Valuable Murillos in a state equal to new. Connoisseurs admitted every Monday and Thursday between four and five p.m." You would never regret it.'

'It would be costly,' repeated the Superior.

The proprietor mentioned a price. The Superior shook his head. In a burst of geniality, the proprietor exclaimed: 'See now! I will fix just one of them, that fine St Joseph yonder, for instance, and charge only for the materials. Then, if you are satisfied, we will agree about the others.'

The Superior said that such devotion found its true reward in heavenly appreciation. 'But as some slight return for such a favour, we will supply you with an assistant. For doubtless you will need a boy to clean the brushes and so forth.'

To watch and not to perform, to clean brushes and not to wield them, to mix paints and not to lay them on was almost more than Plutarco could endure. However, he did endure, observing every stroke and asking a great many questions. As the Novice Master had pointed out, this was a wonderful opportunity for him. A little later, the Novice Master told him that if he were modest and careful and did not waste paint or become vainglorious, he might renovate the remaining old masters. 'But only the backgrounds,' he said, 'and such details as cherubs and feet. For these are all very valuable Murillos. We cannot endanger them. They are works of art and exceedingly antique.'

The use of a forcing-pipe imparts a very steady and accurate hand. Plutarco renovated the backgrounds without infringing by a hair's breadth on the main figures. The new backgrounds were bright and glossy, and wherever possible he introduced lilies, having learned a well-credentialled type of lily from Mother Remedios. By using a great deal of turpentine, which at once made brushwork easier and kept down the cost of the paints, and by avoiding any appearance of vainglory, he won golden opinions. He was allowed to proceed with cherubs and feet. Here, too, he acquitted himself to everyone's satisfaction. Cherubs and feet alike were pink and dimpled, and his renovation of St Margaret's dragon (classed as a cherub) was so striking that he was told to go ahead with the Saint herself. She was not so grateful as her dragon; her nose, in particular, gave him agonies. But when she was completed, there could be no doubt of it: the unrenovated saints made a poor, dowdy appearance in comparison with her.

Plutarco was given a free brush. Month by month the chapel became more bright and bowery. Month by month Plutarco felt his powers expanding, felt himself more enfranchised from dependence upon the original outlines and the old, faded colourings. Now not only did he make blues much bluer, he sometimes made them pink. Countenances that had been austere became smiling and youthful, and his virgin martyrs developed an *embonpoint* at once stately and alluring, as though they were so many celestial circus riders. Everyone was delighted, and the connoisseurs who were admitted, for a small fee, to admire the old masters, now restored to their prime condition, realised as never before the possibilities of heaven, the beauty of holiness.

And then, just as his maturing talents were in full swing, Plutarco Roo was told that there was nothing more that he need paint, unless he cared to give a lick of renovation to the collecting boxes. No more painting? With incredulity he pointed to the expanses of blank wall. There and there he could portray, in fresco, a St Agnes with a far curlier lamb, a St James with infinitely finer legs, a more majestic St Teresa, and a more appealing St Anthony.

'No, my son,' replied the Novice Master, 'that would not do at all. They would not be renovations, you see.'

That night, in a tempest of indignation, Plutarco Roo left the Carmelites, taking with him the paint brushes, all the remaining paints, and a considerable quantity of gold leaf.

It was the act of an artist, impulsive and unpractical. He had no particular intention of theft, but the possession of so much gold leaf was undoubtedly invidious. There was nothing for it: he must leave the town and cast himself, a wandering artist or a wandering pastry-cook, upon the mercies of the countryside.

These mercies proved very slender. Though he found innumerable churches possessing old masters, he could never win a solid commission for renovations; at best, he could contrive an order to brighten up a halo or two with some of the gold leaf. He turned to secular art, offering to paint decorations for shop fronts and taverns. But his style, so intensively nourished upon ecclesiastical subjects, did not lend itself to such commissions. Just as Don Isidro had resented his cake, vintners and saloon-keepers turned up their noses at his beauties and bullfighters. His young ladies, however plump, retained the majesty of virgin martyrs, his toreadors recalled nothing but the Archangel Michael. Client after client said to him: 'It is too idealistic. Such portraits would not sell a glass of lemonade.'

Equally, there was no demand for pastry-cooks in rural districts. Yet because of the gold leaf he did not like to go to a town.

At last, more to get out of Mexico than with any definite hope of doing better elsewhere, he worked a passage to Havana. The voyage made him horribly seasick. Cold and shivering, he sat down in a café near the waterfront and thought to himself that whether he throve or starved on the island, on the island he must remain, for he could never endure another journey by sea. The waiter said to him: 'What you need is a Pernod.'

The waiter was right. The glass was scarcely emptied before Plutarco Roo felt his vitality returning, began to think of his past as a series of interesting adventures, realised himself as the vehicle of an authentic talent maintained with spirit in a rough-and-tumble world, and started to look around on his new environment. At the next table sat two men, both well dressed and handsome, deep in conversation. He studied them with an artist's eye, debating whether they should be put into turbans and become Doctors Disputing in the Temple or whether it would be better to coif them with simple haloes as SS Sebastian and Roch.

'Herbert Spencer,' said one of them, 'an English philosopher. It would be a splendid name for the brand. It would sell it among the English. And they are the kind of cigars that the English are glad to smoke. But the trouble is, there should be a portrait of him inside the lid. And how can one have a portrait if one does not know what the man looks like?'

'I suppose you could get a photograph,' said the other.

The first man shrugged his shoulders. 'And how is one to get a photograph of an English philosopher? It would mean enquiries and research. You know how it is with such affairs. One begins them, but one never ends them.'

'True,' replied his friend. 'One cannot deny it. Perhaps it might be an imaginative portrait?'

'Then the English would know. And these are cigars very definitely for the English market.'

'Yes, they would know. The English are like that.'

After a pause the friend suggested: 'Why not some other English philosopher?'

'I do not know of one. It would mean more enquiries, more research. Besides, I have already printed the bands.'

'Too bad,' said the friend.

Plutarco Roo stepped forward. 'Pardon me,' he said. 'But this is a matter of no difficulty. I am an artist. And I happen to be well acquainted with the features of Herbert Spencer.'

'How foolish one is to worry,' said the first speaker. 'One has only to sit in a café and wait. Will you have a cognac?' he said to Plutarco.

'A Pernod, if you please. I find my best inspiration in Pernod.'

A religious artist, accustomed to rely upon his sense of the befitting for likenesses of saints and martyrs, was not liable to be much troubled in inventing the likeness of a contemporary philosopher. By combining the blandness of St Joseph with the learning of St Jerome, by sweeping the flowing white beard sufficiently to one side to display a Gladstone collar, a blue necktie, and a scarfpin representing a fox's head, and by inserting a monocle, Plutarco Roo provided an excellent likeness of Herbert Spencer. A few palms, a distant volcano, and two emblematical ladies, one holding a telescope and the other leading a lion, supplied the background, and the cigar manufacturer accepted the design with enthusiasm and commissioned others. From that day, Plutarco Roo functioned in his new métier as smoothly as a cylinder in its sleeve, alternating commission and invention, production and payment, in an easy rhythm.

His works were numerous. Many of them can be identified by the initials P. R.

(A Garland of Straw, 1943)

THE HOUSE WITH THE LILACS

IT was in 1937, when they had been settled in their house for over a twelvemonth, had outgrown its first charms and found new ones, and were no longer pained by its demerits, that Mrs Finch, speaking as if she had given the matter long consideration and at last felt justified in announcing her conclusions, said that sometimes she rather wished they had bought the house with the lilacs after all.

'Which house with lilacs, Mother? We looked at dozens. Do you mean the one with the condemned well?'

'No, dear. The house with the lilacs with the lilacs. You remember. It was a white house with a slate roof. We saw it on that very stormy day, and the wind blew a lilac bough against my hat and drenched me. It was the proper lilac, the kind the Turks sent to Vienna.'

'Where was this house?'

'Down a long lane.'

'Yes, but where? What county was it in?'

'Now how can you expect *me* to know that?' She looked at her husband with interest. 'Anyone would think, Henry, that we were spending a week-end at Brighton instead of sitting here with our well-grown family.'

'Why do you wish we had bought that house instead of this? Was it nicer?' This was from Arden, the Finches' twelve-year-old son who was going to be a mathematical genius.

'I don't know that it was nicer. But it had some queer, funny ways that one would have grown very fond of. I liked that old laundry with the stone floor and the round-topped windows and the fig tree growing all along outside. Do you remember? On one side of that bricked yard where there was a grindstone under a sort of thatched canopy.'

'Did the grindstone go with the house?'

'Oh, certainly! That was one of the things I liked, there were so many oddments that went with the house. The yellow pony-cart and the melon-pits and the churn and those thousands of flower-pots in the shed and the bottle tree.'

'Bottle tree, Mother?'

'You know. You've constantly seen bottle trees. Like an iron diagram of a Christmas tree, with spikes in tiers all the way round it, and you put empty bottles on the spikes.'

'But why?'

'Order and tidiness, my child.'

'I can't remember the house at all,' said Cordelia. Clara could not remember it either. No one could remember a house with anything like a bottle tree standing in a bricked yard where stood also a grindstone under a sort of thatched canopy.

'Isn't it extraordinary,' said Mrs Finch, gazing at them as if they were Northern Lights. 'And yet you might be living there at this moment!'

As a conversationalist Mrs Finch was considered hard to follow. Not that she was obscure: she was clear as the cuckoo; but like the cuckoo it was hard to follow her, for one could never be sure into what tree she had flown. Thus it is likely that many of her references to the house with the lilacs went unrecognised, being taken as overtones to measles at the Rectory or death among the bantams; but some statements were categorical. Among the noteworthy aspects of the house with the lilacs was a mulberry tree with a little lawn all to itself, a long-tailed piano in an attic (Mrs Finch herself had thought this rather odd, and had wondered how it had got there), a case of stuffed owls in a linen-cupboard, a little wire staircase (well, iron, if you must be so circumstantial) that went up through the bathroom, and the weathercock, which was a fish.

'I am surprised that you don't remember the fish. Don't you remember the old gentleman telling us that in the gale of 1929 it was blown into a pond?'

'What old gentleman?'

'The old gentleman who lived there with his two sisters. Just as it might be you, Arden, with Cordelia and Clara. One of them was stone deaf and the other wore very large dark spectacles. They were so congenial, and I was so sorry for them for having to leave their house.'

'Why were they leaving it?'

'They were going to Bulgaria to look after their roses. They lived on attar. I mean, it was their income. Not humming-birds. Of course that explained the house being so full of ikons and why, when I saw those owls in the linen-cupboard, I supposed for a moment it was the Holy Family.'

'How much did they want for it?'

'Ten thousand. Yes, Henry, I remember you looked like that at the time. Or was it three? Whatever it was, it gave you exactly that legal expression.'

Nothing likelier, thought Mr Finch, than that he should be wearing a legal expression, since he felt so uncomfortably as if he had been cross-examining a Welsh witness. It would have been a relief to his mind if he could have found Elinor out in a lie. But she was distressingly consistent; though there seemed to be no end to her recollections of the house with the lilac, each as it came dovetailed into the whole with a Mozartian purity. The time of year, the day's weather, the dimensions of the house—every unity was preserved. Apricots never appeared among the lilacs, not a mulberry dropped, the wind still blew from the south, the house continued to face south-east, and the soil remained a light loam. This unshakable consistency (one cannot call it cunning) is one of the qualities that distinguish the person with a delusion from the ordinary liar. In his anxiety to convince himself that Elinor was just ordinarily lying he asked more and more questions; and every question's answer made her seem more resplendently the soul of truth, more transparently the vehicle of what Cordelia called an obsession and Clara referred to as a Thing. To Cordelia and Clara, normal well-brought up girls of their date and station, there was nothing disconcerting in their mother showing signs of madness, it was what their lessons in psychology and physiology had taught them to expect. Arden was too young or too mathematical to mind whether his mother was going mad or telling lies, he just liked hearing about the house. If Arden would not ask so many questions, thought Mr Finch, ten to one the whole thing would die away and be forgotten. What was quite out of the question was that the house with the lilacs should exist and have been inspected: it was asking too much to suppose that he and his two daughters, all three of them perfectly in their senses, should have unitedly mislaid every recollection of the bottle tree, the long-tailed piano in the attic, the two asparagus beds, the bathroom traversed by a little wire staircase, the ikons in every room and the owners who were leaving this unique property for a rose-farm in Bulgaria.

Meanwhile, he must hope that all this would blow over, and that so much evocation of a non-existent house would not unsettle Elinor from the house she was in. It had been trouble enough to decide on it, and now if all those months of journeys in hope and dubious returnings, desks littered with house-agents' hyperboles, keys that didn't fit, punctures in unfrequented byroads, halts to enquire the way from deaf old women and people who were strangers there themselves were to go for nothing . . . However, Elinor did not seem to be growing unsettled, continuing to live in the real and describe the unreal and be none the worse for it.

In the following summer she sprained her ankle, but in a quite rational way, falling off a ladder while picking morello cherries. Her exclamation, too—'Now I can really give my mind to learning the harp!'—was not more eccentric than her usual run of aspirations. Doting on his Elinor in her infirmity (like most husbands, Mr Finch released a peculiar tenderness towards a wife in physical distress), he drove to the county town to see if he could buy a harp, and took his daughters with him, as he did not wish to look like a fool. They could not find a harp; but the disappointment to Mrs Finch was mitigated by two facts: that she had not realised what they had gone to town for, vaguely supposing that it was something to do with a fishpond, and that during their absence she had made a new friend, a young man on a walking tour who had called at the house to ask for a drink of water.

'And isn't it delightful?' she said. 'Mr Doubrov knows the house with the lilacs. He stayed there when he was a child. He remembers everything.'

'It was my godfather,' said Mr Doubrov. 'He is quite shortly dead.' He offered the information as though he were handing his hostess a bouquet. Emitting smiles of tender enthusiasm, he was clearly another of the numerous young men whom Mrs Finch turned the heads of.

'Mr Doubrov was there in July, so he did not see the lilacs. But he ate mulberries and wood-strawberries, and was taken for drives in the pony cart, and he remembers a wooden summer-house, which must have fallen to bits, for it wasn't there when we saw the garden. While he was there the house was struck by lightning.'

Mr Finch, Cordelia, and Clara variously muttered: 'How interesting' and 'How delightful,' and stole hang-dog glances at each other. Mr Finch, in addition, wiped his forehead with his handkerchief.

'Where was this house?' said Cordelia.

'It was on the land. It was altogether on the land. No other houses were there.'

'Down that very long lane,' said Mrs Finch, confirmingly. 'But when Mr Doubrov was there the piano was downstairs, in the room with the french windows and the big bird-cage.'

'But in what part of England, Mr Doubrov? You see, though my mother remembers the house so well, she can't remember what county it was in. None of us can, as it happens.'

Mr Doubrov raised his very black eyebrows and looked sorrowful.

'Ah! Now that I cannot say. I was a stranger, you see. A child. We went by a train from London. We got out. We drove. My mother said to me, Look, what fields! Like parks! Then was I sick. But where was all this, I cannot tell you.'

Sensitive enough to feel that something disastrous had got loose, Mr Doubrov turned with a reassuring look to the only person who felt no need of a reassurance, and said, bowing from the waist: 'If in my tour I shall find this house again, Madame, it will be my pleasure to send you the photograph.'

(*The Museum of Cheats*, 1947)

A VIEW OF EXMOOR

FROM Bath, where Mr Finch was taking the waters, the Finches travelled by car into Devonshire to attend the wedding of Mrs Finch's niece, Arminella Blount. They made a very creditable family contribution—Mrs Finch in green moiré, Cordelia and Clara in their bridesmaids' dresses copied from the Gainsborough portrait of an earlier Arminella Blount in the Character of Flora, Mr Finch in, as his wife said, his black-and-grey. Arden Finch in an Eton suit would have looked like any other twelve-year-old boy in an Eton suit if measles had not left him preternaturally thin, pale, and owl-eyed.

All these fine feathers, plus two top hats, an Indian shawl to wrap around Arden in case it turned cold, and a picnic basket in case anyone felt hungry, made the car seem unusually full during the drive to Devonshire. On the return journey it was even fuller, because the Finches were bringing back Arminella's piping bullfinch and the music box that was needed to continue its education, as well as the bridesmaids' bouquets. It was borne in on Mr Finch that other travellers along the main road were noticing his car and its contents more than they needed to, and this impression was confirmed when the passengers in two successive charabancs cheered and waved. Mr Finch, the soul of consideration, turned into a side road to spare his wife and daughters the embarrassment of these public acclamations.

' "Pember and South Pigworthy",' Mrs Finch read aloud from a signpost. 'The doctor who took out my tonsils was called Pember. It's so nice to find a name one knows.'

Mr Finch replied that he was taking an alternative way home. After a while, he stopped and looked for his road map, but couldn't find it. He drove on.

'Father,' said Cordelia a little later, 'we've been through this village before. Don't you think we had better ask?'

'Is *that* all it is?' said Mrs Finch. 'What a relief. I thought I was having one of those mysterious delusions when one half of my brain mislays the other half.'

Mr Finch continued to drive on. Arden, who had discovered that the bars of the bird cage gave out notes of varying pitch when he plucked them, was carrying out a systematic test with a view to being able to play 'Rule Britannia'. Cordelia and Clara and their mother discussed the wedding.

Suddenly, Mrs Finch exclaimed, 'Oh, Henry! Stop, stop! There's such a beautiful view of Exmoor!'

Ten-foot hedges rose on either side of the lane they were in, the lane went steeply uphill, and Mr Finch had hoped that he had put any views of Exmoor safely behind him. But with unusual mildness he stopped and backed the car till it was level with a gate. Beyond the gate was a falling meadow, a pillowy middle distance of woodland, and beyond that, pure and cold and unimpassioned, the silhouette of the moor.

'Why not,' Mr Finch said, taking the good the gods provided, 'why not stop and picnic?' It occurred to him that once the car was emptied, the road map might come to light.

The Finches sat down in the meadow and ate cucumber sandwiches. Arden wore the Indian shawl; the bullfinch in its cage was brought out of the car to have a little fresh air. Gazing at the view, Mrs Finch said that looking at Exmoor always reminded her of her Aunt Harriet's inexplicable boots.

'What boots, Mother?' Cordelia asked.

'She saw them on Exmoor,' Mrs Finch said. 'She and Uncle Lionel both saw them; they were children at the time. They were picking whortleberries—such a disappointing fruit! All these folk-art fruits are much overrated. And nobody's ever been able to account for them.'

'But why should they have to be accounted for?' Clara asked. 'Were they sticking out of a bog?'

'They were in a cab.'

'Your Aunt Harriet—' Mr Finch began. For some reason, it angered him to hear of boots being in a cab while he was still in doubt as to whether the map was in the car.

'Of course,' Mrs Finch went on, 'in those days cabs were everywhere. But not on Exmoor, where there were no roads. It was a perfectly ordinary cab, one of the kind that open in hot weather. The driver was on the box, and the horse was waving its tail to keep the flies off. They looked as if they had been there quite a long time.'

'Days and days?' Arden asked.

'I'm afraid not, dear. Decomposition had not set in. But as if they had been there long enough to get resigned to it. An hour or so.'

'But how could Aunt Harriet tell how long—'

'In those days, children were very different—nice and inhibited,' Mrs Finch said. 'So Aunt Harriet and Uncle Lionel observed the cab from a distance and walked on. Presently, they saw two figures—a man and a woman. The man was very pale and sulky, and the woman was rating him and crying her eyes out, but the most remarkable thing of all, even more remarkable than the cab, was that the woman wasn't wearing a hat. In those days, no self-respecting woman could stir out without a hat. And on the ground was a pair of boots. While Harriet and Lionel were trying to get a little nearer without seeming inquisitive, the woman snatched up the boots and ran back to the cab. She ran right past the children; she was crying so bitterly she didn't even notice them. She jumped into the cab, threw the boots onto the opposite seat, the driver whipped up his horse, and the cab went bumping and jolting away over the moor. As for the man, he walked off looking like murder. So what do you make of that?'

'Well, I suppose they'd been wading, and then they quarrelled and she drove away with his boots as a revenge,' said Clara.

'He was wearing boots,' said Mrs Finch.

'Perhaps they were eloping,' Clara said, 'and the boots were part of their luggage that he'd forgotten to pack, like Father, and she changed her mind in time.'

'Speed is essential to an elopement, and so is secrecy. To drive over Exmoor in an open cab would be inconsistent with either,' said Mr Finch.

'Perhaps the cab lost its way in a moor mist,' contributed Arden. 'Listen! I can do almost all the first line of "Rule Britannia" now.'

'But, Clara, why need it be an elopement?' Cordelia asked. 'Perhaps she was just a devoted wife who found a note from her husband saying he had lost his memory or committed a crime or something and was going out of her life, and she seized up a spare pair of boots, leaped hatless into a cab, and tracked him across Exmoor, to make sure he had a dry pair to change into. And when Harriet and Lionel saw them, he had just turned on her with a brutal oath.'

'If she had been such a devoted wife, she wouldn't have taken the boots away again,' Clara said.

'Yes, she would. It was the breaking point,' Cordelia said. 'Actually, though, I don't believe she was married to him at all. I think it was an assignation and she'd taken her husband's boots with her as a blind.'

'Then why did she take them out of the cab?' inquired Clara. 'And why didn't she wear a hat, like Mother said? No, Cordelia! I think your theory is artistically all right. It looks the boots straight in the face. But I've got a better one. I think they spent a guilty night together and, being a forgetful man, he puts his boots out to be cleaned and in the morning she was hopelessly compromised, so she snatched up the boots and drove after him to give him a piece of her mind.'

'Yes, but he was wearing boots already,' Cordelia said.

'He would have had several pairs. At that date, a libertine would have had hundreds of boots, wouldn't he, Mother?'

'He might not have taken them with him wherever he went, dear,' said Mrs Finch.

Mr Finch said, 'You have both rushed off on an assumption. Because the lady drove away in the cab, you both assume that she arrived in it. Women always jump to conclusions. Why shouldn't the cab have brought the man? If she was hatless, she might have been an escaped lunatic and the man a keeper from the asylum, who came in search of her.'

'Why did he bring a pair of boots?' Cordelia asked.

'Ladies' boots,' said Mr Finch firmly.

'He can't have been much of a lunatic-keeper if he let her get away with his cab,' Clara said.

'I did not say he was a lunatic-keeper, Clara,' said Mr Finch. 'I was merely trying to point out to you and your sister that in cases like this one must examine the evidence from all sides.'

'Perhaps the cabdriver was a lunatic,' said Arden. 'Perhaps that's why he drove them onto Exmoor. Perhaps they were *his* boots, and the man and the woman were arguing as to which of them was to pay his fare. Perhaps—'

Interrupted by his father and both his sisters, all speaking at once, Arden returned to his rendering of 'Rule Britannia'. Mrs Finch removed some crumbs and a few caterpillars from her green moiré lap and looked at the view of Exmoor. Suddenly, a glissando passage on the bird cage was broken by a light twang, a flutter of wings, a cry from Arden. The cage door had flipped open and the bullfinch had flown out. Everybody said 'Oh!' and grabbed at it. The bullfinch flew to the gate, balanced there, flirted its tail, and flew on into the lane.

It flew in a surprised, incompetent way, making short flights, hurling itself from side to side of the lane. But though Cordelia and Clara leaped after it, trying to catch it in their broad-brimmed hats, and though Arden only just missed it by overbalancing on a bough, thereby falling out of the tree and making his nose bleed, and though Mr Finch walked after it, holding up the bird cage and crying 'Sweet, Sweet, Sweet' in a falsetto voice that trembled with feeling, the bullfinch remained at liberty and, with a little practice, flew better and better.

'Stop, all of you!' said Mrs Finch, who had been attending to Arden, wiping her bloodstained hands on the grass. 'You'll frighten it. Henry, do leave off saying "Sweet"—you'll only strain yourself. What we need is the music box. If it hears the music box, it will be reminded of its home and remember it's a tame bullfinch. Arden, dear, please keep your shawl on and look for some groundsel, if you aren't too weak from loss of blood.'

The music box weighed about fifty pounds. It was contained in an ebony case that looked like a baby's coffin, and at every movement it emitted reproachful chords. On one side, it had a handle; on the other side, the handle had fallen off, and by the time the Finches had got the box out of the car, they were flushed and breathless. His groans mingling with the reproachful chords Mr Finch staggered up the lane in pursuit of the bullfinch, with the music box in his arms. Mrs Finch walked beside him, tenderly entreating him to be careful, for if anything happened to it, it would break Arminella's heart. Blithesome and cumberless, like the bird of the wilderness, the bullfinch flitted on ahead.

'I am not carrying this thing a step further,' said Mr Finch, setting down the music box at the side of the lane. 'Since you insist, Elinor, I will sit here and play it. The rest of you can walk on and turn the bird somehow and drive it back till the music reminds it of home.'

Clara said, 'I expect we shall go for miles.'

Seeing his family vanish around a bend in the lane, Mr Finch found himself nursing a hope that Clara's expectation might be granted. He was devoted to music boxes. He sat down beside it and read the list of its repertory, which was written in a copperplate hand inside the lid: 'Là ci darem la Mano'; 'The Harp that once through Tara's Halls'; the Prayer from *Moïse*; the 'Copenhagen Waltz'. A very pleasant choice for an interval of repose, well-earned repose, in this leafy seclusion. He ran his finger over the prickled cylinder, he blew away a little dust, he wound the box up. Unfortunately, there were a great many midges, the inherent pest of leafy seclusions. He paused to light a cigar. Then he set off the music box. It chirruped through three and a half tunes and stopped, as music boxes do. Behind him, a voice said somewhat diffidently, 'I say. Can I be any help?'

Glancing from the corner of his eye, Mr Finch saw a young man whose bare ruined legs and rucksack suggested that he was on a walking tour.

'No, thank you,' Mr Finch said. Dismissingly, he rewound the music box and set it going again.

Round the bend of the lane came two replicas, in rather bad condition, of Gainsborough's well-known portrait of Arminella Blount in the Character of Flora, a cadaverous small boy draped in a blood-stained Indian shawl, and a middle-aged lady dressed in the height of fashion who carried a bird cage. Once again, Mr Finch was forced to admit the fact that the instant his family escaped from his supervision they somehow managed to make themselves conspicuous. Tripping nervously to the strains of the 'Copenhagen Waltz', the young man on a walking tour skirted round them and hurried on.

'We've got it!' cried Mrs Finch, brandishing the bird cage.

'Why the deuce couldn't you *explain* to that young man?' asked Mr Finch. 'Elinor, why couldn't you explain?'

'But why should I?' Mrs Finch asked. 'He looked so hot and careworn, and I expect he only gets a fortnight's holiday all the year through. Why should I spoil it for him? Why shouldn't he have something to look back on in his old age?'

(*One Thing Leading to Another*, 1984)

THE REREDOS

Nowadays, the Church of England is somewhat prim about the extra-rubrical ornaments of its sacred edifices. Memorial windows, altar frontals, new pulpits for old—all must pass a censorship before they can be allowed in; even such trifles as hassocks have to comply with a doctrinal standard. It was otherwise in the days when Queen Victoria was in the last glow of her Indian summer and Florence Larpent in her prime. There was more latitude then. The Church of England was broader and took a broader view, and when Florence's husband, Geoffrey Larpent, DD, retired from a university professorship to the college living of Woodham Garnish, it did not cross her mind, or anyone else's, that the parish church could be anything but improved by her improvements.

She had not sat through her first Evensong in Advent before she resolved to get the better of those draughts. A fortnight later, the congregation found themselves sheltered, as though in some gigantic pious fourposter, by curtains of the best crimson baize, curtains hanging in abundant folds and lying on the floor in generous, draught-proof rumples. Gratefully sweltering, they looked forward to her next good idea. Their confidence was justified, for it was coconut matting along the aisle. After that came plump hassocks, in place of the old kneeling-boards; hymnbooks in bold type; and an oil heater for christenings. By the time Florence advanced on the chancel, the church council was hers to a man.

While in the nave, Florence had concentrated on the comfort of the congregation. In the chancel, after supplying a nice little Turkey carpet and a suitably Gothic chair for any visiting bishop (it was of oak, richly carved, with the words 'Deus misereatur' in bold relief where the bishop's shoulders might be expected to seek support), she turned her mind to the glory of God, which, first and foremost, demanded a new reredos. The Ten Commandments, almost illegible in yellow lettering on black-painted deal panels, were not at all her notion of the beauty of holiness. She therefore proposed to supplant them by likenesses of the four Evangelists, which she would paint in oils herself.

'Spider and Pawsey quite agree with me,' she said, looking in on Geoffrey in his study to announce her project and borrow the Iconography. (Spider and Pawsey were the churchwardens, and until Florence's advent they had never been in agreement about anything.) Geoffrey, coming half-way out of Saint Ambrose, murmured something about perhaps consulting the archdeacon, just as a matter of civility. Florence replied that of course she would consult the archdeacon—in any case she wanted him for dinner on the thirteenth.

By the close of dinner, the archdeacon was quite ready to assent to the four Evangelists, and to give his approval to some preliminary sketches, which were served with the coffee. He had no idea Mrs Larpent was such a gifted artist—really, most remarkable.

'I have always painted,' said Florence, with the calm of a fish remarking that it had always swum.

Geoffrey added that in the year '81 Florence had exhibited two pictures in the Royal Academy. The archdeacon's 'Really, really! But it does not surprise me' intervened before Geoffrey could state that both the exhibits had been portraits.

New brushes, oil paints and gold leaf were bought, the canvas was stretched, and Florence began on the left-hand side of the composition with a dash at Saint Matthew. She had devoted some thought to the essentials of her design and had settled that Matthew should be in green and crimson, Mark in brown and gold, Luke in grey with touches of purple, and John in shades of blue; that Matthew should be reading his book, John looking upwards for inspiration, Mark and Luke meditating in post-creative calm; and that the evangelical beasts had better be kept small and unobtrusive, since Woodham Garnish was a country parish, where too much interest was taken in animals already. But it was not until she had laid on the first bold swathes of Matthew's drapery that she began to consider the evangelical features. 'Beards,' she muttered. 'How I hate beards! They always remind me of Professor Lothbury.'

Four beards, four full, flowing beards; it was really more than she felt equal to. And must all the beards be grey? A grey beard would ruin the effect of Saint Luke's drapery. If Luke had a brown beard and Mark a black beard, then she could give Mark black eyes and a ruddy colouring, and Luke's eyes could be blue. This would leave hazel eyes for John; and Matthew . . . Could Matthew have green eyes? The thought of a green-eyed Evangelist was rather startling and needed consideration. Perhaps a dark-green eye—and as he would be looking down at his book, not much of it would show.

She was suspended thus when the solution burst upon her. Not for nothing had she two sons and two sons-in-law, and a wonderful talent for catching likenesses. How much more interesting it would be, and how much more in keeping with the great age of religious art, to use her sons, James and Daniel, and her sons-in-law, Pollock and Harold, for the Evangelists. In a second revelation, she knew that Mark must be Pollock, for Mark was the only Evangelist she could imagine with a moustache.

She set to work, and by the next day four portrait sketches enlivened the halos, for which, in order to achieve perfect circularity, she had used a basin.

'Dear me,' said Geoffrey, peering in. 'Dear me! I hope they won't mind.'

'Mind? Why, who should mind what? They'll infinitely prefer it to those battered old Commandments.'

'I was only wondering how Pollock would take it. Army men are sensitive. I don't suppose Harold will object—you've made him extremely handsome, my dear—and, of course, James and Daniel will think nothing of it. I mean, it won't surprise them in the least. They'll be delighted, I'm sure. But Pollock . . . I admit to feeling a little dubious about Pollock.'

'I think he's the best of the lot,' said Florence.

'Oh, yes, he is. Undoubtedly he is. And, of course, he'll have a lion. That will please him. He's shot several. I could never willingly shoot a lion myself.'

Saint Mark might be the best likeness, but Saint Luke was by far the most admired when the finished reredos was set in its place and burst on the congregation for Whitsunday. Such a handsome Evangelist had never been suspected in Woodham Garnish—such flashing eyes, such regular features, and looking, so to speak, such a real gentleman. For, at the time of painting, Harold was very much Florence's favoured son-in-law. The cult spread. During the next twelvemonth, several children were christened Luke on the strength of him. The mother triumphing over the artist, Florence touched up Matthew and John a little and, while she was about it, added some ten years to Mark's age, for Pollock was being rather trying just then, always catching colds and backing the wrong horses, till Cecily was quite fagged out with nursing and economising. Not that Cecily complained. It was the younger daughter, Rosalind, who complained. Like other wives of very hand-some husbands, Rosalind was apt to feel herself neglected, and she had enough of Florence in her to resent being Harold's third leg. Rosalind had even gone so far as to say, her tone of acrimony only slightly disguised by her mouth being full of moss (for, having come down with the children for Easter, she was helping to decorate the church), 'If you knew Harold as well as I do, Mother, I don't think you'd put him in an altarpiece.'

Evading the main issue, Florence replied, 'How disobliging daffodils are! It would be quite easy to alter him, if you don't like him as he is. I've made several changes in Saint Mark, and your father thinks they've been the making of him.'

Rosalind snatched up a bucket and put it down again rather violently, but said no more. It will soon blow over, thought Florence.

It blew over. Saint Luke remained in his prime beauty, and the cult continued, though now, identifications having been established, the votive infants were christened Harold. Except for some dutiful aspir-ations that Geoffrey might now and then be called on to sprinkle a James, a Daniel, or even a Geoffrey, Florence had not a care in the world. As Edward VII succeeded Victoria, and the harmonium gave place to an organ, and the crimson curtains mellowed, Harold's mellowing career in the Civil Service took him and his family to Cairo. It was from Cairo that the telegram came: THIS TIME HAROLD HAS GONE TOO FAR AM RETURNING WITH CHILDREN ROSALIND.

Florence, having read it through, exclaimed, 'Goodness! Geoffrey, do attend. This is from Rosalind, and she says Harold has gone too far and she's coming here with the children. What on earth can she mean?'

'A woman,' said Geoffrey, coming up from Saint Jerome.

Florence said she couldn't believe it; Harold was attractive, but not that kind of man. A letter from Daniel, in the course of which he remarked that there were some odd rumours about Harold going the rounds and that he was afraid poor Rosie would have to open her eyes at last, shook her disbelief, and when it was followed by thirteen closely written pages from Rosalind, with exclamatory postscripts squeezed into all their corners, the last hope of incredulity vanished.

And with an acrobat, too!

The letter with the story of Mlle Zizi came on a Saturday. By the following Wednesday, Rosalind and her children would be arriving at Woodham Garnish. 'I must change everything as much as possible!' cried Florence. 'We can't have the house looking just the same as it did when they were here together. I have decided to turn the spare room into the nursery, and put Rosalind into—' She was about to say '—your dressing-room,' when the thought of a more essential change stopped her breath. Harold could not possibly be left flaunting in the character of St Luke. Too full of purpose to explain her intentions, she hurried off to the church with her paints, brushes and palette, seated herself on the altar, and set to work.

But now something went wrong. Try as she might to expurgate him, Harold continued to exercise a demoniacal possession of Saint Luke. Twice and thrice it seemed to her that she had got him down under quite a new countenance, and each time some final improvement—the arching of an eyebrow, the flaring of a nostril—conjured him back. Realising that she was at the mercy of her talent for catching likenesses, she resolved to base a Saint Luke on Mr Pawsey. This came better. As a basic Saint Luke, Mr Pawsey was everything that a rector's warden should be, helpful yet unobtrusive. Satisfied at last, Florence scrambled off the altar and took the artist's few paces back to view the completed work. It was no use. Draped in Mr Pawsey's cheeks, and leering through Mr Pawsey's mild blue eyes, Harold surveyed her with a sardonic bo-peep.

'Very well!' she exclaimed, addressing only Harold. 'Very well! Have it your own way. Since you insist on being Harold, I'll Harold you!'

Dusk had fallen before she laid on the last strokes. As she gave the renewed Harold a parting inspection, it seemed to her that she had shown him in his true colours.

The pure light of a Third Sunday in Lent revealed an interpretation of Saint Luke that came as a surprise even to the artist, and perfectly outraged the congregation. What had happened to their Beloved Physician? Whatever had come over Mrs Reverend? It seemed to the more imaginative of them that the Devil had got into the church overnight, leaving a strong smell of oil paints and a self-portrait.

'I am very sorry, Florence,' Geoffrey said at luncheon, 'but I cannot possibly conduct divine service under the supervision of that malevolent card-sharper. I quite understand your feelings. As far as they are feelings of a parent, I share them, and as the feelings of an artist, I respect them. All the same, my dear, you must repaint Saint Luke before next Sunday. And before Evensong it would be as well to fill the altar vases with laurel, or some vigorous shrub of that kind.'

Florence readily admitted that Saint Luke had gone beyond the bounds of sacred art. 'The trouble is,' she pleaded, 'I can't paint a face unless it's a likeness. And if it's not to be Harold, who is it to be? I tried Pawsey, but Harold got the better of him—and even if he hadn't, the village might have thought it not quite reverent, and Spider would have had every reason to be jealous and talk about favouritism.'

'It would not be irreverent to paint me,' said Geoffrey. 'I shall sit to you tomorrow afternoon.' On the Fourth Sunday in Lent, the congregation observed that Saint Luke was now the Reverend.

Rosalind had not gone to church. She was not equal to it. The energetic wrath that had whirled her across Europe evaporated in the climate of home. She lay in bed, weeping copiously, refusing all nourishment except cups of strong tea and anchovy toast, and incessantly talking of Harold. Not even the fact that she was bedded in her father's dressing-room was able to distract her from what seemed an inveterate determination to be reminded of Harold by everything she saw or heard, including her father's confident approaches to her door and his sighs of frustration as he went on towards the bathroom. She wept, and talked of Harold's cynicism and her ruined life; and Geoffrey said, 'My poor child, what you need is rest. Try to sleep a little,' and went away; and Florence persisted in expatiating on all the other delightful, stirring things there are in the world besides husbands; and the children, that natural solace for the feelings of an injured wife, were no solace at all, for they had made friends with a pig farmer and talked of nothing but boars and farrowings.

After a week of this, with no letters except letters of sympathy and approval from her sisters-in-law, Rosalind turned to religion, put on a hat, and crept out to sit quietly in the church by herself. Being shortsighted, she was half-way up the aisle before she noticed that a change had taken place in the third Evangelist. She hurried into the chancel for a closer examination. After a minute, she leaned forward and planted her finger on Saint Luke's nose. The rich impasto was still moist.

From the drawing-room window, Florence saw Rosalind crossing the churchyard with a springy, purposeful gait, and rejoiced to think that at last the poor little soul had taken a mother's insinuations to heart and found something better to do than brood on Harold. If by any chance it were the unfolding beauties of nature, and she could be persuaded to take the children for some good, long walks. . . . The springy and purposeful gait now entered the house, the door flew open, and Rosalind came to a violent halt in the middle of the room.

'Mother! This is too much! I have borne a great deal, but there are some things I ought not to be expected to put up with, and will not put up with, and one of them is to be held up to derision in Woodham Garnish. I should have thought you might feel that I had enough to endure already, what with Harold breaking my heart, and that appalling journey, and the children getting so spoiled that they are completely beyond my control, and my health ruined by all these worries, and never able to snatch a wink of sleep because of that odious dovecot below the dressing-room. I must say I didn't expect this. I didn't expect my own mother to turn against me. But now I see that I was wrong.'

'My dear,' Florence said, 'if it's the doves that are troubling you—'

'Doves! Doves! I'm not talking about doves. I never mentioned doves. Poke me away anywhere you like—why not the box room? That's nothing to do with it, I'm quite accustomed to that sort of treatment. But I am still a married woman, and entitled to some respect and consideration, and now to be insulted in this way, held up to ridicule, and published in church like banns—it's outrageous, outrageous, outrageous!'

'Rosalind!'

'Outrageous, I say. To come home, as I did, after all I'd gone through, and then to find my husband obliterated from a reredos! The paint still wet! And not a touch on any of the others, so you can't pretend it's one of your old fiddle-faddle improvements. Quite apart from anything else, I'm positive it's libellous, and if Harold were to sue you, he would be more than justified. What do you suppose people will think? Everyone knew Saint Luke was Harold, and now you go and plaster Father on top of him, and what other conclusions can they come to? I've never been so insulted in my life. And you always pretended to be so fond of him, too. You might have remembered that, even if you've got no consideration for what it all means to me.'

'Don't rant, Rosalind. Your father and I both agreed that in order to spare your feelings—'

'Pooh! I don't for a moment suppose you said a word to him. Father would never want to rob me of my one little crumb of comfort, my only chance of catching a glimpse of Harold's old self.'

'Really, Rosalind, if you can find no better consolation in a visit to church than—'

'What else do you suppose I went for? To glut my eyes on Pollock?'

'I had not expected that Canon Burroughs would be so late,' said Geoffrey, coming in with his watch in his hand and an appearance of not having heard anything out of the usual. 'Well, my dear, I see that you have been for a little turn in the fresh air. It has done you good. You have quite a colour.'

'I'm going out again,' Rosalind said. 'Now. To the post office.'

The front door slammed. Geoffrey said, 'She has gone to send a telegram to Harold, to tell him she's coming back.'

'Poor Rosalind!' said Florence. 'Do you suppose he will want her?'

'I'm sure he will. Men like Harold are always pleased to see a wife come back. My dear, do you suppose she will take the children?'

She did. Thanks to their artless farewells, it was a touching and seemly departure, and after the last wave to the wagonette, Geoffrey and Florence finished the breakfast coffee and turned their minds to the arrangements for Holy Week. As for the reredos, its fangs seemed to have been drawn, until just before Trinity Sunday, when Geoffrey said that Florence must buy a length of some handsome brocade of the correct liturgical green, and make curtains that could be drawn in front of it, after the style of a dossal. For while cutting a bunch of asparagus he had overheard two little girls disputing in the lane, and one of them had said that Saint Luke didn't half look queer now he was the Reverend, and the other had said, correctingly, that when he was Mr Harold, it was Saint Luke, but that now he was the Reverend, it was God the Father.

(*Winter in the Air*, 1955)

HAPPINESS

'THE bathroom's the awkwardest feature,' said Mr Naylor, of Elwes & Sons, house agents, 'being situated on the ground floor. People don't like ground-floor bathrooms. You might say, they just won't hear of them.'

'No, I suppose not. Yet . . .' Lavinia Benton broke off.

'I know what you were going to say, Mrs Benton. You were going to say, Why not convert the dressing room upstairs, leaving the bathroom for what one might call a playroom, or a children's lounge, or a study, if there happened to be no family. Once we'd got the bath out, it could be called ideal for that, being so inordinately large for a bathroom. But then the pipes would have to be carried upstairs. Think of the plumbing, Mrs Benton! Prohibitive! No buyer would contemplate it, not for this class of residence—it isn't as if this were one of those old oak jobs. And I understand you don't want to let the estate in for any extra expense. So there we are, I'm afraid. Back where we started from!'

Mr Naylor had, in fact, scotched a snake that wasn't there. Lavinia's 'Yet' had been provoked by the reflection that an increasingly large acreage of southern England was occupied between 7.30 and 8.30 a.m. by people resignedly bathing on ground level. Not so resignedly, either, since there are always buyers for bungalows. Both Mr Petherick, of Petherick, Petherick & Sampson, and Mr Cox, of Ransom & Titters, had already explained that Aller Lodge, the late Miss Esther Jeudwine's brick-built, two-storey residence in sound repair, would have been easy enough to sell if only it had been a bungalow. All a matter of social psychology, thought Lavinia who, as a columnist on superior Women's Pages, was accustomed to making something out of not much; a mass apprehension of being surprised with no clothes on, which if not primitive, since primitive man had other and more pressing things to be surprised by, must certainly go a long way back, being later reinforced by class distinction—the wealthy are draped, the poor go bare—and Christianity's insistence on modesty; for though a fakir can be venerable in a light handful of marigolds, an archdeacon can scarcely leave off his gaiters. In short, the discomposure of being surprised with no clothes on is, like the pleasurability of possessing a virgin, one of the things long taken for granted—and really even more of an *idée reçue*, being subscribed to by both sexes alike. Yet here was this mass apprehension, fortified by tradition, smoothed by acceptance, part of the British way of life, suddenly ceasing to function when brought into bungalows, where the hazards that might justify it—housebreakers, mad dogs, cars out of control, voyeurs, private detectives, almost anything, in fact, except the atom bomb—would be much more on the cards. But one must remember that bathrooms being so recent an introduction, public opinion could not have made up its mind about them yet, and was bound to be rather hypothetical.

Lavinia became aware that Mr Naylor was observing her with sympathy, but at the same time giving little coughs. Of course. The poor man wanted to go.

'Well, goodbye, Mr Naylor. And thank you for being so helpful. I'm afraid it's a bad lookout, but I'm sure you'll do your best.'

'I'll do my best,' he said, and his voice, being more sincere than hers, sounded less sanguine.

She was almost sorry to see him go, he was so much the nicest of them, and the only one to show the slightest comprehension of the fix she was in. Nothing could have been more straightforward than Cousin Esther's will. Her legacies were proportionate to her estate and left a proper margin for expenses. A short list of remembrance gifts—and she had kept it up to date—was pinned to the will itself. She wished for a funeral service without hymns. She willed her house and personal property, other than the items specified in the attached list, to be sold and the proceeds to form a trust fund for the education of her great-great-nieces, Emily and Jemima Jeudwine, any residue to be divided between them when they reached the age of twenty-one (they were twins); and she appointed Hugh Dickenson Jeudwine and Lavinia Benton as her executors. Unfortunately, Hugh had died of his injuries a few hours after the car crash in which his geat-aunt had been killed, and the house which was to provide the mainstay of the trust for Hugh's three-year-old daughters was proving unsellable.

During the four months of her executorship Lavinia's snatched visits to Aller Lodge, at first so nostalgic and so executive, had become heartless and vacant. The two servants, a married couple named Mullins, had received their legacies and gone off to let lodgings in Felixstowe; the cat, Dollop, had gone with them. The gifts had been dispatched; the best of the furniture, china and books had gone to the auction rooms in the county town, the silver, the Dutch flower paintings and the collection of clocks to Sotheby's. Remarking that this was no era for fish kettles (thereby providing Lavinia with the germ of half a column about the effects of broadcasting in Mandarin English to English listeners who with their native genius for phrase-making would seize on some devitalised term like 'era' and burnish it into a new arrestingness), the local second-hand dealer had removed several miscellaneous van-loads. What remained was just enough to emphasise that the house needed considerable repair and total redecoration.

Being so empty, it seemed brimful of the noise of the traffic speeding past its ironwork railings and the laurel hedge that protected the long narrow garden. 'All those laurels, too,' Mr Petherick had commented. 'Who's going to keep up laurels nowadays? Laurels are O-U-T Out!'

Yet on Lavinia's visits to Cousin Esther she had never noticed the noise of traffic. During the day, they had so much to say to each other; and Lavinia's bedroom was at the back, looking straight into the pear tree.

'Well, child, here we are, all ready for a nice long talk. Sit down, dear. Have you brought any parlour work?'

'Mm petit point.'

'Let me look at it. H'm. Not too bad, not too bad. Is this the same panel you brought last time? Oh, well, no doubt you've got other things to do in London. Now tell me the latest nonsense.'

'Red flannel nightdresses, with long sleeves, high necks and crochet lace edgings.'

'We had featherstitching. Far more practical, and didn't rag out in the wash.' If Lavinia had cited starched ruffs, ankle-length pantalettes or tiffany aprons as being the latest nonsenses it would turn out that

Cousin Esther had worn them, with improvements. 'Will you have a cigar?'

'Not till after dinner, thank you.'

The cigars had begun when Lavinia decided to leave her husband and earn her own living, and they were Cousin Esther's idea. 'You aren't shocked, are you, at my taking a job?' Lavinia had asked. Since childhood, Cousin Esther's approval had been her fortress. And Cousin Esther had said, 'Shocked, dear? Why should I be? Now you can give up those trivial little cigarettes and smoke cigars. I've always liked George Sand. Charming woman, and so capable. But keep to cigars, duckie; you aren't made for de Mussets.'

Now there was only the noise of traffic, for Cousin Esther was in her grave, and the Boulle clock and the clock that played *Partant pour la Syrie* were ticking at Sotheby's; and the house—the only house where Lavinia smoked cigars—was for sale and no one would buy it.

A section of the noise stopped at the gate. The doorbell rang. A possible buyer? But it was Mr Naylor back again, back with something in his jaws: his expression plainly said so.

'Mrs Benton, I've had an idea. I was thinking about those laurels as I drove along, what a job it would be to keep them trimmed. "Another handicap" I said to myself. Handicap! Why, it's the main feature, though I didn't realise it until one of our own "FOR SALE" boards caught my eye, just outside Beck St Mary's. "AMPLE FRONTAGE". Ample frontage! If ever there was ample frontage, we've got it here. So I turned straight round and came back. And here I am.'

'In time for a cup of tea,' she said. 'I'm just making myself one. Do sit down. I won't be a moment.'

She knew and she did not know. What she unequivocally knew was that unless she kept a firm hand on herself, she was going to be silly.

When she carried in the tray, the French windows had been opened and Mr Naylor was walking up the garden, looking pleased as Adam. He came in, rubbing his hands, flowing with kindheartedness.

'Yes, Mrs Benton, it's perfect; couldn't be better. You can forget about that bathroom now. All we've got to do is to apply for a building permit. And you'll get it, never fear. All this end of Long Monkton is scheduled for development, now that we're getting the bypass. Yes, you'll soon be out of your troubles. I've been pacing it. There's ample room for two.'

'Two?' she said, holding on to the teapot.

'Two bungalows,' said Mr Naylor, as though he were promising oranges to a child—to a Victorian child in a pinafore, to whom oranges meant oranges. Two bungalows. Two families bathing in confidence in Cousin Esther's garden.

'Two bungalows?'

'With garages. Up as soon as winking,' said Mr Naylor. 'And double the money you were hoping to get for the place as it is.'

Double the money. And if not double the thankfulness of Hugh's widow—who whatever she might be about to receive would retain a bleak unthankfulness—a possible ten-per-cent abatement in her conviction that because poor Hughie wasn't there to stand up for his children Lavinia would sell the house to the first comer who offered sixpence for it.

'Which I'm not likely to get, you think?'

'To be honest with you, which would always be my wish, not in a month of Sundays.'

A flimsy hope brushed her.

'Unfortunately, I don't think I could afford to build.'

'Build? Heaven forbid! Why, they'd ruin you. No, no, what you've got to do is to sell as building land. Once you've got the permit through, it'll sell before we can say "knife".'

Two rather tipsy butterflies that had been feasting in the buddleia chased each other in through the French window and chased each other out again. Mr Naylor and me saying 'knife', she thought.

'Two bungalows,' she repeated.

'Or it might be three,' said Mr Naylor, wooing her with three oranges, since only a couple appeared to have fallen rather flat with this lady. 'Yes, that's quite a possibility. For the right sort of buyer, someone with enterprise and enough labour, would think nothing of demolishing the house and putting the third bungalow here, where we are sitting. He could use a lot of the bricks; the lead on the roof alone would be worth a fortune. You could ask according, and get it.'

'But the pear tree!'

'True, that's an item. These old trees, their roots get everywhere. But half an hour with a bulldozer—you'd be surprised. Isn't that the front door?'

The lady dotted with mink carried an order to view from Ransom & Titters. 'Sweet old place, isn't it?' she remarked. 'Georgian all over. I never tire of Georgian. It's got so much character.'

'I'm afraid this is Victorian.'

'Oh! Then why does it look so Georgian? I suppose it was an imitation.'

She was so plainly no buyer that Lavinia did not even feel the adulterous embarrassment of being interrupted while drinking tea with one house agent by the client of another. Mr Naylor was not embarrassed, either. Combining tact with business, he returned to the garden and paced it more scrupulously. The dotted lady was scrupulous, too. Before she left, she had gone into every room, opened every closet, asked every question, saying in the tone of one worn out by bestowing benefits, 'Really? Quite quaint!'

Mr Naylor said chivalrously that with ladies of that kind it was hard to tell. Something might come of her.

'Horrible woman!' said Lavinia. By contrast, Mr Naylor seemed such a bosom friend that she allowed her voice to express some of the dejection she felt. If he felt that dejection was a poor response to the happy issue he had opened before her, he did not show it. He remembered something he must be getting along to, thanked her for the tea, said he would leave her to think it over. In the morning, all she would have to do would be to give him a tinkle. He would bring the application forms and see to the rest.

Still fending it off, she went through the house, opening doors and windows. The lady who adored Georgian had a Georgian insensibility to stinks, and her perfume resounded like a cornet. There was the bedroom, the defrauded bedroom in which Cousin Esther had not died. Everything had gone wrong at the last; the house had been robbed of its due.

'I might as well say Done,' she said to herself, at last. 'Say Done, and say Goodbye.'

Goodbye is a thing best said out-of-doors. She went out, and walked up and down the long flower border, being careful not to glance towards the house, to which the opened windows gave a curious air of animation, of a party being held. She looked at the flowers; she noticed the strong growth of late summer weeds. The jobbing gardener she had hired to give the place a tidy-up was not thorough like Mullins. Never mind, never mind! The flowers did not seem to mind, either; the zinnias, the hollyhocks, the velvety dahlias looked exceptionally sumptuous and thriving. One must admit that flowers prefer the company of weeds to the company of a weeder. Their loyalty is to the vegetable kingdom; they are delighted to get away from the fostering, censuring, interfering guardianship of man. All at once, a dahlia shed its petals. She realised that for the last ten minutes she had not been looking at the flowers; she had not even been conscious of them, she had been exploiting them, spinning a true observation into another whimsical paragraph. Never mind, never mind! Come to that, Mullins would have sent them to the flower show. No wonder they felt more at home with their weeds.

Slowly, with hanging head, she walked across the lawn towards the pear tree. It was an old tree. It was said to have been there before Aller Lodge was built; it was already tall and thick-limbed when Cousin Esther arrived, and none could name it. Its fruit, a dark obsidian green, smooth-rinded, narrow, almost cylindrical, ripened very late and kept throughout the winter. Being so old, the pear tree was also rather fitful and cranky. In the spring of last year it had bloomed so abundantly, so triumphantly, that Cousin Esther had telegraphed to her to come and see it. This year, so Mullins reported when she came for the funeral, there had been a very poor show of bloom and no bees. She laid her hand on its rough bark. 'I have sold you,' she said. At the sound of her words, tears of shame started painfully from her eyes. Shaking her head to free her cheeks of them, she looked up and saw something white. It was a cluster of pear blossoms, newly, perfectly unfolded.

It was startling—she need not let it be more. It was the whim of an old tree, and in fact she had seen other such blossomings in other Augusts. To hear a cuckoo would have been much more remarkable. The blossoms' extreme whiteness enforced the sudden presence of dusk. She must go in and shut those windows before dewfall. She sat down on the plank bench that encircled the trunk of the tree. Suppose she bought the house? She could not afford to; she didn't really want to. Suppose she bought the house? Not from sentiment, not from piety, not from resentment of bungalows, but for her own pleasure. She would keep her old bedroom, of course, smelling the pear blossom in the early morning, sharing bees with it, hearing a pear fall, and another pear fall, as she lay under the eiderdown on the first frosty night, and thinking how, first thing in the morning, she would go down and hunt for them in the long grass. After a time—there need be no hurry about it—Cousin Esther's bedroom would become her spare room, and Emily and Jemima, who by then would be old enough to go visiting without their mother, would sleep there, feeling grand in a grown-up bed, as she had felt, and supported by a night light, as she had been. The traffic would not disturb them—besides, by then the bypass would have taken most of it away; the laurel hedge would be a boundary again. She would repaint the white seat. At night she would go round, locking up the house, turning the familiar, heavy, infallible keys, and afterwards she would lie in the ground-floor bathroom, hearing the owls hooting, and looking at the map of Europe, which fortunately even the reluctant fish-kettle remover had refused to take away. If she bought the house, she would buy other things, too. She would buy an inkpot, a penholder, a packet of steel nibs—and never touch her typewriter again. There should be no more clever slavery. To be on the safe side, she would not even keep a diary, and 'LAVINIA BENTON' would vanish from the printed page until it made its curt farewell appearance in the deaths column. Till then, she would be Mrs Benton, an ageing English lady with a winter hat and a summer hat, who sometimes went to church, who sometimes smoked a cigar after dinner, who sat reading by candlelight because it is more restful for the eyes, or for some such decorous reason. The candlelight would be known because its glow would be seen through the gap in the curtains; no one would know the exquisite pleasure she would find in the smell of sweet wax, lingering on into the next morning. No one would know, since she would not speak of it.

As though her moderate intention of churchgoing had encouraged the church clock, it now chimed a quarter. Looking at her watch, she found it was too dark to read its face. Car lights were stabbing through the laurel hedge. Gently, she got up; gently, she laid her lips to the rough bark of the tree, and kissed it a gentle farewell. It had put out its cluster of blossom—a pure statement of spring, since nothing would come of it. It had given her an hour of happiness.

(A Stranger with a Bag, 1961)

TOTAL LOSS

WHEN Charlotte woke, it was raining. Rain hid the view of the downs and blurred the neat row of trees and the neat row of houses opposite which the trees had been planted to screen. This was the third wet morning since her birthday a week ago. There would be rain all through the holidays, just like last year. On her birthday, Charlotte was ten. 'Now you are in double figures,' said Professor Bayer. 'And you will stay in them till you are a hundred years old. Think of that, my Lottchen.' 'Yes, think of that,' said Mother. Charlotte could see that Mother did not really wish to think of it. She was being polite, because Professor Bayer was a very important person at the Research Station, so it was a real honour that he should like Father and come to the house to borrow *The New Statesman*.

Charlotte's cat Moodie was awake already. He lay on the chair in the corner, on top of her clothes, and was staring at her with a thirsty expression. She jumped out of bed, went to the kitchen, breaking into its early morning tidiness and seclusion, and came back with a saucer of milk. 'Look, Moodie! Nice milk.' He would not drink, though he still had that thirsty expression. 'You silly old Moodles, you don't know what you want,' she said, kneeling before the chair with the saucer in her hand. Moodie had come as a wedding present to Mother. His birthday was unknown, but he was certainly two years older than Charlotte. Ever since she could remember, there had been Moodie, and Moodie had been hers—to be slept on, talked to, hauled about, wheeled in a doll's perambulator, read aloud to, confided in, wept on, trodden on, loved and taken for granted. He stared at her, ignoring the milk, and forgetting the milk she stared back, fascinated as ever by the way the fur grew on his nose, the mysterious smooth conflict between two currents of growth. At last she put down the saucer, seized him in her arms and got back into bed. 'We understand each other, don't we?' she said, curling his tail round his flank. 'Don't we, Moodie?' He trod with his front paws, purring under his breath, and relaxed, his head on her breast. But at the smell of his bad teeth she turned her face away, pretending it was to look out of the window. 'It's raining, Moodie. It's going to be another horrible wet day. You mustn't be a silly cat, sitting in the garden and getting wet through, like you did on Tuesday.' He was still purring when she fell asleep, though when her mother came to wake her he had gone. Sure enough, when she looked for him after breakfast he was sitting hunched and motionless on the lawn, his grey fur silvered with moisture and fluffed out like a coat of eiderdown. She picked him up, and the bloom vanished; the eiderdown coat, suddenly dark and lank, clung to his bony haunches. 'Mother, I'm going to put Moodie in the airing cupboard.'

'Yes, do, my pet. That's the best plan! But hurry, because Mr and Mrs Flaxman will be here to fetch you at any moment. They've just rung up. They want you to spend the day with them.'

'And see the horses?'

The cat in the child's arms broke into a purr, as though her thrill of pleasure communicated itself to him. Though of course it was really the warmth of the kitchen, thought Meg.

'Yes, the horses. And the bantams. And the lovely old toy theatre that belonged to Mrs Flaxman's grandmother. You'll love it. It's an absolutely storybook house.'

'Shall I wear my new mac?'

'Yes. But hurry, Charlotte. Put Moodie in the airing cupboard, and wash your hands. I'll be up in a moment to brush your hair.'

She had made one false step. The Flaxmans lived twenty miles away, and if they had just rung up they could not be arriving immediately. Luckily Charlotte, though brought up to use her reason, was not a very deductive child; the discrepancy between the prompt arriving of the Flaxmans and the long drive back to Hood House was not likely to catch her attention. But perhaps a private word to Adela Flaxman—just to be on the safe side.

'Mother! Mother!'

At the threatening woe of the cry, Meg left everything and ran.

'Mother! There's a button off.'

The Flaxmans arrived, both talking at once, and saying what a horrible day it was, and Oh, the wretched farmers, who would be a farmer? in loud gay voices. Mrs Flaxman was Mother's particular friend, but today Mother didn't seem to like her so much, and was laughing obligingly, just as she did with Professor Bayer. As Charlotte stood on the outskirts of this conversation she began to feel less sure of a happy successful day out. She would be treated like a child and probably given milk instead of tea. Moodie hadn't drunk that milk. 'Mother! Don't forget to feed Moodie.'

'Charlotte! As if I would—' At the same moment Mr Flaxman said, 'Come on, Charlotte! Come on, Adela! The car will catch cold if you don't hurry,' and swept them out of the house.

Meg went slowly upstairs, noticing that the sound of the rain was more insistent in the upper storey of the house. The airing cupboard was in the bathroom. She glanced in quickly and closed the door. She gave the room a rapid tidy, went down, and turned on the wireless.

Meg believed in method. Every morning of the week had its programme; and this was Thursday, when she defrosted the refrigerator, polished the silver and turned out her bedroom—a full morning's work. But today she did none of it, wandering about with a desultory, fidgeting tidiness, taking things up and putting them down again, straightening books on their shelves, nipping dead leaves off the houseplants, while the wireless went on with the Daily Service. There was bound to be a *mauvais quart d'heure*. In fact, everything was well in hand; Charlotte was safely disposed of with the Flaxmans, Moodie was asleep in the airing cupboard and the vet had promised to arrive before midday. It would be quite painless and over in a few minutes. But it was, for all that, a *mauvais quart d'heure*. There are some women, Meg was one of them, in whom conscience is so strongly developed that it leaves little room for anything else. Love is scarcely felt before duty rushes to encase it, anger is impossible because one must always be calm and see both sides, pity evaporates in expedients, even grief is felt as a sort of bruised sense of injury, a resentment that one should have grief forced upon one when one has always acted for the best. Meg's conscience told her that she was acting for the best: Moodie would be spared inevitable suffering, Charlotte protected from a possibly quite serious trauma, Alan undisturbed in his work. Her own distress—and she was fond of poor old

Moodie, no other cat could quite replace him because of his associations —was a small price to pay for all these satisfactory arrangements, and she was ready to pay it, sacrificing her own feelings as duty bid, and as common sense also bid. Besides, it would soon be over. The trouble about an active, strongly developed conscience is that it requires to be constantly fed with good works, a routine shovelling of meritorious activities. And when you have done everything for the best, and are waiting about for the vet to come and kill your old cat and can't therefore begin to defrost a refrigerator or turn out a bedroom, a good conscience soon leaves off being a support and becomes a liability, demanding to be supported itself.

The bad quarter of an hour stretched into half an hour, into an hour, and into an hour and a quarter, while Meg, stiffening at the noise of every approaching car and fancying with every gust of a fitful rising wind that Moodie was demanding with yowls to be let out of the airing cupboard, tried to read but could not, looked for cobwebs but found none and wondered if for this once she would break her rule of not drinking spirits before lunchtime. She was in the kitchen, devouring lumps of sugar, when the vet arrived. She took him to the bathroom, opened the cupboard door, heard him say, 'Well, old man?'

'Would you like me to stop? Is there anything I can do to help?'

'If you could let me have an old towel.'

She produced the towel, and went to her bedroom where she opened the window and looked out on the rain and the tossing trees and remembered that everyone must die. At last she heard the basin tap turned on, the vet washing his hands, the water running away.

'Mrs Atwood. Have you got a box?'

'A box?'

He stood in the passage, a tall, red-faced young man, the picture of health.

'Any sort of carton. To take it away in. A sack would do.'

She had not remembered that Moodie would require a coffin. In a flurry of guilt she began to search. There was a brown paper carrier; but this would not do, Moodie could not be borne away swinging from the vet's hand. There was the carton the groceries had come in; but it was too small, and had Pan Yan Pickles printed on it. At last she found a plain oblong carton, kept because it was solid and serviceable. Deciding that this would do, she glanced inside and realised that it would not do like that. Moodie could not be put straight into an empty box: there must be some sort of lining, of padding. She tore old newspaper into strips and crumpled the strips to form a mattress; and then, remembering that flowers are given to the dead, she snatched a couple of dahlias from a vase and scattered the petals on top of the newspaper. The vet was standing in the bathroom, averting his eyes from the bidet, the towel neatly folded was balanced on the edge of the basin, and on the bathroom stool was Moodie's unrecognisably shabby, degraded, dead body. Before she realised what she was saying, she had said, 'If you'll hold the box, I'd like to put him in.'

Yet what else could she say? She owed it to Moodie. She lifted him on her two hands, as she had lifted him so often. The unsupported head fell horribly to one side, lolling like the clapper of a bell. She got the body in somehow, and the vet closed the lid of the carton and carried it away. She knew she ought to have thanked him, but she could not speak. She had never seen a dead body before—except on food counters, of course.

She went downstairs and drank a stiffish whisky. Her sense of proportion reasserted itself. One cannot expect to be perfect in any first performance. She had not behaved at all as she had meant to when Charlotte was born. It was a pity about the makeshift box; it was a pity not to have thanked the vet; but the essentials had been secured, Charlotte was safe and happy at Hood House, Alan was happy and busy in his laboratory; neither of them need ever know what agony is involved in the process of rationally, mercifully, putting an end to an old pet. She would make a quick lunch of bread and cheese, and then be very busy. She heard a distant peal of thunder, and welcomed the thought of a good rousing thunderstorm. Something elemental would be releasing. After a few more long, grumbling reverberations the storm moved away, but when she went to defrost the refrigerator she found it darkened and cavernous, and the current off throughout the house. The power lines on Ram Down were always getting struck. She left the refrigerator to natural forces, and as she couldn't use the Hoover either, she polished the silver and sat down to do some mending. She was a bad needle-woman; mending kept her mind occupied till a burst of sunlight surprised her by its slant. She had no idea it was so late. Charlotte would be back at any moment.

Just as the current had gone off, leaving the refrigerator darkened and cavernous, the support of a good conscience now withdrew its aid. Charlotte would be back at any moment. Charlotte would have to be told. Time went on. Suppose there had been a car smash? Charlotte mangled and dying at the roadside, and all because she had been got out of the house while the vet was mercifully releasing Moodie? Meg's doing —how could one ever get over such a thing and lead a normal life again?

She was sitting motionless and frantic when Alan came in, switching on the light in the hall.

'Well, Meg—Why are you looking so wrought up? Didn't the vet come? Couldn't he do his stuff?'

'Oh, yes, that was all right. But Charlotte's not back.'

'When did they say they'd bring her?'

'Adela didn't say exactly. She said, a good long day. But it's long over that—Adela knows how particular I am about bedtime.'

'Why not ring up?'

'But I am sure they must have started by now.'

'Well, someone would be about. They've got that cook. What's their number?'

She heard him in the hall, dialling. Then he came back saying the line seemed to be dead. Ten minutes later, a car drew up and Charlotte rushed into the house, followed by Mrs Flaxman.

'Mother, Mother! It's been so marvellous, it's been so thrilling. We were struck by lightning. There was a huge flash, bright blue, and the telephone shot across the room and broke ever so much china, and there was an awful noise of horses screaming their heads off and Mr Flaxman tore out to see if the stables had been struck too, and then ran back saying, 'They're all right but our bloody roof's on fire.' And there were great fids of burning thatch flying about everywhere, and Mr Flaxman went up a ladder and I and Mrs Flaxman got buckets and buckets of water and handed them up to him. And I was ever so useful, Adela said so, wasn't I, Mrs Flaxman?'

'I don't know what we'd have done without you, my pet,' said Mrs Flaxman to Charlotte, and to Meg, 'She got very wet, but we've dried her.'

'And then people came rushing up from the village and trod on the bantams.'

'No, nothing's insured except the portraits and the horses. Giles won't, on principle. Yes, calamitous—but it could have been worse. No, no, not at all, it's been a pleasure having her.'

Adela was gone, leaving the impression of someone from a higher sphere in a hurry to return to its empyrean.

For the present, there was nothing to be done but listen to Charlotte and try not to blame the Flaxmans for having let her get so over-excited. Both parents lit cigarettes and prepared themselves for a spell of entering into their child's world; after all, fifteen minutes earlier, they had been fearing for her life. They smoked and smiled and made appropriate interjections. Suddenly her narrative ran out, and she said, 'Where's Moodie?'

For by the time one is ten one knows when one's parents are only pretending to be interested. Back again in a home that had no horses, no bantams, no curly golden armchairs, no portraits of gentlemen in armour and low-necked ladies, was never struck by lightning and gave her no opportunities to be brave and indispensable, Charlotte concentrated on the one faithful satisfaction it afforded and said, 'Where's Moodie?'

Mastering a feeling like stage-fright, Meg said with composure, 'Darling. Moodie's not here.'

'Why isn't he? Has he run away? Has anything happened to him?'

'Not exactly that. But he's dead.'

'Why? Why is he dead? He was quite well this morning. Why is he dead?'

'You know, darling, poor Moodie hasn't really been feeling well for a long time. He was an old cat. He had an illness.'

Charlotte saw Moodie's broad face, and his eyes staring at her with that thirsty expression. Moodie was dead. Mother had explained to her about death, making it seem very ordinary.

'You remember how horrid his breath smelled?'

'Yes. That was his teeth.'

'It wasn't only his teeth. It was something inside that was bound to kill him sooner or later. And he would have suffered a great deal. So the vet came and gave him an injection and put him to sleep. It was all over in a minute.'

Moodie had gone out and sat in the rain. The child's glance moved to the window and remained fixed on the lawn—so green in the sunset that it was almost golden. It was a french window. Without a word, she opened it and went out.

'Poor Charlotte!' said Alan. 'She's taking it very well. I must say, I think you rubbed it in a bit too much. You needn't have said he stank.'

Meg repressed the retort that if Alan could have done it so much better he might perfectly well have done so. In silence, they watched Charlotte walking about in the garden. It was a very small garden, and newly-planted, and the gardens on either side of it were small and newly-planted too, and only marked off by light railings. To Meg, whose childhood had known a garden with overgrown shrubs, laurel hedges, a disused greenhouse and a toad, it seemed an inadequate place to grieve in; but from the eighteenth century onwards people have turned for comfort to the bosom of nature, and Charlotte was doing so now, among the standard roses and the begonias. She walked up and down, round and round, pausing, walking on again. 'Going round his old haunts,' said Alan. Moodie, as Meg knew, shared her opinion of the garden; he used it to scratch in, but for any serious haunting went to Mopson's Garage where he and the neighbourhood cats clubbed among the derelict cars. A sense of loss pierced her; knowing Moodie's ways had been a kind of illicit Bohemianism in her exemplary, rather lonely life. But it was Charlotte's loss she must think of—and Charlotte's supper, which was long overdue.

'I wish she'd come in—but we mustn't hurry her.'

Alan said, 'She's coming now.'

Charlotte was walking towards the house, walking with a firm tread. Her face was still pale with shock, but her expression was composed, resolved, even excited. I must give her a sedative, thought Meg. Charlotte entered, saying, 'I've chosen the place for his grave.'

After the bungled explanations that one couldn't, that the lawn would never be the same again, that it wasn't their garden, that the lease expressly forbade burying animals had broken down under the child's cross-examination into an admission that there was no body to bury, that the vet had taken it away, that it could not be got back, that it had been disposed of, that in all probability it had been burned to ashes as her parents' bodies would in due course be burned; after Charlotte, declaring she would never forgive them, never, that they were liars and murderers, that she hated them and hoped they would soon be burned to ashes themselves had somehow been got to bed, they sat down, exhausted, not looking at each other.

'That damned cat!'

As though Alan's words had unloosed it, a wailing cry came from overhead.

'O Moodie, Moodie, Moodie!

'O Moodie, Moodie, Moodie!'

Implacable as the iteration of waves breaking on a beach, the wailing cries rang through the house. Twice Meg started to her feet, was told not to be weak-minded, and sat down again. Alan ought to be fed. Something ought to be done. The mere thought of food made her feel sick. Alan was filling his pipe. Staring in front of her, lost in a final imbecility of patience, she found she was looking at the two dahlia stalks whose petals she had torn away.

'O Moodie, Moodie, Moodie!'

The thought of something to be done emerged. 'We must put off that new kitten,' she said.

'Why?'

Completing her husband's exasperation, Meg buried her face in her hands and began to cry.

'O Moodie,' she lamented. 'Oh, my kind cat!'

(*A Stranger with a Bag*, 1961)

OXENHOPE

As unfailingly as one knows that the sensation of Venice is called
Venice, of Avila, Avila, William knew that the sensation of Oxenhope was called Oxenhope. He had not been back since he was
seventeen. Now he was sixty-four, and during the interval he had
certainly never heard the name spoken, or spoken it himself except when
he said to Isabel they might go there for their honeymoon (they went to
Aix-en-Provence). He had stayed at Oxenhope for a month. Since then
his life in the Consular Service had made him almost a resident in many
different places; and Isabel was dead, and Isabelita married and settled
in Canada, and a typhoid fever had mauled and telescoped his memories, and recovery had left him feeling like a castaway on the remainder of
what life was left to him. But he could still remember every fibre
of the sensation which was called Oxenhope.

The typhoid fever was not his first experience of brain-mauling. On
the heels of winning a university scholarship, he discovered that all the
facts he had grouped so tidily had dissolved into a broth stirred by an
idiot. Evading his parents' thankful delight, he slunk away on the pretext
of a walking tour. At the station in his Midland town, suddenly
repossessing the name Hawick, he bought a ticket for Hawick. At
Hawick he got out onto a platform raised like a bridge above a river and
saw a rise of ground beyond factory chimneys. He aimed for this, and
presently he was walking up a long steep hill, where there was meadow-
sweet growing in the ditches beside the road. As he had never known its
name, he looked at it with pleasure. Some time after this an evening sky
became a night sky. Unable to remember the name of a single constella-
tion, he lay down among some heather and fell asleep. The next day he
still walked, and a sensation like pleasure hovered somewhere behind

his appalling consciousness of guilt, like the sun behind a fog. That afternoon, following a narrow road that wound beside a river, he saw a farmhouse on the side of a hill, and went to the door and asked for a glass of milk. He was taken into a parlour, where he sat down on a horsehair chair. The woman who brought the milk in a heavy cut-glass tumbler looked at him in silence, then went away and returned with a plate of scones. It struck him that her expression showed concern. Perhaps she was afraid of thunder. For the room had suddenly grown cold and dark, and he remembered how heavy the air had been during the last few miles and how leaden the river had lain between its green banks. He got up, thanking her, shouldering his pack and feeling for his money. 'None of that,' she said. 'If you were a dog you shouldn't go out from here with such a storm gathering.' Before he could answer, a blaze of lightning cut between them.

Like old friends they stood in the doorway watching the storm drive down the valley. Beneath it, the hills seemed shapeless and weltering as waves—those hills he was soon to know by their names, climbing them one after another and looking from their summits to other hills beyond.

All night the rain sang in the gutter pipes and clattered on the corrugated-iron roofs of the farm buildings; and sometimes another kick of lightning lit the wall where there hung a crayon copy of 'The Stag of Eve'. He lay in a narrow bed in an innocent room with a large white chamber pot under the table that held a ewer and basin, a painted deal chest of drawers with a crochet-edged towel laid across the top, and a small swinging mirror on a mahogany stand. Eating his supper among strangers, put to bed in a strange room, he registered nothing except his hostess's calm, large-boned face, which he saw as something irrevocably known, as though immortalised by that first lightning flash. For the rest, there was a husband, a daughter called Maggy, two sons younger than she, and three or four farm servants eating at the same table. The farm, he learned, was called Oxenhope, and behind it, deep-set in the hill, was the Oxenhope Burn.

Next morning, the woman was looking down on his awakening. He began to thank her, to apologise for having overslept. She said, 'And where were you thinking of going on to?'

'Oh, nowhere in particular. Just on. I'm on a walking tour.'

'A walking tour,' she repeated. 'Ah well, you'll be staying here for the present.'

For the first few days, she organised him, telling him to write to his mother, and how to get to the post office, and how to address the postmistress, who was a bit deaf but didn't like to be reminded of it, and where to ford the river, and where to avoid the bull, and not to trust the plank bridge, and where to skirt the hornet's nest. And she gave him odd jobs to settle him—potatoes to scrape, rowanberries to pick for jelly making, knives to sharpen, peats to fetch in. When she judged him able to stand alone, she loosed him to go as he pleased.

If he had been that dog she spoke of, he would have stayed at Oxenhope for the rest of his life. He stayed for a month, bathing in the infinity of time and space. Then he went south, pleased and excited to be going to Cambridge with the scholarship he would soon outgrow as the cuckoo outgrows the nest. For his wits had come back to him and he was no longer intimidated by his learning.

One of the last things she had set him to do was to clean up the family gravestones, lending him a bicycle to cover the eight miles between the farm and the kirk, equipping him with a knife to pick the lichen out of the inscriptions and a toothbrush to brush it away with. It had been a cheerful morning's work, listening to the curlews and the minister's conversational hens, with the wind bringing him the noise of the river from time to time, and he had made a good job of it, so that he took credit to himself—a step back to his rational man.

But it must be a long time now since anyone had cleaned the gravestones.

It took him longer than he expected to find them. As he drove up the valley it seemed to him that it was even more sparsely populated than he remembered. The increase was in the population of the dead. Assuring himself that by now she must be dead, he had not allowed for all the others whom time had raked there and laid in close rows. He was beginning to think she might still be alive when he found himself looking at her name: Helen Sword, Wife to Robert Scott of Oxenhope. She had died in 1942, her husband five years after her. The curlews were crying, the wind was in the same quarter, but blowing more steadily, so that the noise of the river poured into his ears. He took out his knife and began to scratch at her encrusted name. The chiseling was shallow and imprecise compared to that of the earlier names above hers and on the two other stones. It was as if by this date there was not the same expectation of being remembered. A tradesman's van went up the valley as he worked and was back again, so it seemed, in a whisk. Eight miles was not so long as it had been. The Renault 1100 would take him to Oxenhope while his mind was still delaying as to whether or not he would stop at the gate.

It was his mind that carried him past it and on. As the road shook off the manse's windbreak fir plantations and the bare narrowing valley extended before him, he began to boil like a pot in the ecstasy of recognition. There, on the slope of Singlee Knowe, was the dry-stone sheepfold with the dark ring of nettles round it like the woolwork mat under a potted plant. There was the rushy field where the floods carried the hay before the haymakers could. There was the line of crouching alders beside the Drum Pool, and the flashing shoal beyond it. There, under the outcropping of rock, was the boggy cleft where he had found grass-of-Parnassus. There, like a wrinkle on a shaven cheek, was the Oxenhope Burn fissuring the hillside. He drove over the bridge (it was almost too narrow for his car) and past the house, only noticing that the porch was gone and that the herd's cottage had a television mast. The road dwindled on ahead, turning to a grassy track where groups of sheep were feeding. He slowed the car to a standstill. They did not move away. When he sounded his horn they turned their pale fanatic faces toward him, and the foremost of them stamped his hoof pettishly once or twice and then fell to feeding again. Suddenly, for no apparent reason, they all turned and bolted up the hillside. Half a mile farther on he came to another group of sheep, who behaved in identically the same way, and he recalled Jimmie Laidlaw, the Scott's shepherd, remarking that sheep were very regulated animals. For a moment it seemed that Jimmie's actual voice was creaking and whirring in his ears. He sometimes used to find that he heard too much of it; Jimmie, because of his solitary calling, was like an uncorked bottle when he came on a hearer. He talked about sheep, and hard winters, and a black dog that dragged a coffin over Cold Face on Old Year's Night, and a sheepfold that moved with the solstice, so that every time you came to it the opening was a little farther round; and of wildcats, and Covenanters, and lights hovering above the water, moving and staying as the current carried the drowned body, lodged it against an obstacle, worked it free again; and of cholera, and the itch, and an ash tree that cured rickets. But now he rather wished Jimmie would come with his slow shepherd's trudge along the track. Jimmie with his memory extending in all directions was one of those people who need never die; and he would answer questions about Maggy and the two boys, and what changes the unchanging valley had seen, and who was at the post office in these days. But all these questions William could ask later on, and have them answered or not; they were husks of the past, no more.

The past was in the present—the narrowed valley, the steeper hills crowding into it, the river running with a childish voice. On from the junction with the Aila Burn it was scarcely a river at all—just a winding green morass, speechless unless you sank your foot in it. So on the day when he had set out to track the river to its head it was natural that he should have followed the tributary Aila Burn, that ran in a deep crevice, like the Oxenhope Burn, but more steeply. Hauling himself up from waterfall to waterfall, here by a rowan, there by handfuls of heather, he had come to a pool, wide enough to swim a few strokes across, deep enough—though it was so clear that its pebbles seemed within hand's reach—to take him up to the neck. He had stripped and bathed in the ice-cold water, threshing about like a kelpie, and then clambered out on a slab of rock to dry in the sun. He had lain so still in his happiness that after a while an adder elongated itself from the heather roots, lowered the poised head with its delicate, tranquil features, and basked on the rock beside him. There they had lain till a hawk's shadow crossed them, and with a flick the adder was gone.

He could not hope to climb the Aila Burn this time, but for love of the adder he would press the car on till he came within earshot of its waterfalls.

He got out and went as far as the first waterfall, because, like an epicure, he wanted to drink the water at its coldest and most elemental. It thrust into his hand and out again, drenching his sleeve. The plunge of the water into the pool, the stone, mottled like a trout, which it incessantly broke its sleek neck on, the renewed surface, fanning out and smoothly hastening away—he recognised everything. Other recognitions were everywhere around him, tingling in rocks, in soggy patches at the rocks' foot, in the shadow of a hill moving across another hill, in tufts of sheep's wool caught on wire fencing, in the wind's hoo-hooing in the crannies of stone walls, in the seething hiss of dried heather bells. A grouse caught sight of him and cried out, 'Go-back, go-back, go-back!' But the adjuration was beside the point. The past was in the present, and he was back. Where next? If he could not climb, he could walk. Even without deciding, he knew: another drink from the Aila Burn, a ham sandwich in the car; then, circling up the heathery shoulder of Phawp Law, to the Cat Loch. Even if he could not get all the way, he would at least go far enough to look down on it, as he had done on that astonishing first sight. For when one's last backward glance at a river showed it no wider than a skein of darning wool, one does not expect to see a lake lying on the knees of the hills, a lake with nothing running into it or draining out of it, yet complete with a boathouse.

On a later occasion he was to push out of that boathouse—an experience that would have been a solemn rapture if it had not been for the company of Oliphant, the keeper. Oliphant was a harmless enough fellow, but Levitical, and bent on making it clear he wasn't a native. It was for this reason that Major Baxter could allow him to take a rod on the loch from time to time: 'I can trust you not to take out more than three of the trout.' The trout were pink-fleshed and like Oliphant, imported from elsewhere. He was punctilious in seeing that William should have the first casts and polite in saying he was doing well, that all he needed was a little practice. With the fatality of beginners, William caught a fish. It wasn't a large one, but Oliphant netted it as ceremoniously as if it had been a salmon, and killed it by knocking its head against the side of the boat. It went on leaping galvanically, long after—which, according to Oliphant, proved its lineage. They fished on, but it was the only fish they caught.

He had remembered the height of Phawp Law more or less accurately; but he had forgotten to allow for its bulk. Even when the skyline had no more tricks to play on him there was a great stretch of ground to cover. The climb had dizzied him; he had no impetus left. He could only walk by small ambitions—as far as the tuft of rushes, thence on to a farther tuft, thence on under the jut of a peat hag, thence over an expanse of burned and bristling heather. Watching his steps, he was in full sight of the loch before he saw it. It lay in its aureole of rainbow grass and was the same rather sullen blue—the blue of bog water. The boat-house, however, was gone.

Well, there was the Cat Loch, intact and solitary and self-possessing. The blur of Oliphant and Major Baxter and himself had been wiped off it, like breath off a mirror. No one fished there now, unless it were a heron. He sat down and listened to his mind making fragmentary remarks, spaced among his gasps for breath. An uncommonly silly heron. No sensible heron . . . would come so far . . . on the chance of spiking a fish on that shelving rim. 'Old herons go a-fishing there.' . . . Odd, when you come to think of it, that in popular speech the word 'old' is used as a semi-endearment. Not so endearing when you have to nail it into the lonely flesh. He went on listening to his mind's limping trivialities, sheltering against the moment when he would have to admit that the past was draining away out of the present, that Oxenhope, lovely as ever, was irrecoverable, that he would never possess the sensation of Oxenhope again. He had grasped at the substance, and the lovely shadow was lost. For suppose it were possible to implement that sketchy project of finding a house in the valley and ending his days there—what would he do? Take himself out for walks, record the weather in a notebook, suck a rowanberry in autumn, huddle his old bones through the long winters, wonder if he would smell the summer heather again and find the grass-of-Parnassus? He looked at his watch. It had taken him ninety minutes to get here. Another ninety minutes would see him down. He would get into the car and drive away and be at the hotel in time for dinner. As incontrovertibly as she had said, 'You'll be staying here for the present,' the loch said, 'You'll be away by tomorrow.'

He was stirring to get to his feet when he knew, as an animal does, that he was being watched; and like an animal, he became motionless. It was an intense scrutiny: no sheep watches one so; perhaps it was a weasel. Sliding his glance in the direction of the watcher, he saw two brilliant pink flowers lighting a clump of heather: two outstanding ears with the sun shining through them. The boy had concealed himself very well, but his ears betrayed him.

If I had been that boy, thought William, I would have wished the unsuspecting stranger to go away and leave me to trail him. And after a decency-pause he did his part in the transaction. The boy had more strategy than to follow him across the stretch of burned heather. A hare starting up the slope showed that he must have taken a lower course, parallel to William's. Later, a couple of sheep were disturbed. Later still, the boy began to run at full tilt down the remainder of the hillside, dislodging stones, swishing through bracken, leaving a track of sound behind him. When William was down and approaching his car along the grassed road, he saw the boy approaching it from the opposite direction. Though his ears were no longer translucent, they were certainly the same ears.

The sun had left the valley, and the snipe flickered like shadows over the green of the damp grass. The air was full of chill and poetry, and it was the moment to put on an overcoat. Ignoring the boy, who was now standing by the car without appearing to have stopped there, William leaned in and released the lid of the bonnet. The boy started back as he raised it, and exclaimed, 'Mercy!'

'The engine is at the back.'

'Oh, aye.'

'Would you like to look at it?'

'Aye.'

The boy examined the engine carefully but without passion. Clearly, his proper study was man.

'Would you like a lift down the valley?'

'I wouldna mind,' said the boy, falling into the trap.

'Where do you live?'

'At Crosscleugh.'

Having by his countertrap established that William was not a total stranger to the valley, the boy became hospitable. 'Yon's Carra Law,' he said. 'Yon's Cold Face.'

William looked at the one and the other with attention.

'Yon's Scraggie Law. There was a man once, put goats on it. They were Spanish goats. They didna do.'

'One couldn't expect it.'

'This is the Aila Burn,' the boy continued. 'There's a pool halfway up it, no bigger than a barrel. But it's deep. Once it drowned six sheep. There was a snowstorm and they fell in. Then they couldna get out. The burn ran red with blood—the way they fought each other with their feet.'

William had heard that story from Jimmie Laidlaw. 'What's that hill?'

'That's just Phawp Law.'

They looked at each other sternly.

'There's a loch away up there,' the boy said. 'It's called the Cat Loch.'

'Why is it called the Cat Loch?'

'I couldna say. Something to do with a cat, maybe.' A vision transfigured his face as the sun had transfigured his ears. 'There was a man once, set fire to it. He was in a boat, and he set fire to the water. There was flames coming up all round the boat. Like a gas ring.'

Oliphant, interminably rowing about the loch for likely places, had thrust down his oar to check the boat's movement. Bubbles of marsh gas rose to the surface. William saw himself leaning out of the boat and touching off their tiny incandescence with a lighted match.

'What colour were the flames?' he asked.

'They was blue.'

'Jump in,' William said briskly, and turned the car. When the surface allowed, he drove fast, to please the boy. He put him down at Crosscleugh (there was still a white marble dog in the garden) and drove on. There was no call for a backward glance, for an exile's farewell. He had his tenancy in legend. He was secure.

(*The Innocent and the Guilty*, 1971)

A LONG NIGHT

HENRY SPARROW had been directed to the endmost of the two-seat tables in the dining car; and as it had grown too dark to look out of the window and dinner was not yet being served and the young man sitting opposite had not struck him as the kind of fellow-traveller he would enjoy talking to he resumed the dissatisfied speculations which the notice above the young man's seat had been intermittently arousing in him during a course of years:

PRIÈRE D'EXIGER UNE NOTE POUR TOUTE
SOMME VERSÉE

The French official mind emerges from an unswervingly applied education, which includes (under grammar) verse forms, the caesura, *rimes riches* and *rimes suffisantes*, together with admired passages of declamation to be scanned, analysed and learned by heart. So it was natural enough that a notice in a *wagon-restaurant* should open as though it meant to be an Alexandrine. But the author couldn't keep it up; he fell into that torrent of syllables and was swept on, helpless, till he clawed himself back onto the classic manner with his '*versée*'—a preposterous word in the circumstances, thought Henry Sparrow, who had learned during the Medium and Advanced French of his school days to associate it with flowers and tears.

The car had filled up, a man had come round with the basket of rolls, the train had entered the Simplon Tunnel and Henry, who did not like being beaten by a trifle, applied himself yet once again to rescuing that foundered Alexandrine. A bold, but permissible, expedient would be to treat the opening as a half line:

Prière d'exiger
Une note, Messieurs les Voyageurs. . . .

But this only postponed the crisis, besides demanding a larger expanse of public advertising space.

The lights flickered, and went out.

For a moment, no one spoke. The noise of the trains grinding up the incline took over, and was portentous. Someone farther down the car clicked a cigarette lighter; someone else struck a match. A voice from across the table exclaimed, 'Oh, thank God!'

With more clicking of lighters, striking of matches, everyone began to talk. There was a dawn chorus of cheerful expostulations, and car attendants appeared with little lanterns. Under cover of this, Henry said, 'Why? Why "Thank God"?'—for the voice had sounded so abjectly relieved that curiosity was too much for him.

'I always think I've gone blind. Silly, isn't it?'

In the train journey that took Henry to and from his boarding school there had been a certain tunnel—not long enough to warrant lighting up but long enough to impose that darting panic, that interval of accepting the worst. Even when familiarity had taught him not to be an ass he still dreaded the tunnel, because, though it could no longer frighten him, it could remind him how horribly frightened he had been. 'Most people feel like that, at some time or another,' he said. 'Especially when they are young. When one is young, one has a great deal of superfluous fear. Young animals—' He was about to instance colts when the lights came on again, and the attendants began serving the first course.

There sat the young man whom Henry had decided he would not enjoy talking to. A weedy specimen: long, thin neck, high, spotty forehead, callow chin beard—everything about him was weedy. With his shabby-jaunty air, and his pale eyes flinching in their dark circles of sleeplessness, he was at once pathetic and unprepossessing. But a contact had flashed between them; conversation must be kept up.

'I suppose it was a fuse,' Henry said. 'I'm glad they put it right. The tunnel would seem even more interminable if we had to sit in the dark.'

'How long is it?'

'I believe it takes about twenty minutes.'

'Twenty minutes? I don't call that much. I've been through a tunnel in Norway that takes thirty-eight minutes.'

Henry said 'Really?' and hoped the conversation might now languish.

Presently the young man revived it.

'The whole of this journey strikes me as interminable. I loathe these internationalised trains. They're so artificial. . . . *Garçon! Un Coke.*'

'Have you been travelling long?'

'I haven't had a proper sleep for the last four nights. I don't know if you call that long.'

The train had altered its voice. Like an underground stream, it was hurrying down to the valley of the Rhône. Henry, knowing that this was not the solicited inquiry, inquired, 'Have you much farther to go?'

'Liverpool. What's this mess? Veal, I suppose. It's always veal.'

'*A l'Ambassadeur.* In a cream sauce, with mushrooms,' said the attendant, in English.

This is insufferable, thought Henry; I shall get out at Sion. . . . And why not? He had long wanted to hear that venerable organ which had snored and tweedled through so many centuries; he was not particularly expected at home; so why not get out at Sion? All that would be required was the strength of mind to discount the cost of his sleeper and to reclaim his suitcase and passport from the *wagon-lit* attendant. There would be time to finish his veal, which was excellent; then he would assert himself as a freeborn Englishman, rise, pay and escape from the odious young fellow.

Meanwhile the odious young fellow was talking on. 'The only way to travel is on foot. It's the only way you get to know the real country, the real people. Live with peasants and help with the harvest. Drink the local wines. Stay in little fishing ports, go out in the boats, sing, get to know everybody. When I'm in a place like that, I always make a point of going to church.'

'What do you do in Rome?' asked Henry. He knew this would be wasted, and it was.

'Rome? Don't talk to me of Rome. I'd no sooner got into this train than a ghastly slum family was shoved in on top of me—father, mother, three kids, all their earthly belongings in bags and baskets. And they'd come on from Rome—they said so. One of the kids is some sort of cripple, and does nothing but whine and fidget. And his dear Mum does nothing but jump up and down, getting this out of one basket and that out of another, to tempt his appetite. I don't know what they're doing on a rapid. They ought to be in a cattle truck.'

This, too, was overheard by the attendant, who had removed Henry's neat plate and hovered uncertainly over the young man's mauled remains.

'Talking of travelling—yes, take it away, I'm through—I ran into a bit of real life in Turkey. Have you ever been in Turkey?'

'Only on the beaten track.'

'The what? Oh, yes, the beaten track. Well, this wasn't the sort of thing you'd find on the beaten track. It was off in the mountains. I'd been walking all day. I'd seen one shepherd in the morning; after that, no one—just a few eagles. And it had got dark suddenly. You know how suddenly it gets dark in Turkey; even on the beaten track you'd notice that. It looked like a case of under-the-stars for me—not the first time, either—when I saw some tall white things: they were tombstones in a cemetery. And beside it was a broken-down old mosque. Well, I thought, no smoke without fire; where there's dead folks, there's live folks. Sure enough there was a village. Well, knowing how hospitable these mountain Turks are—hospitality's a sacred duty with them—I knocked at a door. No answer. I knocked at another door. No answer. I called. A dog began howling. That was all. There was a storm coming up, and a perishing wind. So I went back to the mosque and curled up just inside. Last thing I knew was the dog howling. When I woke, it was daylight, and the dog was still howling. And the floor of the mosque was covered with stiffs. I must have picked the one place where there wasn't a stiff. And every one of them had spots. Plague spots! Did I hop it? Just think!' said the young man, leaning over the table. 'Just think! If a flea off one of those stiffs had bitten me, I'd have got plague!'

'A near thing,' said Henry. It was the best he could do. The story, told by old Dr Protheroe, had made a deep impression on him when he was eight years old and newly allowed to sit up for Sunday supper. In the Protheroe version it was typhus, and there was no dog. The dog was a good touch, and if the young man had supplied it, it did him credit. *Ars longa*, thought Henry. Two world wars, the Spanish Influenza epidemic, Auschwitz, Hiroshima had gone by and were in process of being forgotten. Old Dr Protheroe's story was as lively as ever; in time it would certainly be told on the moon. Art is long, and tough, and never loses a tooth. This Ninon de l'Enclos of a narrative was fastened in the very flesh of the poor braggart sitting below *Prière d'exiger*. By dint of telling, it had become his story, it had happened to him. His neck swelled, his eyes bulged, there was sweat on his forehead; if one had taken his hand, how horribly clammy the palm would be! Now he would dream about it, and cry out in his sleep. But on reflection, the poor wretch would not be in a way for nightmares; he was spending the night in that crowded compartment with the sickly child and the fidgeting mother.

Coffee was served, the case of liqueurs brought round. Henry had a brandy and offered one to the young man.

'No, thanks. I don't drink alcohol. In any form.' Earlier in the conversation, he had been drinking the wine of the country with peasants—but no matter.

Bills were made out and laid on the tables. The head of the service came round with his cashbox. The young man glanced at his bill, pulled out his wallet, put down a couple of notes. The head of the service, a tout, Father-Christmasy Swiss, shook his head. 'These are lire notes, Monsieur. The charge is in francs.'

When the bill had been settled, the young man said to Henry with a limping smile, 'That's done for my breakfast.' It was the first unfeigned remark he had made since his 'Oh, thank God!' and Henry was completely at a loss how to answer it. 'Unless they'll take these.' With a flourish, the young man threw some Turkish notes on the table and looked at Henry as much as to say, 'There! Now do you believe me?'

Henry was prepared to believe the young man had been in Turkey; he had a vivid mind's-eye picture of him going for a walk beyond a bus stop, trembling at every dog, kite and skin eruption. He knew he ought to ask appropriate questions. He also knew that he ought to offer to change the notes. If he had been asked to, he would have done it willingly enough. However, he was glad he had not been asked, as then he would have put himself under an obligation (for every obligation is two-sided, the one who obliges being tied by the acceptance of the one obliged) and he did not want to be under an obligation to this boasting, flinching mongrel, whom he was now quite inordinately disliking. Besides, it was too late. He had thought about it. Such acts are only possible if one does them suddenly, and Henry was not a person who did things suddenly.

A moment later, the suddenness of his action was as surprising as though a rocket had exploded off his lips. He had said, 'You'll go to pieces if you don't get a night's sleep. I'm going to put you in my sleeper.'

'In your sleeper? Very kind of you, I'm sure. But I'm afraid it's out of the question. I'd really rather not.' The refusal, beginning haughtily, ended coyly. It was clear that he had no doubt of Henry's intentions, and that the coyness was a cautious acceptance of them.

'Where's your compartment?' said Henry. 'Two cars down? Good! Then you can pick up your traps on the way. Come on!'

Watching from the corridor, he saw the look of alarm on the mother's face, and the sadness of her gesture as she woke the child who had stretched out into the vacated seat, gathered him to her and settled his feet on a bundle. The young man jerked down a suitcase from the rack, stumbled over the bundle, stumbled against the man who sat in the inner corner nursing a fiddle case and came away, exclaiming, 'My God, what a pigsty!'

'Come on,' said Henry once more. His rage was now sabled with gloom. Not only was he about to put this young cad into his sleeper, he would also have to explain the transfer to the *wagon-lit* attendant. It would probably turn out to be against the regulations. In which case he would . . . He really did not know what he would do, except that nothing on earth should prevent him from doing a thing he would do with the utmost ill-willingness.

The attendant was sitting in his small apartment, looking monkish. He was an immensely tall man, with an inured expression. When he stood up, he did it with a functional agility, as though he were an expanding ladder and part of the equipment. Henry, concentrating on the matter-of-course aspect of thus disposing of a sleeper, almost forgot whom he was proposing to put into it till, with the words, 'This gentleman here', he glanced back at the young man standing behind him. Dirty, hangdog, apprehensive, the young man looked like a criminal hauled before yet another official person who would presently find him out. Inflamed by that chivalry towards oppressed criminals by which a law-abiding Englishman compounds his law-abidingness, Henry prepared to give battle. The attendant shrugged his shoulders and said he must have the gentleman's passport and ticket. The young man produced them with the affable air of one who has again diddled the authorities, and was conducted to the sleeper.

Henry stood in the corridor waiting to tip. The attendant reappeared. 'I'm afraid I can't offer Monsieur another sleeper,' he said. 'And the train is very full tonight. However, some people may be getting out at

Lausanne. You might find a seat then. It is possible.' His voice had a skin of solicitude over a granite disapprobation. Scratch a Frenchman and you'll find a schoolmistress, thought Henry, quite unfairly. Deciding that he would go back to the restaurant car for another brandy, he began to walk through the train. In the corridor of a first-class a man had pulled down a window and was leaning out. He was so absorbed that he made no attempt to move out of the way, so Henry paused and looked out, too. The train slowed down; then, with the eccentricity of night expresses, it came massively to a halt. The black mountain silhouette remained fixedly against the sky, the improbable sparkles of light on its flanks settled into a social pattern. He could hear the noise of a waterfall. If he had got out at Sion he would have spared himself all this shame of false kindness and futile rage—besides having a bed to look forward to. The train began to move, a woman's voice said, 'For God's sake, Winthrop,' the man went into his compartment. Henry walked on. Almost unawares, he recognised the compartment the young man had quitted.

There they were, the man nursing the fiddle case, the stout man sitting opposite, the family beyond. The two little girls had fallen asleep, clasped together and moving as one body with the sway of the train. Beyond them, the father drowsed. The boy seemed to be asleep, too; at any rate his eyes were shut in his pained, twitching face. Only the mother sat erect and wakeful, supporting the boy's head on her lap. Her face was hidden by the folds of the dull black kerchief tied under her chin, but Henry knew by her attitude that she had composed herself to wakefulness as others compose themselves to sleep. Just as her sad gesture had moved him before, her attitude moved him now. She was small, thin, meanly built; but she was one of those beings whose movements and postures have the infallible aristocracy of a long lineage of labour, hardship and duty. She could no more go wrong with a gesture, he thought, than she could go wrong paring a potato. The boy stirred. She turned her head to look down at him. Her glance went on to the two little girls, to the packages in the rack, to Henry looking in. She leaned forward, careful not to disturb the boy, and touched her husband's knee. Instantly, he came out of his drowse. She said something, and glanced again to the door, and extended her hand palm uppermost over the space between the boy and the stout man in the corner. Henry shook his head, but at the same moment the husband spoke to the stout man, who pulled open the door, saying, 'The Signora says that if you are looking for a seat, there is one here.'

'It is most kind of the Signora,' said Henry. 'But I could not think of disturbing her. I shall certainly find a seat farther on.'

'For that matter,' said the man with the fiddle case, 'if you don't mind waiting a little longer, I shall be getting out at Lausanne, and you can have my seat without disturbing anybody.'

They all did her bidding, as though she were a queen.

Just before Lausanne, the man with the fiddle case came into the corridor, touched Henry's shoulder and said, 'You can go in now.' He obeyed, and sat down beside the two little girls. The woman looked across at him. Her grave, unsmiling face was momentarily expressive of a grave satisfaction; then she looked away and the black drapery hooded her again.

No one spoke. From time to time the boy twitched and moaned. The stout man snored quietly. Then the elder of the little girls, who had woken up, said with a look of delight, 'He's like the sea!'

The mother's finger went up to her lips, but the stout man snored on, and presently the father said to Henry, 'It is natural. Our home is by the sea. Besides, I am a fisherman.'

'A hard life,' said Henry.

'Yes, you are right; a hard life, and a poor livelihood. But it has compensations. One can pick up driftwood on the beach. Sometimes we even find coal. But it does not burn well; the sea has got into it.'

'Once I picked up a toothbrush,' said the little girl.

She was easier to understand than her father, who turned to her when he was at a loss for the Italian for some dialect word. Clasping her sister and swaying in unison with her, she interpreted, and helped on the conversation with comments of her own. They were Sardinians; none of them except the father had been off the island till now, when they were all going to London in England—except Rocco and the hens. Rocco had been coming too but Uncle Dante said that the English customs officers would put him in a prison called the Quarantina; though he had never bitten anybody and had very few fleas.

'The boy's dog, you understand,' said the father. 'A pet. It is because of my poor boy that we are going to London. There is a hospital in

London that can cure such children, so my wife's brother says. He and his family live in London. He keeps a tavern—'

'A restaurant,' corrected the little girl.

'—a restaurant, and students from that hospital go there, and he spoke to one of them about our Gianpaolo. And in the end, suddenly, we heard that all was arranged—the doctor, the bed in the hospital, our permits, our journey. Dante is paying for it all. There is even to be a cabin on the boat. A cabin!' He shook with laughter at the joke of a fisherman going to sea in a cabin.

'Your brother-in-law is a good friend.'

'Oh, yes, Dante is good, very good. And he is rich. He has done very well; he makes a great deal of money.'

The mother, who till now had been silent, looked full at Henry. 'You too are good,' she said in a stern voice. 'You gave up your place in the train to that young man. I saw what was happening. I understood.'

He lowered his eyes. He did not know how to answer. If he was silent, he would appear to concur. He certainly could not enter into the truth; and the usual 'Not at all, it was nothing' would not serve, since there had been an implied reception in her words so that to belittle his merit would be to slight her approval. He was deciding, rather romantically, that the only offering he could make to this remarkable woman would be to leave her her illusion when, raising his eyes, he saw that no answer was called for. Having paid him his due, she had dismissed him from her mind and was offering the child a biscuit.

He wished he could dismiss himself from his own mind. He had felt a glow of pleasure when the stern voice addressed him. The discovery that he had been noticed, pondered on—that he had become a person to her, been received—would have been delightful, if it had not depended on that mistaken word 'good'. After the malice with which he had listened to the young man, and probably envy, too, since he would not have felt such animated dislike for someone nearer his own age; after that arrogant wealthy man's offer of the sleeper, made on an impulse that couldn't have had a spark of kindness in it (since when it was read as an improper advance he was merely glad of another reason for disliking); after the inertia of not getting out at Sion and so retreating with some remnants of self-respect, it was not easy to submit to an imputation of goodness. Yet by degrees it became easier. Her mistake was in no way his doing; it was not even the total condemnation his middle-class conscience felt it to be—a conscience rating goodness at rarity value and shaped from nursery onwards by such estimating phrases as 'good as gold'. These people had a different, perhaps unworldly, outlook on goodness, and apparently did not find it more surprising than, say, rain. A torrential rain comes to be acknowledged as the flood of such or such a year; a torrential goodness comes to be acknowledged as a saint; but apart from extremes, goodness and rain are something naturally to be expected. So the father had agreed that Dante was good, very good; but it was Dante's enabling riches he dwelt on, the riches that were conveying the family to London and Gianpaolo to the hospital. Such an outlook, at once practical and discerning, was very probably quite a common one—at any rate among people who seldom hear the term 'philanthropy' and do not daily receive printed appeals on behalf of the blind, the starving, the homeless, the underprivileged, the unconverted to this religion or that. Very likely the stout man sitting opposite also enjoyed this outlook—which was why he was able to snore so peacefully. The little girl was quite right: he snored like the sea.

The train rushed on through the darkness, and in the darkness waves fell on the beach, broke against the cliffs, and the sea closed and relaxed its embrace of the island. A traveller by air would look down and say, 'I suppose that's Sardinia.' Which way (for one was free to decide) should the plane be travelling—east or west? Henry was nosing his way into sleep when the flash and roar of a train running counter to theirs recalled him to where he was, and why. He realized that it might be possible for him to redeem his imputed goodness. His riches enabled him to command porters.

'I hope there will be someone meeting you at Victoria,' he said to the father.

'Victoria? I don't know about Victoria. Dante will know. He is meeting us at the port of Calais.'

The mother nodded, her face glittering with excitement as though it were a rock dashed with a sudden spray. If Dante resembled his sister, thought Henry, their meeting would be a sight worth seeing. Dante, indeed, was the answer to everything. By asking the address of Dante's restaurant it would be possible to see these people again; perhaps, at last, be of some use to them; at any rate, see them. Meanwhile, he had

entered the restaurant, where Dante was walking about with a peacock
under his arm, feeding it with grapes. Coming up to Henry's table he
said, 'Have you brought my sister's hat? If she is going to be Queen of
Scotland, she will need several hats.' Looking at the peacock, Henry
remarked, 'I suppose that is the Papal Blessing.' Even in his dream, he
felt pleased with this perspicacity: not every Englishman would have
known it. So, in a light slumber, he went lightly from one dream to
another, conscious in another region of his mind that the dreams were
gay and harmless and that he would come to no harm among them.
From time to time, he woke more completely and saw the wakeful
mother, sitting composedly, her hooded head erect and sleek like a
bird's. Not since his childhood, when the wind blew in the chimney
and the black cat lay under the scarlet eiderdown, had he slept so
confidently.

Somewhere in the middle of this strange night without time or
locality, he was nudged awake to share in a meal of bread and stony-hard
sausage and rough sweet wine. The stout man had been awakened, too.
He was a motor salesman. Hearing Henry's English accent, he told how
his cousin, a prisoner in England and working for a farmer, had slashed
his leg with a bill-hook, and how the farmer's wife, leaving all else, had
driven him to the doctor for an anti-tetanus injection. If there was so
much science and good will even in a rough country place, there was no
saying what a London doctor would not be able to do for the little
boy—and should this fail, there was Lourdes.

At the mention of Lourdes, the father's face hardened. Seeing that he
had said the wrong thing, the motor salesman offered peppermints all
round and then produced a very clean handkerchief which he knotted
into a conjurer's rabbit. The rabbit frisked about among the children,
tickling them with its ears and pulling peppermints and coins out of
pockets and hair ribbons. 'Look out, look out! He'll be after your biscuit.
Oho, what has he found now?' A coin fell on the floor. The little girls
made a dive for it. The boy, escaping from his mother's hold, leaned
down, lost his balance and fell. Screaming with pain and terror he lay
writhing among their feet. When his father tried to lift him up he
squirmed away, hideously agile, hauling himself along on his elbows
with his useless legs trailing after him, striking his head against whoever's hand came near him.

'Fool!' said Henry to the motor salesman.

The motor salesman's horrified, crimsoned face did not alter; probably he had not heard, because of the noise the child was making. No one else uttered a word of blame. The mother knelt down beside the child; she made no attempt to touch him but kept up a wordless noise of condolence. Half grunt, half creak, it was more like a tree's voice than a woman's. The boy turned his head and spat at her. Instantly, she had her arms round him and in the same flow of movement had lifted him back onto the seat. 'Brute! Brutes!' he said between sobs.

'*Ciao!*' The father spoke under his breath, with a lifetime of accepted endurance in his voice.

Presently, like reflections in a shaken pond, they settled again, were the same family travelling to London with a sick child, the same pair of well-meaning outsiders. The mother's kerchief, loosened in the struggle, had fallen back. Tears of fatigue ran down her unshielded face. Sleep was mastering her, harsh as death in its oncoming. Twice she reeled forward, twice she jerked herself awake and erect again. Henry got up, saying to the motor salesman that they should move to the corridor. The father misunderstood, and began to apologise for the disturbance.

'The Signora must lie down. She is worn out. You must take the boy from her,' said Henry; and to his amazement he found himself lifting the sleeping child and planting him on the father's lap. As the child's weight was taken away, she put out a groping hand. The elder little girl took hold of it, patted it, and laid it gently back on her breast. She was dead asleep before they had settled her at full length, with a bundle under her head and her feet decently covered with a shawl. Even then, the father made a last attempt at hospitality, pointing out that the two little girls took up no more room than one person, so that with the boy held on his knee there would still be places for the two gentlemen.

Constrained together by what they had been through, Henry and the motor salesman stood in the corridor, keeping up a desultory conversation. Dijon had been left behind; the muteness of the first light was like a reproach to human activities. 'Why go further?' it seemed to say. 'Why all these purposes?' The motor salesman remarked that it would have been better to try Lourdes before London; whatever a person's opinions might be, there was no harm in showing a little civility; and there was no reason to think that the child of Communist parents would not stand as good a chance as any other—even a better chance, as it would be a more beautiful miracle. Henry felt the familiar squirming of inquiry always aroused in him by religious remarks but he had learned from experience that only Dissenters like to have their religious remarks followed up. He praised the behaviour of the two little girls. The motor salesman agreed. Presently they parted.

I shall never see her again, Henry thought, for I can't go back now and ask the name of Dante's restaurant. They would not think it odd. But I should. For a quiet man who minded his own business, he had performed a sufficiency of odd acts during the course of this long night. Since entering Switzerland, he had thrust a young man into his sleeper because he loathed him, prepared himself to fight a *wagon-lit* attendant, compelled a motor salesman out of his corner seat, and fallen in love with a fisherman's wife—who had addressed exactly one remark to him, and that on a false assumption. He had fallen in love with her, and almost immediately had fallen asleep in her presence—as contentedly, as reposefully, as though the physical act of love had taken place between them. A long night!—unquestioned, violent and inconsequential as a dream. Even now, the sun had not risen, and the mists were sleeping in the woodlands, and the odious young man was sleeping in his sleeper.

As he watched, the sky opened like a wound and a glaring tinsel streaked the horizon. Before midday, they would be safe in Dante's keeping. It was too ambitious, it was almost blasphemous, to hope that their breakfast would have escaped Dante's consideration; for all that, he would ask about it after leaving Paris, where the breakfast car came on. The brief glare of sunrising waned and went out; daylight showed a low ceiling of cloud. In Paris it would be raining.

In Paris it was raining. Yellow mackintoshes, white mackintoshes, black mackintoshes emerged from suburban trains and disappeared like a flitting of butterflies. Long dead, and grown quite respectable and undebatable, the French Impressionists continue to paint Paris. The canvases of the Gare du Nord replaced the canvases of the Gare de Lyon. Presently the hand bell would be rung down the corridor. Though he was rumpled and unshaven, he would have breakfast before he faced the odious young man, the disapproving attendant.

The noise of the hand bell approached, its associations so compelling that the smell of coffee seemed to be approaching with it. On the heels of the ringer came a man carrying a breakfast tray. The clatter of crockery ceased, a door was opened, there was an acclaim of voices. The little girls led it, but everyone was talking, and they all sounded happy and unconstrained—as they would be, of course, now that his formalising presence was removed. So Henry went and ate his solitary breakfast, and prolonged the solitude as long as his self-respect would allow him to. When he came to walk past the compartment that was Sardinia, he allowed himself to glance in. The mother was replaiting the younger daughter's hair, the father was rolling a cigarette. No one saw him. There seemed to be a great deal more hand baggage than during the night, but that was because much of it had been taken down from the rack and opened to get things out. When an adventure is over, it is over. Only the adventure's grudging begetter remained—the young man but for whose inability to recognise a peasant family when he met it Henry would not have entered the Sardinian compartment. No doubt he also had been unpacking and expanding. If he starts being grateful to me, thought Henry; if he has the effrontery to utter a word of thanks . . . However, this did not seem very likely.

The *wagon-lit* attendant was in his cell, bundling sheets into a laundry sack. 'Your sleeper's ready for you,' he said. 'I expect you'll be glad to be back in it, and to have it to yourself.' Having watched the first arrow quiver in the outer ring, he aimed the second at the bull's-eye. 'Your friend has left the train, you know. He collected his passport and his ticket to London, and got out at the Gare de Lyon.' Barely glancing at the effect of his words, he showed Henry into his tidied, passionless sleeper and left him to think it over. Postponing emotion, Henry shaved.

Shaving was a thing that Henry did very well, but shave as he might, he was not able to dispel his bristling uneasiness. The event was so exactly what he would have wished that he could not feel satisfied with it. There must be a catch in it somewhere. The young man would reappear, having got out to buy a paper, or hoping to change his Turkish notes. But if so, why did he take his suitcase with him? Suppose he had killed himself in a lavatory?—with a revolver taken from the suitcase? This disposed of the suitcase but not of the young man. His body would be found, the attendant would testify that Henry had put him in the sleeper, a guilty association would be manifest to all, and by the time Henry had extricated himself from the processes of French law, dozens of starving relations would have sprung up in Liverpool. There would be a widowed mother—he was the kind of young man who has 'Widowed Mother' stamped on his brow. Henry had noticed it, along with the pimples, beneath *Prière d'exiger* when the lights came on again in the dining car. '*Prière d'exiger*' ... ominous words. It was going to be one of those transactions you don't get out of till the uttermost farthing has been accounted for. All ill-considered kind actions end calamitously—at any rate, most of Henry's did. One should learn to leave kind actions to the young, who are not endangered by them since they rarely perform them.

Calmed by these general reflections, Henry began to think on broader lines. He thought he would go to sleep. He settled himself, and closed his eyes. They hadn't closed comfortably. He opened them again and saw that the sleeper wasn't quite what it had been. Something was missing. What was missing was the slow wag of his overcoat on its hanger. So that was it! The odious young man had left the train because it was a safe and simple way of stealing a good overcoat. Warm in a good overcoat, he would wait till the next train, and then continue his journey. Henry heaved a sigh of relief. His mind was at rest. He need never give another thought to that odious young man, and when he got to London he would buy a new overcoat.

There was a knock; the door opened. The attendant came in, and he held the overcoat. He had observed, he said with specious tact, that Monsieur's friend had dropped cigarette ash on it. To avert any further mishap, he had taken it away.

The coat was put on the hanger, and resumed its faintly mesmerizing wag. It was a good coat, and Henry was attached to it; under different circumstances he would have been glad to see it again. But now it came as a monitor, and told him he was not done with that young man after all. He would not reappear, he would not be found dead in a lavatory—these silly fancies had gathered up their improbably trailing skirts and fled like ghosts at sunrise. What remained was the real young man, who had left the train with his shabby suitcase, and no good solid overcoat, and no apparent reason. There he stood on the platform, hunching his narrow shoulders against the wet, wolfish cold. No overcoat, no break-fast, no reason. No real reason. No possible reason at all that Henry could see, except a reason which irresistibly imposed itself on his mind, forcing him to admit its validity, its tit-for-tat symmetricality. For if the odious young man had felt a reciprocal dislike, and had nursed it all night, tossing in luxury on a bed he had been forced into, and in the morning had realised that he would be expected to put up some show of thanks to the odious old fellow who at any moment would reappear with his chilblained civility, he might very well have had the courage of his animosity and got out in Paris—as Henry had failed to do at Sion.

(*A Stranger with a Bag*, 1961)

A WORK OF ART

PRIVATE charity still persists in England though mostly it is practised in the disorderly, hole-and-corner style recommended by Jesus. Mrs Bernstein was so far in step with the welfare state that she used a paid administrator, but she did so for reasons of her own. If you have to go about in a wheel-chair, she said, you can't see things for yourself. Moreover, a benefactress of immense weight carried by grunting porters up to attics or down to basements (and misery is seldom domiciled on ground-floor level) is bound to create remark, and bring every cheat, thief, cadger, and social worker, not to mention hosts of other unfortunates, to settle like blowflies on the benefited one. So she availed herself of Miss MacTavish, whose muscular legs and unobtrusive bearing could get her in anywhere. Miss MacTavish had already got herself into a perfectly satisfactory life of her own. She was an artist, and illustrated children's books for a living. It was in the intervals of drawing little girls with turned-up noses offering apples to horses with classical profiles that she went about Mrs Bernstein's business.

Every three months or so, Mrs Bernstein would engage Miss Mac-Tavish in strategic conversation to see if any professional do-goodery had lodged itself in her administrator's outlook. The results were reassuringly negative. The outlook remained that of the artist; no tendency to confuse making people a trifle better off with making people better clouded Miss MacTavish's appraising eye. It was above all betterment that Mrs Bernstein wished to avoid. She had been bettered in her youth and was of the opinion that it would be quite as nauseous to be bettered in maturity or in old age. She was even suspicious of bodily betterment, since the body is the envelope of the soul and not always reliably impermeable. Instead of carrying bundles of blankets and parcels of nourishing food, Miss MacTavish carried pound notes, which are easier both to convey and to conceal. But as one must not muzzle the ox that treadeth out the corn, she was free to give advice—provided that the advice was drawn from her own experience and that the money was given first.

'My Uncle Heinrich,' said Mrs Bernstein, 'did it the other way round. And so I was always being trapped into performing a pound's worth of behaviour and then getting two and sixpence. That's not fair dealing. And one must not do things for them. Even the rich don't trust even the experts who do things for them. For the poor it is impossible. It would crush all the spontaneity of their taking.'

'I wonder that you are prepared to trust me,' said Miss MacTavish.

'Well, yes. Perhaps you'll run off with it. So you wanted it. So that's all right.'

Discovering Mrs Bernstein was an enlarging experience, just as beginning to paint in oils had been, and Fiona MacTavish blessed the day when she had run up to steady the chair which was about to topple sideways into the Serpentine—an act that had led to a conversation about the Loch Ness monster, the best way of cooking carp, and the first of many invitations to lunch.

For several years she acted as Mrs Bernstein's emissary without ever questioning the method laid down for her. This was not mere docility. It seemed to her that the method worked uncommonly well. She saw people looking pleased, and could quit them without any sense of having smudged their pleasure. She saw—which is perhaps rarer—people who regularly received money from her and who met her again without the least trace of fear or calculation. Naturally, she did not always see these wonders, but they occurred oftener than she could have expected. Now and then she gave advice, which was warmly reciprocated in valuable recommendations about health, canaries, geranium cuttings, cockroaches, and so on. And in the course of time she became increasingly attached to Mrs Bernstein, who became increasingly fatter, uglier, richer, and more versed in the *affaire Port Royal*—this last on the ground that it brought her closer to Mme de Sévigné. It was Mr Herzen who drove Miss MacTavish to question the absolute inadmissibility of doing things for those you give money to.

Mr Herzen was solitary, sickly, hypochondriacal, sometimes charming, always shiftless, and never continuing in one stay. When traced to a new lodging, he would explain that he had not been able to pay the rent, or that he had merely forgotten to do so, with the result that he had been cruelly evicted. Quite often, this was not so at all. He had paid, he had gone—the landlady just couldn't account for it. Disappearing thus for months on end and when traced being sicklier, sadder, shabbier, and distinctly reproachful—since he insisted on thinking he had somehow displeased his kind friends and been cast off by them—Mr Herzen drove Miss MacTavish to take a stand.

'I really cannot go on looking for Mr Herzen any longer, Mrs Bernstein.'

'Still lost, poor man?'

'No, no. I've hunted him down again. This time he's in Finsbury.'

'*Mais qu'avez-vous de mourir si souvent?*' murmured Mrs Bernstein.

'In the most frightful hole, with the most appalling landlady. And it seems to me that we—that you—will be compelled into doing something for him.'

'I don't approve of doing.'

'I know you don't. I don't like the idea of it myself. But there are times when there's nothing for it but desperate measures. Now, listen. This is what I suggest. . . .'

In the end, she got her way. A small furnished flat was found, with a pleasant landlady. It was redecorated, and to the landlady it was explained that Miss MacTavish was Mr Herzen's person of business, and that he would pay his rent through her. By thus representing him as someone rich and strange, she hoped to pass off his obvious poverty, settled incompetence, and vagaries of temper. She thought she had done pretty well, but Mrs Bernstein continued to assert that doing didn't do. So convinced was she of this that, though she still paid his rent and his allowance, she ceased to inquire about him—as though she knew by some private information that he was dead, but respected the privacy.

Presently it appeared that Mr Herzen shared Mrs Bernstein's rejection of the Deed. The pleasant landlady, now looking slightly hangdog, said one day, 'You know, dear, you mustn't think I'm taking money under false colours. But that ten bob a week Mr Herzen pays me over and above for cleaning his rooms and so on—well, I'm only too ready to do for him, but he won't hear of it. And how he manages about the dust and the smuts and the carpet sweepings I'm sure I do not know, for he hasn't brought down as much as a teacupful to the dustbin in the yard. And sometimes it really worries me, quite apart from the furniture, for it's as plain as a pikestaff that he's the kind of gentleman who needs doing for.'

Miss MacTavish said that Mr Herzen might be afraid of his papers being disarranged.

'Yes, ducks. I recollect you told me he was consecrated in his work and not to be disturbed. Though I don't know when he does it, really. He's always out. He's gone out now.'

The next time she called, Mr Herzen was out. And the next. Or perhaps it was she who was out—locked out. She had a most distinct impression that on the other side of the door someone was listening. Two could play at that game. Thrusting away all consideration of what Mrs Bernstein would think of such behaviour—besides, Mr Herzen was already an exception—she dropped the envelope with the money in it through the letter slot, walked partway downstairs, continued to pat with her feet, and listened. She heard the envelope being torn open. She heard his cough, exasperated by suppression and now let out to do its worst. Knocking on the door, banging on it and shouting, she at last overthrew the silence that lay behind it like a great mattress propped up to intercept bullets.

'Oh, dear! It's Miss MacTavish. I was asleep. Ah, it would be so. The first sleep I have had for days and days. Unlucky, eh?'

The envelope on the floor, the notes sticking out of his pocket, were the only clean things in the room. Dust lay thick on the furniture, cobwebs trailed from the ceiling and latticed the grimy window. Dirty and unshaven, he stood at bay in his den.

'Isn't it terrible? Isn't it terrible? And I have been so ill, I am still so ill, I cannot sleep because of my cough, and whatever I eat, it comes up again, I am poisoned through and through. And the woman downstairs, she does nothing for me, nothing! She puts milk for her cat and forgets me. Not that I have anything against the poor cat, you understand. If I were not so ill I would move, for it is killing me here. All this dust is so bad for my cough.'

'It must be. Poor Mr Herzen, no wonder you feel ill. Mrs Bernstein will be sorry to hear all this.'

'No, no! Don't tell her. I do not like to be a trouble to my friends. I shall struggle through somehow. Or I shall not. Every herring must hang by his own tail, eh? I do not like to complain.'

'Do you know what I would advise you to do?'

He started, and glared at her.

'What you need is to have this place given a thorough cleaning. You'll never get well breathing up all this dust. And you're certainly not strong enough to tackle it yourself. What you must do is to go to one of those shops where they sell Hoovers and ask them to send a man to demonstrate it.'

His laugh, still a merry charming laugh under its grime of malevolence, rang out. 'That is what I call a genial idea. Then I tell him I'll think it over, eh? Perhaps it would be surer if I paid a first deposit?'

'I didn't.'

'What? You did this yourself? Splendid!'

For he was so abjectly undeserving, so unsuccourably an alien and a misfit, that she had to re-establish some sort of contact, grease the slide for Mrs Bernstein's money to flow into that cold quicksand of a pocket. Loyalty to Mrs Bernstein dictated that. If Mrs Bernstein did not help him, no one else would, since no one could possibly better him. But as she went homeward to her tidy studio, her tiny modest industry, the illustrations for *Jennifer Sees It Through* on her desk and the blue abstract on her easel, she was so filled with discouragement that she seemed to herself to be going nowhere at all.

Locking the door and waiting to make sure that this time the cheating hag's ugly feet had carried her downstairs and away, Mr Herzen savoured the moment when he would turn back to his dirt, his solitude, his paradise and great work of art. He turned. There it was, his own, and grimier and grander than ever before, having been acknowledged by her submission and astonishment. How she had stared, pretending not to stare! And she had not seen the whole. She had not seen his bedroom, the skylight opened to the sooty rain, the spatterings from medicine bottles soiling the walls, the morass of dirty socks left steeping in the wash-basin—a splendid passage, one of his best. She had not seen the kitchenette. But she had seen enough to know what he thought of the bright little reformatory they had designed for him—insulting his misery with light paint and flowery walls—and to know that he was not a man to swallow insults. From the first moment of waking in this bourgeois kennel he had realised what to do with it, he had foreseen the masterpiece that he and time would create between them, stroke by patient stroke. 'How do you like it?' the woman had asked, bringing him his money. And he had replied that every day he liked it better. For even then, though she was blind to it, the masterpiece was taking form and the first cobwebs were mustering in the corners. Slow to get under way, tantalisingly slow and fitful, the process of deterioration had gathered impetus, sweeping him along with it, inspiring him to spill and scorch and knock over, so that whatever he did prompted a new invention of filth and squalor. And then, impalpable as a vapour, the quality of perfection had emerged, grave and austere, wrapping his inventions and contrivances and laboured-at dinginess in a solemn veil of inhumanity. Now when he went out, it was not to escape from the discommodities of creation, the dust that choked him, the fœtor that sickened him, but in order to return like a priest returning to the shrine, like a ghoul entering the rich charnel house and musingly rubbing its palms together as it looks round. Absorbed in his task, he had forgotten the motive that dictated it, the piece of grit round which this black pearl had accumulated.

Though the woman's intrusion had brought him that confirming satisfaction, she was superfluous; he did not require the assent of her dismay. Perfection and the Whole had come before her. He would not open the door again.

But the envelope must be attended to. It lay on the floor, pert, crisp and alien. He set his heel on it, grinding it to and fro on the dirty carpet. A cloud of dust flew up. When he lifted his heel and looked at the envelope, it had learned its place. It subserved a work of art.

(*A Spirit Rises*, 1962)

HOW TO SUCCEED IN LIFE

MANY eminent self-made men have been foundlings or bastards, and Mr Silas Honey was no exception to this rule. His mother was a rather elderly lady's maid who had come down in the world and kept a second-hand clothes shop in Plymouth, and whose appearance was so fusty and forbidding that no one could imagine who was the father of her child, unless, perhaps, he was begotten by an old pair of trousers. She died in labour, and the child was taken to the workhouse, where he was kept, as other oddments are kept, in the hopes that he might be useful later.

At the age of eleven he was placed by the workhouse authorities on a farm in Cornwall, where he was set at once to pick stones out of a field. The farm was a very starve-crow place where lean cattle stood looming out of a sea-mist, and one of Silas Honey's chief employments when he was not actually at work was to hunt for firewood. There were few trees on the farm, and the fields were enclosed with stone walls, so the likeliest place to find fuel was a cove about two miles away where the sea cast up pieces of timber.

One March afternoon, when Silas had been on the farm for five years, he was descending the cliff path on his usual errand when he heard, above the noise of the waves, the sound of a cow mooing. There had been a storm overnight, and the wind blew strongly on-shore. The sound of the cow's mooing came with the wind.

Silas looked down into the cove. He saw a pretty Guernsey cow standing on a rock which was surrounded by breakers. She kept turning about, and her hoofs slipped on the wet rock as she turned. She looked inland, and mooed. Her udder was swollen; she was mooing to be milked.

The tide was rising, he must act quickly. He waded out through the breakers and hauled the shipwrecked cow to land. She struggled when he pulled her down into the water, but he was a strong boy, and accustomed to handling cattle; and after he had hit her on the muzzle two or three times she allowed herself to be rescued docilely enough. When she stood on the beach she trembled, and the blood began to flow from a wound in her leg; but no bones were broken, and though she was quaking with cold, and though the salt sea-water ran from her in streams, her milk was warm and sweet. At first Silas milked her into his cap; but, when he had drunk, he threw down the cap and put his lips to her teats. He had never tasted milk before—real milk; at the farm he was given skim milk from the separator.

He stood erect and elated, as though he had drunk a heady wine. He pulled an old purse from his pocket and counted over the contents —though, indeed, he knew well enough already the sum of his small, hard-wrung savings; and then he turned to the cow, who had begun to crop the salt herbage among the rocks, and drove her before him up the cliff path in the gathering dusk.

Heaven had tossed him this chance; he would take it, and make what he could of it.

Silas Honey turned eastward, and crossed the River Tamar into Devonshire. On the first Sunday in April he entered the small moorland town of St Petrock, walking demurely behind his cow. The cow was in excellent condition; her nerves were quite recovered, and the wound in her leg was healed. Silas also had a sleek, well-suckled air.

The main street was empty, save for a few basking mongrels. A sound of worship came from the Wesleyan chapel, and the yellow dandelions shone like scattered guineas over the small, neglected grass-plot which had once been used as a burial ground. Silas drove his cow into the enclosure and tethered her to a rail. He then entered the chapel, and sat down in the lowest place.

He followed the service with devotion, and knelt on even when the other members of the congregation had left the building. Outside they found the cow, whose appearance there caused no little curiosity and surprise. Her owner heard the surprise, but continued to pray. He was still on his knees, a touching figure, when Mr Ash, the minister, came out of the vestry and walked down the aisle. Mr Ash stepped from the porch, and saw his flock, and the cow feeding in the midst of them.

'What is all this?' he enquired.

A humble voice behind him replied, 'My cow.'

'You should not bring her in here, you know,' said the minister. 'She might cause a scandal.'

'I'm sure I'm sorry, sir. But I am so afraid of losing her. She is all that I have. My dear old mother—' Silas Honey paused, and looked as motherless as possible.

'Come round to my house, and I will see what I can do for you,' said the minister. 'Bring your cow too.'

That night Silas Honey lodged with a devout widow. She reminded him so forcibly of his dear old mother, especially in her method of frying lights and onions, that before going to rest he prayed that God might put it in his way to prove a son to her. He prayed aloud; and as the bedroom wall was very thin, his prayer was heard, and granted. The widow said she would take him as a lodger, and ask no more than three shillings a week till he had found employment. As for the cow, she could be stalled in the empty pigsty where the cat kittened.

'But where will you graze her, my dear soul?' asked the widow.

'In highways and hedges,' he replied.

Mr Ash spoke of finding work for Silas, work on a farm. Silas had no mind for any more of that; work on a farm was not his notion of a successful life. He put off the minister, saying that, as Mrs Gulley was so like a mother to him, the least he could do would be to whitewash her back kitchen, but that he must have a drying day for it, lest the damp walls should give her bronchitis. From bronchitis he led the conversation to his own chest.

'God's pure air would be good for your chest,' said Mr Ash. 'It would do you good to be out of doors.'

'Yes, sir. I was thinking of going primrosing this very afternoon, if the weather keeps up.'

Every morning Silas led his cow out to graze. They wandered through the lanes, enjoying the fine weather and the scenery. Very often the views were so lovely that Silas would lean against a field-gate to admire them befittingly; and presently the gate, being no more securely latched than Devonshire gates commonly are, would yield to his admiration, and he and his cow would wander in a rapt manner into the pasture. They were always back in St Petrock by five o'clock, however, in time for Silas to be on the station platform selling bunches of primroses, bluebells, and horse-daisies to the passengers in the London express. He also sold them Devonshire cream in tins at what he said was four shillings a pound. The tins were secured at a slight profit; for once a week he would go the round of the neighbouring villa residences, undertaking to dispose of their rubbish at twopence a basket-load.

During the harvest season Silas did a little work. He also lent a hand in decorating the chapel for the harvest festival, and shortly after this he added home-made marrow jam to the wares he sold at the station.

About this time he grew a little restless. The work he had done during harvest had, he said, unsettled him. It had put ideas into his head: in particular the idea that he might look for a job. He began to make enquiries about the more distant farms: did they want a cattle man? What sort of stock did they carry? One morning he set off early on a voyage of discovery. The cow went too.

About midday he began to walk more slowly, and to look about him. He had come to a place where there were two gates, one on either side of the road. He looked over the right-hand gate, and the prospect seemed to please him; the cow looked too, and appeared to be as interested as he. Just as he was about to fall into his accustomed trance of admiration he heard voices—a condescending ladylike voice conversing with a respectful gruff one. Silas hurried to a turn in the road and peeped through a hazel-bush. A ray of refracted light flashed on his vision, and another, and another, like signals in morse. He ran back at great speed, opened the left-hand gate, drove his cow into that field, and half-closed the gate on her. Then he dashed across the road and opened the right-hand gate. A small bull bolted out, and would have gone in at the left-hand gate but Silas headed it down the road. At the same moment a bath-chair came round the corner, pushed by an aged man, and containing a lady whose jet bonnet flashed in the sun. When the bull saw the bath-chair it bellowed, and began to paw the ground. Silas ran up and took the bull by the horns while the lady shut her eyes and wished that she had never left Torquay. When she opened them again Silas was closing the left-hand gate and the bull was gone.

'You have acted with splendid promptitude,' exclaimed the lady. Silas panted hard.

'I did what I could, ma'am.'

'When you have got back your breath, please follow me to my house and knock at the back door.'

While Silas was eating cold veal and entertaining the cook with stories about bulls the lady came herself into the kitchen and handed her rescuer an envelope containing a five-pound note. Later in the afternoon he released his cow, drove the bull back into its proper field, and took the homeward way to St Petrock. There was no work to be found anywhere, he told the widow that evening: now that the wild-flower season was over, he did not see how he could continue to pay three shillings a week for his board. He would have to leave her, though to think of such a step made his heart bleed. The widow begged him to stay on at a reduced charge and see what the Lord could do. When the cow proved to be in calf she reminded him of this conversation, and Silas agreed that it was the hand of Providence.

The calf was sold to the butcher for a good price, and in due season another calf was vouchsafed, though not, this time, with such a profitable godmother. In her stead Silas did what he could with Mrs Cholmondeley, whose pedigree Sealyhams were easily led astray and stood in pretty regular need of being returned to their owner at half a crown a time. When Mrs Cholmondeley had a visitor who brought an Alsatian Silas hoped for even better things; for he could see no reason why an Alsatian should not kill a calf as handily as the butcher could, and much more profitably. But this scheme came to nothing, owing to the Alsatian's wrong-headed conviction that Silas was a thief. When Mr Winter, the farmer, saw him clinging to the boughs of a tree while the Alsatian made grabs at him from below, he laughed ill-naturedly, and said, 'I suppose you're grazing my apple-trees, Honey, while your damned poaching cow is grazing my meadow.'

Mr Winter repeated this poor joke to the other farmers, who were as much pleased with it as he. They all hated Silas, and any one of them would have shot the cow long ago if it had not been for the mitigating reflection that as she did unto him she did unto others. Nor was Silas any more popular with the labourers, to whom he now lent small sums of money at a high rate of interest. But his station customers still patronised him, the gentry liked him because he was so respectful and enterprising, and so different from the ordinary working-man, and as for Mrs Gulley, she would have gone through fire and water for him—which was not so surprising, since he was the only man she had ever had to do with who did not get drunk and knock her about. So, balancing one thing against another, Silas managed pretty comfortably.

Just how comfortably nobody knew, for he was very secretive about his money affairs. But at length there came a day when he led the widow into his bedroom, where they could not be overlooked, and having sworn her to secrecy, he opened his wallet and showed her no less than twenty pounds. The widow exclaimed in wonder and thankfulness. He had saved enough to pay for the right to a good pasture, where his cow might graze in all honour and solvency.

Silas Honey bought another cow.

(The Salutation, 1932)

THE NOSEGAY

'So you're doing a bit of mountaineering,' said the voice from over the hedge.

Mary Matlask, standing on a kitchen chair in the middle of her garden path, cast a look of contained hate at her neighbour. A worse neighbour no woman who loved a garden could have. Her hens came through the hedge, her thistledown floated over it; she kept a rolling tomcat and three children who played at ball.

'My roses grow so high,' said Mary Matlask, 'that I can't reach them from the ground.'

She was an old woman, so bleached and brittle that it seemed as though the rays of the sun, beating down on her, might snap her in two. The kitchen chair rocked on the uneven path. Its seat was slippery, it was not easy for her to keep her footing, and to stand so, with her arms stretched above her head, turned her giddy. But there she must stay, impaled on Mrs Colley's ravening gaze. Pride would not let her descend without her flower; malice delayed the gathering of it, for she knew full well that Mrs Colley only waited to see which of the few blossoms she would pick; and so she remained, uneasily poised, snipping off the withered blooms.

At last, yielding to a continuous yelling from her cottage, Mrs Colley withdrew. Smiling disdainfully, Mary Matlask ceased snipping off the withered heads, and watched her go. Then once more she raised her arms, swiftly, excitedly, her uneasy balance forgotten. Her expression had changed. With a look of awed delight she reached for a pink rose-bud, and cut it carefully from the branch.

It was the last bud the tree would put forth that summer. It had only opened that morning, it was still faultlessly virginal and brilliant. She eyed it with solemn satisfaction. It was exactly what she needed, the perfect centre for her nosegay.

All her life Mary Matlask had made nosegays, constructing each after the same pattern—with a central flower, a boss, and round it concentric bands of other flowers, and the whole finished off with a rim of leaves or fern. The materials of the bouquet varied with the season, but the manner was always the same. In spring there might be a centre of blue violets, rimmed with tightly packed primroses, or the first double daffodil ramparted with wallflowers; in the autumn the centre swelled to a massive dahlia with asters and marigolds encircling it, their colours clashing resolutely but their formation strictly preserved. But the best nosegays were the summer nosegays, whose centre could be a rose.

Proud of her art, sure of her mastery, Mary Matlask went on composing nosegays as stubbornly as Cezanne went on painting apples. She gave them to children, to brides, to the bed-ridden, to the dead. She gave them to her landlord when she paid her rent. She gave them to Mr Trudge, who lived in a dusty bungalow writing books on economics, and who never remembered to put them in water. She gave them to Mrs Daniels at the Manor, who lived only for hunting, and to Mrs Cullibere, the rector's wife, who worked on a handloom and felt sure that flowers should look natural. She gave them to the postman, to the baker, to visitors who paused outside her cottage to say it was the prettiest in the village; and during June and July, when the plentifulness of her garden drove her to a frenzy of artistic expression, she gave them to Mrs Colley.

But this nosegay was a different pair of shoes. It had been commissioned, it was, at last, a recognition of her art. This very morning she had received a letter from Mrs Chichester, whose nurse, so long ago, she had been—a letter saying:

'It is ages since I saw you, but I still remember the posies you used to make. Do you still make them? And could you make one tomorrow? For Miss Ursula —my baby daughter—you remember her, but now she is almost grown-up —wants one for a dance. She will drive over tomorrow, with a friend of hers, some time early in the afternoon, on the chance that you can manage to give her one. If you have a rose left in the garden, please put a rose in the middle.'

It was a pity that they had not been able to give her longer notice; she would have liked to meditate the work of art for a previous day or two. And it was a pity that the request had not come earlier in the summer, when the pinks were blooming, and white flowers more plentiful. A nosegay for a young lady should contain a good deal of white, to be suitable. But she had the essential, the rose, the year's last and loveliest. There was a song about that, thought Mary Matlask. '*All its lovely companions are faded and gone.*' And carrying the rose indoors, where it should repose in a basin until the moment of assembling the nosegay arrived, she began to sing, till the thought that Mrs Colley might be listening checked her shrill staggering voice.

This would be one in the eye for Mrs Colley. A car driving up to the door, two young ladies, both in the height of fashion, stepping out, the chauffeur attending on them; and all to carry away a nosegay made by Mary Matlask. Pray God the woman would be at home! Were she not, she would hear about it; such things do not happen in a village without bruit; but seeing would be better than believing.

All that morning, under the scorching sun, Mary Matlask walked up and down her garden, prospecting and pillaging. It was not to be lightly undertaken, this masterpiece. Her most exquisite taste must be invoked. Marigolds, for instance, would never do; their smell could not be permitted in a ballroom. But there were the everlasting peas, pink and white, elegant on their short stalks. There were the montbretias, whose orange sprays would make a delicate sprigged border to the built-up composition. There were the white asters to ring the central rose, and the mauve asters to surround the white; and by picking all she had, and by careful spacing, a further ring of alternate crimson and yellow carnations could be contrived. Carnations were very genteel flowers. Gentlemen wore them in their button-holes, and who knew but that, this very night, some fine young gentleman might not beg one of Mary Matlask's clove carnations from Miss Ursula's nosegay?

The picture of the nosegay became so clear in her mind's eye that when, the materials gathered, she came to build it up, it seemed to her that never had the work of assemblage been so easy, never had she worked so deftly nor so infallibly. But when the completed masterpiece had been firmly bound with wool, and put in a bucket under a damp cloth to stand on the watered cold stone of the outhouse, Mary Matlask was shaking from head to foot and ravaged by such a headache that a cup of tea was all she felt equal to for her lunch.

The clock ticked so loudly that it seemed as though its vibrations would shake down the house. Its pale face stared at her. 'I must go upstairs,' she thought, 'put on my best dress and smarten myself.' Her shaking hands drove the pin of her brooch into her flesh. She dropped the comb and broke it, she spilled the little flask of lavender water.

Downstairs the clock was louder than ever. She began to set the table for tea; for it would only be proper to offer a cup of tea, whether they condescended to it or no. Ladies drank China tea, she knew, and China tea was not to be bought at the local shop; but by making the Indian tea very weak she might be able to offer a cup without offence. Earlier in that long arduous morning she had polished the tea-things and baked scones and rock-cakes. Now it only remained to cut the bread and butter and the lettuce sandwiches. But if the young ladies were coming in the car they might be hungry, they might like a boiled egg with their tea. Mary kept no hens; she dared not go as far as the farm in case the car arrived; for fresh eggs, stooping her pride, she must inquire at Mrs Colley's.

To Mrs Colley's she went, carrying a formal basket, holding up her skirts lest the slops of that threshold should sully them.

'I am expecting visitors,' she said. 'Two young ladies who will come in a car.'

'Haven't they enough to eat at home?' asked Mrs Colley. But in her haughty fat face her eyes sparkled with curiosity, darting in and out like two earwigs in a turnip.

The kettle was set to boil, and the saucepan for the eggs. Delayed by her errand next door, Mary Matlask was in a panic lest the water should not boil before the two young ladies came; and she raked and fed the range till it blazed. Kettle and saucepan had been twice emptied and twice renewed before the car drew up at the gate. There was no chauffeur to spring out and hold open the door. It was a tiny car, open, little larger than the coffin of a motor-bicycle. Only the suddenness of its arrival and the imperious loudness of its horn could uphold it in the watching eyes of Mrs Colley.

But the young ladies, for all they were so queerly dressed, Miss Ursula's friend even in trousers, were grand enough and condescending enough to quell a regiment of Colleys, choosing that moment to hang out their disgracing underclothes on the line, staring for all they were worth. 'Darling old Mat!' cried Miss Ursula, 'of course we should love an egg to our tea. How sweet of you to think of it!' And in the middle of the garden she flung her arms round Mary Matlask and kissed her.

Torn between pride and anguish Mary attended their praising progress round her denuded garden, knowing that Mrs Colley behind the hedge was overhearing every gracious word, knowing that in another minute the eggs (why had she not got four, got six?) would be hard-boiled. Hard-boiled they were. Miss Ursula's friend ate barely more than the top of hers; but for all that the tea-party went with a swing, wave on wave of pride and excitement surging through Mary Matlask as passionately as the waves of her headache crashed each after each to its climax under her neatly combed parting. Such affable young ladies. And the window being open, and their voices so clear, Mrs Colley would certainly overhear every word they spoke.

Now from its stone-floored cloister and its damp veil emerged the nosegay. This should have been the crowning moment, and if admiration could make it so it would have been. But suddenly conscious of a fault in hospitality Mary Matlask realised that the other young lady should have a nosegay too. Not so fine as Miss Ursula's, of course; but still, a nosegay. Trembling, stiffened against the waves of her headache and her fears of doing amiss, of not seeming respectful enough, she heard herself speak the decisive words. 'Oh, Miss Ursula, if you could spare another five minutes, I should so like to gather a few flowers for the other young lady. That is, if she'd accept them.'

'Why, Mat, of course. Another nosegay! How sweet of you. She'd love one. Wouldn't you, Nonny?'

'Adore one,' replied the young lady in trousers. All together they walked into the garden, still raked by Mrs Colley's attention, Miss Ursula most recklessly brandishing her nosegay in the sun. For a while they followed her round, asking the name of this flower and that; then they drew apart, talking to each other, seeking the shade of the elder-tree in the hedge. Eavesdropping Mrs Colley crept nearer. 'She will hear every word,' thought Mary Matlask. 'She will know now how grand they are, even if she didn't know before. For they will certainly be talking of the ball.'

Without their assistance the selection of a second nosegay became easier. At first it had seemed to her that there was not a flower left in the garden; but released into creative solitude she soon became carried away, and it appeared that the second nosegay might almost equal the first, though, alas! for its centre there was no rose, only a begonia.

Absorbed in her art she hurried about the garden, tearing at the fuchsia, gathering and discarding. Now for the final flourish of asparagus fern. It grew near where they were standing, a dense thicket. But they were deep in conversation, they would not mind her coming near. They had no notion, disregarding beings from a higher world, that Mrs Colley, pressed against the hedge, was gulping down their every word.

'Isn't she an old pet?' said Miss Ursula. The gentry spoke like that, tossing away words as they tossed away shillings and half-crowns.

'Enchanting,' answered the friend, 'and makes the sweetest lettuce sandwiches. But, my dear, what will you do with that vegetation? You don't propose to wear it, do you, all chewed up with greenfly, and crawling with earwigs?'

'My God, no! But I wanted a specimen of the genuine Victorian article, for Wallers to copy in proper flowers. I shall drop it with them on the way back. There will be plenty of time.'

'I see,' said the friend. 'Quite a good . . . Hush! Here she comes. Look what she's got for me!'

(More Joy in Heaven, 1935)

IN A SHAKEN HOUSE

AT intervals, a subterranean rumble approached, swelled to a roar, died away. The floor shook, the windows rattled, the glass dome over the clock whiningly vibrated, the curtains sidled as though an invisible hand had twitched them. Directly below No. 27 Ulster Crescent, where Miss Miriam Turner had come to inspect a furnished bedsitting room and kitchenette, ran the Metropolitan and District line. 'Nobody even notices the trains after the first week,' averred Mrs Palmer, the owner of the house, though the recollection that three lodgers in a twelve-month had moved elsewhere because the noise was too much for them made her the readier to 'meet' Miss Turner over the rent. Having met, it seemed a few moments later that the two ladies must immediately part. Holding Miss Turner's card at arm's length as though perspective might enable her to take a broader view of it, Mrs Palmer continued to shake her head. 'Not that *I* object in any way, you understand. I'm interested in that sort of thing, I'm a bit psychic myself. But a professional card on the front door, even though it's the top bell and could be urged as less conspicuous—that's something we've never had before, and I don't know how my other lodgers would take it. We've never had anything but private cards, you see. In fact, it's quite a feature.'

She fell silent. She had chosen a bad moment to do so, for another train was approaching. When it had gone by, having done its worst, Miss Turner asked if the noise was always as bad as this.

'Oh, no! Oh dear, no! It's because of the rush hour.'

Seeing that Miss Turner was now studying the cracks in the ceiling, and aware that very soon another train would approach from the opposite direction, Mrs Palmer read the card aloud. '"Madame Miriam

Turner, Palmiste and Graphologist." I'm sure I don't know. Besides, there's the police. What about them?'

Ostentatiously raising her voice as another rumble swelled to a roar, Miriam Turner said, 'I am not a fortune-teller.'

In fact, that was precisely what she was. And, as one cannot practise fortune-telling without considerable insight into what people are thinking and wishing, she knew that if she held out and let the trains do their work, Mrs Palmer would give way.

After several months Miriam Turner was still noticing the trains—or else noticing that she was not noticing them. In a way, this was the more disturbing. To be unconscious of anything so insistent set her on a level with those clients who were so hard pressed by their desires, their fears, their circumstances, that they had ears for nothing but her words and the portentous silences in between. Such clients were almost invariably single women and no longer young. Miriam Turner was a single woman and in her fifties. But, of course, there was no real similarity. The clients did not notice the trains, because something more urgent was clamouring in their minds. When she did not notice the trains, it was because she was growing used to them. And when other clients, less at the mercy of their feelings, commented on the noise and wondered how she could concentrate on what she was doing, she replied, 'But I don't even notice it,' in a voice which implied that she was above being distracted by anything so trivial. Though it was important to preserve this aura of otherworldliness, her outlook was, in the main, honest and mercantile. People wanted their money's worth, whether in the form of entertainment, excitement, solace, a whiff of the Devil, or plain straightforward flattery; and having found out how they liked it, she did her best to supply it. Even when they came to amuse themselves by catching her out and seeing through her, she would give them a good run for their money. But with those who wept and trembled and besought, and insatiably demanded assurance, and stayed for hours pouring out their troubles and their cravings and their disgraceful rancours—for many were more avid to be told of ill fortune awaiting others than of good fortune awaiting themselves—the process was sometimes oddly reversed, and the good run given to Miriam. In mid-course of guessing what they wished her to supply and supplying it, she would be swept on into a further region that was neither supply nor extemporisation but instead a kind of idiot infallibility, so that she seemed to be reading off their tense faces sentences in a language unknown to her, and only realising how applicable they were by the acceptance with which they were heard. That was how she had first begun—or, as she phrased it in grander moments, had first discovered her gift—sitting in a stiflingly hot tent at the church bazaar; for the usual fortune-teller failed at the last moment, and Miriam Turner, newly an ardent member of the congregation of S. Simon and S. Jude, had volunteered to replace her. Swathed in bright-coloured scarves and not wearing her spectacles, she had gazed into a bowl of violet ink and let herself go, supplying in the generosity of success not only thrilling futures but spells, charms, and incantations. A queue gathered outside the tent, and no less than three pounds seven and sixpence crossed her hand in silver—a testimony that heightened the disapproval of the Turners, who were Chapel by adherence and rationalist by persuasion. 'We shall never hear the last of this,' said Leonard, her half brother. 'Madame Zillah, indeed! As if anyone would take you for a Madame Zillah with Father's nose all over your face.' Leonard was right. Whether it was the rector who betrayed her or the late Mr Turner's nose, the church-bazaar gypsy was soon identified as Miriam and her stepmother's house invaded by strangers clamouring for more spells, since the green ribbon tied to the currant bush had proved so efficacious, or for further light on the future, since a lady from the East and wearing a sari had come in the very day after the new moon and bought an upright piano. A reporter who trapped Mrs Turner on her doorstep got short shrift. Nevertheless, a totally misleading account of the interview came out in the evening paper under the heading 'HOW IT FEELS TO MOTHER A SPHINX', and this led to such a row royal that, having observed an ostentatious fast on the vigil of SS. Simon and Jude, Miriam left home on their feast—heaping added shame on the name of Turner by going to a local hotel as a chambermaid.

From chambermaid to barmaid, from barmaid to dentist's reception-ist, from dentist's receptionist to keeping a second-hand-clothes shop, from that to the post of dresser at a theatre, she went her zigzag course, never foreseeing where she would get to next, and infallibly arriving where, in fleeting contacts, hearts would be opened, tongues loosened, and such subjects as dreams, portents, hares' feet, and the planets come under discussion. Chance or instinct kept her away from professional occultists. When a grateful client (to whom she had supplied, via the planets, racing tips imparted by another client, a bookie who resorted to her in matters of the heart) left her a sum of money that made her semi-independent, Madame Miriam Turner, Palmiste and Graphologist, set up with little more knowledge than Madame Zillah, though with the experience of twenty years' hit-or-miss practice. She knew better now than to discard her spectacles. A grey-haired woman in a woollen cardigan inspires more faith than a seeress in flowing veils. Her only attempt at disguise was to combat her naturally spare physique, since people find it easier to confide in a plump bosom than in a bony one.

Fortunately, starchy foods are cheap.

She picked her first lodgings in the neighbourhood of St Pancras and King's Cross, having in view the hard-headed businessmen from the Midlands—a very profitable line—who would arrive by those termini. It was also a good neighbourhood for cheap, starchy meals; and as time went on, this advantage outweighed the other. The income that in 1953 had seemed so buoyantly supporting was degraded to a pittance in 1958 by the rise in the cost of living. Television had swept away the clients who came from curiosity or for entertainment. Some of her regulars, hopeful to the last that the future had delightful surprises in store for them, had died. Others had left London, saying that London was no longer what it was. Miriam's following was no longer what it was, either. Like London, it was full of foreigners: West Indians, Spaniards, and Italians with labour permits, or refugees from Eastern Europe. Though her approach to the refugees was faithfully correct; though she told herself that they were brave, right-minded, unfortunate, and that it was a mercy they had got away; and though she also told herself that all were fish who came to her net, she never felt easy with them. They daunted her—they, or a sense of their misfortunes. Mutely, they held out a thin palm or a letter in a strange language. Mistrustfully, they watched her, staring as if they would pluck the lie from her mouth before she had spoken it; and as soon as she spoke, they hardened their faces as if whatever she might say would be an insult or a denial.

Yet in almost all of them she sensed a gaping, cavernous credulity that went beyond any she had encountered before, even in the most desperately love-lorn, even in the most desperately hate-ridden. If it could have broken through their rigid mistrust, it might have set free in her the gift that had declared itself at the church bazaar; and then they would have believed her—even if they had only understood one word in ten, their belief would have rushed to meet her. But they kept it penned up like a wild beast, and sat waiting to see how little she could do. Speaking slowly and distinctly and in simple language, she told them that a handwriting showed determination, honesty, a love of music, or that the lines in the hand told of sorrows and dangers in the past, many partings, many journeys—but that a further journey, a journey across an ocean, would bring prosperity and an unlooked-for happiness. Her words vanished into their expectation like straws into a furnace. They paid her, and went away. Some of them implacably came again and again.

She began to sleep badly. She grew thinner; omens pressed themselves upon her attention. She told herself that she was getting imaginative. She bought a budgerigar for company. Like an omen, it died. She bought a flower-pot to bury it in, and a miniature rose to plant above it. The rose drooped, and shed its leaves. She thought she would try going to church—it was a long time since she had been in a church. As she entered, her glance was attracted to a painted window. On a scroll below the figure of a young man seated dejectedly under a small palm tree were the words 'I will arise and go to my Father'. That was it! Leonard! Leonard's common sense, his good, plain, pudding character, was what she needed. She would arise and go to Leonard—for a week or ten days. She did not think she could endure him for longer than that. She spent the rest of the service composing the letter that convention demanded should be addressed to Leonard's Olwen, the young woman with a placid disposition and serviceable legs whom Leonard had married rather late in life. It was a letter that demanded composition, as she had not been near them since they moved out to Rickmansworth ten years back, and at no time had been asked to spend a night under their roof. But by availing herself of former days, the increasing force of family ties as one grew older, often having thought of it before but not implementing the thought because of Olwen's hands being so full with the twins, and a well-placed final admission of sometimes feeling rather lonely and knowing what country air would do, she got the letter settled in her mind before the Blessing and wrote it that same evening. Only after she had dropped it in the pillar box did she remember that Leonard's household included her stepmother. Certainly not longer than a week. Fortunately, she had written 'Love to all', which would cover the old hag. Besides, by now she probably lay down a good deal; Olwen's placid disposition would have seen to that.

Leonard's reply, its envelope still intact, was in her hand when the red-haired refugee strolled in, having found the street door open and walked up the stairs. He was one of those who implacably came again and again. 'So your bird, dead,' he remarked. Though he was not the only red-haired man among these sad clients he seemed to her red-haired *par excellence*—perhaps because red hairs covered his hands and bony wrists, so that in certain lights they glittered as though cased in some reddish metal.

With her mind full of an invitation to Rickmansworth, how soon she could get away, whether she should get a new hat, she found it almost impossible to recollect what she had told him last time; but the journey across an ocean—she could rely on that. It was the one thing that never failed, the one assurance they all wanted to hear and accepted, when they heard it, as though it were a due that was being fraudulently withheld from them. 'When?' 'How soon?' To show such a single-minded impatience to get away from the country that had received them was not, to put it mildly, very polite; but, after all, they had not come to England in order to be polite, so why expect it of them? Once again, Miriam foretold a journey across an ocean, and for good measure foresaw him in a large car beside a lake. He paid her and went away.

Her hands trembled so much that she could hardly tear open Leonard's firmly-stuck-down envelope. How extraordinary to be trembling with excitement because of a letter from Leonard. 'I must be in a worse way than I supposed,' she muttered, and began to read it.

'My dear Miriam, I am very sorry . . .' Leonard was sorry to say that a visit just now would not be practical, as Olwen was feeling rather fagged. If Miriam wanted country air, why not go to the sea and get braced properly? That was what he would advise. The intensity of her mortification forced her to admit the truth. She was indeed in a worse way than she supposed. She was afraid, afraid of this red-haired man and of all he stood for.

Her heart pounded, her knees shook. The few yards between her and the door seemed an insuperable distance, but somehow she crossed it and turned the key in the lock. Instead of making her feel safer, this action impaled her on a sense of guilt. The nonconformist conscience of her upbringing, its cutting edge perhaps all the sharper because for so many years there had been no daily use to abrade it, slashed through her defences. She was afraid because she was guilty. Daunted by these wretched beings, by their maladjustment and their unmanageable misfortunes, and disliking them because their misfortunes were unmanageable, she had gone on cheating and exploiting them, taking their wretched money and blithely promising them happy futures—of what? Of being out of sight and out of mind. But what was she to do? With them on her track and now conscience, too, where could she turn, how could she get away? 'There is nothing else for it!' she exclaimed. 'I must give it all up.'

There is a germ of comfort in every resolution, if only the fact of having got it over and survived. Miriam fell asleep picturing the little cottage where she would live on bread and cheese and pick blackberries on a moor. When she woke, the resolution was still there, and half-way to being an accepted fact. She looked at what was so familiar to her waking eyes—the bleached garlands of the wallpaper, the shabby furniture, the Victorian washstand that did duty for a dressing-table. She would not see them much longer. Good riddance, for they were ugly enough. When she had found that cottage, she would have to buy furniture for it—an item she had forgotten about overnight. Could she afford this? Where should she go to find the cottage? It would have to be somewhere remote, or it would not be cheap enough. Yet it must not be too tumble-down; she could not afford repairs. Perhaps it would be better to find lodgings in a little country town. While she lay drowsing, the answer to all her difficulties entered her mind as calmly as sunlight enters a room. Of course. All she needed to do was to move to some other part of London and pursue her profession as before, but with discrimination, never again cheating any of those unhappy refugees. There was no harm in telling the fortunes of British citizens, and they were often made much happier by it.

Some of her clients so methodically looked to her to be made happier that they came on regular days, and if they could not do so wrote asking for a change of appointment. To these she sent notices of her removal to Ulster Crescent; but she left no address at her former lodgings, explaining that she would be travelling about in search of a cottage and expected to find one in Ireland. She also sent her new address to Leonard, expatiating on the peacefulness and leafiness and airiness of the new neighbourhood, telling him that she was already quite a new being, and hoping that Olwen was no longer feeling so fagged.

In spite of still noticing—or sometimes not noticing—the noise of the trains, the sense of living poised above a recurrence of small earthquakes, her vaunt had gradually come true. She had lost many clients by her removal and new ones were slow to come in. But the interest of beginning again, of building up a career anew, gave her an illusion of youthfulness. As Mrs Palmer said, it was really quite a superior neighbourhood, and with a superior class of residents, since almost all the larger houses had become boarding houses or residential hotels, where elderly people of private means could live in comfort without being worried by the servant problem. It was these elderly people, yawning their heads off in high-ceilinged, cretonne-upholstered lounges, that Miriam had her eye on. In their quieter way, they would be just as good as the hardheaded businessmen arriving from the Midlands; for, however elderly, people never grow tired of hearing about themselves. 'Palmiste and Graphologist' would bring them in. Presently, it was doing so. The line of life, the line of the head, the line of the heart—examining these pink palms, so smooth, so very clean, she fell at times into a professional admiration at the persistence with which the standard pattern was distributed into such a variety of substances and destinies. Etched into those roughened palms that had been mutely held out to her, pencilled on these others like a delicate ornament, the lines, when all was said, were much of a muchness; it was the condition of the hands that told the real story. As for what you said, that was pretty much of a muchness, too, except you varied it to suit. Now, for instance, when she read a journey across an ocean, she put it in the past. 'You have travelled extensively.'

Graphology there was not so much call for. This was a part of the world where people mainly received letters in handwritings too familiar to need any analysis. But here, just as much as anywhere else, she found the clients whom she thought of as 'the real lot'—the famished, the lonely, the insatiably credulous, who hung on her words, who did not notice the trains. These, with their potentiality to release her gift, gave a fillip to an existence that otherwise might have been rather boring.

From time to time, she had nightmares, crude as a film poster, in which there was always a door being broken open and something thrown into the room—a bomb, or a mutilated animal, or a brown-paper parcel with blood oozing from it. Their quality of recurrence made them almost negligible; they were like the noise of the trains clanging their way under the house. Her daily life went on above them, her earnings increased, she made friends with the local shopkeepers. Then, one morning, she had a letter from Leonard. Just like him, she thought, to invite her to Rickmansworth now, when there was no longer any need for it. Leonard, however, proposed coming to see her. He would come next Sunday afternoon.

If it had not been for his clothes, his perpetual, sensible, hard-wearing tweeds, she would scarcely have known him. He was thin, his hair was grey, his face was grey and trenched with lines of worry and misery. He's got cancer, she thought.

'Hullo, Mirrie, old girl. So this is your new place? Good Lord, what's that?'

The rumble swelled to a roar, the floor shook, the windows rattled.

'It's just the trains underneath. The District Line runs right under the house. I never notice it now.'

'Oh well, so long as you don't mind—and it leaves off at midnight, of course. Yes, I should think you've changed for the better. Airier than your last place. Classier, too. How's business?'

'Not too bad.'

'Splendid! And you're looking well. Glad to see that.'

But his gaze, wandering blankly over the room, had not rested on her face. Whatever brought him here, it was not anxiety for her health.

'Clever idea, too, the way the street door opens on its own. That must save you a lot of running up and down stairs.'

And whatever brought him, it was something he was slightly ashamed of, or he would not have been so anxious to wag his tail.

'Yes, I'm glad to find you looking so well. You know, Mirrie, that visit you thought of making us—I was really upset at having to put you off.

But as things are, our house is no place for anyone's holiday. I didn't go into it at the time, but—' He took off his muffler, folded it with extreme care, and laid it down beside his hat. 'It's Mother. She's killing us.' There was an evening paper in his pocket. He drew it out, smoothed it, and laid it near the muffler. 'You never liked her, so it will be no surprise to you.'

'No. I never liked her. She was a bit too managing.'

'Managing! You should see her now. Yes, if you want to know what managing is, you should see her now. Day and night, Mirrie, she's at it. Nothing's done but she must do it all over again. When the table's laid for supper, she'll have everything off because it's the wrong cloth. When that's put right, the beetroot will be in the wrong dish, so it must be changed into the right one, and the first dish washed up and put away before anything else; and after that, she'll have to make a new pot of tea because she's sure Olwen forgot to warm the pot beforehand. We've no sooner got to bed than she hears a mouse, or a tap left running, and has us up to deal with it. Or she'll go down at three in the morning, because she's remembered a pillow slip that wanted darning and must turn out the linen cupboard to get at it. Then there's the telephone—I had it put in to save Olwen, because whenever she went out shopping, when she got home she was sure to find Mother moving all the furniture, or rehanging the curtains, or taking down the pictures, or taking up the carpet. Now Mother's for ever ringing up the tradesmen to counter-order things, or to say they're too expensive, or that she's weighed them and they're short weight. And the way she speaks to them! . . . I suppose it's tragic, really. I suppose it's left over from after Father's death, when she worked so hard and managed so well. But what makes it so awful, Mirrie, is how she complains all the time, and tells everyone how she has to do this and do that, and how all the hard work is left to her, and how she's nothing but a slavey in her old age, and works herself to the bone and never gets a word of thanks for it.'

'Poor Olwen!'

'You may well say so. I tell you, Olwen's life is hell. And she's getting worn out. I never come home from work without expecting to find her dead. It's because of Olwen I've come to you.'

So that was why Leonard had looked so propitiating. Miriam stiffened.

'For her sake, and Leslie's. You see, Leslie's old enough now to have her boy friends, and, naturally, she'd like to bring them to the house. But it's impossible, because of the way Mother behaves. You remember how strict she was with you and Kate? None of that now. If a young man comes to the house, the way she talks and nudges and draws his attention to Leslie—it's downright disgusting. She's worse than any madam in a bawdy house.'

'Why can't Kate take her for a bit? She's Kate's mother, too.'

'That's no go—even if Kate would. You see, when I married, she talked so about old horses turned out to die that I promised we'd always keep a place for her.'

He swallowed, and said, staring at the floor, 'Mirrie! You couldn't give me any idea how much longer she'll last?'

Miriam took a step backward. He followed her, as though it were a figure in a dance.

'I suppose you could say that I've changed my tune. And that considering the past it's a bit late to come to you for this sort of thing. Well, perhaps it is. I'll grant it. But I'm desperate.'

She felt as though her will had been dislocated. A moment before, it had seemed plain that Leonard's intention was to hand over some part of his burden, and she had resolved not to give way. Now it was this. Yet instead of relief, only a different refusal was there.

'You do it for others, Mirrie. Won't you do it for me?'

'I don't see how I can, Leonard. It's not that I don't pity you—but fortune-telling's peculiar. One has to do it one's own way. And a person at Rickmansworth isn't the same as a person sitting opposite one. I'd have nothing to go on.'

'I've thought of that. You know how one sometimes reads in the papers when someone's disappeared, how they take something belonging to that person to a medium, to a clairvoyant. And it puts her on the scent. She sees a wood, or a railway station. Well, I've brought Mother's vest.'

He had it in a paper bag, which he took from his pocket. 'Where shall I put it? Here, on this little table?'

'Oh hell, Leonard, what am I to say? I've never done this sort of thing. Yes, put it on the table.'

'And shall I draw the curtains? Would you like me to wait outside?'

'While I burn some dried toads? No, just sit down and keep quiet. Read your evening paper or something, and don't stare at me.'

'Yes, of course. I'll read my paper. Mirrie! Just a moment. Why are you combing your hair?'

'It helps to concentrate. Now settle yourself, and keep out of it.'

She sat down at the little table, and waited for her reluctance to pass before laying her fingers on the vest. It was a woollen vest, with a darn in it—she'd know that darn anywhere; and it had been worn. Leonard must have pinched it from the washing basket. Cautiously, her fingers descended. An old woman's vest. How long would she last? Which would be the first to wear out, the garment or the woman? A smell of aged flesh, mingled with the scent of violet talcum powder, detached itself from the vest. It made the wearer painfully actual, and Miriam flinched away as though her stepmother's voice had proclaimed, 'It's me.' Intimidated by such vitality of dislike and so much unwillingness to carry out this grisly performance, Miriam was on the brink of saying she could not go on. She looked at Leonard. A train was approaching; she saw him clench his teeth, and remembered how, as a little boy, he used to clench them in just the same way on the taste of his iron tonic. And that mother still had her claws in him. No, she must go on with it! She would go on till the next train, with her fingers on the vest and the smell in her nostrils. How long would its wearer last? How long would this smell make part of the world? She shut her eyes and struggled to make her mind a blank. A blank it remained.

The next train approached. She relaxed and looked round. Leonard had put down his paper and was staring at her with a startled expression. It was as if he had just seen her in some totally new light. Poor Leonard, brought at last to believe in her gift and now to be told that it had no comfort for him. But why should she not say something comforting? She did to others.

'She won't last much longer,' she said.

The rumble swelled to a roar, the floor shook, the windows rattled, and the walking stick he had propped against a chair fell with a clatter. The noise covered their inability to find decent words with which to close a disgraceful transaction.

'I'll make some tea,' said Miriam, rolling up the vest.

'No, thank you, I won't stay. I must get back. Miriam, I can't tell you how grateful I am, what a weight you've lifted off my mind. Thank God I came!'

'Does Olwen know?'

He shook his head. 'I couldn't tell her—the strain. I don't think I shall tell her.'

'Much wiser not.'

'But you'll come—later on, you'll pay us that visit!'

He put the vest in his pocket; he wound the muffler round his neck. Miriam longed to be rid of him, her gull and her partner in an atrocity.

'Your hat. Your gloves. Your paper.'

'Bless my soul! It went clean out of my head. Mirrie, look at this! I read it while I was waiting, and it was all I could do not to interrupt you there and then. No. 17 Olcott Street. That was your old place, wasn't it?'

WIDOW BATTERED TO DEATH

Early this morning, Mrs Sheila Underwood, who lives at 17C, Olcott Street, N.W.1, heard cries for help coming from overhead. She woke her husband, and they ran upstairs. The cries had ceased, but they made their way into the flat occupied by Mrs Flora Gallagher, an elderly widow living alone. Mrs Gallagher was lying on the floor, bleeding from wounds in the head and face. A red-haired man stood beside her, grasping a coal-hammer. 'I said to him,' relates Mrs Underwood, '"You brute, what have you done to her?" He didn't seem to hear me. My husband grabbed hold of him, but he didn't attempt to get away. It didn't seem to occur to him.' The police were summoned, and the man was taken into custody. Mrs Gallagher died on the way to hospital.

'I'm sure she never injured anyone in her life,' said Mrs Underwood later. 'She was a dear old lady and her room was spotless. My children knew her as Grannie, and it has upset them no end.' The police have ascertained that the man is Tibor Keszthely, aged thirty-nine, a Hungarian refugee.

'It might just as easily have been you,' said Leonard.

She nodded. The red-haired man—she was safe from him now. An abject thankfulness distilled from her like a sweat. 'Yes. I suppose it might have.'

'My word, I'm glad you left that place when you did. A widow, too, a poor old widow! Makes you wonder what's become of the Ten Commandments. Well, Mirrie, I must be off. I can't thank you enough. No, don't come down with me. I'll see myself out.'

It was to be hoped he wouldn't start putting widows together.

She walked over to the window and threw up the sash. The room certainly needed airing. It stank of lies, and of blood, and of old women, and of disgrace. But it no longer contained fear. No more nightmares would burrow under her days. When she was sixty and could draw her old-age pension, she would retire, she would wash her hands of the whole thing. Till then, she would reflect on her mercies, and never again say anything definite, anything that a hope could be pinned on, that a hope could be shattered on. There went poor Leonard, running away with his booty. He went faster and faster, almost breaking into a trot, so dazzled by the prospect of his mother's death, in such a hurry to get home and look at her in the light of this new knowledge, that he didn't notice where he was going, and collided with a man who was coming up the street. She could see Leonard apologising, and the man saying nothing. The man came on, walking slowly, and pausing to read the names of the boarding houses, the cards framed in the bell panels. A slow reader—or a man with time to kill. No. 31. No. 30. No. 29. No. 28. Outside No. 27, he seemed to be pausing more attentively. Then he took a step or two backward and stared up at the house, his glance pausing at the first, the second, the third-floor windows, as he had paused before each door. Just when she had recognised him she did not know. All she knew was that in an instant his glance would travel a stage further and that she would be looking down into the face of the red-haired man.

(*A Spirit Rises*, 1962)

SHADWELL

A T HYDE PARK CORNER, Robert Laidlaw halted his taxi, telling the driver that he had changed his mind and would walk the rest of the way. 'Don't trouble about the change,' he added.

'Thank you, sir! *And* I don't blame you. It's a wonderful afternoon, we shan't see many more like it, this year.'

To bestow such an ample tip, and to be assured that the taxi-driver did not blame him, gave Mr Laidlaw's self-respect a fillip which just then it badly needed; for he was bound on a painful errand. That was why he had decided to walk the rest of the way through the park. Not because walking would postpone the moment of climactic painfulness —he was only too anxious to get it over; but he hoped that by immersing himself in the serenity of the autumn afternoon he might achieve a corresponding peace of mind, and a larger outlook on the disagreeable. It was late October. The trees had already shed most of their leaves, which were quietly consuming in bonfires. Those which remained hung motionless, their colours burning against the deep blue of the sky. All the shabbiness of late summer was gone. The grass had renewed its green, the plane trees had stripped off their sooty bark, the picnicking parties contained no inelegant nudes or panting dogs. It was as though summer, after a purgatory of equinoctial rain and gales, had come back ensainted. And despite the taxi-driver's Cockney mistrust of good fortune, there seemed no reason why this spell of Indian summer should not continue for some while yet. For in autumn there is a steadfastness lacking in the other seasons. Autumn is an apple, it is a keeping fruit. The park-keepers thought so, at any rate, for they had brought out the canvas chairs again.

He would have liked to repose his mind on the chairs, but the current of his thoughts swept on, allowing him no dalliance with distractions. Mrs Probus had also been a keeping fruit, persisting in a timeless suspension of old age, gently shrewd, subacidly kindly. Early that morning she had died in her sleep, the death that with an unimpassioned confidence she had proposed for herself. As her lawyer and executor, he had been rung up with the news by Shadwell, her servant. After an interval of grief and recollection—quite apart from her wealth and her hospitality, he had been attached to the old lady—he told his clerk to bring him Mrs Probus's will. And now it was too late to do anything about it. Unchangeably, unanswerably, Mrs Probus had left her ageing trusty servant an annuity of £52 *per annum*.

He was more than half-way across the park, and the noise of traffic along the Bayswater Road swelled in his ears. As though it were a challenge to which he must retort, he said aloud, 'But what could I have done about it?' He had not drawn up the will. That had been done, nineteen years earlier, by his Uncle James. At his uncle's death he had inherited Mrs Probus, and the remains of their long friendship, and had been appointed executor in his stead. At the same time he had inherited many other executorships and trusteeships, for Laidlaw, Larpent and Laidlaw was an essentially testamentary firm. Mrs Probus's will was one among dozens of documents thus refurbished, and no doubt he had read it through, since that was part of the routine. It was no part of the routine to query or suggest, the obligation of an executor is but to execute. In fact, he was already going outside his obligation in the matter by walking across the Park to break the news to poor old Shadwell.

Even in 1934, a pound a week was less than Shadwell's due. Now, it was a mockery. One could not keep a cat on it. At the time when the will was made, Mrs Probus was newly a rich widow, and as such she would naturally consider herself on the verge of starvation. But there had been time to revise that opinion since, and though she had continued to live luxuriously secluded from the life around her ('As far as I am concerned, Mr Laidlaw, there has not *been* a coloratura singer since Tetrazzini. If you want to listen to little English-squeaking kittens, you must go without me. Leave the old woman to her memories, you know.' 'Flying-bombs, Robert? I have forbidden Shadwell to go out, in case she should be killed and I left. I really don't see what more I can do about them'), she had remained sufficiently cognizant of the changes taking place to give up her house and servants and move into a small flat which Shadwell could run single-handed. She was capable of that much revision, and if the rise in the cost of living had been tactfully pressed home . . . There should be a law compelling people of property to bring their wills up to date every five years.

He was now out of the park, and a bus went by him with disgusting speed, as though enforcing the fact that this is a rough world, woe to the vanquished! No doubt wills more unjust, more ungrateful, were made every day, and Shadwell not the only old woman, rendered semi-imbecile by devoted service, to be thrown into the gutter. But they were not this particular will, and did not oblige him to go on this painful errand. Callous, or careless, which? Summarised in *The Times* (for Mrs Probus's fortune was of the dimensions to be summarised in *The Times*), the will would present a rather noble Ancient Roman appearance. Five thousand pounds to a family in Belgium, whose parents had befriended her son, killed during the First World War; to him, her portrait by Wilson Steer, and to his co-executor, a diamond ring; and the rest to be divided between the National Trust and the National Portrait Gallery, subject to an annuity to her servant, Bertha Shadwell. If the amount of the annuity were not disclosed (and he was in honour bound to see what he could do about that), it would seem an exemplary will. But the amount of the annuity must be disclosed to the annuitant, and in less than five minutes he would be doing it. He had no option, the co-executor of the diamond ring being engaged in archaeological research in Sicily, confound her!

The block of flats rose up before him, dowdily sumptuous. 'Twenty years younger than I,' Mrs Probus remarked, when he had incautiously commented on the marbleness of its halls. He entered, and the smell of steam-heating and brass-polish obliterated any sense of the autumn afternoon. The porter got into the lift with him (it was that kind of lift), saying, as he pressed the button, 'A wonderful old lady, sir. A great loss.' He agreed, and the lift was stopped at the third floor with a condoling smoothness and exactitude. He got out, the doors clanged to behind him, the lift went down into its pit unblamed. There he was, on the same level of air as Shadwell and only four doors away. 21, 22, 23, 24. He rang the bell.

Shadwell opened the door, looking just as usual, rubbed unobtrusive as stones are rubbed smooth. She wore her afternoon uniform of black serge, and a short black apron, a form of vestment denoting superior servitude. Her eyes, which that morning had looked on death, retained their shallow brightness, her anteroom appearance was unchanged, her air of being a preliminary to Mrs Probus. So she still considered herself, for her words were, 'You would wish to see Mrs Probus, sir,'—and she preceded him to a door, and opened it, standing back for him to enter. But it was a different door.

Death is a leveller. Irene Probus, lying wrapped in fine linen on her Louis Seize bed, looked like an old peasant woman, or, even more, like a masterpiece of peasant art, as though some village craftsman, with only the truth to guide him, had carved her, with every wrinkle, every blemish of age, and the overall plain statement of death, superlatively rendered in some smooth yellowish wood. This is equal to anything by Epstein, he thought, scarcely able to restrain himself from exclaiming in delighted admiration at the way the heavy wrinkles of the cheek enfolded the plane of the cheekbone and threw into relief the pure sailing arch of the aquiline nose.

'I hope you approve, sir. Mrs Probus did not wish anyone but me to touch her.'

He turned to Shadwell, saying, 'Did *you* do it?' And it was as though he had turned away from the imperious vitality of the work of art to the inadequacy of real life, for Shadwell seemed extinguished, a shabby and negligible dummy, not very firm on its legs. 'It is beautiful, it could not be done better,' he added. She replied, 'I am glad you approve, sir. And I am glad that someone has come to see her.'

It was inevitable, his errand being what it was, that Shadwell should wring his heart, but he could not have foreseen this particular pathos of the neglected artist. He said, before any more assaults could be made on his feelings, 'Shadwell, we must talk a little business.'

With her trained sense of what was befitting, she showed him into the dining-room, and pulled forward a chair.

'Sit down, Shadwell. The business is this. As you know, I am one of Mrs Probus's executors. The other is Miss Grainger, but she is in Italy, so for the present I shall do all that needs to be done. This morning I looked over Mrs Probus's will, which is in our office. I found that she has left you an annuity. "To Bertha Shadwell, if still in my service at the time of my death, an annuity of fifty-two pounds *per annum*"—in other words, for the rest of your life you will have an income of a pound a week.'

'Thank you, sir.'

Preparing himself for what he had to say, he had taken into account what he might have to say next, and how best to reply to shock, to wounded feelings, to resentment, to fear of the future. To this, he could find no answer. Yet he lifted his gaze—it had been resting on Shadwell's long, flat, neatly shod feet—and looked at her searchingly. Perhaps there had been irony in that reply. A woman who could lay out a corpse with such majestic insight must be an artist, and as such, capable of irony, scorching irony. Gladly would he have been scorched. A sprinkle of unmerited suffering would have been positively welcome to him. But the hope was vain. Realising that he had come on purpose to tell her of the annuity, she was thanking him for his trouble.

'Have you any plans, Shadwell?'

'No, sir, I have no plans yet.'

'Then I hope you will be able to stay on here for the next week or so, at any rate until Miss Grainger has come back and seen to the disposal of Mrs Probus's clothes, and so forth. The executors will pay your wages and your expenses. What are your wages, by the way?'

'A pound a week, sir.'

His last sneaking defence, that Shadwell must have salted away some useful savings, went down. He got up from Mrs Probus's table, where he had enjoyed so many *tête-à-tête* dallyings from clear soup to port, and said, gobbling his words a little, 'Well, well, now of course you will be on board wages. They are always rather higher. You will be paid ten pounds a week.'

'It's too much, Mr Laidlaw. I wouldn't take it.'

Feeling as though he were a fishmonger who had asked Shadwell to pay ten shillings for a lemon sole, he climbed down.

'Seven pounds then. A pound a day. You'll need it. Now, Shadwell, don't argue with me. I won't hear another word from you.'

He heard his imperfect imitation of the imperious familiarity with which Shadwell's mistress had been wont to utter such words. Possibly Shadwell heard it too. Her face flickeringly escaped from its respectful composure, and she replied, obliquely quitting the contest, 'May I make you a cup of tea, sir?'

'No, thank you, no, thank you! I must get back to the office. By the way, the valuers for probate will probably come tomorrow. I will let you know when to expect them.'

'Thank you, sir.' She showed him out, and rang the lift bell for him. By the mercy of God, the lift ascended immediately, he was out of the worst of his agony and could go away, with only the painfulness of a painful mission done. As he emerged from the seasonless opulence of the hall, the plenitude and calm of the autumnal dusk overwhelmed him, for he was obliged to compare it with the prospect of Shadwell's wintry decline. He stooped his head, as if under a reproach, and hurried towards the nearest Underground.

Returning to the dining-room, Shadwell straightened the two chairs and removed a few withering blossoms from a potted begonia. These she took off to the trash-bin in the kitchen. Dropping them in, and hearing the lid fall-to with its usual tinny exclamation, she put by her thoughts for the moment, and began looking briskly into canisters, ascertaining what stores would last out for Mr Laidlaw's next week or so, and which would need replenishing. This roused the old canary. He searched himself for lice, and then broke into an abrupt flourish of song. There was a black bow tied to his cage. He had been Mrs Probus's canary until age harshened his coloratura, when he was retired to the kitchen. It was not too harsh for Shadwell. She listened admiringly till he grew tired and gave over. Now there were only the clocks to listen to. The clock on the kitchen dresser rattled on at a cheap gait, and was counter-pointed by the soft whirr-whirr, whirr-whirr, of the French clock in the dining-room. From the street below, the noise of traffic rose up like steam from a cauldron. She laid out a cup and saucer, and clasped a spoonful of tea in the infuser, and put on the kettle. Then she left the kitchen and went into the bedroom, her feet suddenly noiseless on the thick carpet, so that she entered like a ghost.

At the foot of the bed, she paused, and looked appraisingly at the brief masterpiece that in a few hours would be hidden in a coffin. 'He didn't think to bring any flowers,' she said to herself, and shook her head disapprovingly. Old Mr Laidlaw would not have omitted that due courtesy. Her bunch of white carnations, bought that morning, was all that Mrs Probus had. But so it had to be.

From the foot of the bed she went with her ghost's footfall to the dressing-table, massive and ornate as a shrine. Pulling out a drawer, she pressed a hidden spring. The looking-glass slid aside, and disclosed the doors of a little cabinet, which in their turn opened at the twirling of an ivory pillar. There were the jewels, the rings, the brooches, the bracelets. She knew them as well as she knew the contents of her kitchen drawer. She had always taken care of them, cleaning them once a fortnight with jewellers' rouge and putting them back in their velvet lair. Now she took them out for the last time, holding them to the light, watching the coloured flashes leap from the diamonds, feeling the sharp facets of the emeralds and the faint greasiness of the rubies. But they did not tempt her. She examined them only for the pleasure of admiring them, and for a sentimentality of farewell. She laid them back, one by one, and took out the thing she had in mind, a long gold chain on which, at wide intervals, diamonds were set like dewdrops. It was an ornament that Mrs Probus had not worn during her memory; but like the rest, it had been cleaned every fortnight, and once, years ago, while she was polishing it, Mrs Probus had glanced at it, calling it by some foreign name, and saying that it was an old-fashioned thing, which she would never wear again, and really ought to sell; for the stones, though not large, were of a fine water, and Meux would certainly give a thousand for it. Sold one by one—and it would not be difficult to tweak them out of their light claw setting—they would not bring so much, Shadwell supposed; for part of the beauty of the ornament was the exact matching of gem to gem. But by taking a diamond from time to time, sometimes here, sometimes there, and sheltering in her indelible appearance of respectability, she would be able to dispose of them with very little risk. Even if she had been sure of selling one of the more valuable pieces without being detected, she would not have done so. She wanted no more than her due—enough to ensure that she would end her days still retaining her independence and self-respect. As it had not been granted, she had taken it.

She closed the cabinet, pressed the spring. The looking-glass slid into place, offering her the image of her narrow bust and dull, dutiful face, and behind her, the bed, and Mrs Probus lying on it—her hands, with no ornament but the gold wedding-ring, folded under the single bunch of white carnations. Reflecting again, with censure, on Mr Laidlaw's omission—what could he have been thinking of to forget the flowers? He brought them regular enough while Mrs Probus was alive—Shadwell walked over to the bedside and, after consideration, slightly adjusted one of the carnations. Then she went back to the kitchen, where the kettle was now boiling, and made herself a cup of tea.

(Winter in the Air, 1955)

THE PROPERTY OF A LADY

Rooms in London require dusting daily if they are to look like the rooms of a lady. And so, every morning, Miss Amy Cruttwell's rooms were dusted from head to foot, first the bedroom and then the sitting-room; for all things belonging to her must look like the property of a lady, it was their doom and hers. Twice a week the silver was carefully polished, and the china, the Dresden figures and the two millefleur boots entirely encrusted with sharp microscopic forget-me-nots, were washed in the handbasin. While the dusting was being performed Miss Cruttwell was energetic, angry, and contented, the natural rancour of a single woman of sixty living on a small pension flowing easily from her like a sweat. But by eleven o'clock, when all was over, and the brooms and brushes and dusters put away in the ottoman, it was an even hazard whether her pride or her weariness would conquer, whether she would look round with a toss of the head, saying to herself: 'Well, if any one comes, it's ready for them,' or, suddenly prostrated by a longing for a cup of tea, stare at the gas-ring and remember how lonely she was, how old, and how neglected, and how, all her life long, she had kept the lady-standard flying, had been scrupulously clean, scrupulously honest, scrupulously refined, and nothing had come of it save to be old and neglected and lonely.

For though the rooms were so neat, so ready for company, even to having a little bunch of flowers always fresh and daintily arranged, very few people entered them. Sometimes the wife of the clergyman looked in, sometimes the retired matron of the nursing home where Miss Cruttwell's appendix had been removed, sometimes the widow of the gentleman whose secretary Miss Cruttwell had been. They were all nice people, she had never known any but nice people. They appreciated her delicacy of mind and of person, they admired the tea-set, they said how refreshing it was to see a tree from the window; and sometimes, tactfully, they would leave behind a tin of fancy biscuits or a cardboard box containing grapes.

But they did not come often. And when they came, they went. And when they invited her to their houses and she accepted the invitation (she did not always accept) she, too, had to go away; and the warmth of the white wine would evaporate in the bus, and when she had reached home and put away her gloves and shaken her hat and hung up her coat and put her walking shoes on their trees and lit the gas-fire there was not much left but melancholy.

And so things went on till she was sixty-five. Then, almost simultaneously, she had influenza and was given a portable wireless. The wireless came from the widow of the gentleman and with it came a note, saying:

Dearest Amy,
I am so sorry I have not been to see you for such a long time. I am still terribly rushed, I do not quite know when I shall get to you. But with this wireless and all the delightful things which are now being broadcast, I'm sure you will not miss my stupid conversation.
Yours ever affly,
Muriel.

Suddenly enraged by the hollowness of the universe and of all human intercourse, Amy Cruttwell sniffed contemptuously at the wireless as a cat sniffs at milk which it knows to be sour, and turned away; but presently she came back, as a starving cat will, and turned it on. Out came, swimmingly, a polite voice announcing football news. Not interrupting it she went and sat in the farthest corner, stiffly upright, clenching her hands together, darting furious glances about the empty room. So that was what it was all worth, their pretence of friendship! That was all the appreciation one might look for, all the sympathy! —great vulgar wirelesses which they had not even the civility to bring themselves. And every now and then an orange.

'Why should I stay alive?' she asked the announcer. Why, indeed, to buy herrings and the cheapest China tea, to mend old nightdresses, take circulars from the letter-box, dust two rooms daily which no one entered but herself. No one noticed her, she glided through the wet streets unscanned. No one would notice if she died, she said to herself, passionately tasting the sweet strong knowledge of what a to-do her death, her suicide, would create, what stabbing surprise, what pangs of conscience, what convicting self-reproaches among her false friends.

The football news had given place to music on the organ. Those sturdy waves bore her onward, buoying her resolve. And with tears coursing down her cheeks she wrote several farewell letters, letters which would be found after her death, and read at the inquest, and published in the papers. But at last, alas! she must descend from her happiness, she must decide how to kill herself.

Not water, not gas. She rejected those two elements. Her rooms were at the top of the house, but she did not want to die in the street, with people treading in her blood. A seemly death, something dignified. (*She looked so wonderfully peaceful, so inscrutable, lying there, with all her wrinkles gone. But Oh! so sad.*) Aspirin! A whole bottle of aspirin, and she had such. One did not swallow the tablets, one crushed them in water and drank.

'The last time I shall use this teaspoon,' she thought proudly. And the tablets were all crushed, and the drink, chalky white, deadly white, ready in the medicine glass. . . . Like knowing that two and two make four she knew that she had not the courage to drink. Cold with fear, sick with shame, she turned off the wireless and tore up the farewell letters, and emptied the medicine glass into the slop-pail. A whole bottle of aspirin wasted.

It was dusk, and the muffin-bell had gone ringing down the street, when she came out of her despair as out of a terrible slumber. But one thing came with her, a raging resolve to claw her way into those easy minds which could forget her, a living woman, for weeks and then send her a wireless. If she could not get into the papers by one means, she could by another.

So she dressed with her usual exact care, lacing her shoes briskly, smoothing on her gloves; for a lady is always known by her neatness of hand and foot. The drizzle of rain was rather pleasant than otherwise, she felt herself walking lightly and elegantly, comparing well with those other figures bundled in their winter coats, dragging children after them or foolishly pursuing buses. She passed the dairy, and the fish-shop, and the rather vulgar greengrocer with an outside stall where, shopping, she fortified herself with thoughts of Parisian economy. But tonight she had no business with these. She was going to Whiteley's to steal, to be a shop-lifter. Grandly the soft full illumination of Whiteley's flowered on the dowdy Queen's Road. There in the windows were those composition women whose hair never needed cutting, who never felt the cold. In their taper fingers they held silk stockings or dangled silver foxes, and at their feet were scent-sprays and eiderdown quilts and tickets saying neatly, £5 19s. 6d. She would begin by stealing a scent-spray.

Under the floodlit central dome everything was warm and luxurious and orchid-like. The air was sweet, the carpets were soft, the lights, like sharp amorous caresses, pinched little gasps of reflected light from cut-glass bottles and crystal powder-bowls and sleek virgin boxes of cosmetics and rich sleepy cakes of soap. Out of this glittering jungle looked the blueish flesh-tints of the woman behind the counter, thinking she knew Miss Cruttwell, nodding good evening to her. 'Can I assist you, madam?' 'No, thank you,' said Miss Cruttwell and lingered ostentatiously, fingering the clasp of that large useful bag which had been a present from the retired matron of the nursing home. And slowly she walked round, her mind licking the smooth soaps, the flasks of scent, the powder-puffs and the rejuvenating face-creams. This she would have, and that; and when she had finished with that counter she would go on to the adjacent cheap fashionable jewellery, the pearls as large as cherries, the jade earrings; and end up with the gloves.

To one who has led a virtuous life, to sin is the easiest thing in the world. No experience of unpleasant consequences grits that smooth sliding fall, no recollection of disillusionment blurs that pure desire. Like a blackbird singing Amy Cruttwell stole two cakes of soap, a swansdown powder-puff, a scent-spray and a bottle of golden perfume which swayed voluptuously within its glassy walls; and then, going on to the cheap and fashionable jewellery, she stole a brooch on a velvet pad, an enamelled cigarette-case, and a bracelet of weighty false pearls. Theft was in itself such rapture, such calm of paradise, that she forgot that she was stealing for a purpose; it was only at the glove counter, surveying the more serious texture of leather, that she recollected the need to be discovered and arrested and taken to the police and put into the papers. Parading herself, making a slow motion of theft, she took a pair of gloves; but no one noticed. Another pair; and now the bag was full. But it was all right. They never arrested one at the counter because of the unpleasant impression it made upon the other customers. They shadowed one, followed one to the door, struck there. And walking proudly over the dense carpets she reached the swinging doors of glass and metal, and passed into the raw cold outside.

A man came hastily after her, brushed against her, set the bag swinging, and went on.

She waited. She waited. People went in and out, but no one noticed her. Tethered to one of the pillars was a dog, a poodle, whose shaved flanks twitched with cold. It lengthened itself towards her, gave a sniff, sighed disappointedly and turned away again, to sit with patience under the draughty portico on the cold stone. She waited. But no one came, no one noticed her.

At last she began to walk home.

(More Joy in Heaven, 1935)

ONE THING LEADING TO ANOTHER

THE onion, the apple, the raisins, the remains of the cold mutton neatly cubed were simmering over a low heat, and Helen Logie had opened the store cupboard and was about to get down the tin of curry powder when the telephone rang yet again. With a sharply drawn sigh she moved the pan to one side and ran up the basement stairs. The caller was Miss Dewlish, who wanted to consult Father Green about something that might seem rather silly, but something else really quite important might hang on it, so unless he had started lunch . . .

'He's out. Both their Reverences are out.'

But as she spoke, Helen sat down—Miss Dewlish would not be dismissed as easily as that—and as one can rest one's feet and yet be usefully employed, she cast her reviewing eye over the hall, where she noticed that the frayed end of the mat had once more escaped from its binding and that Father Green's snuffbox lay open by the telephone, empty and appealing. She put it in her apron pocket, to be replenished from the tin in the store cupboard. The presbytery was a damp house, and the kitchen was the best climate for snuff. Meanwhile, Miss Dewlish was explaining why the purchase of a different brand of floor polish (costing an extra sixpence, but on the other hand the tin was oval, so it probably held more) from Mr Radbone who kept the small grocery shop at the bottom end of King Alfred Street (at least, from her house it was the bottom end, though from the presbytery it might seem the top end; it depended on the way you looked at it) might bring Mr Radbone back to his duties as a Catholic, for while buying some tapioca (she always felt it a duty to go to small shopkeepers if it was humanly possible) she had discovered that he was a lapsed, so it had immediately occurred to her that if he could be got into Our Lady of Ransom, just to see how splendid his polish looked (she for one would gladly give an extra rub; no doubt the others of the Church Guild would do the same)—well, at any rate, it would be a step, wouldn't it? And we all had the conversion of England at heart, hadn't we?

When there was no reply to these inquiries, she remarked, 'I'm afraid I'm keeping you?' To which Helen vouchsafed in her tight Scotch voice, 'Well, yes, you are, rather, just now. If you don't mind,' and put back the receiver as soon as she could interpose a goodbye among Miss Dewlish's understandings of how busy she was and how wonderfully she managed to do all she did.

Sublimating her feelings into a 'God help his Reverence', she hurried down to the kitchen, put in the rice to boil, stirred up the mutton, and got out the curry powder. The telephone rang again. This time it was the coal merchant, inquiring if it would be all the same if he brought boiler-nuts.

'At six shillings a ton more? It will not.'

He was easier to quell than Miss Dewlish, but for all that, when she returned to the kitchen the rice was just about to boil over. At the same moment she heard the street door open and Father Curtin come in.

'Miss Logie.'

'What is it?' she called back, shaking in the curry powder. Let him bring himself downstairs on his long legs, she thought. He was, God forgive her, but the curate. She heard him doing so.

'Miss Logie, I've a message for you from Mrs Ward. She wants to know—I say, that smells good!'

He approached the stove, and the steam from the boiling rice clouded his spectacles.

'It's about the Catholic Women's Bazaar. She says she's already taken orders for five dozen of your scones, and would you be able to make as many again for sale on the stall, as well as the shortcake and the treacle tarts? And we've been promised another bottle of whisky for the tombola. We'll get those kneelers yet, Miss Logie.'

She drained the rice. Each grain was separate. She stirred the curry. It was thickening to perfection. She would not be eating it—her digestion was not what it was—but it gratified her to see it doing her credit. She loaded the chocolate shape, the custard, the big loaf of bread, and the jug of water on the tray, and started upstairs with it. He did not attempt to take it from her, and she would have been affronted if he had. They had both grown up in good God-fearing homes, and knew their places, his in the sanctuary, hers in the kitchen.

Father Green entered the house, saying 'Well, Helen, that smells very appetising, whatever it is.'

'Mutton curry, your Reverence.'

'Splendid! Any telephone calls?'

'More than enough. But nothing that won't wait till you've had your food.'

When the meal was served, she went back to the kitchen with a clear conscience, saying to herself that the worst half of the day was over.

She had finished her own meal and was about to make the tea when she noticed the tin of snuff on the cooking table. That curate had been after her raisins again, taking out the snuff tin to get at them and forgetting to replace it. Half laughing, half angry, she jumped up to ascertain how far down the raisin jar he'd been. There, on the shelf, was the curry powder!

Never doubting the worst, but as a sort of judicial formality, she went across to the sink, passed her finger over the side of the saucepan, and licked. Yes she had taken the wrong tin; the curry had been made with snuff.

'Mother of God!' she said, and sat down, utterly daunted. How had she come to do such a thing? But it was plain enough. In her flurry she had snatched up the tin that came first to hand; and then, wondering how she would find time for all that extra baking, she had failed to notice any difference in the curry, vaguely thinking to herself that if it looked darker than usual it must be that the onions had caught while the Dewlish body was prating. God forgive her!—it might have been ratsbane and two men of God dying in agonies. As it was, there would be two men of God sitting behind great helpings of curry they couldn't eat—not to mention the waste of a tablespoonful of Father Green's only luxury.

The kettle boiled. 'I'm getting past my work, that's the truth of it,' she said, and rose up as if her limbs were lead, and made the tea and carried it upstairs.

A few grains of rice remained in the dish. Two well-scraped plates had been put by, and the two priests were tranquilly eating their pudding.

All she had meant to say in apology and contrition was annulled. She put down the tea things, collected the used plates, and tried to get away unintercepted. Something in her demeanour struck Father Green. He had inherited her with the presbytery, he knew her worth, he also knew that she must be kept in with. Breaking off an anecdote about a prize begonia, he said, hastily, 'An excellent curry, Helen.'

'Never ate a better one,' added Father Curtin.

'And, Helen. What were those telephone messages?'

'They're down on the telephone pad, your Reverence, all but the last two. The coal merchant, he was trying to foist boiler-nuts on us, but I soon settled his hash. And—and—'

The word 'hash' nearly undid her. If they could eat snuff in a curry, what wouldn't they swallow in a hash?

'Well? What was the other?'

'Miss Dewlish, your Reverence. I just couldn't get all of her down. But the gist of it was that she wants you to buy the church floor polish from Mr Radbone, because he's a lapsed Catholic.'

'Oh, is he? H'mph. But what's the floor polish to do with it?'

'He'd come in, she said, maybe, to admire the floor. Then he'd stay in.'

'It might be worth trying,' said Father Curtin. 'Throw a sprat, you know . . .'

Father Green coughed. 'I'd rather you didn't talk like that, if you please. It's unbecoming. Helen, do you know anything about this Mr Radbone?'

'Only the outside of his shop, and that's no recommendation. The polish is sixpence a tin more.'

'How large is the tin?' asked Father Curtin. 'If it could be stretched out over a fortnight, sixpence more wouldn't be a great obstacle.'

'It might not, your Reverence. But taking away a regular order from Mr Vokes, who never misses Sunday or Saint's Day, and brings that great tail of a family after him, to give it to Mr Radbone, who's never been near the church—and who's to say his polish will fetch him?—I'd call that an obstacle.'

Quenched anew in his zeal for souls, Father Curtin said nothing. Father Green said, 'That's a point, too.'

'Miss Dewlish wouldn't stop to think of that. But new brooms are always on the fidget.'

'Helen, that's no way to speak. There are a great many converts who put us cradle Catholics to shame. Use a pinch more charity, Helen.'

Now why, thought Father Curtin, should Miss Logie, rebuked with this homely and appropriate metaphor, look as if the Devil had entered into her?—unless she was jealous of Miss Dewlish? A simple spinster of canonical age, a Child of Mary, a valued housekeeper, and busy from morning till night, you'd think she'd be over such feelings; but unfortunately, those ones were often the worst.

Helen hated Miss Dewlish as habitually as she scrubbed the doorstep, but in a spirit equally removed from emotions of jealousy. The air of private elation observed by Father Curtin was, in fact, precisely due to private elation, to a surging acknowledgement that she was feeling like a new woman—as though the snuff curry had been a kind of brief holiday to her, a release, a levitation, such as she might snatch from smelling the sea or hearing a skirl of passing bagpipes. Feeling like a new woman, she went through the rest of the day's routine as if she were a blithe stranger to it, a sightseer in her own kitchen. And up in her bedroom at last, standing barefooted for the ease of it, and combing out her hair, as flamingly red and almost as thick as when she was a girl, she found herself staring with a new recognition at the two photographs on her dressing table: Jimmy Stott, whom she had loved so hard and sore and could not marry because he would not give over being a Presbyterian, and Father Ewing, whose housekeeper she had been, here, in this very house, for five proud, blissful years, till he had a call and went off to a mission in Africa, where she could not follow him. Every night she looked at them, every night she remembered them in her prayers, but it was a long time since they had had any reality to her. Now they were real again. Their reality was reflected back from hers, from the unique reality of the woman who had made a snuff curry.

Though the alarm clock, going off as usual at six a.m., reclothed her in the sameness of another day, a new element was at work in her mind. She began to speculate. Snuff was not all. Invention, not mere accident, could play a part in cookery, and that not just with the accepted anomalies—the pinch of salt that seizes the flavour of a chocolate icing, the trickle of anchovy essence that gives life to stewed veal—but by more arresting innovations and bolder departures: caraway seeds in a fish pie, for instance; a lentil soup enriched with rhubarb; horseradish in a tapioca pudding. It would be a way of getting oneself attended to, she thought. The snuff curry, while releasing her into the pleasures of fancy, had also imposed on her a new, raw awareness that to be relied on is not the same thing as being attended to, and that to be relied on by those who do not notice the difference between snuff and Indian spices is no great compliment.

However, she went on being as reliable as before. It was her lot, and there was no escape from it, whether or no she liked it. The gay bubbles of speculative fancy continued to rise and break on the surface of her mind, and harmed no one, since they went no further. And though an almost culinary impulse to vary the sameness of her sins once made her mention in confession that from time to time she got silly fancies, Father Green's assurance that the best way to overcome fancies was to pay no heed to them quelled any faint stir there might have been in her conscience. In fact, when at last one of the bubbles rose beyond the surface of her mind and made its way up to the ground floor, she had been paying so little heed to it that only when she was back in the kitchen again and getting on with the ironing did it strike her that the table spread for their Reverences' tea had not looked quite as usual. Had she perhaps forgotten the sugar tongs? The last of the heavy ironing was done and she was trifling with pocket handkerchiefs when a mental picture showed her that nothing was lacking from the tea table, but that a tureen of mint sauce was there, too.

Though once again she said, 'Mother of God!' and sat down, it was not because she was daunted but because she was so shaken with laughter that she could not stand; and instead of bewailing that she was getting past her work, she exclaimed, 'It'll no be accidental-like next time, that's for sure!' adding, after a moment of rapt consideration, 'Rissoles, is it? That heeltap of the coffee extract will do fine.' Henceforward, the whet of excitement that parishioners got from staking a weekly shilling in the St Thomas à Becket Orphanage Football Pool Helen Logie enjoyed—and without paying a penny for it, either—by laying bets with herself how far she could go before Father Green and Father Curtin noticed anything uncanonical. She kept strictly within her own regulations. She bought nothing out of the usual, and except when she sauced a boiled suet pudding with cough linctus, she used no extraneous ingredients. All was wholesome and homemade, the same thrifty traditional home cooking she had been practising for years. A religious scruple stayed her hand on days of fasting or abstinence, and an innate artistry forbade her to be too emphatic with her personal touches, or too frequent in her offerings. The snuff curry remained her model: something hitherto unthought of but not blatantly uneatable. To serve uneatable food would be waste, and Helen hated waste.

She won every bet. If, instead of betting against herself, she had been betting against St Thomas à Becket at two to one, she would have made at least fifty shillings to add to her savings, where every little helps. After a while, these victories began to pall. She longed, just for once, to lose a bet and gain the substantial crown of an exclamation of horror, a protest, an inquiry—a grimace, even. Having served up a wager, she would hang about, hopefully on the watch, or come back halfway through a meal on the pretext of thinking she had been called, to search their faces for some token of acknowledgement. Sometimes she would seem to catch a glint of disaffection behind Father Curtin's spectacles. Sometimes he would pause and glance inquiringly across at Father Green. But Father Green ate steadily on, and Father Curtin returned to the faith. If it had not been for Father Curtin's intimations of uneasiness, and the fact that he went out to tea more often than of old, and the biscuit crumbs she occasionally found in his bedroom, she would almost have believed that miracles of intervenience were wrought halfway up the kitchen stairs.

She left them unassailed during the holy and taxing season of Christmas, and began again in the new year. But she was no longer laying light bets with herself. Still honourably observing her own regulations, she now staked her soul on the event, and lay awake half the night racking her brains for some new abnormality, some arresting concoction that would extort from the two men she served an acknowledgement, if not of her skill, then at least of her labours, an outcry of wrath and amazement that would prove their occasional attention to what she cooked and they consumed. As one of Father Curtin's New Year resolutions had been to subdue the flesh and not think so much about what he liked or did not like eating, she had not even the support of a biscuit crumb. She cooked. They ate. That was all there was to it.

'I'll just waste no more pains on them!' In those words she accepted and disguised defeat. It was necessary to disguise defeat, since she did not like to admit herself inferior to Miss Dewlish in moral stamina; for when Father Green had remarked, 'Well, Miss Dewlish, after thinking it over for this long time, I've come round to your opinion, so we'll try that Cinderella polish,' and then dashed the cup of victory from her lips, and in front of all the Guildswomen, too, by adding, 'But for the present we'll get it from Vokes.' Miss Dewlish had not relinquished her purpose, and had since been engaged in trying to bring back Mr Radbone by calling on him daily for small quantities of groceries and reasoning with him over the counter. 'He's weakening. She'll have him yet' was the report of Willy Duppy, who, being employed as errand boy by the fishmonger opposite Mr Radbone, was able to keep a close observation on this fight for a soul. Father Green's flock included a number of Irish immigrants, and Willy Duppy, the youngest son of a widowed mother, was a favoured lamb. On the mornings when Willy served at Mass he got his breakfast in the presbytery kitchen; and if his reports from the Radbone sector of the Catholic Front were a trifle over-sanguine it was not to be wondered at. His heart was in it, and other military correspondents have been the same.

It was the middle of February, and Father Curtin was gratefully discovering that it was easier than he would have supposed to subdue the flesh and eat what was set before him without considering whether or no he liked it, and a packet of candles had appeared in Mr Radbone's window—which showed, said Willy, what his mind was dwelling on, since why should they be there otherwise?—and people with time for it were having influenza and others were just keeping about with bad colds, and Father Green under doctor's orders had been forced out of the ranks of the latter and been put to bed, when a last belated bubble of fancy rose in Helen's mind. Twelve dozen Seville oranges had simmered in the copper and she was about to begin on the business of scooping out the pulp and chopping the rinds, when it occurred to her that a dash of mustard might make an interesting addition—not to the marmalade she made for sale (her marmalade was in great demand and brought in almost as much to the parish funds as her baking did) but to an experimental pot for use upstairs. It was a poor weak bubble, and by the time it had weakly exploded she had already lost interest in it. There was a long afternoon's work before her, and the best she could hope was that by the time she had done with scooping and chopping and stirring she would be too tired to worry about that ache across her shoulders.

She was not at Mass next morning. She's down with influenza, thought Father Curtin. Though he was slightly appalled at the thought of being neither led nor fed, he was young enough to like the idea of showing his single-handed worth. However, the living-room fire was burning, the breakfast table was laid, and from below came the sounds and smells of breakfast preparing. He warmed his hands at the fire and waited. Steps approached. The door was pushed a little way open, and a tray appeared in the opening. He waited for Miss Logie to follow the tray. The tray remained where it was, and Miss Logie's voice—crisper, he thought, than usual—announced, 'Here you are, your Reverence. Your breakfast.'

As there presently seemed nothing else to do, he advanced, and took hold of the tray. As he took it, he nearly dropped it. It was proferred to him by what seemed at first sight a perfectly unknown woman with a great deal of rather tousled red hair streaming over her shoulders.

'I can't get it up,' she said. 'I've the rheumatism in my shoulders, and I can no more reach to the back of my head than to this ceiling.'

'I daresay I could tie it back for you, Miss Logie, if I had a piece of string.'

He set down the tray and began searching in his pockets. At the same time, he began searching in his mind, for there was something else, to do with Miss Logie's hair and yet not to do with it, that should be dealt with immediately if he were to prove his single-handed worth. 'I've got a rubber band.' At the sound of a cough overhead, he realised what it was that had to be dealt with. 'I'll tell you what I can do. I'll take up Father Green's breakfast.'

It was harder than he supposed to carry a tray upstairs; as for shutting the door after him with his foot, he could not manage it at all. It must be one of those womanly knacks that a man has no need for. At the clatter of the sliding crockery, Father Green opened his eyes.

'Miss Logie has got a touch of rheumatism, so I thought I'd spare her the tray.'

'Well, well. That's very kind of you. I'm glad it doesn't prevent her from cooking.'

Father Curtin felt that he had shown both presence of mind and good judgment. The doctor had spoken of a strain on the heart. It could have been a very dangerous shock to Father Green to see his housekeeper looking like the repentant Magdalen—partially, at any rate. From the chin down, she was as neat and buttoned-up as usual, though, oddly enough, this didn't make her appearance a whit less disquieting; it made it more so.

When he came in to lunch, her hair was up, though it did not look very secure. He commented on this—at least, he expressed his relief that her rheumatism was better.

'It's no better at all, your Reverence. It's just the best that Willy could do, when he brought the kippers.'

'Oh! Isn't there anyone else who could—'

'And he's coming again tonight, to take it down. And early tomorrow, so that I can get to Mass.'

He could not feel that this arrangement was very suitable, but he did not feel that to question it would be very suitable either. That evening —an impulse of chaperonage impelled him to sit up later than usual —he heard Willy being let in at the back door. Willy seemed to be staying a long time, as long as if he were putting Helen's hair up instead of taking it down—which the force of gravity made ridiculous. At last he could bear it no longer. He went unobtrusively to the head of the kitchen stairs. He heard a steady mutter of two voices, apparently conversing with phenomenal glibness. Going a step or two down the stairs, he realised that Helen and Willy were saying the rosary. Well, that was very nice. But what was that other recurrent, swishing sound? It could not be . . . But it was. It was Willy brushing Helen's hair. A moment later, Father Curtin heard himself being called from above stairs. The call was sharp, and urgent. Father Green must be having a heart attack. He hurried to the bedroom.

'Who's that downstairs at this hour of night?'

'It's Willy Duppy.'

'Well, what's he doing? He's been there for hours.'

'He's taking down Miss Logie's hair.'

'What?'

It was a comfort to disburden himself, for there are certain problems that only an experienced priest can deal with, and an experienced housekeeper is one of them. They were still talking when Helen, her two plaits finished off with two blue bows—Willy had a grateful heart, and took this opportunity to show how much he appreciated the breakfasts —went past on her way up to bed. The door was shut. But without straining her ears or disgracing herself by stopping to hear more, she heard enough to know that she was being talked about—she herself, not just her ability to provide bacon and eggs.

'I wouldn't care to cross her,' the younger priest said.

And the elder replied, 'We'll have no crossing, I hope. But you're right, all the same. She hasn't got that red hair for nothing.'

'She's what I'd call sensitive.'

'Well, that would be one word for it. Anyway, the best thing you can do is to keep out of it, for she's got more tricks up her sleeve than you'd be equal to.'

So that was the secret! All a woman need do to get herself attended to was to have a fit of rheumatism that would make it impossible for her to put her hair up. Well, now she knew it. And if she didn't rivet their attention this time, she'd have only herself to blame.

Next morning, Father Curtin inquired after Helen's rheumatism—but cautiously—and said nothing of carrying up Father Green's breakfast. With a grieved face and a dancing step, she went up with the tray, and as she needed both hands to carry it, she could do nothing when another hairpin lost its footing and fell out.

'Good morning, Helen. What's all this about your hair?'

'Good morning, your Reverence. I hope you had a better night.'

'Passable, passable. I don't mind telling you, your hair kept me awake for part of it.'

'I'm sure I'm sorry to hear that. Your Reverence has enough to worry you, without thinking about me. What's a little rheumatism? It doesn't prevent me from cooking, or washing or ironing, or the housework, except that I can't dust above my head. But that's no matter. Don't give it another thought, your Reverence. As for my hair, what's her hair to a woman of my age? Nothing, nothing at all.' She shook her head disclaimingly, and several more hairpins fell out.

'And what's all this about Willy?'

'Yes, indeed. It's Willy I have to thank that I could get to Mass this morning. He came round early on purpose, to put it up for me. He's a very obliging lad, your Reverence. There's nothing he wouldn't do to help us.'

'Willy's well enough. But he's got other things to do than put your hair up.'

'A true word. That's what makes it so obliging of him.'

'And take it down again, when he ought to be in bed and asleep. Besides, it's not properly up at all, as far as I can see.'

'Poor Willy! He does the best he can.'

'If you can't manage it yourself, you ought to get some other woman, who'd know how to do it.'

'Well, yes, I daresay. But I wouldn't care to flout Willy, when he's been so obliging. As I've heard your Reverence say, Willy's a boy in a thousand.'

'Some other woman—'

'Excuse me, your Reverence. That's the street bell.' She turned to the door, and her movement shook down a long tress.

'Helen, stop! You can't answer the door, looking like . . .'

But it was too late. Looking like a comet with a burning tail, Helen was gone.

When the doctor came, later in the day, Father Green gave him a searching look and inquired if he knew of a quick cure for rheumatism. The doctor, a rather prosy man, replied that there were a great many different kinds of rheumatism, and that the more one studied the disease, the more mysterious it became. For instance, some people got rheumatism if they drank cider; others if they drank cider were cured of it. After a while, he perceived that his patient had lost interest in the subject and introduced a new topic.

'Remarkable hair your housekeeper has got. I've never seen it down before. She told me she'd been washing it.'

It was a fine explanation, but scarcely one for daily use. When on the morrow Helen's rheumatism quitted her as abruptly as it had seized on her, she was not sorry. She could always recall it if she wished. Meanwhile, it was a comfort to have her hair, and Willy, too, firmly back in their right places. Willy was a good quiet boy, but their Reverences had spoiled him, and he must not be encouraged to suppose himself indispensable.

It seemed, however, as though she were in a way to be as much attended to with her hair in its usual knob as when it flowed unconfined. Father Curtin and Father Green, who was now up and about again, rejoiced in her recovery and showed a great deal of solicitude in warning her not to sit in draughts, get wet feet, or do anything beyond her strength. It was but solicitude, though sharpened by anxiety, that impelled Father Green—after Willy, in the course of delivering a smoked haddock, had stayed for half an hour at the back door, imparting how Mr Radbone had sent away three of his regular suppliers without ordering as much as a packet of starch—and what could that mean but a mind distracted towards more spiritual things?—to inquire what on earth Willy had been chattering about for so long.

'Willy?' said Helen, in affable tones. 'Willy? Oh, aye, I remember. He came while Miss Dewlish was upstairs talking to your Reverence. But I didn't pay any attention, my mind wasn't on him at all. I was wondering when Miss Dewlish would go, so that I could get on with cleaning the parlour windows. But there, she stayed on, so I must just do it tomorrow. Tomorrow'll do as well.'

She could afford to be affable. Tomorrow would see her rheumatism back, and his Reverence dancing and praying for Willy Duppy to come again, and no questions asked, either.

Father Green did not see himself as dancing and praying. It seemed to him that he was exercising a proper amount of authority, while keeping his temper remarkably well for a man who had only just got over influenza.

'Helen, I am sorry to see you are having trouble with your hair again. And I don't think Willy Duppy is a fit person to put it up for you. It needs a woman to deal with it. So you had better ask one of our good neighbours—one of the ladies of the Women's Guild, for instance.'

'Your Reverence, I wouldn't have one of them touch me.'

'Your rheumatism may be painful. I daresay it is. But I can't believe you're as sensitive as all that. In any case, we can't go through life avoiding pain.'

'I'm thinking of the talk. They'd say it was dyed.'

'Helen, this is ridiculous. You must either consent to have your hair put up or—'

'Or what, your Reverence?'

'Or you must stay in your bedroom.'

'Oh well—if your Reverence insists . . .' Helen spoke with more submission than he had dared to expect. Her glance, avoiding his, strayed about the room and lighted on the wastepaper basket, which needed emptying. She picked it up; then, with a shake of the head and a sigh, she put it down again and moved slowly towards the door.

'If you need the tin opener, it's on the dresser, your Reverence.'

Three days, she judged, would be about right. Less than three days would not give them adequate time for repentance. More than three days would mean such havoc in the kitchen that she, too, might be driven to repent.

Three days' leisure took some getting rid of, but she passed the time by overcoming a great heap of darning, and writing letters to her relations. At due intervals she crept downstairs, sad and unshriven, to get herself something to eat. She timed her descents to the kitchen so that she would either find Father Curtin getting a meal or Father Green and Father Curtin together washing up. Abashed and silent, she would then hang about in the doorway, a shameful spectacle that would not intrude itself upon them by any offers of help or advice; and after a minute or two retire, until the kitchen was vacated, when she could have a grim look round on the aftermath, cook something with a strong declamatory smell, like toasted cheese, and leave whatever she had used in a state of ostentatious cleanliness, polished and shining like a good deed in a naughty world.

Three days, as it turned out, was a little too long, for on the evening of the third day they disconcerted her by being invited to supper by Mrs Ward, who was celebrated for keeping a good table. When Helen served breakfast the next morning with her flowing locks back where they should be, she sensed that the situation had curdled, and that next time she would have to go about it more circumspectly. When Mrs Ward's car drove up just before lunchtime and Mrs Ward stepped out of it carrying a covered basket, she knew what had happened. She was no longer the only cook in their Reverences' lives.

So it was unfortunate that, less than a week later, Helen should wake up with another attack of rheumatism in her shoulders, as genuine and inhibiting as the first. Gritting her teeth, and calling on St Jude, the patron of seemingly lost causes, she somehow managed to bundle her hair into a chignon and fling a scarf over her head. St Jude had also provided Willy. Though this was not one of Willy's mornings, the usual Thursday server had failed, Willy had been called to replace him, and was now at the back door, waiting to be let in for breakfast, and bursting to communicate the latest news about Mr Radbone.

'Trying to sell the business? Hoots, why should he want to do that? I don't believe it.'

'It's true as I stand here. And ready to take whatever he can get for it, he's that wild to get away.'

'Where does he want to go, then?'

'Anywhere out of here. The fact of it is—' Willy lowered his voice and glanced behind him. 'The fact of it is—and I wouldn't like to be telling anyone but you, Miss Logie—the fact of it is . . .'

'Oh, hurry, boy, don't make so many bobs at it. And twist harder than that, or it will never stay on my head.'

'The fact of it is, it's her. She's been going at him too hard, every day and twice a day, and telling him in front of the commercial traveller that she's put another novena on him, till it's got so that he breaks out into a sweat every time she goes in for a tin of cocoa or a pennyworth of birdseed. No, she's been too savage for him; she'll never get him now, he's lost.'

'Well, now! That will fair break Miss Dewlish's heart,' said Helen briskly, and went off with the breakfast tray.

People rapturously savouring the misfortunes of others cannot help betraying it by an expression of morbid primness. When Father Curtin looked up to say 'Good morning', he found himself recalling the occasion when it seemed to him that the Devil had entered into Miss Logie. But this morning it appeared as though the Devil had been comfortably lodged in her for some time.

Father Green also said 'Good morning', but did not look up. He did not want to look at Helen, he did not want to hear her voice, he did not want to be aware of her in any shape or form except in the form of works. Ever since the day when she had shot madly from her sphere—her befitting womanly sphere of being his housekeeper—and turned into a baleful, red-maned comet, she had compelled far too much of his unwilling attention, forcing him to struggle not only with her vagaries but with, on his own part, an obsessive, uncomfortable, and totally unmanly exasperation. He looked at his plate of porridge, so calm and daily, and then he unfolded his newspaper and propped it against the teapot and looked at that.

Thus, when Reggie Mendoza, the son of a local landowner, and in the tadpole stage of conversion, arrived that afternoon for an hour's instruction, and was shown in by Helen with her hair in a state of nature, Father Green was unprepared for the shock, and said, 'Sit down, Reggie' with such controlled force that Reggie felt with a delicious thrill that he was really being addressed by the Voice of the Church, and almost knelt down instead. Reggie's reason for becoming a convert was that he doubted the validity of Anglican Orders, and as Father Green did not even give them the benefit of the doubt, one might have supposed that everything would be straightforward. People who feel such doubts, however, do not like to have them too emphatically endorsed; at an unwary assent, the doubter will fly to the defence of what he is proposing to abjure, as when if too heavy a weight is cast on one end of a seesaw the person at the other end will fly upward and possibly fall off. Though Reggie did not fall off, the conversational seesawing required patience and delicate adjustment, and Father Green, with the thought of Helen hammering in his brain, found these much harder than usual to supply. At long last, he got Reggie to the doorstep and saw him off with a blessing. Then, after a pinch of snuff and a couple of reviving sneezes, he summoned Helen to his study.

'Shut the door, Helen,' he began, in much the same compressed tones as when he said, 'Sit down, Reggie'. She was, in fact, already shutting it, but in this conversation he wished to assert his authority from the start. There she stood, her unrepentant tresses flowing and her small grey eyes fixed on him—a revolting, an embarrassing, spectacle.

He had decided on a preliminary pause—such as he made use of, on solemn occasions, in the pulpit. The pause was broken by Helen saying, 'Well, your Reverence?'

He disregarded this, and continued to pause. Helen continued to stare. Then her glance veered to his snuffbox, and her lips curled slightly, as though she were sneering at his only self-indulgence.

'Ahem! What I have to say can scarcely come as a surprise to you. Your conscience will have told you already that I have cause for uneasiness—painful uneasiness.'

'My hair, I suppose.' Her Scottish intonation, dragging out the word 'hair', gave this a cynical ring. 'Or would it be my rheumatism?'

'I have spoken about this already. I had hoped not to have to speak again. But I see I must. Helen, this cannot go on. I cannot have you going about with your hair streaming down your back. It is unseemly. I don't like it.'

'I don't like it myself, your Reverence. But what way can I get it up if my rheumatism won't let me and I mayn't have Willy?'

'It is not your rheumatism that stands in your way, Helen. It is your obstinacy. The parish is full of women who would put your hair up for you.'

'It can be fuller yet, your Reverence, before I'd let one of them near me.'

'Think twice, Helen. Do you seriously mean those words?'

'Indeed and I do.'

'Very well. In that case, there's only one way out.· Your hair must be cut short.'

'Cut off my hair? Never! I don't know what your Reverence is thinking of. St Peter said women should keep their hair long.'

'St Peter said nothing of the sort. And if it's St Paul you want, St Paul said that a God-fearing woman doesn't adorn herself with plaited hair, but with modesty, sobriety, and good works.'

'Let them plait their hair that can get their hands round to it! See for yourself if I can plait my hair!' She wrenched up her arms with such fury and vehemence that the pain made her cry out.

The door opened. Father Curtin looked in. 'Is there anything wrong? Has something happened to Miss Logie?'

'Just this—that I've come to the end of my patience. And both your

Reverences can hear what I've got to say. Here and now, I'm giving you a month's notice.'

She stamped out of the room, her face white as a bone and her hair streaming like a banner.

Father Curtin turned to Father Green for reassurance. He got none. Father Green's face was purple, the veins stood out on his forehead, and he was breathing like an embattled ram. Presently he glanced at his watch. 'About time to say our vespers.'

On the morrow, Father Green rang up Mrs Ward and said in a voice that was perhaps a trifle calmer and louder than ordinary that he would be grateful if she would help him to find a new housekeeper. To her condolences he replied that it was indeed quite a blow, and that he had no doubt Helen's baking would be missed throughout the parish, but that the work was getting beyond her strength and that she had well earned a reposeful old age.

The news that Helen was going made a considerable stir, but the news, coming soon after, that Mr Radbone had gone, nobody knew where to, made a greater, since there was also Miss Dewlish's frustration to be canvassed, and the question of what she would take up next.

Presumably, Helen was relieved to be out of the limelight; at any rate, about the time of Mr Radbone's departure she was observed to grow less morose, and as Lent wore on, her disposition sweetened to such an extent that instead of triumphing over Mrs Ward's failure to catch a housekeeper, she mentioned a Cousin Isa, who would come on trial if their Reverences thought fit, learn what was required, and, if she gave satisfaction, take over after Helen went. As there was now less than a fortnight left of Helen's month, this was agreed to.

Isa arrived, gave satisfaction, and was engaged. Wearing a new suit and an unexpectedly dashing going-away hat, Helen made a round of farewell calls, in the course of which she said a great deal that was proper and civil, and nothing that was informative. Her demeanour was so grave and reserved that a number of people believed she had been dismissed for some sudden lapse it would not be kind to inquire into, and some among them even thought that Father Green had been too hasty with an old servant.

Her farewells appeared to be final, so it was a pleasing surprise when, soon after Easter, Mr Radbone's redecorated shop opened its doors for the sale of light refreshments, cooked meats, cakes, jams, scones, and bannocks, and there was Helen presiding over it, assisted by Willy Duppy. The business throve, the money she had borrowed to complete the purchase was soon paid back, and Willy was felt to be as good as made, since Helen allowed it to be known that when he had learned the trade, and put by a decent nest egg in the Post Office Savings, and married a nice steady girl, he would become her partner and ultimately inherit the business. True, Willy's vocation to the priesthood, which at one time had seemed so promising, was mislaid in all this; but as Willy himself had never felt altogether sure of it, things were probably for the best.

(*One Thing Leading to Another*, 1984)

MY FATHER, MY MOTHER,
THE BENTLEYS, THE POODLE,
LORD KITCHENER,
AND THE MOUSE

THE first bed, the bed in which I was got and born, was made of brass, with shiny knobs and a starched white valance usually stencilled with dogpaws. By the time I was in my teens it looked shockingly old-fashioned, and my mother decided to replace it by a fourposter, replicated under the influence of Lutyens from some chaste Georgian original. This cost a great deal of money and was made of solid oak. The groans of the men who carried its limbs upstairs and put them together testified to the solidity.

It was because of the uncouthness of the groans, my mother averred, and the powers of association in the canine mind that our poodle concluded that the fourposter was some kind of lofty machine expressly invented for the oppression of poodles, and refused to sleep in the same room with it. Bidden to lie down and be a good dog, he would twitch in a martyred silence till the light was turned off; then he would rise to his feet and begin what my mother, whose childhood was spent in southern India, called Dead-Hindoo-ing. Dead-Hindoo-ing is uttering a succession of those flesh-creeping howls which end in a tremolo. My mother could do it very eloquently herself, and when I was younger had enlarged my mind by telling me how the chief jackal proclaims, 'I've found a dead Hindoo-oo-oo!' to the rest of the pack, who, sitting round on their haunches in the slashing jungle moonlight, bark out, 'Where?

Where? Where?' But to have the poodle Dead-Hindoo-ing in nocturnal Middlesex was inappropriate. After several nights of this, the poodle was persuaded to sleep in my father's study, and my mother was able to give her whole mind to enjoying the fourposter.

A few nights later she woke up to hear more animal noises. These were well in keeping with Middlesex, for they came from a mouse. It scampered around the room in a lighthearted, flippant way, pausing at intervals to crunch. Trying to compose herself by the force of Reason, my mother remembered that while she was still striving to rescue the poodle from being a prey to superstition, she had tried biscuits. He must have left some crumbs about, and the mouse had come after them. This was shocking, as it meant that Rose did not really sweep. Rose, on the other hand, darned linen as no housemaid of my mother's had ever darned before; she made her darns adornings. Shaping the diplomatic approach which would indicate the biscuit crumbs without unsettling such a good darner, my mother got over her morbid interest in the mouse, and presently fell asleep again.

The *aide-mémoire* to Rose passed off without mishap, and that night, having ascertained for herself that there were no crumbs, my mother lay down in the fourposter thinking how pleasant it is to fall asleep with a quiet mind. She was still dwelling on the quietness of her mind when she heard the mouse again. This time—umbraged, perhaps, by finding no crumbs—it was in a sterner mood. It approached with a resolute gait and began to gnaw a leg of the bedstead. My mother leaned out of bed and said in an undertone, 'Shoo!' The gnawing ceased, but the mouse did not go away, and presently it began to gnaw again. The rest of the night was spent antiphonally between my mother and the mouse, who formally acknowledged her shooings by brief silences, after which he gnawed on. But by sunrise my mother's voice, strained by the effort of reiterating 'Shoo' in an undertone, was almost exhausted, whereas the mouse, each time it returned to the attack, gnawed more vigorously, as though it were inflamed by rage and defiance.

All through these painful hours, my mother did not think of waking my father. On weekdays he had to get up at quarter to seven, and as he seldom went to bed before midnight, she had strong views about the sacredness of his slumbers. I don't doubt that she would have lain bleeding to death beside him, or racked with the most compelling of sudden thoughts, rather than make a move to waken him. But in the small hours of the following night she prodded him with her elbow and said, 'George! Did you feel the bed shaking just then? Hush. Don't make a sound. It's a mouse.'

As usual, my mother was right. It was a mouse, and it was gnawing. 'There it is!' she exclaimed. 'Did you feel it then? It's shaking the whole bedstead.' No man of intellect cares to base an argument on the obvious. While my father, scorning to assert that a bedstead which four men could only carry with groans could not be shaken by one mouse, was casting about for some more controvertible and interesting disagreement, she continued, 'This has been going on night after night. And always the same leg—the near hind leg. There's nothing else for it—you must fetch Lord Kitchener.'

Lord Kitchener, the only cat I ever knew who chewed his own moustachios, was our respected tabby, and he had become very much of a recluse and spent most of his time in the boiler room. It was from the boiler room that my father carried him, mutely and sullenly resisting, upstairs. 'Mice, Kitchener, mice! Go seek!' cried my mother, who had no real vocation for cats. Lord Kitchener gave her one blighting monosyllabic glance, removed all traces of my father with a few smart licks, and resumed his slumbers. My father watched this with wistful veneration. He, too, would have been glad to resume his slumbers, having washed off some trifling bloodstains and a haunting smell of boiler room. But it was not to be.

'No wonder this house is overrun by mice,' said my mother bitterly. 'Tomorrow I shall go to the Army and Navy and buy a mongoose. But now, as you are up, darling, would you mind fetching the poodle. *He's* not so fat he can't move.'

It was not that we had omitted to choose a name for our poodle; we had chosen too many, none of them had stuck, and in the end he was spoken of as the Poodle, just as one says the Pope, or at that date said the Tsar. A willing, romantic animal, he came upstairs enthusiastically prepared to do whatever feats might be expected of him—short of sleeping with that fearful fourposter. On the threshold he cringed. But finding himself propelled into a lighted room where my mother was sitting up in the machine for the oppression of poodles and making encouraging noises, he suddenly developed the valour of the terrified, the acumen of the warrior. There was the cat. This, however wild and unprecedented, was what was expected of him. With a yell, he launched himself on Lord Kitchener. Lord Kitchener scratched his nose with lightning nonchalance and sprang on to the mantelshelf, whence he dislodged several family photographs and Lady Hamilton as a Bacchante. There, if he had not been dragged from his own boiler room, the encounter might have ended, for he was temperamentally a Quietist and asked only for peace with honour. But now, having twice been so rudely disturbed, he needed to shake the black bile off his liver, which he did by rushing round the room at furniture level, scattering destruction as he went, while the poodle bounded in his wake through a hail of pincushions, powder bowls, nail scissors, cardcases, pomade pots, copies of the *Christian Year*, glove stretchers, trinket boxes, small ornaments, cough lozenges, and anything else that Lord Kitchener found available for self-expression.

Roused by the shindy, I was wondering if I would be well received if I joined the family circus when I heard the spare-room door opened, and Mr and Mrs Bentley, who were staying with us at the time, consulting together as to what they ought to do. They were a pair of earnest, high-minded numbskulls, so it was only a matter of a few sentences before they knew that they should do their duty. The passage light flicked on. Mr Bentley, tactfully raising his coughs above the tumult of voices and crashes, crossed the landing and tapped on the bedroom door. As he did so, there was another splintering crash, and the poodle left off baying and began to sneeze.

'Warner, I say, Warner. Is anything wrong?'

Except for the poodle's sneezes, everything had become arrestingly silent, and Mr Bentley's inquiries must have been plainly audible through the door. But there was no answer. He spoke again, much louder, and rather jerkily. 'I say, Warner! Is there anything wrong?'

My father, speaking as though he had a clothespeg on his nose, answered in what would have seemed untroubled tones except for the effect of the clothespeg. 'Thank you, thank you. There's nothing wrong. We had to intimidate a mouse, that was all. I'm sorry if we disturbed you.'

Mr Bentley said, 'Not at all,' sneezed, and went back to Mrs Bentley.

A minute later, the bedroom door was opened from within, and Lord

Kitchener and the poodle came out, walking soberly side by side in an odour of aromatic ammonia—for the last victim of Lord Kitchener's self-expression had been my mother's bottle of strong smelling salts.

When the Bentleys came down to breakfast, it was plain that they had agreed to draw a veil. It was also plain that my mother had been made aware of the graces of contrition.

'Coffee or tea? Thank God they both seem pretty strong. I'm sure we all need it after such an appalling night.'

Parrying this implication that both Bentleys had been sleeping in my parents' bedroom, Mrs Bentley said that she and Eustace preferred tea—and took it weak.

'I'd hate you to think that I'd make such a fuss about any normal mouse,' my mother said. 'But this one has been persecuting me for ages, and last night it came to a head.'

'A mouse?' Mrs Bentley spoke as if she belonged to some cool, calm world into which mice never climbed.

'It ground its teeth like a sawmill. I wonder you didn't hear it.'

'No.'

'Really,' my mother said, as though speaking from some world into which no Ginevra Bentley with her adenoids would ever climb, and turned to Mr Bentley. 'You heard it, though. At least, you heard something, for you came to our help. It was very kind of you.'

'I heard the dog barking. It struck me that your room might be on fire. That's all. One reads of such things.'

'Yes, doesn't one? Dear angels! And whole slum families saved, poor wretches!—though one sometimes wonders what for.'

My father, seeing that Mrs Bentley was about to burst out of her ice cavern, remarked that this angel was barking at the cat, and that he was very sorry the Bentleys should have been disturbed.

Mr Bentley, scrupulously just, said that my mother had been disturbed, too. Mice could be quite disturbing.

My mother suddenly looked very happy. 'Of course! Now I understand why it upset me. It was gnawing the leg of the bed, and at the back of my mind I must have thought it was that Indian mouse. You know—it gnaws the root of the tree which holds up the world. I expect our butler, Ragaloo, told me. He knew a lot of stories.'

'The tree Ygdrasil,' said Mrs Bentley. 'But isn't it in Scandinavian mythology? And isn't the mouse an adder?'

'Sanskrit first,' said my mother. 'And a mouse. Indians know too much about snakes to suppose they gnaw. They'd ruin their poison fangs. I can remember my ayah finding a clutch of cobra's eggs in a broken wall, and how she took a stone and smashed each egg— squashed them, really. The eggs are soft, like kid gloves. Then she picked me up and ran full tilt down a hillside covered with small dahlias, in case the mother cobra should come after us. That must have been in the Shevaroy Hills, where I saw gold fern and silver fern.' She looked at the Bentleys as serenely as if they were not there, though in fact it was she who had gone away, carried off face downward under a never failing bangled arm.

My mother's recollections of her childhood in India were so vivid to her that they became inseparably part of my own childhood, like the arabesques of a wallpaper showing through a coating of distemper. It was I who saw the baby cobras writhing as the stone hammered the flaccid eggs. It was to me that the man fishing in the Adyar River gave the little pink-and-yellow fish which I afterwards laid away among my mother's nightdresses, alone in a darkened room under a swaying punkah. It was I who made sweet-scented necklaces by threading horsehair through the tamarind blossoms which fell on the garden's watered lawn. I was there when the ceiling cloth broke and pink baby rats dropped on the dining-room table; when the gardener held up the dead snake at arm's stretch and still there was a length of snake dragging on the ground; when the scorpion bit the ayah. It was my bearer who led me on my pony through a tangle of narrow streets, and held me up so that I saw through a latticed window a boy child and a girl child, swathed in tinsel and embroideries and with marigold wreaths round their necks, sitting cross-legged on the ground among small dishes of sweetmeats, and who then made me promise never to tell my parents—which I never did. It was I whom the bandicoot visited in my night nursery, nosing in my palm for titbits—another thing which I kept to myself, bandicoots having a bad name among elders and servants. It was I, wearing a wreath of artificial forget-me-nots, who drove to St George's Cathedral to be a bridesmaid, with an earthenware jar in the carriage, from which water was continually ladled out and poured over my head; for this being an

English wedding it had to take place in the worst heat of the day. It was I, though I blushed for it, who, coming back past the jail from my early-morning rides, used to put out my tongue at the prisoners. It was I whom the twirling masoola boat carried through the surf to the P & O liner, on that first stage of a journey towards an unknown land which was called home.

The harshness of an English winter and of an English nurse disabled my mother like a mortal sickness, snapping the continuity between the adored precocious child in Madras and the stupefied little malapert in Hampshire—whose skin was yellow, whose legs were spindleshanks, who could not even repeat the alphabet, because she was one of those unfortunate Indian children. What was the use of remembering everything when you could recall nothing? Only when she had a child of her own, a confidante and a contemporary, was she able to repossess herself. Then she began to unpack this astonishing storehouse, full of scents and terrors, flowers, tempests, monkeys, beggars winding worms out of their feet, a couple of inches a day, not more, or the worm broke and you had to begin again, undislodgeable holy men who came and sat in the garden, the water carrier's song—and as she talked as much for her own pleasure as mine, and made no attempts to be instructive or consecutive, I never tired of listening. I remember being rather puzzled why we never went to India, since we often went to London; the journey to London took less than an hour, and India would have been more interesting.

Another misconception lasted longer. Though I don't recollect how it came out that for years I had supposed that the groom in the photograph of my grandfather's charger was my grandfather himself, I remember her plain, factual correction: 'Your grandfather had a white skin and was a much smaller man.'

(*Scenes of Childhood*, 1981)

SCENES OF CHILDHOOD

S PACE is subject to time. The garden I recall was an oblong, twenty by fifteen yards, perhaps; the garden I remember was more than twice as long as the morning shadow of the almond tree and as wide as America; it contained a sweetbriar, a city of reversed flowerpots, a central prairie where bird food was scattered in winter, a Gloire de Dijon rose, a rubbish heap, two paths, and a group of white lilies, where I had to stand on tiptoe in order to get my nose adjusted to the heart of the scent and smudged with pollen.

There was a dark path and a light path. Along the light path ran a low dividing fence, and beyond the fence was the neighbouring garden and Mr Scudamore. I suppose the neighbouring garden was the same size as ours, since the houses were identical; but it seemed commandingly larger because Mr Scudamore gardened so earnestly and kept down the weeds and tied up annuals and always called flowers by their botanical names. Our cat visited his garden pretty regularly—cats prefer a nice clean tilth to scratch in—and when circumstances compelled, Mr Scudamore and my father would converse without bitterness across the fence. The rubbish heap was at the end of the dark path, which began as a narrow arched passageway where the dustbins stood, continued on under a high containing wall, and was shadowed by a row of black poplars growing at a higher level in the builder's yard beyond. Horseradish grew here in morbid profusion, but not much else.

It was on the rubbish heap that I transcended existence. It was higher than usual, augmented by the garden debris of late summer. A bundle of old peasticks had been thrown there. I climbed it, and trod on the peasticks, and heard them snap under my feet, and felt the rubbish heap sidling as I moved. I stared at the wall, and the poplar trees rustled, and the rubbish heap became a raft, and the ocean where it floated directionless was all around—and I left myself and was gone.

I don't remember what it was like being gone. I remember being startled back by a voice from the house calling me in because it was my bedtime. It was like the raw agony of recovering from frostbite.

I believe it is exceptional to have had only one experience of this sort of thing during a whole childhood. But I was an unimaginative child —solitary and agnostic as a little cat, and mistrusting other children to a pitch of abhorrence, as cats do. Adults, if unfamiliar, often had charms. There was, for instance, Major Beldam—an unforgotten brief garden ornament.

Major Beldam was, as my mother's fashion magazine would have put it, a simple confection in red and grey. His face was red, he wore a suit of grey flannel—baggy and rather grubby. His pale-blue eyes were blood-shot. He was a large heavy man and walked with a limp. He had a grey walrus moustache. He owned a small unprofitable estate in Dumfries-shire, called Wolfshawes, and during the greater part of the year he lived there, supporting life on porridge and whisky, reading *The Field*, and singing 'Annie Laurie'. This I learned when I was older and have no warrant for the truth of it. All I knew at the time he came into the garden was that he made a yearly trip south to watch cricket matches at Lord's and, as we lived conveniently near London, invited himself to stay with us—which my mother resented and my father encouraged, laying in more whisky, addressing him, *Scotice*, as Wolfshawes, and trying to water down my mother's resentment by saying that Wolfshawes had no harm in him, and wasn't a classical scholar, and called a snapdragon a snapdragon, and hadn't got a wife with legs like a horse, and was in every way more congenial than Scudamore, besides being merely occasional.

As Major Beldam was busy all day with cricket matches, and as I had to be in bed by half past six, I knew him mainly as a loud voice and a heavy tread and the concomitant phenomena of my mother raising her eyebrows and the maidservants giggling. But cricket matches were not played on Sundays, and early one Sunday morning there was a thump on my night-nursery door and a husky voice saying, 'I say, little girl —what's your name? Sylvie?—you shouldn't be in bed on a morning like this. Hurry up and dress yourself! Don't waste time on washing. It's a splendid morning—too good to miss.' I wasted no time on washing.

Outside my door was Major Beldam with a finger to his walrus moustache. 'Come on out,' said he. 'Sh-h-h! Not a word.'

It did not seem a moment for the front door. I led him down the kitchen stairs and out by the back door, past the dustbins and so into the garden.

The garden had that brand-new look of early morning. The morning had the unmistakable reserve of a Sunday. I allowed Major Beldam his coup d'oeil. Then I began to show him round. Calculating my effects, I began with the dark path and the builder's yard; halting him among the horseradish I pointed out the exact spot by the hepaticas where my two dormice lay buried. As there was nothing to say about the rubbish heap, I said, 'This is the rubbish heap,' and showed off the flowerpots and detached a few snails for him to look at. The snails did not keep him long; when he had replaced them we turned sharply to the left, past the hop vine growing on the Wilbrahams' wall, past the Gloire de Dijon, and turned once again into the vista of the light path and the view beyond the dividing fence. Here I repeated to him a poem our cat had composed, in a rather 'Moab is my washpot' tone, about the Scuda-mores' garden. Then we came to the almond tree, and the lilies, and the kitchen window, where I picked him a sprig of sweetbriar to rub in his fingers.

It seemed to me that I had earned my reward. It was disconcerting when Major Beldam exclaimed, 'Now let's play at desert islands!'

Condescending to his childishness, I replied, 'Let's.'

'The first thing to do,' said he, 'is to build a fire to frighten away crocodiles.' Limping about the garden he collected twigs and stalks and tufts of dry grass and an old bird's nest, and supplemented these by raiding the dustbins and coming back with a quantity of straw bottle cases, potato peelings, newspaper, and a handkerchief full of cinders. With these additions he laid a fire in the middle of the central prairie. Bypassing that nonsense about crocodiles, I said, 'Let's cook something. Wait till I get a frying pan.' I came back with the frying pan and some dripping and a kipper which was lying about in the larder serving no useful purpose. Major Beldam charged the frying pan, settled it in, and lit the fire, which went out. He knelt down, relit the fire, and puffed. As he knelt down, he groaned, and between the puffs he continued to groan. Without a shade of compassion, but seeing my reward almost within my grasp, I said consolingly, 'Does it hurt, your poor leg?' He said it hurt like the devil but couldn't be helped. I didn't want philosophy, I wanted certainty. Tuning my rapacity to tones of dovelike concern, I asked if I might see it. He looked astonished but touched. Rising from his knees with more groans, he rolled up a grey flannel trouser leg over a hairy calf and displayed a varicose ulcer. I gazed. I made small moans of sympathy. And Major Beldam said I was a kind child, and rolled up more trouser leg to display the ulcer to better advantage.

Unwatched, the frying pan heeled over. The kipper and the dripping spilled into the fire, which blazed up. Wreaths of kipper-scented smoke rose into the morning air, crackles and splutterings broke the Sunday silence; and a window was thrown up with a bang and Mr and Mrs Scudamore leaned out and saw Major Beldam in the posture of a martyr, exhibiting his leg to my enraptured gaze. . . . A moment later, a matching window opened, and my parents saw Major Beldam, etc. But as they also saw the Scudamores seeing it, they refrained from comment. And remarkably little was said about it afterwards.

(*Scenes of Childhood*, 1981)

THE YOUNG SAILOR

R EADING last week in some family papers how 'the Bishop did them in whole railsful with both hands'—my grandmother's fastidious Scotch account of a mass confirmation in St Paul's—I was glad that the mellowing influence of some fifty years had intervened between the ceremony she described and a similar ceremony in which I played my modest part. If she had objected, her objection would have had the force of an ex cathedra; my grandfather had been well esteemed as a preacher and my grandmother had written all his sermons, which made her the family authority on matters of church discipline. But she did not object. I was confirmed in St Paul's, and I do not in any way regret it.

I was sixteen at the time, and not in a state of religious exaltation. We were not a religious household. But the due preliminaries had been attended to. I had some conversations on theology with a clerical friend of my parents, a man of signal goodness of heart but without much dialectical address. (I remember him saying, 'And, of course, there's the Atonement.') My father ascertained that I was acquainted with the Thirty-Nine Articles and knew the Church Catechism by heart, and drew my attention to a text (Isaiah 40:31) that implies that it is less taxing and remarkable to mount up like eagles than to go on walking, which, considering the perseverance I had put into learning the Catechism, I thought unkind. My mother gave much anxious consideration to how I could possibly combine wearing a veil with wearing spectacles.

And on a fine May morning (I know it was May; May is an unlucky month for marriages but not for confirmations) I was punctually in my place in the nave of St Paul's without an uneasy thought in my mind, for the incompatibility of my veil and my spectacles (I had insisted on retaining the spectacles) was—as, thanks to the spectacles, I soon discovered—a handicap shared by a number of other candidates, and anything like stagefright was abolished by my being one of such a number that all I had to do was to do as all the others did. It was not as if I were in one of the front rows. I was well situated, somewhere about the middle. Best of all, there was no one within sight whom I had ever set eyes on before.

I sat in tranquil anonymity, waiting for the Bishop to appear and the service to begin. I listened to the organ, which was rolling about in one of those somnolent extemporizations that Church of England organists do so well. I looked towards the dome, and there it was. I glanced across the central aisle, which sexually differentiated the candidates, and thought it was hard for boys not to be granted veils; one feels so ensconced in a veil. Our parents, godparents, and other confirmed members of the Church of England sat well to the back of the building in, as it were, a sort of hallowed pit, and this added to my satisfaction, partly because it meant that my mother could not get at me for any last-minute pinnings or admonitions, and partly because it was agreeable to think of them being kept in their place—a comfortable, respectable place, but not the operative one. My memory assures me that they were held back by some red ropes. But I do not think this was actually the case; the ropes were probably incorporeal. Anyhow, they could not get in among us; they were no part of the flock.

I had very powerfully the sensation of being one of a flock, in an exceedingly handsome fold. We were such a large flock (I daresay there were five hundred of us, culled from the metropolitan diocese, and perhaps more) that the handsomeness of the fold did not seem beyond our deserts, and yet, on the other hand, the fold's classical stature and magnificence, and the absence of fuss with which Sir Christopher Wren did his business, countervailed any tendency to self-importance or egoistic exaltation. It is in school chapels that confirmation candidates have visions and see doves hovering with marked solicitude over particular heads—usually their own heads. With the best will in the world (not that I was set on it, or thought it very likely), I could not anticipate such a distinguishing dove's being requisitioned for the ceremony about to take place. Flocking, I felt, was the main thing. And any specifically pious thoughts I had were all of security, continuity, and conformity, with a musing awareness that in the Book of Common

Prayer the service of Confirmation is followed by the Solemnisation of Matrimony, and that, in turn, by the Visitation of the Sick and the Burial of the Dead.

Meanwhile, the organ had rolled into a more purposeful measure, the Bishop had entered, and the service had begun.

In the Book of Common Prayer, the Order of Confirmation is brief and compact (making prudent allowance, as I had learned, for the length of time required for a Bishop's reiterated 'Defend, O Lord, this Thy Child,' etc.). I had been somewhat taken aback to discover from the leaflet provided that the Prayer Book text was to be considerably bulked out by the inclusion of hymns and two Addresses from the Bishop, one before the 'Defend, O Lord's, and one after—by which time, considering what railfuls there were of us, he might reasonably have been expected to be rather out of breath and disinclined for further talking. But it was not this that prejudiced me against the Bishop. It was his habiliments that I was disappointed in. Reared on the engravings of Gillray and Rowlandson, I had expected his lawn sleeves to be much puffier. I may even subconsciously have been expecting him to wear a full-bottomed wig. As it was, I judged that he looked meagre, and that his cassock should not have shown so much of his boots, and that those boots should not have been—however nicely blacked—such plainly secular boots. But the state of being in a flock, secured by those ropes and impersonally brooded over by that ravishing echo, which turns the squeak of a chair into psalmody and into which coughs and sneezes ascend and are instantly beatified into mild hallelujahs, kept me in a decent frame of mind, and when the Bishop began his first Address, I took pains to sort him out from the squeaks, coughs, and sneezes, and to attend to what he might have to say.

'The Wages of Sin Is Death.' That was his text, and perhaps he thought we were not familiar with it, for he repeated it pretty frequently. I was thinking about the grammatical oddity, which at some time or other had been explained to me, and trying to recall the explanation, when a new ingredient was cast into the echo. It came from the further side of the sexually dividing aisle, and was contributed by a young man wearing the uniform of a rating in the Royal Navy. He was edging his way past the knees and among the feet and the hassocks of the half-dozen or so candidates seated between him and the aisle. Though he was doing it carefully and considerately, he could not do it silently, and his face wore that expression of contained, unwilling woe that designates the truebred Englishman when he knows he is making himself conspicuous. Once disentangled, however, he looked cheerful, and walked lightly and briskly down the aisle and eventually out of the building.

We were all too well-conducted to seem to notice this, and the Bishop was also too well-conducted to waver in his peroration or interpolate a pastoral recall. We behaved as though nothing had happened. But the recording echo had not failed to gather up those departing steps, and we were all of us perfectly aware that the young sailor had got up and gone away.

Afterwards my parents and I often discussed this strange incident, each of us, as usual, with his own theory. According to my mother, the young sailor had never meant to be confirmed. He had gone into St Paul's for a little sightseeing and, finding it too much for him, had sat down in what was at that moment a nice, empty public building and fallen asleep. A young sailor could sleep through anything; we had Shakespeare's word for it, and Shakespeare was always right. So the young sailor slept on, peacefully as though upon the high and giddy mast, while the confirmation candidates mustered round him, and the service began, and got as far as halfway through the Bishop. Then, catching some view-halloo note in the Bishop's oratory, the young sailor had woken, realised his peril, and got out just in time. Nelson would have been delighted—my mother rated Nelson only one below Shakespeare. My father disagreed; in fact, he disagreed twice. My mother, he said, took Shakespeare too literally, and did not make allowance for speaking in character. A king might very well suppose that a wet sea-boy could sleep like a dormouse on the masthead during a storm, and a king suffering from insomnia would be all the more inclined to take this view, but that was not to say that Shakespeare thought so himself. By my father's reading of the incident, the young sailor had gone, or been taken, to St Paul's like any other of the candidates, only he had not been sufficiently prepared—prepared for the length of the service. A call of nature had been too strong for him; he had gone out to find a public convenience and then felt too self-conscious to come in again. I considered both these theories ingenious but wrong. In my view, the young sailor decided that he did not care about being confirmed, and had the courage of his opinions.

I did not add, for it is no use going into that sort of thing with even the most emancipated parents (and mine were remarkably emancipated from the usual parental duty to quell their child), that the young sailor's action had filled me with such admiration for his independent mind and such shame at my own sheepish conformity that though I went on being confirmed, I was to all intents and purposes unconscious of it. One can never know beforehand what isn't going to happen to one, or, as a hymn expresses it, 'Sometimes a light surprises the Christian while he sings.' A light had surprised me. A dove had descended where I was least expecting it. A profound spiritual experience had taken place—though a little prematurely—during my confirmation. And by the time my mother had produced my hat from a paper bag and we were lunching very late in a City restaurant, I knew that I would follow the young sailor out.

(*Scenes of Childhood*, 1981)

THE ONE AND THE OTHER

✦✦✦

WHEN the baby was lifted from the cradle, he began to whimper. When he felt the rain on his face, he began to bellow. 'Nothing wrong with his lungs,' said the footman to the nurse. They spread their wings, they rose in the air. They carried the baby over a birchwood, over an oakwood, over a firwood. Beyond the firwood was a heath, on the heath was a grassy green hill. 'Elfhame at last,' said the nurse. They folded their wings and alighted. A door opened in the hillside and they carried the baby in. It stared at the candles and the silver tapestries, left off bellowing, and sneezed.

'It's not taken a chill, I hope,' said the footman.

'No, no,' said the nurse. 'But Elfhame strikes cold at first.' She took off the swaddling clothes, wrapped the baby in gossamer, shook pollen powder over it to abate the human smell, and carried it to Queen Tiphaine, who sat in her bower. The Queen examined the baby carefully, and said he was just what she wanted: a fine lusty baby with a red face and large ears.

'Such a pity they grow up,' she said. She was in her seven hundred and twentieth year, so naturally she had exhausted a good many human babies.

'And what is he to be called, Madam?' asked the nurse.

Tiphaine considered. 'It's quite six decades since we had a Tiffany,' she said. 'Let him be named Tiffany. And see to the seven weasels.'

Elfhame is in Heathendom. It has no christenings. But when a human child is brought into it there is a week of ceremonies. Every day a fasting weasel bites the child's neck and drinks its blood for three minutes. The amount of blood drunk by each successive weasel (who is weighed before and after the drinking) is replaced by the same weight of a distillation of dew, soot, and aconite. Though the blood-to-ichor transfer does not cancel human nature (the distillation is only approximate: elfin blood contains several unanalysable components, one of which is believed to be magnetic air), it gives considerable longevity; up to a hundred and fifty years is the usual span. During the seven days, the child may suffer some sharpish colics, but few die. On the eighth day it is judged sufficiently inhumanised to be given its new name.

'Dear little thing,' said Tiphaine. 'I hope he won't age prematurely.' For when grey hairs appear on the head of a changeling he is put out of the hill to make the rest of his way through the human world; which is why we see so many grey-haired beggars on the roads.

Mrs Tod, the baker's wife, did not notice the difference between her baby which had been stolen away and the elf-baby left in its stead. She was busy making sausage meat and pork pies that day; and this was not her first child, to be studied like a nonpareil. Indeed, it was her ninth, though not all of them had lived. It was Ailie, the servant, who noticed that the baby had lost flesh all of a sudden.

'Well, if you won't, you won't,' said Mrs Tod, putting it from her breast. 'I can't wait all day for you. There's the paste to raise and the master's supper to get. Here, Ailie! Give it the milk rag.'

Ailie washed out the rag, dipped it in milk, and offered it to the baby. It would not take it, and looked at her with staring green eyes. This put it into her head to lay it among the cat's kittens. The baby sucked the cat, who purred and laid her paw over it. So it went on for three days, the baby refusing Mrs Tod's breast and Ailie pretending it took the milk rag—for she did not care to speak of the cat. On the fourth day Mrs Tod said to her husband, 'We'll lose this Adam like we did the other. It must be christened before it slips away.'

The Minister named the child and poured water on it. It lay in his arms, neither stirring nor uttering. He looked grave, and poured on more water. Still the child neither stirred nor uttered. 'God forgive me,' said the Minister, 'but I think I have baptised a changeling!'

Taking the parents aside, he explained to them that as the child had made no remonstrance at the water, there could have been no sin to be driven out of it; therefore, it must be an elfin, a soulless being between Heaven and Hell and of no interest to either. So the best thing to hope for was that the changeling, already sickly and peevish, should die.

But it did not. Between Ailie and the cat, it strengthened, took broth and spoon meat, cut its teeth, learned to speak plain. It was the Minister who died. The thought that he had baptised a changeling so preyed on his mind that he took to walking in his sleep, stumbled into a beehive, and was stung to death. Lacking his sad looks to remind them, the Tods thought less of their misfortune in having a changeling child. Adam was doing well enough. The Minister might have been mistaken. No other person knew of it. Within a handful of years they had no doubt but that the boy was their own child and likely to be a credit to them.

In Elfhame everyone agreed that Tiffany was the prince among all the other stolen children. His cheeks were polished every morning like prize apples. His motions were examined by the court physician. He had a new suit once a month, gold boots, a Shetland pony to ride, and a drum to beat on. He was everybody's pet and pleasure and his every wish was indulged—save one. From the day when he saw the under-nursemaid spread her wings and fly off to fetch a pillowcase, he was wild to be given a pair of wings. His tutor explained to him that wings cannot be fastened to a human back, and told him the story of Icarus. His governess assured him that flying is a horrible sensation and would certainly make him sick. Both these persons had wings but kept them neatly folded away. Servants, grooms, stable lads, people who went on errands flew because it was their lot in life; they were brought up to it and it did not make them sick. But in court circles no one dreamed of using his wings unless in an extreme emergency. In all her seven hundred and twenty years Tiphaine had never been known to leave the ground.

In spite of these examples and admonishments, Tiffany thought there could be nothing so glorious, so marvellous, as the act of flying. The ease of the performance convinced him that, wings or no wings, if he gave his mind to it he could go flying himself, as he already did in his dreams; and to study how it was done, he took to frequenting flying company, slinking off to the stables or the kitchen quarters whenever he got the chance. This was reported to Tiphaine. Unannounced and terrible, she came into the servants' hall. 'Tiffany,' she said. 'Come away. I wish to speak to you.'

Half the servants fell on their knees. The other half flew up into the rafters, where they felt pretty sure their angry Queen would not follow them. Glancing neither upward nor downward, Tiphaine went silently along many passages and up several flights of stairs to her bower; and Tiffany followed her with his heart in his boots.

'Shut the door,' said she. 'I do not wish anyone to hear you rebuked.' She looked so beautiful that he trembled. 'I did not have you fetched to Elfhame,' said she, 'to gape after wings and keep company with people who, however useful and necessary they may be, are no better than sparrows. You must put all thought of flying out of your head. If you do not, you will be sent away and never see me again.'

His face, his neck, his hands turned scarlet. His ears stood out like flags in a gale.

'Promise me, Tiffany.'

He promised with all his heart. She laid her hand on his hot cheek. 'There's my good Tiffany! It would have made me sad to send you away. Tomorrow, you shall have your first billiard lesson. And when you put on your next new suit of clothes we will have a banquet.'

It was a splendid banquet. New clothes were issued to all. People in corridors murmured to each other, 'I shouldn't be surprised if—' and, 'I've thought so for a long while.' All agreed that Tiffany had every qualification for the Green Ribbon—though some of the court ladies did so rather wistfully. For the Green Ribbon tied about a boy's waist denotes that when he is old enough he will be the Queen's love and that in the meantime no woman may lay a finger on him.

Duly, at the banquet, the Green Ribbon was tied round Tiffany's waist by the Lord Chamberlain and the Ambassador from Thule.

After the old Minister died, a new one came. He was called Guthrie. His wife was sickly and hadn't enough strength in her arms to knead dough, so he bought bread from Tod's bakery. One day he noticed Adam, who was drawing 'A's and 'B's on the floor with a wet finger. 'Your boy's young to know his alphabet,' he said.

'I wouldn't say that he knows his alphabet,' answered Mr Tod, 'but he copies the letters off the advertisements. I wish he were as forward in walking. His legs are rickety, that's the truth of it.'

Adam could not fly. Elfindom is an aristocratic society, and jealous of its privileges. Before an elf-baby is sent into the human world its wings are extirpated and it is dosed with an elixir of mortality, compounded from the tears and excrement of changelings. Neither process is wholly satisfactory. The transfers die, but tardily and with extreme difficulty, and some have been known to hover briefly in the air—a phenomenon called levitation and usually ascribed to saintliness.

Mr Guthrie said that when the boy was old enough to walk so far he would take him into the school. Next day, Adam had crawled to the doorstep. Though he was the youngest child in the class, he was soon at the head of it. In his fifth year he was learning the Hebrew alphabet, and so set on scholarship that in the great snowfall of that winter he cajoled his eldest brother into making him a pair of stilts, and got to school that way. After the snow came a long hard frost. Ice formed on the river. The boys went sliding and played ice hockey. One afternoon when they were tussling together and whacking at each other's shins, the ice cracked and parted beneath them. It was a shallow reach of the river, and they got off with nothing worse that a wetting, except Jimmie Guthrie, who had measles coming out on him. His mother had forbidden him to go out, and he was afraid to go home and be whipped for disobedience, so he hung about waiting for his clothes to dry. By the time they dried, he was in a fever, and soon after then he was dead.

His schoolmates went to the funeral, Adam among them. Adam's attention wandered. He was counting the lozenge panes in the window when he heard his name spoken by the Minister. 'For as in Adam all die' were the words. He was not the only Adam in the village, but he felt sure that the words had been spoken of him. It was as if he had heard an important secret. Thinking it over, he decided he must be the Angel of Death. He had often heard his mother and Ailie say he was not like the others. As they had as often told him not to boast or think himself remarkable, he kept the important secret to himself.

Since he was so quick at his books and so undersized, it seemed meant that he should go into the Ministry. Mr Guthrie began to teach him theology. They soon got to the Fall of Man, and the true sense of the text in First Corinthians. Adam was glad he had kept his fancy about the Angel of Death to himself. If he had told of it, he would have been laughed at. But the word 'Death' had somehow taken root in his mind—as if he might have a special vocation or talent for the subject. As a step in the right direction, he studied epitaphs and watched pig killings. In his heart he thought he would rather be a surgeon than a minister; but it was by his excellence in theology that he won a bursary and was admitted (for all he was under age) to the Dollar Academy.

When he came home for the half-year holiday, the first person he met was Ailie. She was weeping. 'You should have got here an hour earlier,' she said. 'She waited on for you, poor old Pussy! But you're too late. She's gone. Pussy Bawdron's gone.'

She took him into the woodshed, and there, beneath a cloth, was the dead cat.

'Under God, you wouldn't be here if it hadn't been for her,' said Ailie with another outbreak of weeping.

He looked at the body. He felt in his pocket. There was the knife; and there, where the teats protruded from the shabby fur, was the place where he would make the first incision.

'I must have her,' he said. 'Fetch me a bowl of water and some rags.' And he turned back his sleeves.

When Ailie came back, he had already laid the body on the chopping block and cut open the belly. Ailie said no word. She had two things in the world to love: one was the boy, the other the old cat. In an hour, she had lost them both.

It was the custom of Elfhame that when the Queen tired of a lover she sent him a willow leaf. The Willow Leaf was conveyed privily by her confidential woman, and within an hour everyone at court knew about it. Tiffany's tenure of the Queen's love lasted so long that people gave up speculating when the Willow Leaf would be delivered. A year, two years, four years, seven years: even in a timeless society such a span of love causes remark. The aspiring Green Ribbon wearers began to grow impatient at their protracted virginity and to despair of ever getting into any bed. The livelier court ladies felt their Queen's fidelity (one would not, of course, call it infatuation) slightly scandalous. The nurse who had purloined him from the bakery said she had foreseen it from the moment Tiphaine set eyes on him and exclaimed that he was just what she wanted. Even the malcontents admitted that Tiffany was fit to set before a Queen. His black eyes glanced and danced in his ruddy face like black cherries bobbing in claret cup. He was large of limb, light of foot, sweet-breathed. He had a baritone voice, and his large red fingers were light as butterflies on the strings of a lute. He was also a brilliant mimic and could make Tiphaine laugh. He was perfectly good-natured and just stupid enough to be delightful. His demeanour, his unaffected enjoyment of a rewarded sensuality, made him as popular as a song.

For thirteen years, Tiffany was the Queen's love.

Shortly before the Willow Leaf dismissed him, a girl baby was born to one of the handsomest ladies at court. Fertility is rare among the Elfin aristocracy, though common enough among working fairies. Some speculative thinkers put this down to the fact that working fairies use their wings, pointing out that wrens, tits, sparrows, etc., are notoriously fertile, whereas the pedestrian dodo is extinct. Be this as it may, aristocratic fairies are passionately fond of children and a birth in court circles is an occasion for much rejoicing. Titania (so this baby was named) was on show daily from two to four. At her naming ceremony she was attended by ninety-nine sponsors, headed by Tiphaine and Tiffany hand in hand. Her parents were given a pension and the Order of the Pomegranate, Tiphaine made her a cowslip ball, and the working fairies, who were quite as much excited about her as if they had no babies of their own, clubbed together and presented a Noah's ark, imported at great expense from the outer world.

Tiffany, who was rather at a loose end after receiving the Willow Leaf, spent many an empty hour playing with Titania, sitting on the floor for her dolls' drinking bouts, playing carpet bowls, pretending to be a bear who would hug her to death, and pulling hideous faces to amuse her. She was a courageous, tyrannical child. The bear could never growl loud enough nor hug fiercely enough to satisfy her, the faces had to be intimidating before she would be amused by them. Tiffany frowned till his brows ached while she sat smirking like a snowdrop. Her governess complained that he overexcited the child, who was hoyden enough already. But he flattered the governess and kept his entry to Titania's nursery, and to her schoolroom. Even when she was going through her awkward age and people were finding her a nuisance and being disappointed in her, he still kept her as a pet, fished her out of scrapes, and shot snipe for her dinner.

Of course, she was not his only interest. The Willow Leaf had dispensed him from his vassalage to Tiphaine. He had enjoyed several bachelor friendships and several love affairs as well as improving his average at golf. The latest of his ladies was a stickler for traditions. Now it was the thirteenth of February and he still had not completed the valentine he ought to send her. He was sitting in the North Gallery, where he hoped to be undisturbed, and considering rhymes to 'azure' when he saw Titania steal in at the farther end of the gallery and come towards him. He signalled to her to be quiet. For once, she was in a biddable mood. She sat down and busied herself with her embroidery. He had decided on 'embrasure' and was modelling a sentiment to include it when there was a sudden Crack! and a whirr, as though a fan had been flirted open. He looked up. Titania was overhead. Five times she flew down the whole length of the gallery and back again. She folded her wings and alighted beside him, as dexterously as though she had spent her whole life flying on errands. 'Titania!' he exclaimed. 'What ever will you do next? You know you mustn't fly.'

'Don't tell on me,' she said.

He could no more resist her than he could fly himself. For when he looked up and saw her swallow flight up and down the gallery, his old fascinating rapture at the act of flying exploded like a rocket. Crack! Whirr! He was in love with Titania.

From that hour, he was her delighting, miserable slave. All his other loves, the affairs since the Willow Leaf, his thirteen years with Tiphaine, seemed no more than music lessons or practices on the putting green, preliminaries merely to equip him for the reality of love. In fact, these lessons were of little use, except for the patience and tact he had learned with Tiphaine. He had every need of these. Titania was wilful as a kitten, tart as a green fruit. She established a bond of mutual guilt between them: her reckless indecorum of flying, his disloyalty of consenting to it. There could not have been a worse moment for such behaviour. Under the influence of her latest love (the eighth since Tiffany's day) Tiphaine had set about reforming the court. Regulations were tightened up, etiquette insisted on. If it were known that Titania flew, her reputation would be lost. She knew this as well as he did. She placed a high value on her reputation, since her future pleasures must depend on it. But future pleasures were not so interesting to her as the present pleasure of tossing Tiffany between agonies of anxiety lest she should take to the air and agonies of rapture when she did. She grew so brazen about showing her wings that she even flew in public rooms, hovering overhead during state functions and harp competitions. Sometimes he dreamed of some blessed turn of events by which Titania would be expelled from Elfhame and he would follow her: they would wander over the heath, living on mushrooms and cloudberries, and perhaps take up with the gypsies. More often, he wished himself dead.

It was she, viewing him from above, who saw he was going grey. She had the grace to be embarrassed, and did not tell him. He was left to find out for himself, dully growing aware that his friends were not so friendly as they had been, appeared to shun his company, turned their backs on him when he spoke; that ladies whispered in groups, eyeing him through the sticks of their fans; that servants were impertinent. But as all he thought of was Titania, he supposed he was in disgrace because she had been caught flying and he was suspected of having seduced her into it.

One evening, during a pause in the music, the Lord Chamberlain came up to Tiffany, holding a tray covered with a black cloth. The cloth was lifted. On the tray was a lock of grizzled wool, a large pair of spectacles, and a miniature pair of crutches. Every face was averted as Tiffany was led to the door in the hillside and put out, to make the rest of his way through the mortal world.

Ailie outlived Mr Tod and his wife. By then she wasn't good for much. She helped herself to a ring off Mrs Tod's finger and bought a lottery ticket. It was the winning number, so she finished the rest of her days better than she ever expected to.

While she was still at the bakery she saw Adam three times. Each time he gave her a guinea. She took the guineas but felt no gratitude. The cat lay between them.

Adam could ill afford the guineas. He gave them out of pride, to show that he did not come home as a Prodigal Son. For all that, both his parents considered him such. If he had kept to the path laid down and swept for him, he would have been in the Ministry by now, with a manse, and printed books of sermons to his credit. Since they would only sigh at him, he went to brag of his travels to Mr Guthrie. One time it was Montpellier, in France; the next, Ratisbon; the next again, far Finland to see the aurora borealis. Mr Guthrie enjoyed the traveller's tales; they were as good as a coal fire in the grate. After Adam had gone, he knelt down and prayed that Adam might not be led into becoming a Papist.

Travelling costs money. Adam hired himself out as a travelling tutor to sons of good families and showed the testimonials he had got from the Dollar University, all praising his learning and steady character. For a time, Adam and the boy would travel very sociably; then Adam would grow tired of this, and load the boy with lessons, keep him in, and allow him to eat nothing till he could ask for it in Latin, wake him before sunrise to study mathematics; and then, when he judged the moment ripe, send him out to buy a hat. The boy would see his chance and run away. Then Adam wrote a sorrowing letter to the parents and went off on his own devices.

Mostly he walked. He was as strong as a flea, and had an engaging manner with strangers. In his knapsack he carried a magnifying glass, his testimonials, and the skull of a marmoset. If he had been asked what he was in search of, he would have been hard put to it to say. He used his intellect as he used his legs: to carry him somewhere else. He studied astrology, astronomy, botany, chemistry, numerology, fortification, divination, organ building, metallurgy, medicine, perspective, the kabbala, toxicology, philosophy, and jurisprudence. He kept his interest in anatomy and did a dissection whenever he could get hold of a body. He learned Arabic, Catalan, Polish, Icelandic, Basque, Hungarian, Romany, and demotic Greek. He had no religious feeling, didn't drink, was an early riser, and cared only for very large women. Every time he crossed over a bridge the rumbling echo seemed to admonish him. But it was an inarticulate admonition, and as what he valued was exact knowledge, he disregarded it.

It was in Cracow that he heard a Rosicrucian speak of the transcendental elements—among them, of magnetic air, which runs in the veins of sylphs, and gives them their buoyancy and immortality. Adam listened as though the echo under the bridges had suddenly become articulate, reiterating the sentence which had struck him during Jimmie Guthrie's funeral: 'For as in Adam all die.' He had been too hasty in putting by his first interpretation of those words. In a deeper sense, it was true: all his journeys and learnings and languages and dodges, his nights under the stars and with very large women, had accumulated and died in him. He was a compendium of deaths. Death, then, must be his proper study. To understand death, he must approach it through its opposite: the incapacity to die. He must catch a fairy, draw blood from it, identify that special element of magnetic air.

Having bought a fleam and practised phlebotomy, he spent the next thirty years haunting dells, fountains, forests, fairy rings on lawns and in pastures, caves, tumuli—every place where fairies were said to resort.

Yearly, as Midsummer Eve drew on, he was in a fever of anticipation. Nothing came of it, except that he was forty years more travelled and forty years uglier. Otherwise, he felt no older. He was active and limber as ever he had been, and, for all the nights he had spent in dells and damp pastures, without a trace of rheumatism: it was almost as though magnetic air ran in his own veins. He decided to lower his ambition and pursue Brownies; they, too, were of the fairy kind, though vulgarised and more like Lars. Brownies were common in Scotland, so to Scotland he went, and lodged in a wayside inn near Dumfries. A noisy brook ran beside it. Wakened during his first night by shouts and mutterings, he thought he was hearing a Kelpie. Kelpies are fierce immortals; Brownies would be easier to deal with; yet a Kelpie within a stone's throw ought not to be neglected. While he was debating this, he came to distinguish between the noise outside the house, which was the brook contesting with its rocky bed, and the noise within it, the voice of someone raving in a high fever, so near at hand that he could hear the bedstead creak as the sick man tossed and turned. In the morning he complained of this disturbance to the woman of the inn.

'I don't suppose you'll be troubled with him much longer,' said she. 'But if you like, I'll move him to the out-house. I only took him in for pity's sake. One doesn't want the scandal of a tramp dying on one's doorstep. He's a big man, though, and his fever makes him as awkward as a ram. Perhaps you'd lend a hand with him?'

'Willingly,' said Adam.

It was the remains of a handsome man that lay on the bed, and of a man who before age and beggardom had broken him must have belonged to the gentry. When they began to pull away the blanket, he came out of his stupor, sat up, and said arrogantly, 'What now?'

'We're just moving you,' said the woman.

'Leave me alone, please,' said the sick man. 'Kindly leave me alone, so that I may get back my strength. For I'm on my way to Elfhame, I must be there before nightfall. Leave me alone, woman—and you, whoever you may be. Leave me alone, I tell you. Aren't I in torment enough?' His fever came back, he began to cry and boo-hoo, and clutched the blanket to his breast.

'Elfhame,' said Adam. 'Where may that be? Is it far from here?'

'It's no place for a respectable man to go to,' said the woman, tweaking away the blanket. 'That's all I care to know of it. But he's forever raving about how he's on his way back there.'

'Let him be for a day longer,' said Adam. 'Mercy never comes amiss.' He could scarcely believe his luck.

He put some money in the woman's hand. When she had gone, he sat down to listen. Presently the man began to rave again.

'Titania! Titania! What have they done to your wings? Why don't you fly to me? Why don't you come, you cruel child? Oh, they've caught her! They've tied her! O Titania, my little love, what have they done to you? My bird's in a cage, and the cage has a black cloth over it. The Chamberlain of Elfhame put it there. Wait till I get at him! Don't flutter so, my bird. Sit patiently till I come. I'm on my way. I'll be home before nightfall. I'll knock on the hill—it's all brambles now—the door will open. There they'll all be, singing and dancing like bees in a hive. Elfhive. Elfhame. They'll make me welcome. But I won't speak to one of them, no, not to Tiphaine herself, till I've pulled off the black cloth and kissed your wings. Titania! Titania! O my darling!' He hugged the bolster to him, so hard that the feathers burst out of it. Adam sat and pondered.

Fairies can take any shape they will; so much is agreed by the best authorities. Yet if this derelict greybeard were indeed a fairy, why did he lie bemoaning on a dirty bed instead of resuming himself and flying to that Titania he called on? If he were a fairy, threescore years and ten would be nothing to him—so there was no need to be precipitate. But again, if he were a fairy, in a flash he might cast off his disguise of mortality and fly to Elfhame, taking the secret of his unexplored blood with him. And if he were not, it would be waste of time to hang about waiting for a dying man to declare his mortality by dying.

This last consideration settled it. That night, when all were asleep, Adam took his fleam and his vials and his test tubes and a basin and a candle and went to the bedside. There lay the man, talking gently to the bolster. The fleam pierced the vein, the blood spurted out. Adam carried the basin to a corner of the room and set to work. It was poor blood, even for such an old, undernourished man; indeed, it was more than half water. It contained an unaccountable deposit of carbon. It tasted slightly bitter. It was totally unmagnetic. Adam repeated his analysis several times. Either Master Hieronymus of the Rosy Cross was wrong about the transcendental element of magnetic air or the man on the bed was no fairy. Adam now glanced towards the subject of his experiment. He had not plugged the vein sufficiently after the phlebotomy. The bed was soaked in blood. A lagging trickle still flowed from the wound. Ceased. Began again. Ceased. With the last impetus of the heart, a few gouts of blood emerged, till the last of them sealed the wound. So the poor wretch was not a fairy; and the bedding would have to be paid for. But if the body could be got to the anatomists in Edinburgh, thought Adam, taking heart again, I shall break about even. He straightened it, put his things together, and went to bed.

(*Kingdoms of Elfin*, 1977)

THE FIVE BLACK SWANS

※ ⭓⭔⭓ ※

PORTENTS accompany the death of monarchs. A white horse trots slowly along the avenue, a woman in streaming wet garments is seen to enter the throne room, vanishes, and leaves wet footmarks; red mice are caught in the palace mousetraps. For several weeks five black swans had circled incessantly above the castle of Elfhame. It was ninety decades since their last appearance; then there were four of them, waiting for Maharit, Queen Tiphaine's predecessor. Now they were five, and waited for Tiphaine. Mute as a shell cast up on the beach, she lay in her chamber watching the antics of her pet monkey.

The mysterious tribe of fairies are erroneously supposed to be immortal and very small. In fact, they are of smallish human stature and of ordinary human contrivance. They are born, and eventually die; but their longevity and their habit of remaining good-looking, slender and unimpaired till the hour of death have led to the Kingdom of Elfin being called the Land of the Ever-Young. Again, it is an error to say 'the Kingdom of Elfin': the Kingdoms of Elfin are as numerous as kingdoms were in the Europe of the nineteenth century, and as diverse.

Tiphaine's Kingdom lay on the Scottish border, not far from the romantic and lonely Eskdalemuir Observatory (erected in 1908). Her castle of Elfhame—a steep-sided grassy hill, round as a pudding basin—had great purity of style. A small lake on its summit—still known as the Fairy Loch, and local babies with croup are still dipped in its icy, weedless water—had a crystal floor, which served as a skylight. A door in the hillside, operated by legerdemain, opened into a complex of branching corridors, one of which, broadening into a set of anterooms, led to the Throne Room, which was wainscotted in silver and lit by candles in crystal sconces. It was a circular room, and round it, like the ambulatory of a cathedral—and like the ambulatory of a cathedral fenced off by pillars and a light latticing—ran a wide gallery where the courtiers strolled, conversed, and amused themselves with dice, *bouts-rimés*, news from other Kingdoms and the outer world, needlework, flirtations, conjectural scandal and tarot. The hum of conversation was like the hum of bees. But at the time of which I write, no one mentioned the five black swans, and the word 'death' was not spoken, though it lay, compact as a pebble, in every heart.

Dying is not an aristocratic activity like fencing, yachting, patronising the arts: it is enforced—a willy-nilly affair. Though no one at Elfhame was so superstitious as to suppose. Tiphaine would live forever, they were too well-mannered to admit openly that she would come to her end by dying. In the same way, though everyone knew that she had wings, it would have been *lèse-majesté* to think she might use them. Flying was a servile activity: cooks, grooms, laundresses flew about their work, and to be strong on the wing was a merit in a footman. But however speedily he flew to the banqueting room with a soup tureen, at the threshold he folded his wings and entered at a walk.

In these flying circles of Elfhame, Tiphaine's dying was discussed as openly and with as much animation as if the swans were outriders of a circus. A kitchen boy, flying out with a bucket of swill for the palace pigs, had been the first to see them. On his report, there was a swirl of servants, streaming like a flock of starlings from the back door to see for themselves. The head gardener, a venerable fairy, swore he could distinguish Queen Maharit in the swan with the long bridling neck: Maharit had just such a neck. Tiphaine's servants were on easier terms with death than her courtiers were. They had plucked geese, drawn grouse and blackcock, skinned eels. They had more contact with the outer world, where they picked up ballads and folk stories, flew over battlefields, and observed pestilences. The mortals among them, stolen from their cradles to be court pets and playthings, and who, failing in this, had drifted into kitchen society, seldom lived into their second century, even though on their importation they were injected with an elixir of longevity, as tom kittens are gelded for domestication. Thus death was at once more real to them and less imposing. Every day their loyalty grew more fervent. They said there would never again be such a queen as Tiphaine, and had a sweepstake as to which lady (Elfindom inverts Salic law) would be the next.

In Elfindom the succession is determined by the dying ruler naming who is to come after her. If, by some misadventure, the declaration is not made, resort is had to divination. At sunrise half a dozen flying fairies are sent up to net larks—as many larks as there are eligible ladies, with a few over in case of accidents. During the morning the larks, one to each lady, are caged, ringed, and have leaden weights wired to their feet. On the stroke of noon the court officeholders—Chancellor, Astrologer, Keeper of the Records, Chamberlain, and so forth—wearing black hoods and accompanied by pages and cage bearers, go in torchlight procession to the Knowing Room, a stone cellar deep in the castle's foundations, where there is a well, said to be bottomless. One by one, the larks are taken from the cages, held above the well while the name of their lady is pronounced, and then dropped in. The weights are delicately adjusted to allow the larks a brief struggle before they drown. Its duration is noted with a stopwatch by the Court Horologer and when one by one the larks have drowned, the lark which struggled longest has won the Queenship for the lady it was dedicated to. The officials throw off their mourning hoods and go back to the Throne Room, where they kiss the hand of the new Queen and drink her health from a steaming loving-cup of spiced and honeyed wine which recovers them from the cramping chill of their ordeal in the Knowing Room.

At Elfhame, however, all this was hearsay: Tiphaine and the two Queens before her had been named. Lark patties and the loving-cup were all anyone expected.

Early in the new year the weather changed. Rain pock-marked the snow that lay in rigid shrouds over the black moorland; the swans were hidden in a web of low-lying cloud. Suddenly they reappeared; the wind had shifted into the north and there it would stay, said the head gardener who remembered Queen Maharit, through the three long months ahead—the starving months, when shrew mice feasted underground, and deer and cattle wandered slowly in search of food, eating frozen heather, rushes, dead bracken, anything that would stay the craving to munch and swallow.

It was warm in the castle, where the walls of solid earth muffled the noise of the wind. Chess tables were laid out in the gallery: matches lasted for days on end, protracted by skilful evasions, long considerings before the capture of a pawn. From the musicians' room came intermittent twangings and cockcrowings, flourishes of melody broken off, begun again, broken off again, as the court band of harps and trumpets rehearsed the funeral and coronation marches which would soon be needed. In Tiphaine's chamber the Head Archivist sat by her bed, waiting to take down her dying command about her successor. Every morning he was brought a new quill pen. Every night he was replaced by the Sub-Archivist, who had a peculiar aversion to monkeys, unfortunate but also convenient, since it kept him reliably awake.

The monkey's life depended on Tiphaine's. Royal favourites are seldom popular in court circles. The monkey had amusing tricks but dirty habits; few would put in a good word for it when Tiphaine's death plunged the court in sorrow. Nothing at all could be pled for Morel and Amanita, Tiphaine's latest importees from the mortal world. Strictly speaking, they were not changelings, for they had been bought with good fairy gold. This in itself was against them; but, however got, they would have been detested. They were twins, and orphans; their parents had been burned as heretics during the Easter festivities in Madrid, and the Brocéliande ambassador, on his way back from the Kingdom of the Gaudarramas, had stolen them from the convent of penitents to which they had been assigned. Tiphaine had bought them from him. For a while she was devoted to them—as devoted as she had been to the still remembered changeling Tiffany, who for thirteen years she had kept as her lover. Tiffany, in his mortal way, was tolerable. Morel and Amanita were intolerable from the start. They thieved, destroyed, laid booby traps, mimicked, fought each other like wildcats, infuriated the servants, and tore out the Chief Harpist's hair. (Custom dictated that it be worn long and flowing as in olden days.)

For as in the kitchen loyalty grew daily more ardent and more undiscriminating, in the gallery it developed a sense of historical perspective. There had been some regrettable incidents in the past —blown up by scandal, of course; but there is no smoke without fire. Tiphaine was indiscreet in her choice of Favourites—the fault of generous character, no doubt, but she was often sadly deluded. Admittedly, she was headstrong—but to live under the rule of a vacillating Queen would be far more exhausting. Beauty like hers could atone for everything—or almost everything. Perhaps her complexion had been a shade, just a shade, too florid? 'You would not think that if you saw her now,' retorted the Dame of Honour.

'I suppose so, I suppose so.' The words sounded slightly perfunctory. The speaker was looking at the chessboard, where Morel and Amanita had rearranged the pieces.

By now, it was the end of March and cold as ever.

The Sub-Archivist had entered the bedchamber, seated himself, wrapped a foxskin rug over his knees, taken the virgin parchment, the day's quill pen. The monkey sat hunched before the fire. Dwindled, mute, a dirty white like old snow, Tiphaine lay among her snow-white pillows, and did not notice the replacement. She was remembering Thomas of Ercildoune.

It was May Day morning, and she rode at the head of her court to greet the established spring. Doves were cooing in the woods, larks sang overhead, her harness bells rang in tune with them. She pulled off her gloves to feel the warm air on her hands. The route took them past a hawthorn brake and there, lolling on the new-grown grass, was a handsome man—so handsome that she checked her horse's pace to have a completer look at him. She had looked at him and summed him up when suddenly she realised that he had seen her and was staring at her with intensity. *Mortals do not see fairies.*

She spurred her horse and rode fast on from the strange encounter.

That night she couldn't sleep, feeling the weight of her castle stopping her breath. An hour before sunrise she was in the stables, scolding a sleepy stableboy, had a horse saddled, and rode at a gallop to the hawthorn brake. And he was not there and he did not come. She rode on over the moor. The sun was up before she saw him walking towards her. She reined in her horse, watching him approach. Keeping her pride, she looked down on him when he stopped beside her. 'You're out early, Queen of Elfhame,' he said. She couldn't think of anything to say. He put his arms round her and lifted her from the saddle, and she toppled into his embrace like a sheaf of corn. The dew was heavy on the grass, and when they got up from their lovemaking they were wringing wet and their teeth chattered.

From then on it was as though she lived to music. To music she followed him barefoot, climbed a sycamore tree to look into a magpie's nest, made love in the rain. Once, they came to a wide rattling burn, with a green lawn on the further bank. He leaped across, and held out his hand for her to catch hold of. It was too wide a leap for her and she took to her wings. It was the first time in her life she had flown, and the sensation delighted her. She rose in another flight, curling and twirling for the pleasure and mastery of it, as a fiddler plays a cadenza. She soared higher and higher, looking down on the figure at the burnside, small as a beetle and the centre of the wide world. He beckoned her down; she dropped like a hawk and they rolled together on the grass. He made little of her flying, even less of her queenship, nothing at all of her immense seniority. Love was in the present: in the sharp taste of the rowanberries he plucked for her, in the winter night when a gale got up and whipped them to the shelter of a farm where he kindled a fire and roasted turnips on a stick, in their midnight mushroomings, in the long summer evenings when they lay on their backs too happy to move or speak, in their March-hare curvettings and cuffings. For love-gifts, he gave her acorns, birds' eggs, a rosegall because it is called the fairies' pincushion, a yellow snail shell.

It was on the day of the shell, a day in August with thunder in the air, that she asked him how it was he saw her, he who had only mortal eyes. He told how on his seventeenth birthday it had come to him that one day he would see the Queen of Elfhame, and from then on he had looked at every woman and seen through her, till Tiphaine rode past the hawthorn brake. In the same way, he said, he could see things which had not happened yet but surely would happen, and had made rhymes of them to fix them in his memory. She would live long after him and might see some of them come true.

With one ear she was listening for the first growl of thunder, with the other to Thomas's heartbeats. Suddenly they began to quarrel, she railing at him for his selfish mortality, his refusal to make trial of the elixir of longevity. He flung away from her, saying she must love him now, instantly, before the lightning broke cover. A time would come when he would grow old and she would abhor him: he could tell her that without any exercise of prophecy. The storm broke and pinned them in the present. When it moved away they built a cairn of hailstones and watched it melt in the sunshine.

The Sub-Archivist woke with a start. The Queen was stirring in her bed. She sat up and said fiercely, 'Why is no one here? It is May Day morning. I must be dressed.'

The Sub-Archivist rushed to the door and shouted, 'The Queen has spoken! She wants to be dressed.'

Courtiers and women servants crowded in, huddling on their clothes. There was a cry of 'Keep those two out', but Morel and Amanita were already in the room. They saw their hearts' desire—the monkey. The monkey saw them. It screamed and sprang onto Tiphaine's bed, where it tried to hide under the coverlet. The Court Physician hauled it out by the tail and threw it on the floor. While the court ladies crowded round the bed, chafed the Queen's hands, held smelling salts to her nose, urged her not to excite herself, and apologised for their state of undress, Morel and Amanita seized the monkey. At first they caressed it; then they began to dispute as to which of them loved it best, whose monkey it should be. Their quarrel flared into fury and they tore it in half.

The smell of blood and entrails still hung about the room when the Sub-Archivist took up his evening watch. Everything had been restored to order: the bed straightened, the floor washed and polished, a fresh coverlet supplied. Tiphaine had been given a composing draught, and was asleep. That deplorable business with the monkey had made no impression on her, so the Court Physician assured him. She might even be the better for it. Morel and Amanita had been strangled and their bodies thrown on the moor as a charity to crows. With every symptom so benign, they could hope she would return to her senses and name her successor.

As the virgin parchment had been crumpled during the scuffle, the Sub-Archivist was given a new one, and left to himself.

The room was so still that he could hear the sands draining through the hourglass. He had reversed it for the third time when Tiphaine opened her eyes and turned a little towards him. Trembling, he dipped the quill in ink.

'Thomas—O Thomas, my love.'

He wrote this down and waited for her to say more. She grunted once or twice. The room was so still he could hear the swans circling lower and lower, and the castle beginning to resound with exclamations and protesting voices. The swans rose in a bevy, and the chant of their beating wings was high overhead, was far away, was gone.

No one at court had a name remotely resembling Thomas, so preparations for the ceremony of divination were put in hand.

(Kingdoms of Elfin, 1977)

ELPHENOR AND WEASEL

꙳⁓꙳⁓✠⁓꙳⁓꙳

THE ship had sailed barely three leagues from IJmuiden when the wind backed into the east and rose to gale force. If the captain had been an older man he would have returned to port. But he had a mistress in Lowestoft and was impatient to get to her; the following wind, the waves thwacking the stern of the boat as though it were the rump of a donkey and tearing on ahead, abetted his desires. By nightfall, the ship was wallowing broken-backed at the mercy of the storm. Her decks were awash and cluttered with shifting debris. As she lurched lower, Elphenor thrust the confidential letter inside his shirt, the wallet of mortal money deeper in his pocket, and gave his mind to keeping his wings undamaged by blows from ripped sails and the clutches of his fellow-passengers. Judging his moment, he took off just before the ship went down, and was alone with the wind.

His wings were insignificant: he flew by the force of the gale. If for a moment it slackened he dropped within earshot of the hissing waves, then was scooped up and hurled onward. In one of these descents he felt the letter, heavy with seals, fall out of his breast. It would be forever private now, and the world of Elfin unchanged by its contents. On a later descent, the wallet followed it. His clothes were torn to shreds, he was benumbed with cold, he was wet to the skin. If the wind had let him drown he would have drowned willingly, folded his useless wings and heard the waves hiss over his head. The force of the gale enclosed him, he could hardly draw breath. There was no effort of flight; the effort lay in being powerlessly and violently and almost senselessly conveyed—a fragment of existence in the drive of the storm. Once or twice he was asleep till a slackening of the wind jolted him awake with the salt smell of the sea beneath him. Wakened more forcibly, he saw a vague glimmer on the face of the water and supposed it might be the light of dawn; but he could not turn his head. He saw the staggering flight of a gull, and thought there must be land not far off.

The growing light showed a tumult of breakers ahead, close on each other's heels, devouring each other's bulk. They roared, and a pebble beach screamed back at them, but the wind carried him over, and on over a dusky flat landscape that might be anywhere. So far, he had not been afraid. But when a billow of darkness reared up in front of him, and the noise of tossing trees swooped on his hearing, he was suddenly in panic, and clung to a bough like a drowning man. He had landed in a thick grove of ilex trees, planted as a windbreak. He squirmed into the shelter of their midst, and heard the wind go on without him.

Somehow, he must have fallen out of the tree without noticing. When he woke, a man with mustachios was looking down on him.

'I know what you are. You're a fairy. There were fairies all round my father's place in Suffolk. Thieving pests, they were, bad as gypsies. But I half liked them. They were company for me, being an only child. How did you get here?'

Elphenor realised that he was still wearing the visibility he had put on during the voyage as a measure against being jostled. It was too late to discard it—though the shift between visible and invisible is a press-button affair. He repressed his indignation at being classed with gypsies and explained how the ship from IJmuiden had sunk and the wind carried him on.

'From IJmuiden, you say? What happened to the rest of them?'

'They were drowned.'

'Drowned? And my new assistant was on that ship! It's one calamity after another. Sim's hanged, and Jacob Kats gets drowned. Seems as though my stars meant me to have you.'

It seemed as though Elphenor's stars were of the same mind. To tease public opinion he had studied English as his second language; he was penniless, purposeless, breakfastless, and the wind had blown his shoes off. 'If I could get you out of any difficulties—' he said.

'But I can't take you to Walsham Borealis looking like that. We'll go to old Bella, and she'll fit you out.'

Dressed in secondhand clothes too large for him and filled with pork pie, Elphenor entered Walsham Borealis riding pillion behind Master

Elisha Blackbone. By then he knew he was to be assistant to a quack in several arts, including medicine, necromancy, divination, and procuring.

Hitherto, Elphenor, nephew to the Master of Ceremonies at the Elfin Court of Zuy, had spent his days in making himself polite and, as far as in his tailor lay, ornamental. Now he had to make himself useful. After the cautious pleasures of Zuy everything in this new life, from observing the planets to analysing specimens of urine, entertained him. It was all so agreeably terminal: one finished one thing and went on to another. When Master Blackbone's clients overlapped, Elphenor placated those kept waiting by building card houses, playing the mandora, and sympathetic conversation—in which he learned a great deal that was valuable to Master Blackbone in casting horoscopes.

For his part, Master Blackbone was delighted with an assistant who was so quick to learn, so free from prejudice, and, above all, a fairy. To employ a fairy was a step up in the world. In London practice every reputable necromancer kept a spiritual appurtenance—fairy, familiar, talking toad, airy consultant. When he had accumulated the money, he would set up in London, where there is always room for another marvel. For the present, he did not mention his assistant's origin, merely stating that he was the seventh son of a seventh son, on whom any gratuities would be well bestowed. Elephenor was on the footing of an apprentice; his keep and training were sufficient wages. A less generous master would have demanded the gratuities, but Master Blackbone had his eye on a golden future, and did not care to imperil it by more than a modest scriptural tithe.

With a fairy as an assistant, he branched out into larger developments of necromancy and took to raising the Devil as a favour. The midnight hour was essential and holy ground desirable—especially disused holy ground: ruined churches, disinhabited religious foundations. The necromancer and the favoured clients would ride under cover of night to Bromholm or St Benet's in the marshes. Elphenor, flying invisibly and dressed for the part, accompanied them. At the Word of Power he became visible, pranced, menaced, and lashed his tail till the necromancer ordered him back to the pit. This was for moonlight nights. When there was no moon, he hovered invisibly, whispering blasphemies and guilty secrets. His blasphemies lacked unction; being a fairy he did not believe in God. But the guilty secrets curdled many a good man's blood. A conscience-stricken clothier from a neighbouring parish spread such scandals about the iniquities done in Walsham Borealis that Master Blackbone thought it wisest to make off before he and Elphenor were thrown into jail.

They packed his equipment—alembics, chart of the heavens, book of spells, skull, etc.—and were off before the first calm light of an April morning. As they travelled southward Elphenor counted windmills and church towers and found windmills slightly predominating. Church towers were more profitable, observed Master Blackbone. Millers were rogues and cheats, but wherever there was a church you could be sure of fools; if Elphenor were not a fairy and ignorant of Holy Writ he would know that fools are the portion appointed for the wise. But for the present they would lie a little low, shun the Devil, and keep to love philtres and salves for the itch, for which there is always a demand in spring. He talked on about the herbs they would need, and the henbane that grew round Needham in Suffolk, where he was born and played with fairies, and whither they were bound. 'What were they like?' Elphenor asked. He did not suppose Master Blackbone's fairies were anything resplendent. Master Blackbone replied that they came out of a hill and were green. Searching his memory, he added that they smelled like elder-flowers. At Zuy, elderflowers were used to flavour gooseberry jam—an inelegant conserve.

At Zuy, by now, the gardeners would be bringing the tubs of myrtle out of the conservatories, his uncle would be conducting ladies along the sanded walks to admire the hyacinths, and he would be forgotten; for in good society failures are smoothly forgotten, and as nothing had resulted from the confidential letter it would be assumed he had failed to deliver it. He would never be able to go back. He did not want to. There was better entertainment in the mortal world. Mortals packed more variety into their brief lives—perhaps because they knew them to be brief. There was always something going on and being taken seriously: love, hate, ambition, plotting, fear, and all the rest of it. He had more power as a quack's assistant than ever he would have attained to in Zuy. To have a great deal of power and no concern was the life for him.

Hog's grease was a regrettable interpolation in his career. Master Blackbone based his salves and ointments on hog's grease, which he bought in a crude state from pork butchers. It was Elphenor's task to clarify it before it was tinctured with juices expressed from herbs. Wash as he might, his hands remained greasy and the smell of grease hung in his nostrils. Even the rankest-smelling herbs were a welcome change, and a bundle of water peppermint threw him into a rapture. As Master Blackbone disliked stooping, most of the gathering fell to him.

It is a fallacy that henbane must be gathered at midnight. Sunlight raises its virtues (notably efficacious against toothache, insomnia, and lice), and to be at its best it should be gathered in the afternoon of a hot day. Elphenor was gathering it in a sloping meadow that faced south. He was working invisibly—Master Blackbone did not wish every Tom, Dick, and Harry to know what went into his preparations. Consequently, a lamb at play collided with him and knocked the basket out of his hand. As it stood astonished at this sudden shower of henbane, Elphenor seized it by the ear and cuffed it. Hearing her lamb bleat so piteously, its mother came charging to the rescue. She also collided with Elphenor and, being heavy with her winter fleece, sent him sprawling. He was still flat on his back when a girl appeared from nowhere, stooped over him, and slapped his face, hard and accurately. To assert his manly dignity he pulled her down on top of him—and saw that she was green.

She was a very pretty shade of green—a pure delicate tint, such as might have been cast on a white eggshell by the sun shining through the young foliage of a beech tree. Her hair, brows, and lashes were a darker shade; her lashes lay on her green cheek like a miniature fern frond. Her teeth were perfectly white. Her skin was so nearly transparent that the blue veins on her wrists and breasts showed through like some exquisitely marbled cheese.

As they lay in an interval of repose, she stroked the bruise beginning to show on his cheek with triumphant moans of compassion. Love did not heighten or diminish her colour. She remained precisely the same shade of green. The smell, of course, was that smell of elderflowers. It was strange to think that exactly like this she may have been one of the fairies who played with Elisha Blackbone in his bragged-of boyhood, forty, fifty years back. He pushed the speculation away, and began kissing behind the ear, and behind the other ear, to make sure which was the more sensitive. But from that hour love struck root in him.

Eventually he asked her name. She told him it was Weasel. 'I shall call you Mustela,' he said, complying with the lover's imperative to rename the loved one; but in the main he called her Weasel. They sat up, and saw that time had gone on as usual, that dusk had fallen and the henbane begun to wilt.

When they parted, the sheep were circling gravely to the top of the hill, the small grassy hill of her tribe. He flew leisurely back, swinging the unfilled basket. The meagre show of henbane would be a pretext for going off on the morrow to a place where it grew more abundantly; he would have found such a place, but by then it was growing too dark for picking, and looking one way while flying another he had bruised his cheek against a low-growing bough. At Zuy this artless tale would not have supported a moment's scrutiny; but it would pass with a mortal, though it might be wise to substantiate it with a request for the woundwort salve. For a mortal, Master Blackbone was capable of unexpected intuitions.

The intuitions had not extended to the reverence for age and learning which induced Elphenor to sleep on a pallet to the windward. Towards morning, he dreamed that he was at the foot of the ilex; but it was Weasel who was looking down at him, and if he did not move she would slap his face. He moved, and woke. Weasel lay asleep beside him. But at the same time they were under the ilex, for the waves crashed on the screaming pebble beach and were Master Blackbone's snores.

At Zuy the English Elfindom was spoken of with admiring reprehension: its magnificence, wastefulness, and misrule, its bravado and eccentricity. The eccentricity of being green and living under a hill was not included. A hill, yes. Antiquarians talked of hill dwellings, and found evidence of them in potsherds and beads. But never, at any time, green. The beauties of Zuy, all of them white as bolsters, would have swooned at the hypothesis. Repudiating the memory of past bolsters, he looked at Weasel, curled against him like a caterpillar in a rose leaf, green as spring, fresh as spring, and completely contemporary.

She stirred, opened her eyes, and laughed.

'Shush!'

Though invisible, she might not be inaudible, and her voice was ringing and assertive as a wren's. She had come so trustingly it would be the act of an ingrate to send her away. Not being an ingrate he went with her, leaving Master Blackbone to make what he would of an early-rising assistant. They breakfasted on wild strawberries and a hunk of bread he had had the presence of mind to take from the bread crock. It was not enough for Weasel, and when they came to a brook she twitched up a handful of minnows and ate them raw. Love is a hungry emotion, and by midday he wished he had not been so conventional about the minnows. As a tactful approach, he began questioning her about life in the hill, its amenities, its daily routine. She suddenly became evasive: he would not like it; it was dull, old-fashioned, unsociable.

'All the same, I should like to visit it. I have never been inside a hill.'

'No! You can't come. It's impossible. They'd set on you, you'd be driven out. *You're not green*.'

Etiquette.

'Don't you understand?'

'I was wondering what they would do to you if they found out where you woke this morning.'

'Oh, that! They'd have to put up with it. Green folk don't draw green blood. But they'd tear *you* in pieces.'

'It's the same where I come from. If I took you to Zuy, they might be rather politer, but they'd never forgive you for being green. But I won't take you, Weasel. We'll stay in Suffolk. And if it rains and rains and rains—'

'I don't mind rain—'

'We'll find a warm, dry badger sett.'

They escaped into childishness and were happy again, with a sharpened happiness because for a moment they had so nearly touched despair.

As summer became midsummer, and the elder blossom outlasted the wild roses and faded in its turn till the only true elderflower scent came from her, and the next full moon had a broader face and shone on cocks of hay in silvery fields, they settled into an unhurried love and strolled from day to day as through a familiar landscape. By now they were seldom hungry, for there was a large crop of mushrooms, and Elphenor put more system into his attendances on Master Blackbone, breakfasting soundly and visibly while conveying mouthfuls to the invisible Weasel (it was for the breakfasts that they slept there). Being young and perfectly happy and pledged to love each other till the remote end of their days, they naturally talked of death and discussed how to contrive that neither should survive the other. Elphenor favoured being struck by lightning as they lay in each other's arms, but Weasel was terrified by thunder—she winced and covered her ears at the slightest distant rumble—and though he talked soothingly of the electric fluid and told her of recent experiments with amber and a couple of silk stockings, one black, one white, she refused to die by lightning stroke.

And Master Blackbone, scarcely able to believe his ears, madly casting horoscopes and invoking the goddess Fortuna, increasingly tolerant of Elphenor's inattention, patiently compounding his salves unassisted, smiling on the disappearances from his larder, was day after day, night after night, more sure of his surmise—till convinced of his amazing good fortune he fell into the melancholy of not knowing what best to do about it, whether to grasp fame single-handed or call in the help of an expert and self-effacingly retire on the profits. He wrote a letter to an old friend. Elphenor was not entrusted with this letter, but he knew it had been written and was directed to London. Weasel was sure Master Blackbone was up to no good—she had detested him at first sight. They decided to keep a watch on him. But their watch was desultory, and the stranger was already sitting in Master Blackbone's lodging and conversing with him when they flew in and perched on a beam.

The stranger was a stout man with a careworn expression. Master Blackbone was talking in his best procuring voice.

'It's a Golconda, an absolute Golconda! A pair of them, young, in perfect condition. Any manager would snap at them. But I have kept it dark till now. I wanted you to have the first option.'

'Thanks, I'm sure,' said the stranger. 'But it's taking a considerable chance.'

'Oh no, it isn't. People would flock to see them. You could double the charges—in fact you should, for it's something unique—and there wouldn't be an empty seat in the house. Besides, it's a scientific rarity. You'd have all the illuminati. Nobs from the colleges. Ladies of fashion. Royal patronage.'

The stranger said he didn't like buying pigs in pokes.

'But I give you my word. A brace of fairies—lovely, young, amorous fairies. Your fortune would be made.'

'How much do you want?'

'Two-thirds of the takings. You can't say that's exorbitant. Not two-thirds of the profits, mind. Two-thirds of the takings and a written agreement.'

The stranger repeated that he didn't like buying pigs in pokes, the more so when he had no warrant the pigs were within.

'Wait till tonight! They come every night and cuddle on that pallet there. They trust me like a father. Wait till they're asleep and throw a net over them, and they're yours.'

'But when I've got them to London, suppose they are awkward, and won't perform? People aren't going to pay for what they can't see. How can I be sure they'll be visible?'

Master Blackbone said there were ways and means, as with performing animals.

'Come, Weasel. We'll be off.'

The voice was right overhead, loud and clear. Some cobwebs drifted down.

Elphenor and Weasel were too pleased with themselves to think beyond the moment. They had turned habitually towards their usual haunts and were dabbling their feet in the brook before it occurred to Elphenor that they had no reason to stay in the neighbourhood and good reason to go elsewhere. Weasel's relations would murder him because he was not green, Master Blackbone designed to sell them because they were fairies. Master Blackbone might have further designs: he was a necromancer, though a poor one; it would be prudent to get beyond his magic circle. Elphenor had congratulated himself on leaving prudence behind at Zuy. Now it reasserted itself and had its charm. Prudence had no charm whatever for Weasel; it was only by representing the move as reckless that he persuaded her to make it.

With the world before them, he flew up for a survey and caught sight of the sea, looking as if ships would not melt in its mouth—which rather weakened the effect of his previous narrative of the journey from IJmuiden to the ilexes. Following the coastline they came to Great Yarmouth, where they spent several weeks. It was ideal for their vagrant purposes, full of vigorous, cheerful people, with food to be had for the taking—hot pies and winkles in the marketplace, herring on the quayside where the fishing boats unloaded. The air was rough and cold, and he stole a pair of shipboy's trousers and a knitted muffler for Weasel from a marine store near the Custom House. He was sorry to leave this kind place. But Weasel showed such a strong inclination to go to sea, and found it so amusing to flaunt her trousers on the quayside and startle her admirers with her green face, that she was becoming notorious, and he was afraid Master Blackbone might hear of her. From Yarmouth they flew inland, steering their course by church towers. Where there is a church tower you can be sure of fools, Master Blackbone had said. True enough; but Elphenor tired of thieving—though it called for more skill in villages—and he thought he would try turning an honest penny, for a change. By now he was so coarsened and brown-handed that he could pass as a labouring man. In one place he sacked potatoes, in another baled reeds for thatching. At a village called Scottow, where the sexton had rheumatism, he dug a grave. Honest-pennying was no pleasure to Weasel, who had to hang about invisibly, passing the time with shrivelled blackberries. In these rustic places which had never seen a circus or an Indian pedlar, her lovely green face would have brought stones rattling on their heels.

Winter came late that year and stealthily, but the nights were cold. Nights were never cold in Suffolk, she said. He knew this was due to the steady temperature under the hill, but hoping all the same she might be right he turned southward. He had earned more than enough to pay for a night at an inn. At Bury St Edmunds he bought her a cloak with a deep hood, and telling her to pull the hood well forward and keep close to his heels he went at dusk to a respectable inn and hired the best bedroom they had. All went well, except that they seemed to look at him doubtfully. In his anxiety to control the situation he had reverted to his upper-class manner, which his clothes did not match with. The four-poster bed was so comfortable that he hired the room for a second night, telling the chambermaid his wife had a headache and must not be disturbed. It was certainly an elopement, she reported; even before she had left the room, the little gentleman had parted the bed curtains and climbed in beside the lady. After the second night there was no more money.

They left on foot, and continued to walk, for there was a shifting, drizzling fog which made it difficult to keep each other in sight if they flew. Once again they stole a dinner, but it was so inadequate that

Elphenor decided to try begging. He was rehearsing a beggar's whine when they saw a ruddy glow through the fog and heard a hammer ring on an anvil. Weasel as usual clapped her hands to her ears; but when they came to a wayside forge the warmth persuaded her to follow Elphenor, who went in shivering ostentatiously and asked if he and his wife could stand near the blaze: they would not get in the way, they would not stay long. The blacksmith was shaping horseshoes. He nodded, and went on with his work. Elphenor was preparing another whine when the blacksmith remarked it was no day to be out, and encouraged Weasel, who stood in the doorway, to come nearer the fire.

'Poor soul, she could do with a little kindness,' said Elphenor. 'And we haven't met with much of it today. We passed an inn, farther back'—it was there they had stolen the heel of a Suffolk cheese—'but they said they had no room for us.'

Weasel interrupted. 'What's that black thing ahead, that keeps on showing and going?'

The blacksmith pulled his forelock. 'Madam. That's the church.'

They thanked him and went away, Elphenor thinking he must learn to beg more feelingly. The blacksmith stood looking after them. At this very time of year, too. He wished he had not let slip the opportunity of a Hail Mary not likely to come his way again.

The brief December day was closing when they came to the church. The south porch, large as a room, was sheltered from the wind, and they sat there, huddled in Weasel's cloak. 'We can't sleep here,' Elphenor said. For all that, he got up and tried the church door. It was locked. He immediately determined to get in by a window. They flew round the church, fingering the cold panes of glass, and had almost completed their round and seen the great bulk of the tower threatening down on them, when Weasel heard a clatter overhead. It came from one of the clerestory windows, where a missing pane had been replaced by a shutter. They wrenched the shutter open, and flew in, and circled downward through darkness, and stood on a flagstone pavement. Outlined against a window was a tall structure with a peak. Fingering it, they found it was wood, carved, and swelling out of a stem like a goblet. A railed flight of steps half encircled the stem. They mounted the steps and found themselves in the goblet. It was like an octagonal cupboard, minus a top but carpeted. By curling round each other, there would be room to lie down. The smell of wood gave them a sense of security, and they spent the night in the pulpit.

He woke to the sound of Weasel laughing. Daylight was streaming in, and Weasel was flitting about the roof, laughing at the wooden figures that supported the crossbeams—carved imitations of fairies, twelve foot high, with outstretched turkey wings and gaunt faces, each uglier than the last. 'So that's what they think we're like,' she said. 'And look at *her*!' She pointed to the fairy above the pulpit, struggling with a trumpet.

Exploring at floor level, Elphenor read the Ten Commandments, and found half a bottle of wine and some lozenges. It would pass for a breakfast; later, he would stroll into the village and see what could be got from there. While he was being raised as the Devil at Walsham Borealis, he had learned some facts about the Church of England, one of them that the reigning monarch, symbolically represented as a lion and a unicorn, is worshipped noisily on one day of the week and that for the rest of the week churches are unmolested. There was much to be said for spending the winter here. The building was windproof and weatherproof, Weasel was delighted with it, and, for himself, he found its loftiness and spaciousness congenial, as though he were back in Zuy—a Zuy improved by a total removal of its inhabitants. He had opened a little door and discovered a winding stone stairway behind it when his confidence in Church of England weekdays was shaken by the entrance of two women with brooms and buckets. He beckoned to Weasel, snatched her cloak from the pulpit, and preceded her up the winding stairs, holding the bottle and the lozenges. The steps were worn; there was a dead crow on one of them. They groped their way up into darkness, then into light; a window showed a landing and a door open on a small room where some ropes dangled from the ceiling. Weasel seized a rope and gave it a tug, and would have tugged at it more energetically if Elphenor had not intervened, promising that when the women had gone away she could tug to her heart's content. Looking out of the cobwebbed window, he saw the churchyard far below and realised they must be a long way up the tower. But the steps wound on into another darkness and a dimmer lightness, and to another landing and another door open on another room. This room had louvred windows high up in the wall, and most of its floor space was taken up by a frame supporting eight bells, four of them upside down with their clappers lolling in their iron mouths. This was the bell chamber, he explained. The ropes went from the bells into the room below, which was the ringing chamber. There was a similar tower near Zuy; mortals thought highly of it, and his tutor had taken him to see it.

Weasel began to stroke one of the bells. As though she were caressing some savage sleeping animal, it presently responded with a noise between a soft growl and a purr. Elphenor stroked another. It answered at a different pitch, deeper and harsher, as though it were a more savage animal. But they were hungry. The bells could wait. The light from the louvred windows flickered between bright and sombre as the wind tossed the clouds. It was blowing up for a storm.

They would be out of the wind tonight and for many nights to come. January is a dying season, there would be graves to dig, and with luck and management, thought Elphenor, he might earn a livelihood and be a friend to sextons here and around. Weasel would spare crumbs from the bread he earned, scatter them for birds, catch the birds, pluck and eat them: she still preferred raw food, with the life still lively in it. On Sundays, she said, they would get their week's provisions; with everybody making a noise in church, stealing would be child's play. The pulpit would be the better for a pillow, and she could soon collect enough feathers for a pillow, for a feather mattress even: one can always twitch a pillowcase from the washing line. The wine had gone to their heads; they outbid each other with grand plans of how they would live in the church, and laughed them down, and imagined more. They would polish the wooden fairies' noses till they shone like drunkards' noses; they would grow water-cresses in the font; Elphenor would tell the complete story of his life before they met. Let him begin now! Was he born with a hook nose and red hair? He began, obediently and prosily. Weasel clamped her eyes open, and suppressed yawns. He lost the thread of his narrative. Drowsy with wine, they fell asleep.

He woke to two appalling sounds. Weasel screaming with terror, a clash of metal. The bell ringers had come to practise their Christmas peal, and prefaced it by sounding all the bells at once. The echo was heavy on the air as they began to ring a set of changes, first the scale descending evenly to the whack of the tenor bell, then in patterned steps to the same battle-axe blow. The pattern altered; the tenor bell sounded midway, jolting an arbitrary finality into the regular measure of eight.

With each change of position the tenor bell accumulated a more threatening insistency, and the other bells shifted round it like a baaing flock of sheep.

Weasel cowered in Elphenor's arms. She had no strength left to scream with; she could only tremble before the impact of the next flailing blow. He felt his senses coming adrift. The booming echo was a darkness on his sight through which he saw the bells in their frame heaving and evading, evading and heaving, under a dark sky. The implacable assault of the changing changes pursued him as the waves had pursued the boat from IJmuiden. But here there was no escape, for it was he who wallowed broken-backed at the mercy of the storm. Weasel lay in his arms like something at a distance. He felt his protectiveness, his compassion, ebbing away; he watched her with a bloodless, skeleton love. She still trembled, but in a disjointed way, as though she were falling to pieces.

He saw the lovely green fade out of her face. 'My darling,' he said, 'death by lightning would have been easier.' He could not hear himself speak.

The frost lasted on into mid-March. No one went to the bell chamber till the carpenter came to mend the louvres in April. The two bodies, one bowed over the other, had fallen into decay. No one could account for them, or for the curious weightless fragments of a substance rather like sheet gelatine which the wind had scattered over the floor. They were buried in the same grave. Because of their small stature and light bones they were entered in the Register of Burials as *Two Stranger Children*.

(*Kingdoms of Elfin*, 1977)

THE REVOLT AT BROCÉLIANDE

WACE, a Norman poet of the mid-twelfth century, had heard so much about the fairy Kingdom of Brocéliande, in Brittany, that he went to see its wonders for himself; and found nothing, except that he had gone on a fool's errand:

> Là allai je merveilles querre,
>   Vit la forest et vit la terre,
> Merveilles quis, mais ne trovait:
>   Fol m'en revins, fol y allai,
> Fol y allai, fol m'en revins:
>   Folie quis, por fol me tins.

His intention defeated his purpose. His mind was full of preconceived ideas of what he was in search of, so his eyes saw nothing.

Mortals do not see fairies—the generalisation is as nearly a rule as anything in this turning world can be. It is certain that they cannot be seen by those who are looking for them. If a fairy of Brocéliande were seen, it was by some peasant whose mind was taken up with his own concerns—hunger, a leaky roof, a lost cow. He saw it out of the tail of his eye, and wished he hadn't, since to see a fairy is unlucky. It was on a day in mid-winter, with the north wind thundering in the forest and hail spiking the air, that the turf-cutter's son who had been sent out to find enough wood to warm a Sunday dinner saw his fairies: two fat men, dressed in scarlet, who sat under a live oak, holding hands and weeping. He ran home in terror, hitting his frostbitten feet against tufts of frozen grass, and told his parents. Before the end of the week he was dead of fever—which proved again that it is unlucky to see a fairy.

But this was long before Wace's expedition. Seeing nothing, he suffered no more than a passing mortification, and lived to versify the story of King Arthur and the Round Table.

Brocéliande was the foremost Elfin Court in all Western Europe, the proudest and most elegant. It claimed that it had preserved the pure tradition of ancient Persia, where the elfin race originated. Its queens wore a pink turban instead of the usual crown; the royal wand was of cedarwood from the banks of the Euphrates, so massively encrusted with jewels that it took a team of courtiers to wave it; its ladies-in-waiting distilled an exquisite rosewater; it kept a particular breed of long-furred cats and an astrologer. It was peculiar in having preserved a belief in a supernatural world, peopled by spirits of incalculable power, called Afrits. The obligation to worship these Afrits, while at the same time averting their intervention, was carried out by quarterly ceremonies of propitiation. These ceremonies were preceded by a round of pious cockfights, after which the victor cock was sacrificed.

Apart from the element of piety, court life at Brocéliande was much the same as in other Kingdoms. There were fashions of the moment —collecting butterflies, determining the pitch of birdsongs, table-turning, cat races, purifying the language, building card castles. There were expeditions to the coast to watch shipwrecks, summer picnics in the forest, deer hunts with the Royal Pack of Werewolves.

Ambassadors from other courts complained that the palace, situated in the depth of that immense forest, was sombre and damp; even so, they admitted that everything was carried on in the best of taste, and that its peculiar mixture of piety and fickleness was enchanting. It was, of course, an expensive embassy. There was not a corner of the palace where a wager was not in progress: which of two hailstones would be the first to melt, the span of a cat's whiskers, which way it would jump. And every debt was a debt of honour.

There was a regular programme of racing events—the Scullery Cup, the Laundry Half-Mile, the Staff Handicap. Lineaged fairies, who would rather be seen dead than seen flying, felt a practical admiration for the speed of those who flew on errands or obeyed the summons of a silver whistle. Servants who excelled in pace or endurance were transferred to the specialised seclusion of race horses and exercised morning and evening; a famous valet who had the misfortune to break a wing was kept at stud and sired several winners.

It was a custom that each new queen should introduce a fresh Persian tradition. When Queen Melior assumed the pink turban she was at a loss for Persian traditions till, gazing at her eyebrows in a looking glass, she realised, with the amazement with which one contemplates the dullness of one's predecessors, that no one had thought of eunuchs. She called an assembly and announced, her wand being waved before her, that she proposed to add eunuchs to her retinue. For the present, two would be enough.

There were loud murmurs of approval, low murmurs of doubt. Who was she going to pick on? Obviously some working person; yet here, too, there were difficulties. The calm balance of society depended on people remaining in their proper stations.

The wand was waved again. Queen Melior continued. From each, she said, according to his disposability. The eunuchs should be drawn from the ranks of the changelings, whose abundance could always supply another pair if anything went wrong with the first experiment.

Fairies are constructed for longevity, not fertility. Many of the aristocracy do not breed at all; those who do, at long intervals. But this does not prevent them from delighting in small children. Couriers are sent prospecting, and where they see a baby left unguarded make off with it. Strong ruddy babies are most in request; their unlikeness to the fairy race makes them engaging. They grow up as court playthings, fondled, indulged, and kept much cleaner than they would be in human homes. Some penurious Kingdoms, like Elfhame in Scotland, injected them with a drug which prolonged their natural span. This was never done at Brocéliande, where the freshness of youth was the prime desideratum.

All went smoothly. Two handsome well-matched boys in their early teens were chosen. The castration was performed by a skilled surgeon who flew from Constantinople. A special uniform was designed; they were given a course in etiquette and deportment, learning to walk with measured steps and stand still without fidgeting, and a new rank was invented for them, between the Directors of Piety and the Ladies of Honour. Their names were Ib and Rollo.

They were not altogether happy in their advancement. Their feet swelled and their backs ached from so much standing about in their attendance of the Queen. Other changelings laughed at them. Some of the Ladies of Honour were offended that mere mortals should take precedence of them, and affected to shudder at the proximity of anything so unnatural as a eunuch; others, less squeamish, were sorry for the poor creatures and questioned them maternally. Their outstanding friend at court was the Royal Favourite. Male companionship, however imperfect, was a support to him. He was handsome and silly, and when Melior was cross they repaired his self-esteem. By the time he was replaced and the new Favourite, who was handsome and intensely musical, had set the whole court to singing in four-part harmony, Ib and Rollo had ceased to be novelties. Their traditional significance—which was in fact as meaningless as a vestigial button on a suit—was forgotten. However, they were for the time being useful, as they reinforced the soprano voices in the part-singing.

Persons deprived of their sex are deprived of their intuition: there is no leap of the heart, towards or against. They cannot even make mistakes. Existing in the equable winter of reason, the best they can do is to see clearly and arrive at a correct judgment. Sometimes in dreams both Ib and Rollo returned to the pell-mell spontaneity of their young selves and were delighted, infuriated, embarrassed before they could say why. But time went on—a clock that never lost a minute, never ran down. The dreams came less often, the waking was less lacerating. Eventually, it was not lacerating at all. They woke remembering that there was something further to be observed, an unaccountable smile, gesture, tilt of the voice to be considered and fitted into the correct judgment of a character or a situation. It is this imperturbable power of judging and assessing which makes eunuchs so powerful in court intrigues and palace revolutions. But that is in mortal courts. At Brocéliande there was a perfect loyalty to things as they were.

The boredom of court life closed in on them—the boredom in which one stares, day after day, at the same face in a tapestry hanging. Their function kept them together, idling about till some occasion called them to stand on either side of the throne. They did not talk much: there was nothing much to talk about; they exchanged comments, and agreed with each other. They were figures in the tapestry—rather portly figures by now, for their mortal origin made them large eaters. One evening Rollo remarked, 'We have not seen the Astrologer since the new moon. I wonder what he does, sitting alone in his tower. He can't watch the stars by day.' After a pause for thought, Ib said, 'I suppose he sleeps.' This degree of speculation was so unusual that it pricked them into an impulse. Melior had taken a new Favourite and gone early to bed. Their absence from the tapestry would not be noticed. They climbed the long stairway to Master Tarantula's apartment at the top of the tower, and knocked on his door. It swung open, and closed behind them. In the middle of the room was a table, spread with a meal for two. Master Tarantula was playing solitaire. 'Sit down,' he said. 'I was expecting you.' It was not so surprising that they had been expected: he was a Magian, cast horoscopes, read future events in the stars. What took them aback was to find themselves welcomed and drawn into conversation. They began to talk, found they had things to say, found themselves listened to. The moon shone in through the open uncurtained window. Clouds sailed across it, moving smoothly and rapidly on a steady wind. Suddenly Master Tarantula got up, threw off his cloak, and unfurled a pair of large wings. With one powerful stroke, he was out of the window, breasting the air like a strong swimmer. They watched him soar upward, vanish in a cloud, emerge from it, a black speck against the moonlight blue of the sky, vanish.

They were still speechless when he returned, neatly diving into the room with his wings packed to his sides, and finished the wine in his glass. Breathlessly (Master Tarantula was not in the least out of breath) Ib asked, 'How do you find your way back?' 'I call that a very sensible question,' said Master Tarantula. 'I will explain when we next meet. But now I must send you away. It is already daybreak in Bohemia.'

Next week the great Winter Candle was lit and everyone went into furs. After the festivities had died down, Master Tarantula sent a message to the Queen asking for a private audience. Leaning on a stick and looking very old, he made his bow and explained his purpose. The stars had warned him that it would be a very unpropitious winter, with a number of Afrits about. He was an old man, his powers were failing. The last Afrit had almost got the better of him, slipping between his spells. He had managed to divert its malignancy to a village west of the forest, now in ashes, but he could not hope to keep off the next assault single-handed. Would Her Majesty grant him a couple of assistants? They need not be experts in Art Magic: he could supply all that himself; all he asked was that they should be strong and obedient. And virgin.

The least flaw in virginity would provoke the Afrits to fury. And here lay the difficulty. Young people are careless of their virginity; one day they may have it and the next not. What was needed was a trustworthy, an inexpugnable virginity. Would Her Majesty lend him her eunuchs? It had been well drummed into Melior in her girlhood how strongly Afrits feel about virginity. She handed over Ib and Rollo without demur.

For many years they lived happily in Master Tarantula's tower, playing three-handed whist, learning a few tricks of magic, listening to his conversation, keeping off the Afrits, and becoming almost as agnostic as he. Because he respected nothing, they began to respect each other, finding each other likeable instead of merely habitual. At the propitiatory ceremonies they attended him as formerly they had attended the Queen. Sometimes he feigned weakness and leaned on them. In fact he was uncommonly strong and limber, which he put down to the fresh air and exercise of his nocturnal flights. One night, he failed in his usual neat entry and made several blundering essays before he got through the window. His teeth chattered, his clothes were wet through. When he recovered his breath he asked for brandy. With his teeth knocking on the glass, he told them he had been badly mauled in a thunderstorm. They got him to bed and heaped blankets on him. He was no sooner asleep than he began to leap like a fish in a net. Towards morning, he opened his eyes and did not recognise them. Death was hearsay to them, and seeing him fall into a quiet sleep they supposed he was recovering, till the old bedmaker came with her broom and bucket, and told them he was dying and would be gone by nightfall. She had been his servant since his college days and thought the world of him. At dusk she came again. He seemed to be dying easily and contentedly. 'There. He's gone,' she said, and held a mirror to his lips. His wings started out; he looked like a dead crow. But such deathbed erections are not unusual, she said. The wings are folded back, and nothing said of it.

The new Astrologer wanted no assistants. Ib and Rollo resumed their former service. They had been absent from court life for so long that they felt out of date. New niceties of etiquette had been introduced and these, familiar to everyone else, left them at a loss. With Master Tarantula they had got into a way of talking quite freely, questioning, contradicting, saying whatever came into their heads. It was difficult to discard this; they talked too much, and laughed, and were thought impertinent, or they could find nothing to say and were thought stockish. It was held against them, too, that they were inseparable.

The ladies who had taken offence when these mortal beings were thrust into court society had not forgotten their grudge (the Elfin memory is proportioned to Elfin longevity), and petitioned the Queen that Ib and Rollo should be included in the next batch of elderly changelings to be deposited on the Island of Repose—a reef off the Pointe du Raz, covered in seaweed, lashed with spray from Atlantic cross-currents, a place of no return. Bretons knew it as the Isle of the Dead, and fishermen reported hearing the howls of souls in Purgatory there. Melior objected. Ib and Rollo were part of Brocéliande's precious heritage of Persian traditions: old and smelly they might be, but they were still her eunuchs, and she could not possibly appear on state occasions without them; but she would give them new suits.

The next state occasion was the Snuffing of the Winter Candle, when everybody put off furs and began to carry fans. The weather was appalling. Gales raged round the castle, the forest clanged with the ice frozen on to trees, the servants could only venture out on foot. In the midst of all this an Afrit eluded the new Astrologer, changed its shape into a starving weasel, got into the palace mews and killed all the fighting cocks.

During the following tumult of rage, consternation, suggestions, objections, counter-suggestions, the Chancellor's daughter said to her bosom friend (she was at the age of bosom friends), 'Why don't they have a eunuch fight?' She had not meant to be overheard, but a low voice catches every ear. Her remark was considered the height of absurdity or else marvellously witty, but within a few days the idea of a eunuch fight was being seriously discussed. It would be something to bet on and something to laugh at.

Living with Master Tarantula, Ib and Rollo had lost the knack of observing and forming correct judgments. When Aquilon, Master of the Werewolves, affably appealed to them to lighten the gloom of life without cocking by a small set-to between themselves, they were flattered, saw a chance to win their way back into favour, said that if they were younger, almost agreed. They were nailed to agreement by Aquilon's friends assuring them that a great deal of money had been staked.

The fight took place in a ring of cheering spectators. As they could not be expected to fight to the death, a referee was appointed, who would ring his bell after a round of five minutes (no one expected them to last out longer). They had, of course, witnessed a great many ceremonial cockfights, and noticed that fighting cocks aim at the eye. They flinched at this, but buffeted each other's face. When Rollo drew blood from Ib's nose, there was great applause. It swelled to a storm when the flustered Ib miscalculated his aim and hit Rollo's eye. The eye swelled and closed. The referee rang his bell, declared the fight over and Ib the victor. Congratulating spectators swarmed into the ring and supervised the combatants being revived with hot towels and vinegar.

There is always a charm about amateur efforts: they are at once so silly and so sincere. Ib's nose, Rollo's black eye, the bruises that came out on their soft skins, roused an almost genuine solicitude in their backers. They were given a punchball, bottles of liniment, tonic pills; each was privately urged not to clench his teeth in the next fight. For somehow —they did not quite know how—there was going to be another fight.

It was not such a success. In their anxiety not to hurt each other's face they repeatedly hit below the belt. There was laughter and some booing. The referee declared the match a draw.

This peaceable decision angered them. For the first time in their lives, they quarrelled—quarrelled to the quick, because they had been humiliated. In a desolate reconciliation they vowed they would never fight again, never betray the friendship which was all, in a society of flippant, arbitrary, alien beings, they could rely on. And a couple of days later each had betrayed it, for each had been separately approached and told that the other had agreed to a third fight—a fight to settle all, since by then the new cocks would be arriving from Morocco. Furious with each other for having been tricked, they consented with indifference to the proposal that for this last fight they should be spurred— symbolically, of course: the spurs would be blunted.

Embarrassed by these toy-sized weapons fastened to their heels, they walked stiffly into the ring, bowed to the spectators, bowed to each other. Every male in the palace—courtiers, servants, changelings—had been ordered to attend, and it was known, though not mentioned, that Melior and her ladies were in the screened gallery above, pressed together like hens on a perch. The referee stepped out of the ring and struck his bell. They turned on each other and began to fight.

They fought with the frenzy of the betrayed; they fought and would not leave off. They tore out each other's hair, wrenched at each other's arms, set their teeth in each other's flesh and worried it, kicked at each other's shins. The spurs had not been blunted. They discovered how to use them, and blood spurted out. The applause was incessant. Suddenly it was dominated by a frightful caterwauling as the two eunuchs began to scream at each other. Maddened by the sound, the spectators fell to fighting among themselves, Rollo's backers shouting defiance at Ib's, Ib's trying to get at Rollo's. So many old scores were being wiped out, so much dissembled loathing gratified, that for some time nobody noticed that the caterwauling had ceased. But when the spectators left off fighting and glanced towards the centre of the ring, they saw a man who grovelled and a man who stood over him, and thought, though they could not be sure, that the standing man was Rollo and the grovelling man Ib, hamstrung by Rollo's battering spur.

Fortunately, the Moroccan cocks arrived next day. They were splendid birds. Their proud strut, their eyes glittering like sequins, ennobled everyone's spirits and redeemed Brocéliande from an inelegant memory. A black eye here or there was ignored; scratched faces were restored with very becoming strips of black court plaster. The principal Director of Piety explained that whatever had happened—he himself had seen a certain indecorum—was undoubtedly the work of the same Afrit who had come among them in the disguise of a weasel. The Chancellor's daughter, who had started it all, was questioned before Melior by a panel of Ladies of Honour, but exonerated, as she had only meant to be helpful. When she had left the room, the Ladies of Honour turned to the Queen and begged to renew their former petition, which earlier she had graciously refused. They did not dispute the traditional importance of her eunuchs, but she really could not be attended by a cripple and a stammering idiot. Surely the time had come when they should be retired to the Island of Repose. Melior assented. The Ladies of Honour spread the news.

Apparently, the Afrit had not finished his work. Aquilon, using such words as 'shabby' and 'iniquitous', declared that Ib and Rollo had suffered enough, and threatened to resign his Mastership of the

Werewolves if they were now deported to the Island of Repose. His friends supported him; the changelings banded themselves under his leadership, saying that they had been downtrodden for too long and were stolen property anyway. The Ladies of Honour urged Melior to be firm, the Directors of Piety begged her to be prudent, the Favourite took mandragora. When the Queen called an assembly, several of the team of Wand Wavers, bowing, put their hands behind them. The revolt spread to the servants, who refused to fly and went about their duties at a leisurely walking pace. This was the last straw. The Ambassador from Blokula—a formalist from a petty northern Kingdom who would be delighted to report that Brocéliande was in a state of insurrection—was hourly expected. Melior gave in. A disused hermitage was reroofed and simply furnished, and Ib and Rollo installed, with a reliable groom of Aquilon's to see to their needs. There, not long after, they ended their days, Ib surviving Rollo by less than a year.

(*Kingdoms of Elfin*, 1977)

VISITORS TO A CASTLE

MYNNYDD PRESCELLY is the westernmost mountain in Wales. It is of only moderate height but its sweeping contours, rising from a gentle countryside, dominate the skyline. Sometimes it is there, sometimes not. Giraldus Cambrensis, who wrote the 'Itinerarium Kambriae', must often have looked inquiringly towards it from his birthplace, Manorbier Castle. In the 'Itinerary', however, all he has to say of Prescelly is that a man dwelling on its northern slope dreamed that if he put his hand into a certain spring he would find a rock and beneath it a golden torque; and being covetous, did so, was bitten by a viper, and died. It may be that Giraldus wrote more fully about Prescelly in a lost chapter of the 'Itinerary'; otherwise, this is another instance of his credulity distracting him from more serious matters.

Since time out of mind, there has been a small Elfin Kingdom of Castle Ash Grove, which lies in a valley of Mynnydd Prescelly. Its name harks back to a time when its inhabitants did not care to build and had not developed a social hierarchy of flying servants, strolling gentry. At nightfall, regardless of class distinctions, they flew up into the boughs of an ash grove and slept there.

They were still sleeping in trees when a mortal came among them, a civil old man in a single garment, very coarse and verminous, who had voyaged from Ireland into St Brides Bay on a slab of granite. This he told them, while they hospitably combed the lice from his single garment. True hospitality includes receiving travellers' tales, and they asked him how he had made the granite slab seaworthy. He replied, 'By Faith'. The word was new to them. He preached them a sermon on the nature of Faith, and how its apartness from knowledge, its irreconcilability with all human experience, proved that it was a spark of the heavenly mind.

'Faith can remove mountains!' he exclaimed. But Faith was not for them. Being Elfins, they had no souls. Without souls, they could not enjoy the advantages of Faith, not so much as to say to a pebble, 'Be thou removed'.

Till now, they had listened politely. But at this last statement their Welsh pride put up its hackle. They did not contradict him to his face, but when he had limped on to convert the heathen in Carmarthenshire they exploded with resentment and set themselves to disprove it, each and all saying to his chosen pebble, 'Be thou removed!' Not a pebble stirred. They decided that pebbles were too small to be worth removing anyway, and that it would be simpler to work on Mynnydd Prescelly. Prescelly did not comply; their Welsh pride would not yield. Matters were at a deadlock when the Court Poet's nephew said that if they seriously wished to remove Mynnydd Prescelly they must sing. There is nothing so powerful as singing. Everyone who sings knows this with an inward certainty.

He was a stout young fairy with a light tenor voice. Previously, no one had paid much attention to him. Now he assumed command. When they proposed to sing immediately, he quelled their impatience: they must give their voices, hoarse and ravelled from shouting at pebbles, a chance to recover. Not a note till sundown tomorrow; meanwhile, a light supper and early to bed after a gargle of blackberry juice and honey. For his part, he would compose a special Removal Song, to be sung without accompaniment, and of narrow compass so that all could join in it.

At sundown precisely, they met to sing. Not a cough was heard among them. The Poet's nephew mounted a stool and took them through the Removal Song till they had it by heart. The tune, as he had promised, was one they all could join in. It was in a three-beat measure and within the compass of a sixth. The words 'Mynnydd Prescelly, Be thou removed' they knew already, and after a few niceties had been attended to he signalled them to a pause and said, 'Now, all together. One, two, three!'

They began with their gathered breaths. At first, they sang in unison. Then they sang in thirds. As the power of song took hold of them, they threw in some spontaneous descants. When they realised that the song could be sung in canon, like Three Blind Mice and Tallis's Evening

Hymn, their joy knew no bounds. They sang. They sang. The Poet's nephew, singing himself and conducting with both hands, led them from an ample *forte* to a rich *fortissimo* and tapered them down to a *pianissimo espressivo* and roused them again and again calmed them. Each sang, putting his whole heart into it as though everything depended on him, and at the same time felt the anonymous ardour of those singing with him. They sang so intently that they did not hear the ash trees rustle as though a solemn gale blew over them. When the Poet's nephew had brought them back to a unison and slowed them to a close, they looked round on each other as though on well-met strangers. Glorified and exhausted by a total experience, they ate an enormous supper, climbed into their ash trees, and slept till well past sunrise.

It was as though they had woken in a new country. Rubbing their eyes, they stared at an unfamiliar aspect of day. The mountain was gone. When they flew up to see what had happened to it, they saw the distant coastline and the mysterious pallor of the sea.

A dandelion clock could not have vanished more peacefully. There was no sign of uprooting; the hare tracks printed their established pattern but on level ground, the brook ran in its same bed, but unhurrying. Wherever the mountain had gone to, it had gone without ill will.

Three nights later it came back, unobserved, and was settled in its old place before day.

Its return was more sobering than its departure had been. It had gone because they had willed it to do so. It came back of its own will. The Court Poet in his Welcoming Ode compared it to bees, cats, pigeons, and other animals with homing instincts, but it was felt that he was using too much poetic licence. There were stories from the Kingdom of Thule of individualistic underground springs which burst into towering activity and deluged everybody with hot water and cinders. Though nothing of that sort had ever happened in Wales, neither had a disappearing and reappearing mountain. But Mynnydd Prescelly embraced its inhabitants as quietly as ever, and sheltered them as reliably from the north wind, and bumblebees hummed up and down its slopes, and harebells grew where they always did. Presently the more light-minded and scientific fairies began to experiment in removal by Faith—not the mountain, of course, but rocks and stones which nobody needed—and when there was a small landslide, nothing would content them but another singing assembly. Again the mountain disappeared—this time in a heavy sea fog; and again it came back, looking, as one might say, unmoved. Before five centuries had passed, moving the mountain had become a regular ceremonial, carried out because the mountain would expect it. By then, research had established what happened. Mynnydd Prescelly rose up in the shape of a cloud, and travelled to Plynlimon. There it descended as a heavy rain, and after it had rained on Plynlimon for the inside of a week, the cloudy Mynnydd Prescelly would travel back, fall as rain, solidify as mountain. And human beings who had noticed its absence from the skyline would say, 'There's Mynnydd Prescelly again, so we'll start harvesting.'

Whether one sleeps in an ashtree cradle or under the thatch of a modest castle, a moist mountainy air is a better soporific than any good conscience. The Elfins of Castle Ash Grove prided themselves on being good sleepers, and had remarkably inoffensive consciences. Music was their preoccupation. They brewed an incomparable mead. They also prided themselves on being good neighbours: if a peasant's cow strayed into their park, they allowed it to graze; if a peasant's horde of children wandered into their valley, they sat in trees and watched them with benevolence. This did not happen very often, however; it was a poor countryside and thinly populated. As the martyred Irishman's teaching spread among the descendants of his hearers, being an Elfin good neighbour became less easy: women pestered them with offerings, tied dirty rags on their trees, and dipped scrofulous babies in their brook; men threw stones at them, aiming in the direction of their voices. But the music and the mead continued, and the link with Plynlimon, and the satisfaction of knowing that they were instrumental in swelling the baby Severn into a real river. For though it rains copiously on Plynlimon, the contributions of their own Mynnydd Prescelly must surely count for something: if they had not all sung so powerfully to confute the Irishman and for the honour of Wales, the mountain—extraordinary thought! —might never have removed.

Perhaps it aided time to slip away so peacefully that all their queens were called Morgan. There was the notorious Morgan le Fay. There was Morgan Philosophy, whose long scholarly amour with Taliesin taught him to be a salmon and acquainted him with Alexander the

Great. There was Morgan Breastknot of Music, whose page, grown old, wept on his death bed because all living memory of her singing would perish with him. The reign of her successor, Morgan Spider (so titled because of her exquisite fine spinning), saw a new manifestation of Castle Ash Grove's devotion to music. Ignoring the traditional Elfin aloofness from mankind, a party of music lovers democratically disguised themselves as mortals and went to Worcester Cathedral, masked and in riding mantles, to hear Thomas Tomkins play on the organ; and later, wearing bonnets and top hats, attended a performance of the Messiah at the Three Choirs' Festival.

By now we are within sight of the twentieth century.

It was a fine autumn evening in 1893. The mountain had just come back from Plynlimon. Morgan Spider and some of her court were strolling in the park, saying how pleasant it was to feel sheltered from the outer world again, when they heard an astonishing assortment of noises—a frantic ting-a-ling, a metallic crash, loud mortal bewailings and cries for help. They moved cautiously towards the cries. Where their valley curved under the slope of a steep hillside they saw a massive young woman in a dark-blue uniform sprawled on the grass, weeping convulsively and draped in what seemed to be a tattered metal cage —and was, in fact, a bicycle.

In order not to alarm her, they made themselves visible, as they had made themselves visible at Worcester and the Three Choirs' Festival in order not to be sat on.

'I'm afraid you're in some trouble,' said Morgan Spider.

'I should think I am in some trouble,' replied the young woman. 'My brake wouldn't hold and my bike's smashed and my knee's cut to the bone. And I'd like to know what's been going on here,' she continued, glaring at them. 'It wasn't like this last week.'

Consulting among themselves, they agreed that this was not the moment in which to explain about the mountain.

The young woman launched into a resentful narrative of a road which went on going uphill, so she knew it must be the wrong one, of the track she had turned into which led to a bog, of other tracks leading nowhere, of exhaustion, desolation, bulls, gnats, distant cottages which turned out to be sheepfolds, birds that got up behind her with a noise like a gun, vipers that threatened her with their stings, and never a sign of life and always uphill. 'And if that wasn't enough—' She broke off and exclaimed, 'Where's my bag?'

A large black bag lay nearby. Morgan Spider's page picked it up and handed it to her.

When she opened it, they all started back in horror at the appalling smell that came out. She pulled up her skirts, rolled down a black stocking, and displayed a bloodied knee. She unstoppered a small bottle. The appalling smell was redoubled. Dame Bronwen fainted. The mortal poured a well-known disinfectant on a wad of cotton wool, laid the wad (with howls) on her knee, and tied on a white bandage very deftly. Looking up, she saw them ministering to Dame Bronwen. 'One of those who can't stand the sight of blood,' she remarked. 'My job wouldn't suit her.'

A mortal who delighted in the sight of blood was not the guest they would have chosen. But hospitality is a sacred duty among Elfins. Trying not to inhale her, they supported the young woman to the castle, sat her down in the parlour, and gave her a glass of mead. There was a rather long silence. Morgan Spider looked out of the window and saw Dame Bronwen approaching, and the page doing his best with the bicycle and the bicycle retaliating. And she looked at the tranquil darkening sky, and then at the massive, reddening young woman, who was twirling her glass.

But hospitality requires more than refilling a glass. Morgan Spider mentioned that the mead was homemade, and the young woman commented that they were quite old-fashioned, weren't they.

'And where do you come from? Is it far away?'

'Nottingum.'

A beatified simper spread over the young woman's face, and she dwelt on the word as though it were a jujube. 'Nottingum,' she repeated, and held out her glass dreamily. 'Born there. Educated there. And look at me now. All my qualifications, and they've sent me to this back-of-beyond district. And that Mrs Jones I saw last week sends a message to say she's taken unexpected and would I come soon as I could. And if I lose her, I suppose they'll blame me. Slave driving, I call it.'

'Where does this Mrs Jones live?' demanded Morgan Spider. The young woman started. She groped in her pocket and handed over a screw of paper. 'It's in Welsh. Even if I could say it, it wouldn't get me there. It's my poor bike I'm worrying about.'

While she wept, Morgan Spider told the page to fetch her muff—for it would be a cold night to fly in.

'Madam, Madam! Your Majesty's surely not going to fly?'

'The woman's in labour. Do you expect me to go in a procession?' She snatched the muff and ran out. They saw her flicker down the valley like a bat. The uppermost thought in every heart was envy.

When Morgan Spider returned, rosy with triumph and night air, she heard singing. As she entered, it broke off. Her whole court was assembled round the District Nurse, who lay on the floor dead drunk, with her right hand clenched on a pair of scissors.

After her departure, they explained, the mortal talked about lockjaw and said she must renew the dressing on her knee. The bandage was peeled off and rerolled with exactitude. The bottle was unstoppered, the wad soaked and reapplied. As before, she howled, but now a great deal louder. Brandishing a pair of scissors, she staggered round the room trying to get at the page in order to cut the grin off his face, tripped over the Keeper of the Archives—a slow mover—and subsided on the floor. There she had lain ever since. All felt she should be removed. None was willing to approach her, in case she might come to. The Keeper of the Archives, with a quotation from Vergil, said that in special difficulties one should turn to tradition. For a great many centuries the mountain had been removing itself unprompted, but he supposed the Removal Song would be as effective as ever. After a few false starts, they remembered the tune. Altering the words so that there should be no misunderstanding, they began singing, and had been singing for an hour and three-quarters:

> 'Nottingum, Nottingum,
> Be thou removed.'

Morgan Spider said they must put more life into it. It was a fine old tune, and would stand up to a little impiety. Joined by their Queen, the singers did better; some almost believed they saw the dark-blue mass rise a few inches from the floor.

Morgan Spider clapped her hands. 'Stop! I see what's wrong. We're

barking up the wrong tree. "Nottingum, Nottingum, Be thou removed"
means nothing to her.'

They objected that the mortal had said 'Nottingum'.

'She said she was born there. Wherever it is, it's just a place.'

One of the younger ladies said, with a giggle, 'Suppose it's working
there?'

'That's no affair of ours. It isn't working here. But if we can't remove
her, we can remove ourselves. So we'll have a quick supper and then fly
to Plynlimon.'

She spoke to be obeyed. On the morrow, glittering in the rays of the
newly risen sun, they descended like a swarm of fireflies on the vast,
green, featherbed expanse of Plynlimon.

When they had recovered from the fatigue of the journey, they found
themselves delighted to be there. Even Elfins are susceptible to the
Zeitgeist. The Zeitgeist of the day was to resort to the Simple Life
—nature, nuts, sleeping out-of-doors, an escape from convention and
formality. Plynlimon afforded exactly that. Doing nothing, they were
never at a loss for something to do. They snared rabbits and roasted
them over a wood fire they had rekindled from the ashes of a fire
abandoned by travelling gipsies. Collecting enough fuel to keep the fire
going was a labour of love, eating rabbit with their fingers was a feat.
When the Keeper of the Archives found a thrown-away iron cauldron in
a ditch, they cooked gipsy stews, flavouring the rabbit with chanterelle
mushrooms and wild garlic, and supping the broth from snail shells. All
these things called for much time and invention and were achievements
—unless they went wrong, when they were things to laugh about. The
more active went for immense walks. Others picked watercress and wild
strawberries or sat talking on large subjects. At night, they admired
the stars. Their feet were usually wet and they were all in perfect
health.

Morgan Spider, but for whom they would not have come to Plynlimon, disclaimed any particular hand in it. It was a mass rising, she said;
she had chanced to speak first, but the thought was in every mind. The
voice of Nature had said, 'Be thou removed', as it spoke to swallows and
cuckoos and ice-cream vendors and nightingales; and the happy migrants obeyed. When the voice of Nature directed, they would fly back to
Castle Ash Grove, and settle down for a comfortable winter, telling

stories and brewing more mead. Every trace of the visitor would have been broomed and aired out of the castle. It had been left in the care of reliable changelings, who had detested Nottingum as only blood relations can.

One thing only slightly troubled her—Dame Bronwen's incapacity to delight in what everyone else found so delightful. At the announcement that they would remove to Plynlimon, Bronwen had welcomed the idea, so impatiently that she wanted to start at once. On their first day there, she was the earliest to be up and about, as excited as a child by the change of air, the change of scene, the prospect of an entirely new way of life. By midday, the bright morning clouded over. Politely admiring, politely enjoying, she remained aloof. Though Morgan Spider had for the time shaken off the responsibilities of a queen, she still felt the obligations of a hostess. It occurred to her that Bronwen was sulking because she felt in some way slighted.

A little favouritism might put this right. Noticing the tufts of wool which brambles and thistles had plucked off passing sheep, she had idly planned to take home the best of them to card and spin during the winter. She invited Dame Bronwen to come woolgathering. Sometimes they wandered together, sometimes apart. The air was perfectly still. There were a great many flies about, which they beat off with bracken whisks. Morgan Spider fell behind to pull some particularly fine tufts from a thorn brake. Beyond the thorn brake, she came on Dame Bronwen, who was standing motionless in a cloud of flies. She whisked her bracken frond. Dame Bronwen started violently; it was as if she had been found out in some atrocious fault.

'A penny for your thoughts, Bronwen.'

It was the wrong thing to say. Dame Bronwen locked up her face, and after a pause remarked on the flies, saying that they were the only drawback to Plynlimon; adding politely that they were only a nuisance on windless days.

They walked on together, Morgan Spider making experimental conversation and getting nothing but a Yes or No for her pains. There was a crooked sloe bush ahead of them, and she said to herself, 'Before we reach the sloe bush I'll get it out of her.' But they were level with the bush before she said, 'Bronwen, what ails you?'

Bronwen said, 'A bad smell.' She pressed a branch of the sloe to her bosom as though its thorns would help her to speak. 'Do you remember the smell that came out of the bottle?'

'And was so appalling that it made you faint? Of course I remember it. But by the time we go back, Castle Ash Grove will have been cleaned and aired. I shall send the page ahead of us to make certain; we won't start till he tells us the smell is gone.'

'It will never be gone.'

Dame Bronwen pressed the branch so hard to her bosom that a sloe burst and its juice spurted out.

'When I fainted it was because of what was shown me. I saw trees blighted and grass burned brown and birds falling out of the sky. I saw the end of our world, Morgan—the end of Elfin. I saw the last fairy dying like a scorched insect.'

She was mad. But she spoke with such intensity it was impossible not to believe her.

(*Kingdoms of Elfin*, 1977)

WINGED CREATURES

WHEN, after many years of blameless widowhood devoted to ornithology, Lady Fidès gave birth to a son, no one in the fairy Kingdom of Bourrasque held it against her. Elfin longevity is counterpoised by Elfin infertility, especially in the upper classes, where any addition to good society is welcomed with delight. Naturally, there was a certain curiosity about the father of Fidès' child, and her intimates begged her to reveal his name so that he, too, could be congratulated on the happy event. With the best will in the world, Fidès could not comply. 'My wretched memory,' she explained. 'Do you know, there was one day last week—of course I can't say which—when I had to rack my brains for three-quarters of an hour before I could remember "chaffinch".'

The baby's features afforded no clue. It resembled other babies in having large eyes, pursed lips, and a quantity of fine fluff on its head. When the fluff fell out, Lady Fidès had it carefully preserved. It was exactly the shade of brown needed for the mantle of a song thrush she was embroidering at the time. As an acknowledgement, she called the baby Grive. Later on, when a growth of smooth black hair replaced the fluff, she tried to establish the child in its proper category by calling it Bouvreuil. But Grive stuck.

In a more stirring court these incidents would have counted for nothing. Even Fidès' lofty project of decorating a pavilion with a complete record of the indigenous birds of France in needlework, featherwork, and wax work would have been taken as something which is always there to be exhibited to visitors on a wet day. Bourrasque preferred small events: not too many of them, and not dilated on. The winds blowing over the high plains of the Massif Central provided all the stir, and more, that anyone in his senses could want.

Indeed, Bourrasque originated in a desire for a quiet life. It was founded by an indignant fairy whose virginity had been attempted by a Cyclops. Just when this happened, and why she should have left the sheltering woodlands of the Margeride for a bare hillside of the Plomb du Cantal, is not known. Apparently, her first intention was to live as a solitary, attended only by a footman and a serving-woman, but this design was frustrated by friends coming to see how she was getting on. Some decided to join her, and a settlement grew up. In course of time, working fairies raised a surrounding wall. A palace accumulated, a kitchen garden was planted, and terraces were set with vines. The vines flourished (it was the epoch of mild European winters); the population grew, and a group of peasants from the northward, disturbed by earthquakes, migrated with their cattle and became feudatories of the Kingdom of Bourrasque. That was its Golden Age. It ended with a total eclipse, which left the sun weak and dispirited, and filled the air with vapours and falling stars, rain and tempests. Late frosts, blight, and mildew attacked the vines. Fog crawled over the harvest before the crops could be gathered, and from within the fog came the roar and rumble of the winds, like the mustering of a hidden army. Bourrasque dwindled into what it afterward remained—a small, tight, provincial court of an unlegendary antiquity, where people talked a great deal about the weather, wore nightcaps, and never went out without first looking at the weather-cock. If it pointed steadfastly to one quarter, they adjusted their errands. If it swung hither and thither like a maniac, they stayed indoors.

It was not really a favourable climate for an ornithologist.

Fairies are celebrated needlewomen, and do a great deal of fancy-work. From her youth up, Fidès had filled her tambour frame with a succession of birds in embroidery: birds on twigs, on nests, pecking fruit, searching white satin snow for crumbs. The subjects were conventional, the colouring fanciful, and everybody said how lifelike. On the day of her husband's death (an excellent husband, greatly her senior) Fidès entered the death chamber for a last look at him. The window had been set open, as is customary after a death; a feather had blown in and lay on the pillow. She picked it up. And in an instant her life had a purpose: she must know about birds.

At first she was almost in despair. There were so many different birds, and she could be sure of so few of them. Robin, blackbird, swallow, magpie, dove, cuckoo by note, the little wren, birds of the poultry yard—no others. The season helped her. It was May, the nestlings had hatched, the parent birds were feeding their young. She watched them flying back and forth, back and forth, discovered that hen blackbirds are not black, that robins nest in holes. When no one was looking, she took to her wings like any working fairy and hovered indecorously to count the fledglings and see how the nests were lined. As summer advanced she explored the countryside, and saw a flock of goldfinches take possession of a thistle patch. She picked up every feather she saw, carried it back, compared it with others, sometimes identified it. The feather on her husband's pillow, the first of her collection, was the breast feather of a dove.

An eccentricity made a regular thing of ceases to provoke remark. Public opinion deplored the freckles on Fidès' nose, but accepted them—together with her solitary rambles, her unpunctuality, and her growing inattention to what was going on around her—as a consequence of her widowed state. Her brother-in-law, her only relative at Court, sometimes urged her to wear gloves, but otherwise respected her sorrow, which did her, and his family, great credit.

As time went on, and the freckles reappeared every summer and the feathers accumulated to such an extent that she had to have an attic made over to hold them, he lapsed from respecting her sorrow to admiring her fidelity—which was just as creditable but less acutely so. When she made him an uncle he was slightly taken aback. But it was a nice peaceful baby, and not the first to be born to a bar sinister—which in some Courts, notably Elfhame in Scotland, is a positive advantage. With a little revision Fidès was still creditable: to have remembered with so much attachment the comfort of matrimony through so long and disconsolate a widowhood was undeniably to her credit, and his late brother would have taken it as a compliment.

But as a persuasion to Fidès to stay quietly indoors the baby was totally ineffective. She was no sooner out of childbed than she was out-of-doors, rambling over the countryside with the baby under her arm. 'Look, baby. That's a whinchat. Whinchat. Whinchat.' A little jerk to enforce the information. Or 'Listen, baby. That's a raven. "*Noirâtre*," he says. "*Noirâtre*."' The child's vague stare would wander in the direction of her hand. He was a gentle, solemn baby; she was sure he took it all in and that his first word would be a chirp. If her friends questioned her behaviour—Wouldn't the child be overexcited? Wouldn't it be happier with a rattle?—she vehemently asserted that she meant Grive to have his birthright. 'I grew up without a bird in my life, as if there were nothing in the world but fairies and mortals. I wasn't allowed to fly—flying was vulgar—and to this day I fly abominably. Birds were things to stitch, or things to eat. Larks were things in a pie. But birds are our nearest relatives. They are the nearest things to ourselves. And far more beautiful, and far more interesting. Don't you see?'

They saw poor Fidès unhinged by the shock of having a baby that couldn't be accounted for, and turned the subject.

The working fairies, chattering like swifts as they flew about their duties, were more downright. 'Taking the child out in all weathers like any gipsy! Asking Rudel if he'll give it flying lessons! Gentry ought to know their place.'

Only Gobelet spoke up for his mistress, saying that weather never did a child any harm. Gobelet spoke from experience. He was a changeling, and had lived in the mortal world till he was seven, when Fidès' husband saw him sucking a cow, took a fancy to his roly-poly charm, and had him stolen, giving him to Fidès for St Valentine's Day. Gobelet grew up short-legged and stocky, and inexpugnably mortal. No one particularly liked him. To prove satisfactory a changeling must be stolen in infancy. Gobelet's seven years as a labourer's child encrusted him, like dirt in the crevices of an artichoke. He ate with his fingers. When he had finished a boiled egg he drove his spoon through the shell. If he saw a single magpie, he crossed himself; if anyone gave him a penny he spat on it for luck; he killed slow-worms. He was afraid of Fidès because he knew he was repulsive to her. Yet once he made her a most exquisite present. She had gone off on one of her rambles, and he had been sent after her with a message. He found her on the heath, motionless, and staring at the ground with an expression of dismay. She was staring at the body of a dead crow, already maggoty. Forgetting the message, he picked it up and said it must be buried in an anthill. She had not expected him to show such feeling, and followed him while he searched for an anthill large enough for his purpose. When it was found he scrabbled a hole and sank the crow in it. What the maggots had begun, he said, the ants would finish. Ants were good workmen. Three months later he brought her the crow's skeleton, wrapped in a burdock leaf. Every minutest bone was in place, and she had never seen a bird's skeleton before. In her rapture she forgot to thank him, and he went away thinking she was displeased.

Grive's first coherent memory was of a northeasterly squall; a clap of thunder, darkened air, and hailstones bouncing off the ground. He was in his mother's arms. She was attending to something overhead. There was a rift of brilliant March-blue sky, and small cross-shaped birds were playing there, diving in and out of the cloud, circling round each other, gathering and dispersing and gathering again, and singing in shrill silken voices. The booming wind came between him and the music. But it persisted; whenever the wind hushed, he heard it again, the same dizzying net of sound. He struggled out of his mother's arms, spread his wings, felt the air beneath them, and flew towards the larks. She watched him, breathless with triumph, till a gust of wind caught him and dashed him to the ground. She was so sure he was dead that she did not stir, till she heard him whimper. Hugging him, small and plump, to her breast, she waited for him to die. He stiffened, his face contorted, he drew a sharp breath, and burst into a bellow of fury. She had never heard him cry like that before.

He had come back to her a stranger. Though she still hugged him, the warmth of recognition had gone out of her breast. The angry red-faced stranger buffeting her with small soft fists was just another Elfin: he had never been, he could never become, a bird. She must put the idea out of her head, as when, deceived by candlelight, she stitched a wrong-coloured thread into her embroidery and in the morning had to unpick it.

It had slipped her memory who had fathered him, but she could be sure of the rest. An Elfin called Grive, he would grow up clever and sensible, scorning and indulging her, like her kind parents, her good kind husband, her brother-in-law. He would know she was crazy and make allowances for her; he might even feel a kind of love for her. She could never feel love for him. Love was what she felt for birds—a free gift, unrequired, unrequited, invulnerable.

The angry stranger wriggled out of her arms. She watched him making his way on hands and knees over the wet turf. Even when he paused to bite a daisy, there was nothing to remind her that she had half-believed he might become a bird. Presently, she could say, quite calmly, quite sensibly, 'Come, Grive! It's time I took you back.'

She told no one of this. She wanted to forget it. She had her hair dressed differently and led an indoor life, playing bilboquet and distilling a perfume from gorse blossoms. By the time the cuckoo had changed its interval, she was walking on the heath. But she walked alone, leaving Grive in the care of Gobelet—an uncouth companion, but wingless.

Gobelet pitied the pretty child who had suddenly fallen out of favour. He cut him a shepherd's pipe of elder wood, taught him to plait rushes, carved him a ship which floated in a footbath. By whisking up the water he raised a stormy ocean; the ship tossed and heeled, and its crew of silver buttons fell off and were drowned. On moonlight nights he threw fox and rabbit shadows on the wall. The fox moved stealthily towards the rabbit, snapping its jaws, winking horribly with its narrow gleaming eye; the rabbit ran this way and that, waving its long ears. As the right-hand fox pursued the left-hand rabbit, Grive screamed with the excitement of the chase, and Gobelet said to himself, 'I'll make a man of him yet.'

When these diversions were outgrown, they invented an interminable saga in which they were the two last people left alive in a world of giants, dragons, and talking animals. Day after day they ran new perils, escaped by stratagems only to face worse dangers, survived with just enough strength for the next day's instalment. Sorting and pairing feathers for Fidès for hours on end, they prompted each other to new adventures in their world of fantasy.

But the real world was gaining on them. Gobelet had grown stout. He walked with a limp, and the east wind gave him rheumatism.

The measure of our mortal days is more or less threescore and ten. The lover cries out for a moment to be eternal, the astronomer would like to see a comet over again, but he knows this is foolish, as the lover knows his mistress will outlive her lustrous eyes and die round about the time he does. Our years, long or short, are told on the same plain-faced dial. But by the discrepancy between Elfin and mortal longevity, the portion of time which made Grive an adolescent made Gobelet an aging man. Of the two, Gobelet was the less concerned. He had kept some shreds of his mortal wits about him and felt that, taking one thing with another, when the time came he would be well rid of himself. Grive lived in a flutter of disbelief, compunction, and apprehension, and plucked out each of Gobelet's white hairs as soon as it appeared. Elfins feel a particular reprobation of demonstrable old age. Many of them go into retirement rather than affront society with the spectacle of their decay. As for changelings, when they grow old they are got rid of. Grive, being measured for a new suit, thought that before he had worn it out Gobelet would be gone, discarded like a cracked pitcher, left to beg his way through the world and die in a ditch with the crows standing round like mourners, waiting to peck out his eyes.

Grive was being measured for a new suit because the time had come when he must attend the Queen as one of her pages. It was his first step up in the world, and having determined he would not enjoy it he found himself enjoying it a great deal. At the end of his first spell of duty he returned to the family apartment, full of what he would tell Gobelet. Gobelet was gone. As furious as a child, Grive accused Fidès of cruelty, treachery, ingratitude. 'He was the only friend I had. I shall find him and bring him back. Which way did he go?'

Fidès put down the blue tit she was feathering. 'Which way did he go? I really can't say. He must have gone somewhere. Perhaps they know in the kitchen, for I said he must have a good meal before he started. As it is, I kept him long after he should have been got rid of, because I knew you had been fond of him. But one can't keep changelings forever. Anyhow, they don't expect to be kept. Be reasonable, dear. And don't shout.' She took up the blue tit and added another feather.

'How it must distress you to think of getting rid of the Queen,' he said suavely. It was as if for the first time in his life he had shot with a loaded gun.

Queen Alionde had felt no call to go into retirement. She brandished her old age and insisted on having it acknowledged. No one knew how old she was. There had been confidential bowerwomen, Chancellors sworn to secrecy who knew, but they were long since dead. Her faculties remained in her like rats in a ruin. She never slept. She spoke the language of a forgotten epoch, mingling extreme salacity with lofty euphemisms and punctilios of grammar. She was long past being comical, and smelled like bad haddock. Some said she was phosphorescent in the dark. She found life highly entertaining.

When the pestilence broke out among the peasantry, she insisted on having the latest news of it: which villages it had reached, how many had died, how long it took them. She kept a tally of deaths, comparing it with the figures of other pestilences, calculating if this one would beat them, and how soon it would reach Borrasque. Working fairies were sent out to look for any signs of murrain among cattle. They reported a great influx of kites. Her diamonds flashed as she clapped her hands at the news. And rats? she asked. Few rats, if any, they said. The reflection of her earrings flitted about the room like butterflies as she nodded in satisfaction. Rats are wise animals, they know when to move out; they are not immune to mortal diseases as fairies are. If the pestilence came to the very gates of Bourrasque, if the dying, frantic with pain, leaped over the palace wall, if the dead had to be raked into heaps under their noses, no fairy would be a penny the worse. Her court was glad to think this was so but wished there could be a change of subject.

Exact to the day she foretold it, the pestilence reached Bourrasque. Her office-holders had to wrench compliments on her accuracy out of their unenthusiastic bosoms, and a congratulatory banquet was organised, with loyal addresses and the young people dancing jigs and gavottes. Fires blazed on the hearths, there were candles everywhere, and more food than could be eaten. The elder ladies, sitting well away from their Queen's eye, began to knit shawls for the peasantry. By the time the shawls were finished, they were thankful to wrap them round their own shoulders.

Bourrasque, complying with the course of history, had come to depend on its serfs for common necessities. The pestilence did not enter the castle; it laid siege to it. Fewer carcasses were brought to the larderer's wicket, less dairy stuff, no eggs. The great meal chest was not replenished. Fuel dues were not paid. There was no dearth in the land; pigs and cattle, goats and poultry, could be seen scampering over the fields, breaking down fences, trampling the reaped harvest—all of them plump and in prime condition for Martinmas. But the men who herded and slaughtered, the women who milked the cows and thumped in the churns, were too few and too desperate to provide for any but themselves. Others providing for themselves were the working fairies, who made forays beyond the walls, brought back a goose, a brace of rabbits, with luck an eel from under the mud of a cow pond. They cooked and ate in secret, charitably sparing a little goose fat to flavour the cabbage shared among their betters.

On New Year's morning the Queen was served with a stoup of claret and a boiled egg. The egg was bad. She ate it and called a Council. Hearing that they had hoped to spare her the worst, she questioned them with lively interest about their deprivations, and commanded that Bourrasque should be vacated on the morrow. She had not lived so long in order to die of starvation. The whole court must accompany her; she could not descend on her great-great-great-nephew in Berry without a rag of retinue. They would start an hour after sunrise.

Somehow or other, it was managed. There was no planning, no consultation, no bewailing. They worked like plunderers. The first intention had been to take what was precious, like jewellery, or indispensable, like blankets. This was followed by a passion to leave nothing behind. Tusks, antlers, a rhinoceros horn, some rusty swords, two voiceless bugles, a gong, and an effigy of Charlemagne were rescued from the butler's pantry. The east pavilion was stripped of its decorations. They tore down velvet hangings to wrap round old saucepans. Cushions and dirty napkins were rammed into a deed chest, and lidded with astrological charts. By dawn, the wagons stood loaded in the forecourt.

A few flakes of snow were falling.

The courtiers had gathered at the foot of the main staircase. Many of them had put on nightcaps for the journey. Alionde was brought down, baled in furs, and carried to her litter. Behind its closed screens she could be heard talking and giving orders, like a parrot in its cage. A hubbub of last-minute voices broke out—assurances of what had been done, reassurances that nothing had been overlooked. Grive heard his mother's voice among them: 'I don't think I've forgotten anything. Perhaps I'd better have one last look.' She brushed past him, stared up the wide staircase, heard herself being told to hurry, turned back, and was gone with the rest. He stood at the window, watching the cavalcade lumber up the hillside, with the piper going ahead and playing a jaunty farewell. A gust of wind swept the noise out of earshot. Nothing was left except the complaining of the weathercock.

He was too famished to know whether he had been left behind or had stayed. Like his throstle name-giver, *Turdus philomelos*, he was shy and a dainty feeder; rather than jostle for a bacon-rind or a bit of turnip, he let himself be elbowed away. Now, though he knew that every hole and corner had been ransacked for provision for the journey, he made a desultory tour of inspection. A smell of sour grease hung about the kitchen quarters. He sickened at it, and went into the cold pleasure-garden, where he ate a little snow. He returned to the saloon which had been so crowded with departures, listened to the weathercock, noticed the direction of the snowflakes, and lay down to die.

Dying was a new experience. It was part of it that he should be sorting feathers, feathers from long-dead birds, and heavy because of that. A wind along the floor blew him away from the feathers. It was part of dying that a dragon came in and curled up on his feet. It seemed kindly intentioned, but being cold-blooded it could not drive away the chill of death. It was also part of dying that Gobelet was rocking him in his arms. Once, he found Gobelet dribbling milk between his jaws. The milk was warm and sent him to sleep. When he woke he could stretch himself and open his eyes. There was Gobelet's hand, tickling his nose with a raisin. So they were both dead.

Even when Grive was on the mend he remained light-headed. Starvation had capsized his wits. If he were left to sleep too long he began to twitch and struggle; wakened, he would stare round him and utter the same cry: 'I had that dreadful dream again. I dreamed we were alive.'

Gobelet was not distressed at being alive; on the contrary, it seemed to him that his survival did him credit. It had been against considerable odds. It was the lot of changelings to be dismissed on growing old. He had seen it happen to others and taken it for granted; he did so when it was his turn to be packed off to find a death in a world that had no place for him. But he had been a poor man's child, and the remembrance of how to steal, cajole, and make himself useful came to his aid. He was too old for cajolery to apply, but he flattered, and by never staying long in one place he stole undetected. He had forgotten the name of his birthplace till he heard it spoken by a stranger at the inn. Then everything flashed back on him: the forked pear tree, the fern growing beside the wellhead, his mother breaking a pitcher, the faggot thrust into the bread oven. Knowing what name to ask for, he soon found his way there. Everyone he had known was dead or gone, but the breed of sheep was the same. Here he hired himself as a farmhand and for a couple of years lived honest, till the sudden childhood memory of a gentleman on a horse who drew rein and asked how old he was so unsettled him that he knew he must have another look at Bourrasque. By then the pestilence had reached the neighbourhood. He hoped to evade it, but it struck him down on the third day of his journey. Shivering and burning, he sweated it out in a dry ditch, listening to the death-owl screeching to the moon. In spite of the owl, he recovered, laid dock-leaf poultices on his sores, and trudged on through the shortening days. He knew he was nearing Bourrasque when he met an old acquaintance, Grimbaud, one of the working fairies, who was setting a snare. From him he heard how the peasants were dying and the palace starving. He inquired after Lady Fidès. Grimbaud tapped his forehead with two fingers. He could say nothing of Grive.

He rose in the air and was gone, lost in the winter dusk.

'Starving, are you?' Gobelet shouted after him. 'No worse than I. And you can whisk off on your wings. No limping on a stiff knee for you.' He felt a sudden consuming hatred for the whole fairy race. He took a couple of steps, caught his foot in the snare, and fell, wrenching his knee. It was his good knee. He crawled away on all fours, and made a bracken hut, where he spent a miserable week nursing his knee, changing and unchanging his mind, and listening to the kites mewing in the fog. In the end he decided to go forward. There was nothing to be got by it, but not to finish his wasteful journey would be worse waste. To look at Bourrasque and turn away would clear the score.

The fog lifted and there it was—larger than he remembered, and darker. The gates stood open. A long procession was winding up the hillside, the piper going ahead. The Queen must be dead at last! It was odd that so many wagons, loaded with so much baggage, should be part of the funeral train. But no doubt, freed from her tyranny, the court would bury her and go on to being better fed elsewhere. He watched the procession out of sight, stared at the smokeless chimneys, and renounced Bourrasque, which he had come such a long journey to renounce. As he was turning away, it occurred to him that he owed himself a keepsake, and that one of Lady Fidès' birds would do. He limped on, and entered the palace by the familiar gully where the waste water flowed away. The east pavilion was stripped bare. He remembered other things he had admired and went in search of them. Some furniture remained in the emptied rooms—gaunt beds with no hangings, cabinets with doors hanging open. Meeting his reflection in a mirror, he started back as if it accused him of trespassing.

He was hurrying away when he saw Grive lying in a corner.

There was time to remember all this during Grive's convalescence, when the excitement of winning him back to life was over and the triumphs of stealing provisions from the homes of the dead had dulled into routine. He compared Grive's lot with his own: no one had tended him in his ditch, and never for a moment had he supposed it better to be dead than alive. What succour would a dying Grive have got from a dead Gobelet? The comparison was sharpened because the living Gobelet was afraid. The survivors outside the walls railed against the palace people, who had done nothing for them, feasted while they starved, danced while they were dying, deserted them. If this angry remnant invaded the palace—and certainly it would—Grive and he would be done for.

They got away as smoothly as they did in their serial story. It was a clear frosty night, a following wind helped them uphill, and in the morning they took their last look at Bourrasque, where the villagers, small and busy as ants, were dragging corpses to the plague pit.

With that morning Gobelet began the happiest epoch of his life. As nearly as possible, he became a fairy. He lost all sense of virtue and responsibility and lived by pleasures—pell-mell pleasures: a doubled rainbow, roasting a hedgehog. And, as if he shared the hardiness and resilience of those who live for pleasure, he was immune to cold or fatigue, and felt like a man half his age. Grive had made an instant and unashamed recovery. Most of the time he was high overhead, circling while Gobelet walked, sailing on the wind, flying into clouds and reappearing far above them. From time to time he dived down to report what he had seen. There was a morass ahead, so Gobelet must bear to the left. Another storm was coming up, but if Gobelet hurried he would reach a wood in time to take shelter. He had seen a likely farm where Gobelet could beg a meal. He had seen a celandine.

A day later there were a thousand celandines. The swallows would not be long behind them, remarked Gobelet: swallows resort to celandines to clear their eyesight after spending the winter sunk in ponds; they plunge in, all together, and lie under the mud. All together, they emerge. What proves it is that you never see a swallow till the celandines are in bloom. On the contrary, Grive said, swallows fly south and spend the winter in some warmer climate where they have plenty of flies to prey on. This had been one of Lady Fidès' crazy ideas: no one at Bourrasque credited it, for why should birds fly to a foreign shore and encounter such dangers and hardships on the way when they could winter comfortably in a pond?

Grive and Gobelet were still disputing this when the swallows came back, twirling the net of their shadows over the grass. By then it was hot enough to enjoy shade. They moved away from the uplands, and lived in wooded country, listening to nightingales. Grive had never heard a nightingale. It was like the celandines—the first single nightingale, so near that he saw its eye reflecting the moonlight, and the next day thousands, chorus rivalling chorus; for they sang in bands and, contrary to the poets, by day as well as by night. Fairies, he said, were far inferior to birds. They have no song; nothing comes out of them but words and a few contrived strains of music from professional singers. Birds surpass them in flight, in song, in plumage. They build nests; they rear large families. No fairy drummer could match a woodpecker, no fairy militia manoeuvre like a flock of lapwings, no fairy comedian mimic like a starling.

He spoke with such ardour that it would not do to contradict him, though privately Gobelet thought that if Grive could not sing like a nightingale he could praise as fluently and with more invention. Grive was as much in love with birds as ever Lady Fidès had been, but without the frenzy which made her throw the lark pie out of the window—which was fortunate, as there were many days when the choice of a meal lay between pignuts and an unwary quail spatchcocked. He left provisioning to Gobelet; whether it was begged, stolen, caught, Grive found everything delicious, and sauced by eating it with his fingers. In other respects he was master. It was part of Gobelet's happiness that this was so.

All this time they were moving eastward. It was in the Haute-Loire that Grive suddenly became aware of bats. As the narrow valley —scarcely wider than the river with its bankside alders—brimmed with dusk, bats were everywhere, flying so fast and so erratically that it was hard to say whether there were innumerable bats or the same bats in a dozen places at once. As birds surpass fairies, he said, bats surpass birds.

They were the magicians of flight. With a flick, they could turn at any angle, dart zigzag above the stream, flicker in and out of the trees, be here, be gone, never hesitate, never collide. They were flight itself. Trying to fly among them he was as clumsy as a goose. They did not trouble to scatter before him, they were already gone.

The valley was cold at night, and stones fell out of the hillside. It seemed to Gobelet that wherever he went a fox was watching him. If it had not been for Grive's delight in the bats, he would have been glad to move on. Instead, he set himself to catch a bat. He had seen it done in his childhood; it was not difficult. He took the bat to Grive. Daylight had meekened it. It let itself be examined, its oiled-silk wings drawn out, its hooked claws scrutinised, its minute weight poised in the hand. It was, said Grive, exactly like Queen Alionde—the same crumpled teats, the same pert face. But verminous, said Gobelet loyally. Grive said that if fairies did not wash they would be verminous; he had read in a book that the fairies of Ireland are renowned for the lice in their long hair.

He looked more closely at the bat, then threw it away. It staggered and vanished under a bush. As though a spell had snapped, he said that they must start at once.

He flew ahead, shielding his eyes from the sun to see more clearly. Circling to allow time for Gobelet to catch up, he felt an impatient pity for the old man scrambling up hillsides, gaining a ridge only to see another ridge before him, obstinate as a beetle, and as slow. Gobelet thought he was making fine speed; they had never travelled so fast since the wind blew them uphill on their first morning. It was not till they sat together on the summit of the last ridge that Grive relaxed and became conversational. They sat above a heat haze. Beneath and far away was the glimmer of a wide river. He heard Grive's wings stir as if he were about to launch himself towards it, but instead he rolled over on the turf and said, 'Tonight we will sup on olives.' And he told Gobelet that the river was the Rhône, wide and turbulent, but crossed by a bridge built by pigeons. All they had to do now was to follow it, and then bear eastward. 'Where to?' asked Gobelet. 'To the sea.' All Gobelet's happiness in being mastered (it had been a little jolted by that abrupt departure from the bat valley) flowed back. More than ever before he acknowledged the power and charm of a superior mind.

Later on, when they were walking over the great bridge of Saint-

Esprit, he remembered Grive's statement. It seemed to his common-sense thinking that not even eagles, let alone pigeons, could have carried those huge stones and bedded them so firmly in the bellowing currents. He had to bellow himself to express his doubts. Grive repeated that pigeons had done it; they were the architects and overseers, though for the heavier work they might have employed mortals.

For the work of provisioning their journey he still employed Gobelet. They were now among Provençal speakers, but the beggar's tune is the same in all languages, theft is speechless, and bargaining can be conducted by signs and grimaces. Gobelet managed pretty well. One evening he begged from a handsome bona roba (light women were always propitious), who laughed at his gibberish, put money in his hand, ogled Grive, and pointed to an inn. They sat down under an awning, the innkeeper brought bread and olives and poured wine into heavy tumblers. Grive had just begun to drink when he leaped up with a scream, dropped the tumbler, and began frantically defending himself with his hands. A sphinx moth had flown in to his face and was fluttering about him. The innkeeper came up with a napkin, smacked the moth to the ground, and trod on it. On second thought, he made the sign of the cross over Grive.

Gobelet was ashamed at this exhibition of terror. Grive, being a fairy, was not. Trying to better things, Gobelet said it was an alarmingly large moth—as big as a bat. Had Grive thought it was a bat?

'An omen!' gasped Grive, as soon as he could unclench his teeth. 'An omen!'

That night they slept under a pine tree. The moth hunted Gobelet from dream to dream; the stir of the tree in the dawn wind was like the beating of enormous black wings. He sat up and rubbed his eyes. Grive was sleeping like a child, and woke in calm high spirits. After his usual morning flight, when he soared and circled getting his direction, they continued their journey. Of all the regions they had travelled through, this was the pleasantest, because it was the most sweet-smelling. Even in the heat of the day (and it was extremely hot, being late August) they were refreshed by wafts of scent: thyme, wild lavender and marjoram, bay and juniper. There was no need to beg or steal; figs, olives, and walnuts were theirs for the picking. Here and there they saw cities, but they skirted them. Here and there mountains rose sharply from the plain, but there was no need to climb them; they appeared, threatened, and were left behind. The only obstacle they met in these happy days was a fierce torrent, too deep to ford till they came to a pebble reach, where it spread into a dozen channels. It was here that Grive had his adventure with the doves. They were abbatial doves, belonging to a house of monks who lived retired from the world with the noise of the torrent always in their ears. Grive saw the doves sitting demurely on the platforms of their dovecote. He made a quick twirling flight to entertain them, and as he alighted waved his hand towards them. They came tumbling out of their apertures and settled on his raised arm. He stood for a while talking to them, then shook them off. As if they were attached to him by some elastic tether, they flew back and settled again. He cast them off, they returned. He walked on, they rode on him. He flew and they flew after him, and settled on him when he returned to earth. 'Make yourself invisible,' said Gobelet. 'That will fox them.' He did so. The doves stayed where they were, placidly roo-cooing. Gobelet clapped his hands, Grive pranced and rolled on the ground; nothing dislodged them, till a bell rang and a monk came out shaking grain in a measure. They looked startled, and flew back to be fed.

Grive was pleased but unastonished. It was natural, he said; a matter of affinity. The doves felt his affection flow towards them and had responded. He tried the experiment again, with plovers, with fieldfares. Sometimes it worked, sometimes it did not. Once he fetched down a kestrel from the height of its tower. It landed on him, screaming with excitement, and drew blood with its talons. Flock after flock of birds streamed overhead, flying high up; but he had no power over these, they were migrants bent on their journey. One morning he came down from his prospecting flight, having caught sight of the sea, lying beyond a territory of marsh and glittering waterways. Travelling east of south they skirted another city, another mountain. There was a change in the quality of the light, and large birds, flying with effortless ease and not going anywhere in particular, swooped over the landscape; and were seagulls.

'When we get to the sea, what shall we do then?'

Gobelet hoped the answer would speak of repose, of sitting and looking around them, as they had done in the spring.

'Find a ship going to Africa. And that reminds me, Gobelet, we must have money for the passage.' He snuffed the air. 'That's the sea. Do you smell it? That's the sea.' Gobelet smelled only dust and oleanders and a dead lizard. But he had an uninstructed nose; he had read no books to tell him what the sea smelled like.

Two days later he felt he had never smelled anything but the sea, nor would ever smell anything else, and that the smell of the sea was exactly paralleled by the melancholy squawking cry of the seagulls. He sat on a bollard and rubbed his knee. It pained him as much as it did when he was turned out of Bourrasque. Grive had flown so fast that morning, and paused so impatiently, that he had had to run to keep up with him. The port town was noisy, crowded, and lavish, and ended suddenly in the mournfulness of the quays and the towering array of ship beside ship. In all his inland life Gobelet had never seen anything so intimidating. Their hulls were dark and sodden, their slackened sails hung gawkily, they sidled and shifted with the stir of the water. Black and shabby, they were like a row of dead crows dangling from a farmer's gibbet. At the back of his mind was another comparison: the degraded blackness of the sphinx moth after the innkeeper had smacked it down and trodden on it. In one of these he must be imprisoned and carried to Africa, where there would be black men, and elephants. Yet it depended on him whether they went or no, for he must steal for their passage money. A cold and stealthy sense of power ran through him. And a moment later he saw Grive coming towards him and knew he had no power at all. Grive had found a ship which was sailing to Africa tomorrow at midday. He talked to her captain; everything was arranged. Presently they would take a stroll through the town, prospecting likely places for Gobelet's thieving. But first Gobelet must come and admire the ship. She was a magnificent ship, the swiftest vessel on the Inland Sea, and for that reason she was called the Sea-Swallow.

'The Sea-Swallow, Gobelet. You and your ponds!'

He walked Gobelet along the quays with an arm round his neck. A swirl of gulls flew up from a heap of fish guts; he held out his other arm and they settled on it, contesting for foothold. He waved them off and they came back again and settled, as determinedly as the doves had done, but not so peaceably as the doves. They squabbled, edged each other away, fell off and clawed their way back. The Sea-Swallow was at the end of the line. The crew was already making ready for departure, coiling ropes, clearing the decks, experimentally raising the tarred sails. With one arm still around Gobelet and the other stretched out under its load of gulls, Grive stood questioning the captain with the arrogant suavity of one bred to court life. With the expression of someone quelled against his reason, the captain answered him with glum civility, and stared at Gobelet. Asserting himself, he said that anyone happening to die during the voyage must not look for Christian burial. He would be dropped in the sea, for no sailors would tolerate a corpse on board; it was certain to bring ill luck. Of course, said Grive. What could be more trouble-saving?

He shook off the seagulls, and they went for a stroll through the town. It wasn't promising. The wares were mostly cheap and gaudy, sailor's stuff, and the vendors were beady-eyed and alert. Grive continued to say that a gold chain with detachable links would be the most convenient and practical theft. A begging friar stood at a corner, and a well-dressed woman coming out of church paused, opened her purse, and dropped a gold coin into his tray. Grive vanished, and a moment later the coin vanished too. Gobelet felt himself nudged into a side street, where Grive rematerialised.

They had supper at an inn, eating grandly in an upper room, whence they could watch the shipmasts sidling and the gulls floating in the sky. The wine was strong, and Grive became talkative and slightly drunk. Gobelet forgot his fatigue and disillusionment in the pleasure of listening to Grive's conversation. Much of it was over his head, but he felt he would never forget it, and by thinking it over would understand it later on. The noise of the port died down, voices and footsteps thinned away; the sighing and creaking of the ships took over. They found a garden on the outskirts—garden or little park, it was too dark to tell—and slept there.

The next morning, all that remained was to acquire the gold chain with detachable links. Grive had displayed such natural talents for theft that Gobelet suggested they should go together. But he was sent off by himself; Grive had a headache and wanted to sit quietly under the trees.

The gold chain was so clear in Gobelet's mind that he felt sure of finding it. It would be in one of the side streets, a shop below street level with steps down into it, the shopkeeper an old man. When he had located the chain, he would walk in and ask to be shown some rings.

None would quite do, so the shopkeeper would go off to find others. With the chain in his pocket, he would consider, say he would come again, and be gone—walking slowly, for haste looks suspicious. In one of the side streets there was just such a shop, and looking through the lattice he saw gold buttons that would serve as well or better. But the chain was so impressed on his mind that he wandered on, and when he began to grow anxious and went back for the buttons he could not find the side street. Blinded with anxiety, he hurried up and down, was caught in a street market, collided with buyers and sellers. A market-woman whose basket of pears he knocked over ran after him demanding to be paid for them. He dived into the crowd, saw a church before him, rushed in, and fell panting on his knees. Looking up, he saw the very chain before him, dangling within reach from the wrist of a statue.

A ceremony was just over, the congregation was leaving, but some still dawdled, and a beadle was going about with a broom, sweeping officiously round Gobelet's heels. There hung the chain, with everything hanging on it. There he knelt, with every minute banging in his heart. When at last he was alone, he found that the chain was fastened to the statue; he had to wrench it off. He burst through the knot of women gossiping round the holy-water stoup, and ran. The usual misfortune of strangers befell him; he was lost. Sweat poured down his face, his breathing sawed his lungs. When he emerged on the quay, it was at the farther end from the Sea-Swallow. He had no breath to shout with, no strength to run with. His legs ran, not he.

Grive was standing on the quay. The Sea-Swallow had hoisted anchor and was leaving the port. A rope ladder had been pulled up, the gap of water between her and the quayside was widening. Grive shouted to the captain to wait. The captain spat ceremonially, and the crew guffawed.

Grive leaped into the air. As the sailors scrambled to catch him and pull him on board he spread his wings and vanished. A throng of screaming gulls followed him as he flew up to the crow's nest, and more and more flocked round and settled, and more and more came flying and packed round those who had settled, all screaming, squalling, lamenting, pecking each other, pecking at him. Blood ran through their breast feathers, their beaks were red with blood. The ship was free of the port, her mainsails were hoisted and shook in the wind. The exploding canvas could not be heard, nor the shouts of the sailors, nor the captain's speaking trumpet. The ship moved silent as a ghost under her crown of beating wings and incessant furious voices. She caught the land breeze, staggered under it, heeled over, and recovered herself. The people who stood on the quay watching this unusual departure saw the gulls slip in a mass from the crow's nest and fly down to the water's face. There they gathered as if on a raft. Their raft was sucked into the ship's wake and they dispersed. The onlookers saw the old man who had stood a stranger among them pull something bright from his pocket, drop it into the dirty clucking water, and turn weeping away.

(*Kingdoms of Elfin*, 1977)

THE DUKE OF ORKNEY'S LEONARDO

THE child, a boy, was born with a caul. Such children, said the midwife, never drown. Lady Ulpha was cold to the midwife's assurances; the same end, she said, could be reached by never going near water. She was equally indifferent to the midwife's statement that children born with a caul keep an unblemished complexion to their dying day. Lady Ulpha had long prided herself on her unblemished decorum. The violent act of giving birth, the ignominy of howling and squirming in labour and being encouraged by a vulgar person to let herself go, had affronted her. Seeing that encouragements were unwelcome, the midwife did not mention that cauls are so potent against drowning that mortals making a sea voyage will pay a great price for one. The child was washed and laid in the cradle, and a nurse given charge of it. As for the caul, by some mysterious negotiation it got to Glasgow. There it was bought by the captain of a whaler and subsequently lost at sea.

Sir Huon and Lady Ulpha were fairies with a great deal of pedigree, pride to match it, and small means for its upkeep. On the ground that it does not do to make oneself cheap, they seldom appeared at the Court of Rings, a modest Elfin kingdom in Galloway, preferring to live on their own estate, small and boggy, and make a merit of it. When the boy was of an age to be launched into the world, it would be different.

He was still spoken of as The Boy, because he had been named after so many possible legacy leavers that no one could fix a name on him, except his nurse, who called him Bonny—a vulgar dialect term which would get him nowhere. He was the most beautiful child in the world, she said, and would grow into the handsomest elfin in all Scotland.

Looking at her child more attentively, Lady Ulpha decided that though he was now an expense, he might become an asset.

His first recollection of his mother was of being lifted onto her high bed to have his nose pinched into a better shape, his ears flattened to the side of his head, and his eyebrows oiled. As time went on, other measures were imposed. He had to wear a bobbing straw hat to shield him from getting freckles, and was forbidden to hug his pet lamb in case he caught ticks. In winter a woollen veil was tied over his face. This was worse than the hat, for it blinded him to his finer pleasures: the snow crystal melted in his hand, the wind blew the feathers away before he had properly admired them. Baffled by the woollen grating over his eyes, he came indoors, where sight was no pleasure. The veil was pulled off and he was set to study an ungainly alphabet straddling across a dirty page.

It was in summer that he got a name of his own. A trout stream ran through the estate, and as he couldn't be drowned he was allowed to play in it, provided he kept his hat on. Sir Glamie, Chancellor of the Court of Rings and an ardent fly-fisher, had permission from Sir Huon—who knew he would otherwise poach—to fish there on Wednesdays, provided he threw back every alternate fish. Having scrupulously thrown back a small trout, Sir Glamie approached a pool where he knew there was a large one. A ripple travelled towards him, and another. He saw a straw hat, and advanced on the poacher. Under the hat was a naked boy, whose limbs trailed in the pool. The boy was not even poaching, merely wallowing, and scaring every trout within miles; but as Sir Glamie drew nearer he saw that the boy was winged. 'Are you young what's-his-name?' he asked. The boy said he thought so. Sir Glamie said he was old enough to know his name. The boy agreed, and added, 'It used to be Bonny.' Sir Glamie replied that Bonny was a girl's name, and wouldn't do. Overcome by the boy's remarkable beauty, he had a rush of benevolence, and casting round in his mind remembered the worms, small and smooth and white, that fishermen called gentles, and impale on the hook when the water is too cloudy to use a fly. 'I shall call you Gentle,' he declared. By force of association, he took a liking to the boy, extricated him from Lady Ulpha's clutches, and took him to Court, where he was made a pet of and called Gentil.

It was not the introduction his parents had intended: it was premature, since clothes had to be bought for him and he would outgrow them;

it was also patronising, and made their heir seem a nobody. But as none of the legacies they invoked had responded, they submitted, called him Gentil, made him learn his pedigree by heart, and loyally attended banquets.

Gentil was scarcely into his new clothes before he grew out of them. A fresh outfit was under consideration when the need for it was annulled: the Queen made him one of her pages, and a uniform went with the appointment. For the first time in his life he was aware of his beauty, and gazed at his image in the tailor's mirror as though it were a butterfly or a snow crystal—a snow crystal that would not melt. At intervals, he remembered to be grateful to his parents, but for whose providence he might still be admiring the veined underwater pebbles without noticing his reflected face. It needed no effort to be grateful to his new friends at Court: to the Queen, who stroked his cheek; to her ladies, who straightened his stockings; to his fellow-pages, who shared their toffees with him; to Sir Glamie, who chucked him under the chin with a fishy hand and asked what had become of the hat; to Lady Fenell, the Court Harpist, who sang for him

> I love all beauteous things,
> I seek and adore them

—an old-fashioned ditty composed for her by an admirer, which exactly expressed his own feelings. For he, too, was a beauty lover, and loved himself with an untroubled and unselfish love.

Fenell's voice had grown quavering with age—she had actually heard Ossian—but her fingers were as nimble as ever, her attack as brilliant, and young persons of quality came from all over Elfindom to learn her method. The latest of these was the Princess Lief, Queen Gruach's daughter from the Kingdom of Elfwick, in Caithness. She had the air of being assured of admiration, but there was nothing beautiful about her except the startling blue of her eyes: a glance that fell on one like a splash of ice-cold water. During the reception held to celebrate her arrival, the glance fell on Gentil. It seemed like a command. He came forward politely and asked if there was anything she wanted. After a long scrutiny, she said, 'Nothing,' and turned away. He felt snubbed. Not knowing which way to look, he caught sight of Sir Huon and Lady

Ulpha, whose faces expressed profound gratification. He knew they did not love him, but he had not realised they hated him.

If it had not been for Lady Ulpha's decorum, she would have nudged Sir Huon in the ribs. All that night they sat up telling each other that Gentil's fortune was made. There could be no mistaking such love at first sight. Gentil would be off their hands, sure of his future, sure of his indestructible good looks, with nothing to do but ingratiate himself with Queen Gruach and live up to his pedigree. And, as the castle of Elfwick stood on the edge of a cliff, the caul would not be wasted. The caul might count as an asset and be included in the marriage settlement.

It was just as they foresaw. Lief compelled Lady Fenell into saying she had nothing more to teach her (the formula for dismissing unteachable pupils), assaulted Gentil into compliance, and bore him off to Elfwick, where, after a violent set-to with Queen Gruach, she had him proclaimed her Consort and made a Freeman of Elfwick.

The ceremony was interrupted by the news that a ship was in the bay. Every male fairy rushed to the cliff's edge. Narrowing his eyes against the wind, Gentil was just able to distinguish a dark shape tossing on the black-and-white expanse of sea. He was at a loss to make out what the others were saying, except that they were talking excitedly, for they spoke in soft mewing voices, like the voices of birds of prey. Gulls exploded out of the dusk, flying so close that their screams jabbed his hearing, They, too, sounded wild with excitement. The sea kept up a continuous hollow booming, a noise without shape or dimension, unless some larger wave charged the cliff like an angry bull. Then, for a moment, there seemed to be silence, and a tower of spray rose and hung on the air, hissed, and was gone. Ducking to avoid a gull, Gentil lost sight of the ship. When he saw it again, it was closer inland. He saw it stagger, and a wave overwhelm it, emerge, and be swallowed by a second wave. There was a general groan. A voice said something about no pickings. A flurry of snow hid everything. He heard the others consulting, their voices dubious and discouraged. They had begun to move away, when a shriller voice yowled, 'There she is, there she is.' They gathered again, peering into the snow flurry. When it cleared, the ship was plainly visible, much smaller and farther out to sea. Everyone turned away and went back to the castle, where the ceremony was resumed, glumly.

When he said to Lief that he was glad to see the ship still afloat, and hoped no one on her was drowned, she said, embracing him, that he would never be drowned—that was all she cared for. He learned that Elfwick had rights over everything that came ashore—wreck, cargo, crew: the east wind blew meat and drink into Elfwick mouths. Next day she walked him along the cliffs, and showed him where the currents ran—oily streaks on the sea's face. A ship caught in a certain current would be carried, willy-nilly, onto a rock called the Elfwick Cow, which pastured at the entrance to the beach, lying so temptingly in the gap between the cliffs. She pointed to a swirl of water above the rock, and said that at low tide the Cow wore a lace veil—the trickle of spray left by each retreating wave. He clutched at his retreating hopes. 'But if a sailor gets to shore alive—' 'Knocked on the head like a seal,' she said, 'caul or no caul. Cauls have no power on land.' Seeing him shiver, she hurried him lovingly indoors.

Her love was the worst of his misfortunes. He submitted to it with a passive ill will, as he submitted to the inescapable noise of the sea, the exploitation of a harshly bracing climate. Wishing he were dead, he found himself at the mercy of a devouring healthiness, eating grossly, sleeping like a log. 'You'll soon get into our Elfwick ways,' Queen Gruach remarked, adding that the first winter was bound to be difficult for anyone from the south. She disliked her son-in-law, but she was trying to make the best of him. If Gentil had inherited his parents' eye for the main chance, he could have adapted himself to his advantages, and lived as thrivingly at Elfwick as he had lived at Rings—where everyone liked him, and he loved himself, and was happy. At Elfwick, he was loved by Lief, and was appalled.

The first winter lasted into mid-May, when the blackthorn hedges struggled into bloom and a three-day snowstorm buried them. The storm brought another ship to be battered to pieces on the Elfwick Cow. This time, the cold spared her plunderers the trouble of dispatching the crew. The ship was one of the Duke of Orkney's vessels, its cargo was rich and festive: casks of wine and brandy, a case of lutes (too sodden to be of any use), smoked hams (none the worse), bales of fine cloth. In a strong packing case and wadded in depths of wool was an oval mirror. Lief gave it to Gentil, saying that the frame—a wreath of carved ivory roses, delicately tinted and entwined in blue glass ribbons—was almost lovely enough to hold his face. She was in triumph at having snatched it from Gruach, who had the right to it. He thanked her politely, glanced at his reflection, saw with indifference that he was as beautiful as ever, and commented that he was growing fat. The waiting woman who had carried the mirror stood by with a blank face and a smiling heart. To see the arrogant Princess fawning on an upstart from Galloway was a shocking spectacle but also an ointment to old sores.

Baffled and eluded, Lief continued to love her bad bargain with the obsession of a bitch. She beset him with gifts, tried to impress him by brags, wooed him with bribes. She watched him with incessant hope, never lost patience with him, or with herself; she was so loyal she did not even privately make excuses for him. If anyone showed her a vestige of sympathy, she turned and rent him. This and quarrelling with her mother were the only satisfactions she could rely on.

At first, she hoped it was winter that made him cold. Summer came, and Gentil was cold still—cold like a sea mist and as ungraspable. If she had believed in witches, she would have believed he was under a spell; but Caithness was full of witches—mortals all, derided by rational elfins. He was healthy, could swim like a fish, leap like a grasshopper —and none of this was any good to him, for he was without initiative, and had to be wound up to pleasure like a toy. The only thing he did of his own accord was sneak out and be away all day. Sometimes he brought back mushrooms, neatly bagged in a handkerchief. Otherwise, he returned empty-handed and empty-headed, for if she asked him what he had seen, he replied, 'Nothing in particular.'

And it was true. He could no longer see anything in its particularity —not the sharp outline of a leaf, not the polish on a bird's plumage. It was as though the woollen veil had been tied over his face again, the woollen grating that had barred him from delight. He saw his old loves with a listless recognition. Another magpie. Another rainbow. More daisies. They were the same as they had been last summer and would be next summer and the summers after that.

It was another April, and Gentil, wandering through the fields, was conscious only that a cold wind was blowing, when he heard a whistling —too long-breathed for a thrush, too thoughtful for a blackbird. The whistler was a young man, a Caithness mortal. He was repairing a tumbled sheepfold. Each time he stooped to pick up a stone, a lappet of black hair slid forward and dangled over one eye. Gentil was accustomed to mortals, took them for granted, and never gave them a thought. At the sight of the young man he was suddenly pierced with delight. The lappet of hair, the light toss of the small head that shook it back, the strong body stooping so easily, the large, deft hands nestling the stones into place were as beautiful and fit and complete as the marvels he had seen in his childhood. Weakened by love, he sat down on the impoverished grass to watch.

He went back the next day, and the morning after that he got up early and was at the sheepfold in time to collect some suitably sized stones and lay them in a neat heap at the foot of the wall. Love is beyond reason, and when the young man took stones from the heap as though they had been there all the time, Gentil was overjoyed. Civility obliged him to attend the celebrations on Gruach's birthday, telling himself furiously that no one would notice if he was there or not. On the morrow, he woke with such a release into joy and confidence that he even dawdled on his way to the sheepfold. It was finished, the young man was gone. Gentil took to his wings and flew in wide circles, quartering the landscape. A flash of steel signalled him to where the young man was laying a hedge.

This task had none of the scholarly precision of mending a dry stone wall. It was a battle of opposing forces, the one armed with a billhook, the other armoured in thorns. It was an old hedge, standing as tall as its adversary; some of the main stems were thick as a wrist, and branched at all angles with intricate lesser growths. Here and there it was tufted with blossoms, for the sap was already running. The young man, working from left to right, chose the next stem to attack, seized it with his left hand, bent it back, and half severed it with a glancing blow of the billhook. The flowing sap darkened the wound; petals fell. Still holding the upper part of the stem, he pressed it down, and secured it in a plaited entanglement of side branches, lesser growths, and brambles. Then he lopped the whole into shapeliness with quick slashes of his billhook. The change from dealing with stone to dealing with living wood changed his expression: it was stern and critical—there was none of the contented calculation which had gone with rebuilding the sheepfold.

It changed Gentil too—from a worshipper to a partisan. He hovered above the hedge, watching each stroke, studying the young man's face—how he drew down his black eyebrows in a frown, bit his lip. Secure in his invisibility, Gentil hovered closer and closer. They were moving on from a completed length of hedge when a twig jerked up from the subdued bulk. 'Look! Here!'—the words were almost spoken when the young man saw the twig and slashed at it. The bright billhook caught Gentil in its sweep and lopped off half his ear. Feeling Gentil's blood stiffening on his hand, the young man licked the scratch he had got from a thorn and went on working. Another length of hedge had been laid before Gentil left off being sick, and crept away.

Several times he trustingly lay down to die. The trust was misplaced; the cold shock and loss of blood forced him to rise from the ground into the clasp of the sunny air and walk on. When he tried to fly, he found he could not: the loss of half an ear upset his balance. He walked on and on, vaguely taking his way back to Elfwick and wondering how he could put an end to his shamed existence. He could not drown, but he remembered a place where a ledge of rock lay at the foot of the cliff, and if he could get that far he could let himself drop and be dashed to pieces. But he must make a detour, so that no one from the castle would see him.

Lief, impelled by her bitch's instinct, was there before him, not knowing why but knowing she must be. In any case, it never came amiss to look seaward: there might be another ship. He went past without seeing her. She grabbed him. As they struggled on the cliff's edge, she saw the bloody stump of his ear but held him fast.

As time went on Lief sometimes wondered whether it would not have been better to let him have his way. But she had caught hold of him before she saw what had happened, and her will to keep him was stronger than her horror at his disfigurement. So she fought him to a finish, and marched him back to the castle.

The return from the cliff's edge was perhaps the worst thing she had to endure. There were no more people about than usual but it seemed to her that every Court elfin was there, gathering like blowflies to Gentil's raw wound, turning away in abhorrence. It was natural, she accepted it. Elfwick had never lost the energy of its origin as an isolated settlement, embattled against harsh natural conditions: cold and scarcity, wind and tempest. Its savagery was practical, its violence law-abiding. Though it had grown comfort-loving, it had never become infected with that most un-Elfin weakness, pity. She herself nursed Gentil through his long illness without a tremor of pity traversing her implacable concern. She risked her reason to save him, exactly as the wreckers risked their limbs to snatch back a cask from the undertow, and she recognised the rationality and loyal traditionalism of the public opinion she defied. The mildest expression of it was Gruach's. 'He must be sent back to Rings.' While he was thought to be past saving (for the stump festered and his face and neck swelled hideously) there was hope. But the swelling went down and Gruach visited the sickbed to remonstrate in a motherly way against Lief's devotion. 'I chose him. I shall save him,' said Lief.

'But have you considered the future? It's not as though you were saving a favourite hound. He is your Consort, remember. How can you appear with such an object beside you? How could you put up with the indignity, the scandal, of his mutilation?' Lief replied, 'You'll see.' She put a bold front on it, but at times she despaired, thinking that if Gentil once left her keeping, public opinion would soon do away with him.

As it happened, this problem did not arise. No one was more horrified by his deformity than Gentil himself. He refused to be seen, he would have no one but Lief come near him. If she had to make an appearance at Court, he insisted that she lock him in and keep the key between her breasts. She still did not know what had happened. When she questioned him he burst into tears. She did not risk him again, for by then she was as exhausted by his illness as he, and only wanted to sit still and say nothing. They sat together, hour after hour, saying nothing, she with her hands in her lap, he fingering his ear.

The oncome of winter was stormy; two profitable ships were driven onto the Cow, the castle resounded with boasts and banquetings. Then for months nothing happened. A deadly calm frost clamped the snow, waves crept to the strand and immediately froze, the gulls flew like scimitars through the still air. Gentil sat by the fire, fingering his wound.

The smell of spring was breathing through the opened casement when he suddenly raised his head, looked round the room and on Lief, and said passionately, 'Everything is so ugly, so ugly!' Casting about for something to please him, Lief remembered her mother's gold and silver beads, which the Duke of Orkney had thought to hang round a younger neck. Schooling herself to be daughterly and beguiling, she persuaded Gruach to unlock her treasure chest, questioned, admired, put on the gold and silver beads, and asked if she could borrow them. And though Lief had never shown the least interest in the Duke of Orkney's importations, except when she carried off the oval mirror, Gruach thought she might be returning to her right mind, and handed over the beads and some other trifles. Gentil tired of running the beads through his fingers; a jewelled bird trembling on a fine wire above a malachite leaf and a massive gold sunflower with a crystal eye were more durable pleasures. Later, he was spellbound by a branching spray of coral. At the first sight of the coral, which to Lief was nothing to marvel at, since there was no workmanship about it, he gave a cry of joy that seemed to light up the room.

But this, too, eventually went the way of the sunflower and the bird. And when she brought fresh rarities to replace it, he thanked her politely and ignored them. Except for sudden fits of rage, when he screamed at her, he was always polite. The fits of rage she rather welcomed; they promised something she could get to grips with. It never came. He sat by the fire; he sat by the window; the maimed ear had thickened into an accumulation of flaps, one fast to another, like the mushrooms, hard as leather, that grow on the trunks of ageing trees and are called Jew's-ears. A scar extended down his cheek. The rest of him was lovely and youthful as ever.

Nothing deflects the routine of a court custom. The Freemen of Elfwick had no particular obligations except to wear a badge and have precedence in drinking loyal toasts at banquets; but in times of emergency they were expected to rally and attend committee meetings. Gentil was now summoned to such a meeting. Naturally, he did not attend. The emergency was still in the future, but it was inevitable, and must be faced with measures of economy, tightening of belts, and finding alternative sources of supply. For the Duke of Orkney was mortal, and over sixty—an age at which mortals begin to fall to bits. His heir was a miserly ascetic, always keeping Lents; there would be no more casks of wine and brandy, no more of those delicious smoked hams, no more candied apricots from Provence, fine cloth from Flanders, spices to redeem home-killed mutton from the aroma of decay; the Cow would advance her horns to no purpose, the Elfwick standard of living would fall catastrophically. The meeting closed with a unanimous recommendation to make sure of the Duke of Orkney's next consignment.

It could be expected before the autumnal equinox. Spies were sent out for hearsay of it, watchers were stationed along the cliffs, where they lolled in the sun, chewing wild thyme. It had been an exceptionally early harvest; rye and oats were already in stooks, rustling in the wind. It was a lulling sound, but not so to the Court Purveyor. For it was a west wind, and though it was gentle it was steady. Of all the quarters the wind could blow from he prayed for any but the west. With a west wind keeping her well out to sea, the Duke's ship would be safe from those serviceable currents that nourished the Cow. Elfwick would get nothing.

Subduing his principles, consulting nobody, the Purveyor put on a respectable visibility and sought out the nearest coven of witches. They were throwing toads and toenails into a simmering cauldron; the smell was intolerable, but he got out his request, and at the same time got out a purse and clinked it. 'A wind from the east?' said the head witch. 'You should go to my sister in Lapland for that.' He answered that he was sure a Caithness witch could do as well or better. She threw in another toad and said he should have his will. Handing over the purse, he asked if there was anything else he could supply. A younger witch spoke up. 'A few cats . . . seven, maybe.' 'Alive?' 'Oh, aye.' He carried the hamper of squalling cats to the place they commanded, and fled in trust and terror.

The storm which impaled the Duke of Orkney's ship on the Elfwick Cow did so at a price. Hailstones battered down the stooks and froze the beehives. A month's washing was whirled away from the drying yard. Shutters were torn from their hinges, fruit trees were uprooted, pigs went mad, the kitchen chimney was struck by lightning, the Purveyor, clutching at his heart, fell dead. Lief stepped over him on her way out. The clamour of wind and voices, the reports of a superb cargo, of a cargo still at hazard, had been more than she could withstand. Settling Gentil with a picture book, she locked him in, put the key in her bosom, and ran to the cliff's edge. Bursts of spray made it difficult to see what was going on. She caught sight of a Negro, fighting his way to shore against the suck of the undertow. He was down, he was up again, still grasping an encumbering package. It was wrenched from him by the undertow; he turned back. When she could see him again, he had retrieved it. Curious to know what it was he guarded so jealously, she descended the path. By the time she reached the strand, he had been dispatched, and lay sprawled over his package—an oblong wooden box, latticed with strips of iron—as though he would still protect it. She tried to pull it from under him, but it was too heavy for her to shift. More and more plunder was being fetched ashore. She stood unnoticed in the jostle till one of the Freemen tripped over the Negro. He started at seeing Lief there, and panted out felicitations: never had the Cow done better for Elfwick. She told him that the Negro's box was hers, under the old law of Finders Keepers; he must call off one of the wreckers to carry it after her to the castle.

On the cliff's summit she stopped to look back. Twitches of lightning played incessantly over the sea. Remade by wind and tempest, she felt a lifetime away from Gentil; when the grunting porter asked what to do with the box, she had forgotten it existed.

Yet in the morning the box was the first thing in her mind. Gentil had a cat's pleasure in anything being unpacked: had a crate been large enough, he would have jumped in and curled up in it. The box was brought to her apartment, the castle's handyman called in. Practised in such duties, he made short work of it. The iron bands were eased and tapped off, screw after screw withdrawn. At intervals he remarked on the change in the weather. The wind had fallen as suddenly as it had come up, and when he had finished the box he would see to the shutters, and then the pigsties, which the pigs in their frenzy had torn through like cannonballs. This box, though, was a different matter. Made of solid mahogany, it would baffle the strongest pig in Scotland. He laid the screws aside and raised the lid. Whatever lay within was held in place by bands of strong twine and wrapped in fold on fold of waxed linen. The handyman cut the twine, bowed, and went away. Gentil came out of hiding. Kneeling by the box, Lief lifted the oblong shape and held it while Gentil unwound the interminable wrappings. The oblong turned into a frame, the frame held a padding of lamb's wool. Gentil folded the linen and smoothed it affectionately. Pulling away the lamb's wool, he was the first to see the picture.

It was the half-length portrait of a young man, full face and looking directly before him. Behind him was the landscape of a summer morning. Wreaths of morning mist, shining in the sun, wandered over it. Out of the mist rose sharp pinnacles of mountain, blue with distance yet with every rocky detail exactly delineated. A glittering river coiled through a perspective of bronzed marshes and meadows enclosed by trees planted in single file, each tree in its own territory of air. It was as though a moment before they had been stirring in a light wind which now had fallen. Everything lay in a trance of sunlight, distinct, unmoving, and completed. Only the young man, turning his back on this landscape, sat in shadow—the shadow of a cloud, perhaps, or of a canopy. He was not darkened by it; but it substantiated him, as though he and the landscape belonged to different realities. He sat easily erect, with his smooth, long-fingered young hands clasped like the hands of an old man round a stick. His hair hung in docile curls and ringlets, framing the oval of his face. He had grey eyes. In the shadow which substantiated him, they were bright as glass, and stared out of the canvas as though he were questioning what he saw, as smilingly indifferent to the answer as he was to the lovely landscape he had turned his back on.

Lief tired under the effort of holding up the picture. She propped it against a chair, and went round to kneel beside the kneeling Gentil and discover what it was he found so compelling. The likeness was inescapable: Gentil was gazing at himself in his youth, at the Gentil who had come forward and asked if there was anything she wanted; she had said, 'Nothing', and nothing was what she had got. Tears started to her eyes and ran slowly down her cheeks. She shook her hand impatiently, as if to dismiss them. He turned and looked at her. The sun shone full on her face. He had never seen her cry. The glittering, sidling tears were beautiful, an extraneous beauty on an accustomed object. He shuffled nearer and stared more closely, entranced by the fine network of wrinkles round her eyes. She heard him give a little gasp of pleasure, saw him looking at her with delight, as long ago he had looked at an insect's wing, a yellow snail shell. Cautiously, as though she might fly away, he touched her cheek. She did nothing, said nothing, stretched the moment for as long as it could possibly last. They rose from their knees together and stood looking at the picture, each with an arm round the other's waist.

Love—romantic love, such as Lief had felt for Gentil, Gentil for the young man at the sheepfold—was not possible for them. In any case, elfins find such love burdensome and mistrust it. But they grew increasingly attached to each other's company, and being elfins and untrammelled by that petted plague of mortals, conscience, they never reproached or regretted, entered into explanations or lied. This state of things carried them contentedly through the winter. With the spring, Gentil astonishingly proclaimed a wish to go out-of-doors, provided he went unseen. Slinking out after midnight, they listened to owls and lambs, smelled honeysuckle, and ate primroses chilled with dew.

After the sweetness of early morning it was painful to return to the stuffiness of the castle, its oppressive silence shaken by snores. Gentil planned stratagems for escaping into daylight: he could wear a sunbonnet; they could dig an underground passage. But the underground passage would only deliver him up to the common gaze, the sunbonnet expose him to a charge of transvestism—more abhorrent to Elfwick than any disfigurement, and certain to be more sternly dealt with. Seeing him again fingering his ear and staring at the morning landscape behind the young man in the painting, Lief racked her brains for some indoor expedient which might release him from those four walls. Build on an aviary? Add a turret? The answer swam into her mind, smooth as a fish. The court library! It was reputed to be a good one, famous for its books of travel. And was totally unvisited. She had heard that some of the books of travel were illustrated. Gentil enjoyed a picture book. The midsummer mornings which had curtailed their secret expeditions now showed a different face: no one would be about at those unfrequented hours of dawn.

No one was. The snores became a reassurance and even a blessing, since they could be timed to smother the squeaks of the library door. Gentil sat looking at the travel books and Lief sat listening to the birds and looking at Gentil. One morning, he gave a cry of delight, and beckoned her to come and see what he had found. It was a woodcut in a book about the Crusades—a battle scene with rearing horses and visored warriors. It was unlike Gentil to be so pleased with a battle scene, but he was certainly in a blaze of joy. He pointed to a warrior who was not visored, whose villainous dark face was muffled in a wimplelike drapery, whose eyes rolled from beneath a turban. 'That . . . that . . . that's what I need, that's what I must have!' She said it would be ready that same evening.

Having embraced Islam, Gentil found a new life stretching before him. Turbaned and wimpled, he appeared at Court, kissed the Queen's hand, sat among his fellow-Freemen, studied sea anemones. This was only an opening on wider ambitions. It seemed excessive to go to Mecca, and Lief did not wish to visit his parents. But they went to Aberdeen, travelling visibly and using the alias of Lord and Lady Bonny. From Aberdeen they took ship to Esbjerg and inspected the Northern capitals. As travellers do, they bought quaint local artifacts, patronised curiosity shops, attended auctions. One has to buy freely in order to discover the run of one's taste. They discovered that what they most liked was naturalistic paintings. They concentrated on the Dutch School, Lief buying seascapes, Gentil flower pieces, and by selling those which palled on them they made money to buy more. In course of time, they acquired a number of distinguished canvases, but never another Leonardo.

(*One Thing Leading to Another*, 1984)